ANGEL DUST

LORNA DOUNAEVA

ALSO BY LORNA DOUNAEVA

The McBride Vendetta

FRY

Cold Bath Lane

Other Books

The Perfect Girl

Simply for Denis.

ACKNOWLEDGMENTS

A big thank you to Rob Barker & Virginia Malcolm.

Editors
Hayley Sherman
Maria Dounaeva

Cover
Coverquill

Copyright © 2018 by Lorna Dounaeva

All rights reserved.

No part of this book may be reproduced in any form or by any electronic or mechanical means, including information storage and retrieval systems, without written permission from the author, except for the use of brief quotations in a book review.

ANGEL DUST

PROLOGUE

I climb out of the car and run down the garden path.
"Mum, come and play with me!" I call.
"Not now, Angel. I need to get dinner on."
"Why can't you play first?" I say. "I'm not even hungry yet."
"Later, darling."
She disappears into the kitchen. I can see her in there, flipping through a magazine as she waits for the kettle to boil. She isn't cooking. She just doesn't want to play with me. I might as well go and look at the rock pools and see if there are any crabs out there today. Mum would freak if she knew I go down to the beach on my own, but it's alright. I'm a strong swimmer, one of the best in my class. She doesn't have to worry.

I stand on the edge of the rocks and enjoy the cool ocean spray on my face. A little crab scuttles out from behind a rock. I run after it, but it wants to play hide and seek. I climb from one rock pool to the next, venturing further and further out, until a big wave rises out of the ocean and almost knocks me off my feet.
"Careful!"

I look in the direction of the voice. He has a special smile, like he knows a secret and wants to share it.

"The water's rough out there today," he warns, over the roar of the waves.

He puts out his hand to steady me. I don't really want to touch him, but it seems rude not to.

"The tide's coming in," he says, as we clamber back onto the beach. He whistles loudly, a really cool, musical whistle, and a little dog flies up the beach, showering us with sand. He looks like a cuddly toy, with his doe eyes and long, droopy ears.

"He's so cute!" I say, bending down to stroke him. "What's his name?"

"Dog," the man says.

"Seriously?"

"I wasn't born with the gift of imagination," he says, looking down at his shoes.

"I think it's funny," I say.

"You're most kind. What's your name?"

"Lauren," I say. "But I'm not supposed to talk to strangers."

He laughs. "We're not that strange, are we, Dog?"

The little dog licks my foot.

"I really have to go," I say, glancing back at the house. "I'm not supposed to be out."

"I'll walk with you," he says. "My caravan's just over there."

"You live in a caravan?" I say in wonderment.

"That's right."

"Wow, I've never been in a caravan," I tell him. "My mum's not keen on camping. Daddy says she can't function without a hairdryer."

He laughs again. He has a nice laugh, loud and hearty.

"You can come and see inside if you want," he says.

I hesitate. I've never been inside a caravan before, but it feels a bit weird.

Angel Dust

"Go on!" he says. "I don't mind."

"Sorry, I have to go," I say. "I've got judo tonight. Can't be late."

"Another time, then," he says with a smile.

"Definitely," I promise.

"Oh, and Lauren? Don't tell your mum."

As if I would.

1

The alarm shatters the night. I open one eye. It's pitch black.
"Deacon," I hiss, springing from the bed. "Deacon!"
Deacon murmurs something in his sleep. I shake him violently.
"DEACON!"
"Wha ..."
"Get up!" I say, urgently.
"I'm up! I'm up!"
The bed creaks as he swings his legs over the side.
I pace six short steps to the door and turn the knob, grabbing a towel from the laundry basket to protect my hand, in case it's hot.
"No lights," Deacon calls, as we fumble along the corridor to Lauren's room.
"I know!"
"Get up! Get up!" I yell, shining my phone at the wall above Lauren's cabin bed.
"Get up!" I repeat, in a tone that's not to be messed with. "Quickly!"

I climb up onto her chair and reach into her cabin bed to shake her. I can't even see her, just a mass of hair and the hunch of her shoulders.

"I'm tired," she moans. "What time is it?"

"Grab your torch," I say.

I wait nervously while she climbs down the rungs.

"Faster!" I yell.

Picking up on my urgency, she jumps the last bit, and I pull her out into the hallway.

"Come on," Deacon says. "Down the stairs."

We race down two flights of stairs, wary of the slight dip in the third one from the bottom. We wait frantically as Deacon fumbles with the lock.

"What about Fluffy?" Lauren cries, her green eyes glistening.

"There's no time to get him," Deacon says.

A lump forms in my throat. I've had Fluffy longer than we've been married. I shine my phone around the kitchen, but there's no sign of him.

"He was on my bed," Lauren says. "I could go and …"

"No," says Deacon. "Absolutely not."

We burst outside. The night air is bracing, and an owl screeches overhead.

The door slams shut behind us.

"Come on!" I gasp, clinging to Lauren's hand as we bolt down the garden path. I throw open the gate and pull her across the road. I glance back at the house as we race across the deserted car park and down the steps to the beach. It's paramount that we get as much distance between us and the burning building as possible.

A few more metres and we'll be clear.

"Get down!" Deacon shouts. "Take cover!"

The three of us flatten ourselves against the gristly sand. As we lie there, panting, a blob emerges out of the darkness.

"Fluffy!" Lauren cries, flinging her arms around him.

"You followed us!" I say, stroking his mottled fur.

Deacon pulls out his phone. "Three minutes twenty," he reports. "Not bad, but we haven't beaten our record."

"I'm cold," Lauren moans.

I pull a piece of seaweed out of my hair and lob it towards the ocean. The wind flings it right back at me and I shudder as I peel the quivering mass off my leg. I'm wearing flip-flops, but they're neither warm nor comfortable. If this were a real fire, I wouldn't even have stopped to put these on, but for tonight I draw the line at bare feet. At least Fluffy is dressed for this. I envy his long, thick coat.

Deacon resets the fire practice app on his phone. It's programmed to go off at random a few times a year. The last time was a couple of weeks before Christmas, so I thought that would be it for a while. My mistake.

"It's freezing out here," Lauren whines, as we plod back to the house. "I bet I'm going to get the flu after this."

"Oh, don't be so melodramatic," I say. "We have these practises for a reason. It's important you know what to do if you ever encounter a real fire."

"I do know," she says impatiently. "You're always banging on about it. But Sophia and Robyn don't have to get up in the middle of the night for no reason, so why do we?"

I look at Deacon, but now isn't the time.

"You need to remember to wrap up warm at night," I chastise her. "You're not dressed for an emergency."

"I didn't know there was going to be an emergency."

She sticks out her bottom lip, like she did when she was a toddler.

"That's just it," I say. "You never know."

"Come on," Deacon says. "Let's get back to bed."

The central heating is a welcome treat as we shuffle back inside and lock the door. Lauren stands in front of the radiator, warming herself, back and front. I give her a couple of minutes, then coax her back up the stairs to bed.

"I'm thirsty," she says, as I stand on the chair to tuck her into her cabin bed.

I heave a sigh, but I take her water bottle to the bathroom and fill it up. She takes it, but she doesn't drink.

"Mum?" she says.

"What?" I ask, my face screwed up in a yawn.

"If we didn't get out in time, would we all burn to death?"

My spine tingles as I remember the toxic taste on my tongue. It wouldn't be the flames that got us. The smoke would penetrate our nostrils and work its way down our throats, making it impossible to breathe. Lungfuls of awful toxic smoke would render us unconscious. We would all be dead in minutes.

"That wouldn't happen," I tell her fiercely. "We're prepared."

"OK."

But the fear on her face doesn't entirely dissolve.

"Goodnight, darling." I kiss her cheek and step down from the chair, switching out the light. I can't see her face. Maybe I should have said something more comforting, but I'm so damned tired. We both are. We can talk about it more in the morning.

Deacon's body is warm beside me as I slip back into bed. I shift him over slightly, but he immediately rolls back into the same position, his hand draped affectionately across my waist. I pull the cover over me. I'm mystified as to how he stays so warm when I'm so cold. There are goose bumps all down my thighs.

I lie awake, questioning the choices we've made. Are we doing the right thing with all these practise drills? Do we really want Lauren to see the ugliness of the world, as we do? Do we want her to live in fear? Before I can come to any conclusions, the gentle rhythm of sleep takes over. I imagine I am lying in a rowing boat, gently rocking in the ocean. The sun shines down on me, warming my body with its rays. Gradually, the boat rocks faster and faster, until I'm aware of someone nudging me, tipping me into the ice-cold water. My eyes snap open.

"I can't sleep."

Lauren is standing by the side of my bed. Her tangled hair hangs over her eyes.

"Back to bed," I grunt.

I never allow her to come into bed with us, because if I did, we'd never get her back into her own bed. Instead, I nudge her back towards her room and up the ladder once more.

"Come on, get in," I say, pulling back her duvet.

Her lip trembles. "There are monsters under my bed."

"Can't be," I say. "I sprayed anti-monster repellent under there."

"But, Mum, I think they've found an antidote."

She's playing me. She's fine. And just when did we go from 'Mummy' to 'Mum'?

"Please, Mum, you've got to spray some more. Use a different one this time."

I go into the bathroom and open the cleaning cupboard. I find a can of cherry blossom air freshener and spray it around Lauren's room. It has a pungent smell, but Lauren doesn't mind.

"Go to sleep," I say. "There are no monsters, I promise you."

I give her a hasty kiss on the cheek and leave the room before she can argue.

Deacon is still sound asleep when I return to bed. I get in beside him again and close my eyes, but my relaxing dream has gone, replaced by flames that burn my eyes. I force myself to picture the ocean again, the way my therapist advised. It isn't so hard to do, with the real thing just outside my window. Back and forth, back and forth …

2

When my alarm goes off in the morning, there's a figure slumped in the doorway between my room and the corridor. She has her Hello Kitty duvet tucked around her and her pillow under her head. Gently, I shake her awake. Her eyelids flutter and she looks up at me. Her eyes are several different shades of green: darker on the outside and lighter towards the middle, where they blend in a swirl of yellow and hazel. I don't think anyone in the world has such beautiful eyes, and I'm not just saying that because I'm her mother.

"Morning," I say, softly. "How long have you been there?"

Lauren shrugs. Perhaps, in the cold light of day, she's too embarrassed to talk about monsters.

I catch a glimpse of myself in the mirror and see that my face looks pale. Nothing that a dab of foundation and a stroke of blush won't cure, but not quite the peaches and cream complexion I aspire to. Lauren looks a little pale too. I offer her a hand to help her up, but she waves me away.

"Can I walk to school with Sophia today?" she asks.

"No," I say, removing a strand of hair from her mouth. "You're too young."

"But everyone else does it," she insists. "It's only a few streets away. It's not like I have to cross any big roads."

"I'm sorry, but the answer's still no," I say in my firmest voice.

"It's not fair!" she wails, stamping her bare foot. "Why do you always treat me like a baby? Sophia's allowed to walk by herself."

"Sophia lives closer to the school," I point out. "And she's six months older than you."

"So, I can walk with Sophia when I'm nine?" she says, seeing a window.

"I didn't say that."

"When then, Mum? You have to let me some time."

"Let me discuss it with your dad," I say.

I don't want her walking to school without me, ever. But I can't tell her that.

Lauren sticks out her bottom lip and flops back down under her duvet, like one of those hermit crabs she loves so much. I step over her and march into her room to pull her school uniform out of her wardrobe. I lay it out on her chair for her. She's more than capable of doing it for herself, but it's quicker this way.

"I'm going to have a shower," I tell her. "You get dressed."

When I emerge from the shower, Lauren is sitting at her desk, making something out of cardboard. The clothes that I laid out so neatly for her now lie discarded on the floor.

"Come on!" I say, crossly. "Put your uniform on! And stop sucking your hair!"

"This chair's so uncomfortable," she moans.

"No one's asking you to sit on your bottom!" I reprimand her. "Pick up your clothes and get them on. It's nearly breakfast time."

"I need to finish this," she says, without looking up.

I feel my blood pressure rising. "I'm serious, Lauren. Get ready. Now!"

Her teddy bears look at me with disproval. I feel bad for shouting, but if I don't shout, she doesn't listen. It's got to the point where I practically have to bellow for her to take any notice. I don't really know why I bother. Children are like cats – they have no sense of urgency. They won't be chivvied.

I towel dry my hair. Gone are the days when I had all morning to straighten and style it. Now I wear it wavy and natural, with just a blob of serum to manage the frizz.

I jump as the smoke alarm goes off. I lean over the bannisters to see Deacon hitting the alarm with the broom. The smell of charred toast fills the air. That's the way Deacon likes it – burned to a crisp.

When I enter the kitchen, Deacon is clattering about in the cutlery drawer, looking for Lauren's favourite spoon – the purple one.

"Aha!" he cries, as I slide into my seat. He holds up the perishing spoon, like it's King John's lost treasure, and places it next to Lauren's purple bowl.

"Bucket of tea?" he asks. His hair flops over his eye, Hugh Grant style. He never gets it cut until he has to.

"Please."

I sit down at the table and work on the consent forms for Lauren's upcoming school trip to Stratford-upon-Avon. That's something they don't tell you at the antenatal classes – how much paperwork children come with. I could do with a personal assistant to keep on top of all the forms I have to fill in, all the cakes I have to bake and all the costumes I have to make. Every week there's another demand from that blasted school.

Fluffy lets out a hoarse purr and rubs up against my legs. His black fur has a grey tinge these days. He's rusting, as Lauren puts it. And he can't run as fast as he used to. If he spots a mouse, he saunters casually after it, then gives up halfway up the garden.

I turn over the form and fill in the name and address of Lauren's doctor, details the school already has but asks for time and again, regardless. I hope she learns something on this damn trip. The only thing I got out of her after her trip to the Science Museum was that the gift shop had cool notebooks. Oh, and there was an ice-cream van outside.

Deacon sets steaming mugs of tea on the table and spreads marmalade on his toast. There is a mini poinsettia plant on the table, and another larger one on the counter. I once mentioned that I liked them, and now he buys them for me whenever they're in season.

"I left you the last Weetabix," he says, putting a bowl in front of me.

"Thanks," I murmur, pouring the milk. I'm not hungry, but I force a bit down anyway, to show I appreciate the gesture.

"Lauren's taking her time," he observes.

"Lauren!" I holler. "Breakfast!"

No response.

"Lauren!"

I hear the sound of a baby elephant charging down the stairs, then Lauren appears in the kitchen. She's wearing her school uniform, but her tights are white, as opposed to the regulation grey. I bite my tongue. Sometimes you have to choose your battles.

"How did your rehearsal go yesterday?" Deacon asks, as she sits down.

"Alright, I suppose," she says, wriggling in her chair. She's always been incapable of sitting still.

"You don't sound very excited?"

"I wanted to be the wolf," she complains, "but instead I have to be the second little pig."

"That's a decent part," he says. "You ought to be pleased."

"Everyone knows the first and second little pigs are morons," she tells him, scornfully. "Only the third one's bright enough to build his house out of bricks."

"Maybe it's an insurance scam," he says, catching my eye. "The first two pigs probably did well out of having their houses blown down. They'll have their own private yachts by now."

"Dad!" she says, rolling her eyes.

"Well, you never know," he says. "Hey, did Sophia get a part in the play?"

"Her class is doing Goldilocks and the Three Bears," she says. "Sophia's going to be porridge pot number three."

"And you're whingeing about being a pig?" he chuckles and swallows the last of his toast. "Well, I'd better be going," he says, getting to his feet. He looks remarkably fresh given our midnight fire practise.

"See you later," I say.

He gives us each a kiss and he's out the door. I hear his Bentley pull out of the gravel driveway and resent how easy it is for him to leave the house. I turn my attention to my daughter, who is playing with her toast, examining it as an entomologist might study a new species.

"What's wrong with it?" I ask, flatly.

"Too bready," she complains.

I take it from her and pop it back in the toaster for a minute.

"There," I say, chucking it back on her plate.

"Now it's all burnt," she says, sulkily.

"Have some cereal then," I say in exasperation. "You know where the cupboard is."

"Cereal makes me feel sick," she complains. "Except for Shy Boyz flakes."

"I'm not buying them," I say, firmly. "They're a waste of money and full of sugar."

I push my bowl away and clear the table, shoving the milk back in the fridge and leaving the cups and plates to soak in the sink.

"Right, are you ready?" I ask, locating my keys.

"No, I have to finish making my Tudor house," Lauren says.

"What, now?"

"It's my homework."

I narrow my eyes "When's it due?"

"This morning."

I feel steam coming out of my ears. "Why didn't you tell me before? There's no way you can do it now!"

"But I won't get to go on the trip if I haven't done it."

My eyes bulge. "Oh, you've got to be kidding me! What would you even make it out of?"

"I'll show you."

She runs up to her room and returns with the cardboard box she was tinkering with earlier.

"Right," I say, glancing at the clock. "We've got five minutes, max."

I run out to the recycling bin and pull out some toilet roll tubes. Back inside, I place them on top of the box and try to visualise how it's supposed to look.

"Come on, Mum," Lauren chastises me. "It doesn't have to be good!"

I grab the glue and within minutes we've made the world's crumbiest replica of a Tudor house.

"What do you think?" I ask.

"It looks craptastic," she says, with a smile on her face.

"The roof needs a quick trim," I say, cutting along the top with the kitchen scissors. "Ow!"

"Oh, Mum! Don't get blood all over the roof! You're ruining it!" she wails.

"Go and get me a plaster, then."
She stands there looking at me.
"What?"
"You didn't say please."

"Can I sit in the front?" she asks, as I carry her artwork out to the car.
"No. The back seat is safer."
"Just this once?" she cajoles.
"In the back!" I bark. "And hurry up. We're late."
I place the Tudor house on the passenger seat and wait for her to get in, but she stands stubbornly by the car.
"One," I count, "two, three …"
This used to work when she was younger, but not so much these days.
"… nine …"
Quick as a flash, she opens the door and scoots into her seat.
I bite my lip to stop myself saying, 'Was that so hard?'
I switch on the radio, hoping a bit of music will brighten the mood, but when I glance in the rear-view mirror, Lauren is covering her ears. She doesn't think much of my 'Mum music'.
I spot Hilary next door, gawking from behind her net curtains.
How long has she been watching us?
I avoid making eye contact as I start the car and manoeuvre round their caravan. It's been there since Christmas, blocking the pavement and making it a pain to get in and out of our driveway. I'm tempted to wind down the window and yell at her to move it, but I don't want to make a scene in front of Lauren.
I head onto the coast road and enjoy the ocean view for a

few minutes, until I have to turn onto the road that leads to the school. The barriers are down at the level crossing and we are forced to sit and wait for the train to pass.

"I'm going to be late," Lauren huffs. "This wouldn't happen if you let me walk with Sophia. It's much quicker."

"This wouldn't happen if you hadn't left your homework until the last minute," I shoot back, checking my make-up in the mirror. The barrier comes up, but none of the traffic moves. I lean out the window to see what's happening.

"I don't bloody believe it!" I say.

"What?" Lauren asks from the back.

"There's a funeral procession. At this time in the morning! Can't the dead wait until after the school rush?"

I drum my fingers on the steering wheel as the procession moves by at a respectful pace. Then, once the road is finally clear, the car refuses to start. The vehicles behind beep their horns at us.

"Oh, for Christ's sake!" I cry. "Just move, you stupid car!"

Yelling works. The Picasso splutters to life and we pull away. There's a loud cheer from behind.

"Is the car OK now?" Lauren asks. I choose not to notice that she's painting her fingernails with a pink highlighter pen.

"I don't know," I say. "I'll have to get Uncle Julio to take a look later."

By the time we reach the school, it's already gone nine. The receptionist tuts and makes us sign the late book before I can take Lauren through to her classroom.

"Bye, darling!" I try to plant a kiss on her forehead, but she neatly dodges.

"Mum!" she hisses, sounding embarrassed.

"Sorry!" I murmur.

I watch her carry her craptastic Tudor house into class. Actually, it doesn't look any worse than some of the others. I wave goodbye, but she doesn't turn around. Her teacher, Mrs Darley, motions to me to shut the classroom door.

3

I drive round to Gerry's Motors after work. I always liked the smell of the garage, that earthy combination of oil and Swarfega. I can't see Julio, but I find Gerry, the owner, a man who lives in orange boiler suits and has a pencil stub tucked permanently behind his ear. He's balding and pushing fifty, but he still thinks he's the dog's bollocks.

"Is Julio about?" I ask.

He looks at me with a weary half-smile. "Got man flu, last I heard. Hasn't been in for a couple of days."

"Oh. I didn't know."

I picture Julio at home under a pile of blankets. I wonder if he's really ill or if he's just got carried away with his PlayStation. I wouldn't put it past him to pull a sickie. He thinks he's entitled to two weeks sick a year. He treats it as extended holiday.

"I wanted him to have a look at my starter motor," I explain. "Is there anyone else who can help?"

"Not right now, love," he says. "We've got a lot on, what with your brother being off and all."

"Oh, I suppose …"

"If you're going round there, tell him to get his arse back to work, will you?"

I smile awkwardly. "I wasn't planning to." But maybe I should pop round. After all, what's the point of having a mechanic for a brother if you can't get him to fix your car?

Julio's house is in an old neighbourhood that has been untouched by the recent modernisation in the town. His Range Rover is in the driveway, so I park up and walk down the path to his house. While most of the buildings round here are council flats or bungalows, Julio has a rectangular two up, two down that doesn't look like any of the other houses in the street.

I stand at the door and peer through the frosted glass. The lights are on in the hallway, and I hear loud, repetitive base. I lean on the doorbell. There are shadows on the stairs, then the door swings open.

Bristles protrude from his chin and his usually minty-clean breath smells like rotting flesh.

"So, you are ill then?" I say, eyeing his tatty old t-shirt and pyjama bottoms.

"I'm fine." He sounds defensive.

"Then why aren't you at work?" I ask. I wrinkle up my nose. It's not just his breath that stinks. His whole body reeks like a sweaty stomach ache.

He rubs his bloodshot eyes. "Didn't feel like it."

I look past him into the hallway. A chair lies on its side and there are pizza boxes piled up on the table.

"Can I come in?" I ask, more gently.

A dark look flickers across his face. "I don't feel like company."

"Why not?"

"Just don't."

It's like we're teenagers again and I've walked into his room unannounced.

"Oh, come on, what's up? Did Nina dump you?" I ask, hopefully.

"Piss off!"

"So, you and Nina are fine?"

"Of course."

I study his face, trying to figure out what's different. He doesn't look ill exactly, but he doesn't look well either. He keeps shifting his weight from one foot to the other.

"Can I get you anything?" I ask, trying to sound more sympathetic.

"No thanks," he says.

He puts his hand on the door, ready to close it.

Bloody rude, really.

"I need you to look at my car," I say. "There's something wrong with the starter motor."

"Later," he says.

"Shall I come back this evening?"

He stares blankly at the space behind me. I glance in the same direction, but there's no one there, just the wind whistling in the trees.

"This evening?" I prompt.

"Can't."

"Well, when then?" I struggle to keep my tone civil. He can be a mardy sod sometimes.

"Some other time."

"Thanks for nothing," I say loudly, not caring what his neighbours might think.

Why do I even bother?

I traipse back to the car, the wind scattering leaves in all directions, like pages from a burning book.

Goddammit, Lauren's form! I completely forgot. I never put it in her school bag. It'll still be sitting on the kitchen table – Lauren would never think to pick it up for herself. And it's the deadline today. I'll have to go back for it on the way to pick her up.

My car coughs a little when I start the engine, but I'm able to get it going. It's not far to my place, as long as I get there before the roads get busy.

FLUFFY LAUNCHES himself at me the minute I open the front door and clings to my leg like a foot-muff. I bend down and stroke his head. He might be old, but he's still got a killer grip. I pick up Lauren's form from the table and try to leave, but Fluffy dives in front of the door, mewing loudly.

"For crying out loud, I'll be back in a minute." I tell him. "I've got to get Lauren from school."

He continues to pester, nudging me towards the kitchen and the cupboard where I keep his food. I take out a box of cat biscuits and shake some out, at which point he loses all interest in me, and all I see is his tail sticking out of the bowl. Clutching Lauren's form, I rush back to the car.

Everyone and his mother is out there now. I get stuck behind a tractor on the coast road. Then, to my annoyance, the amber light flashes on the level crossing.

"Oh, come on!"

The barriers come down and I wait for the train. It takes forever to come through, and still the barriers don't go up. Glancing down the line, I see another train leaving the station. The car behind me toots. Wazzock!

Finally, the barriers lift and I drive up to the school. The road is crammed by now, but I see a car pull out, so I reverse into the empty space before anyone else can.

The playground is teeming with people, so I can't be that late. A couple of mums have set up a stall selling second-hand uniforms and there's quite a throng around them. I stride towards Lauren's classroom. Her teacher, Mrs Darley, is standing outside, talking to another mum.

"Sorry I'm late," I interrupt, peering past her into the classroom. "Where's Lauren?"

Mrs Darley narrows her eyes. "She left five minutes ago."

I suck in my breath. "What?"

She frowns. "She left with her cousin, Sophia. I thought you knew?"

I stare at her. "Lauren's not allowed to walk home!"

She looks confused. "But you phoned the office."

Panic rises in my chest. I have an unsettling awareness of my own heartbeat.

"No. I didn't."

Mrs Darley is still talking, but I blank her out. My hands tremble as I dial Kate.

"Kate? Is Lauren there?"

"No," she says, sounding confused. "Why would Lauren be here?"

"What about Sophia?" I ask, urgently.

"She's not home yet. What's going on?"

My legs propel me forward. I run down the street, weaving my way through a sea of parents and children.

"Have you seen my daughter?" I call to the lollipop lady. She knows them all by face, if not by name.

She shakes her head, her eyes wide with concern.

If Lauren set off with Sophia, they'd be heading down the road, towards Sophia's house. It's on the way to ours. God, I wish Lauren had her phone, but it's against school rules.

"Watch it!"

Several mums shoot me venomous looks as I hurtle through the crowd. I reach my car and hover on the grass verge beside it. Should I continue on foot or would it be better to drive? I look down the road at the turning that leads towards Kate's. There's a footpath. Is that the way they went?

That's when I see the skirmish. I hear Lauren's voice, loud

and indignant. I turn, just in time to see a tangle of limbs and a flash of her green and grey uniform. Her hair has come loose from its ponytail and her voice rises, louder and louder, as she is pulled inside a white van.

"Lauren!" I scream. Every muscle in my body floods with adrenaline. "Lauren!"

There's another stifled yell in response. Then the screech of tyres as the van peels away.

4

The ground sways below me. People flood the pavements as I fight my way back to my car.

"Excuse me!"

I push past a group of slow-moving children, only to stumble over a dog lead that's helpfully tied to a buggy. The mother gives me a dirty look, but I don't care. My car is just yards ahead.

"Oy!"

A boy on a scooter rides into me as I cross his path. I don't even stop. I'm at the car. I grab the door handle and fall inside like a drunk. I press the power button and start to edge out of my parking space. The car beeps at me to put my seatbelt on.

"Move!" I scream in frustration at the vehicles in front of me. "Come on, move!"

My voice feels like it's coming from someone else. I punch the horn like a crazy person, but it has little effect. The road is too congested for anyone to move at any pace. I grip the steering wheel. My foot feels like concrete on the pedals. I can still see the white van. I think about getting out, but then the traffic lurches forward, giving me the room I need to pull out. I glance around. If I don't do it now, it might be too late.

Angel Dust

My ears ring with the sound of Lauren's screams. I wipe my face on my sleeve, trying to stem the flow of unhelpful tears that blur my vision. I reach for my phone and dial 999. I am connected straight away.

"What service do you require?" the call handler asks.

"Police!" I gasp. "My daughter …" I struggle to find words to express the enormity of the situation. "My daughter's been snatched from Queensbeach Primary School. I'm following in my car."

"Can you describe the vehicle?"

The call handler's voice is calm and reassuring, like this sort of thing happens all the time.

"It's a white van with tinted windows," I say. "It has a yellow licence plate, but I can't see the registration because there are other cars in front of me."

I pause. Each breath feels like an effort. I feel a surge of nausea and I hang onto the steering wheel as the world tips around me. There are cars and people everywhere, but the van is all I concentrate on. My life is in that van.

I think of Mrs Darley. Did she call the police? If so, they'd be on their way by now. I hear a helicopter overhead.

Please let it be them.

The traffic stops and starts. I still don't know whether to stay in the car or get out. I'm worried that if I do get out, the traffic will move and the van will be gone.

The call handler has stopped speaking. I glance at the phone and see that the screen's gone blank. Stupid thing. I dial again while I shunt the car forward. Most of the vehicles in front of me turn into the road on the right, but the van goes straight on, heading for the level crossing. My eyes go to the lights and then back to the van.

There's only one car between us now. I can see the van more clearly. It's covered in a thick layer of dust and someone has sketched a lewd drawing on the back. I can make out some of the number plate: T26 something. I want to sound the horn, but if I do, the driver will know I'm in pursuit.

Can you see me, Lauren?

I can't see anything through the van's tinted windows, but if she looks back, Lauren should be able to see me. She could be looking at me right now, begging for help. I glance at the lights again.

Please ...

To my amazement, they turn amber and the warning alarm sounds.

"No!" I scream, as the van shoots through. The car behind it tears through too, just before the barriers come down. I'm stuck behind the crossing. I bite down on my lip and taste my own blood.

Rather than wait for the crossing, the car behind me makes a right turn. Quickly, I put my car into reverse and move back as far as I dare. Then I glance at the tracks again. Still no train. I suck in my breath and hit the accelerator hard. In the next instant, I crash through the barrier. It breaks like a biscuit. I drive on, but the car bounces up against the second barrier and grinds to a halt in the middle of the tracks.

A noise like a death rattle reaches my ears. I can't look, but I feel the vibrations of the train rumbling down the track.

"Oh God! Oh God! Oh God!"

The second set of barriers is directly in front of me, blocking my exit.

I try to start the car again, but it has stalled.

There's no time.

I should get out of the car, but my legs have turned to jelly.

"Come on!" I shriek.

Finally, the car jolts into life and I stamp down hard on the accelerator, my eyes tight shut as I crash through the barriers. I feel a gush of wind as the train flies past, a hair's breadth from my car.

I made it.
I dare to look up, through the cracked windscreen.
The van has gone.

THE CAR SPLUTTERS and comes to a complete stop.
"God, not now!" I groan. I try to start it again, but to no avail.
People rush to help.
"Are you alright?"
"What the hell were you doing?"
"You could have killed yourself, you silly mare!"
I open my mouth to speak, but it's all too much.
"Are you hurt?"
I fall forward onto the steering wheel. I don't feel anything – only despair. Every precious second, Lauren is being carried further and further away from me. And I'm not doing anything to stop it. I can't function. Can't think.
My phone. Where is my phone?
With effort, I pull myself into a sitting position.
"Easy," someone says.
The people on the pavement are clamouring to see inside. I'm not sure if they're trying to help or if it's morbid curiosity on their part. Their voices drill through my throbbing head as they argue amongst themselves.
"We have to get her out."
"No, we shouldn't move her."
The door is wrenched open and kind hands reach in to help me. That's when I see my phone lying on the floor. The screen is so badly cracked, I can't make anything out.
"Police!" I manage.
"The police are on their way," someone says. "Ambulance too."
I hear the helicopter again.

Please tell me they're tracking her.

I emerge, trembling, from the car and look in the direction of the van.

"Did anybody see anything?" I ask the crowd. "Did anybody see the van?"

I'm met with a variety of blank stares.

"I didn't see no van," an old man tells me. "Only you and that train. I almost had a heart attack."

They don't even know what I'm talking about. They all think I'm cracking up.

"My daughter," I say through chattering teeth. "They took her. Someone must have seen?"

5

A neon-yellow ambulance pulls up in front of me. The paramedics are kind. They ask my name and try to keep me calm. I cling to them, in the hope that they will help me.

"My daughter's been taken," I say. "Please …"

They show too much concern for me and my injuries, and keep asking me simple questions. They're not sure I'm in my right mind.

"Can you tell me your name, luv? What's today's date? Do you know what happened?"

"Lauren, my baby!" I stutter. I can't think straight, can't form a coherent sentence.

I look around for the police.

"Try to keep your head still," the paramedics tell me. But I don't listen. What does it matter?

A police car arrives just as they are loading me into the ambulance. A female officer gets out and walks towards me. I grab onto her arm, determined not to let go.

"My daughter has been kidnapped," I croak. "She's in a white van, registration T26 …"

"What make?" she asks, taking a notebook from her pocket.

"I don't know. It was a white van."

I realise the futility of what I'm saying. There are so many white vans. I didn't even see the driver.

"What's your daughter's name?"

"Lauren. Lauren Elizabeth Frost. They might have got her cousin Sophia, too." It's the first time I've thought of this. "Unless she got away. There's a chance she got away."

My heart pounds as I consider the possibility: Sophia, running off into the woods; Sophia, reaching home and telling Kate, giving the police a proper description. Sophia is a sensible girl, wise beyond her years. Maybe Sophia saw what I didn't. Maybe Sophia can save Lauren.

The paramedics are set on taking me to the hospital, but I don't have time.

"I'm not hurt," I say, a bit louder than I intended. I feel ridiculous as they strap me to the stretcher and immobilise my head. The crowd on the pavement has grown. They gawp, even as the paramedics try to shoo them away.

"My name's Kirsty," the policewoman says. "You can tell me everything on the way. My colleague's already radioed for backup."

"Fine," I relent.

The paramedics continue to fuss over me, patching up the blood that trickles from my forehead. I'm not that bad, at least I don't think I am. I'm not sure I'd feel it if I were.

"Did you see the driver?" Kirsty asks. "Was it a man or a woman?"

"I don't know," I say. "I didn't get a good look. It all happened so fast."

The paramedics shut the door and I'm forced to lie back as the ambulance whizzes through the town. I'm grateful for their urgency, but I feel every bump in the road. Clutching Kirsty's hand, I tell her everything I can.

"Are you getting all this?" I ask, because my head is foggy and there's a danger that I might forget some important detail.

"Yes," she assures me. "Try not to worry, Isabel."

Could she say anything more insane?

"What about your husband?" she asks. "We can contact him for you."

"I don't know his number," I admit. "It was programmed into my phone, but he works at the hospital. Deacon Frost. He's a doctor."

When we reach the hospital, the paramedics open the doors and pull out my stretcher. I squeeze my eyes shut as they wheel me inside. I don't want people looking at me. If I had the strength, I'd get out and walk, but my legs are like rubber.

When I open my eyes again, I feel a fresh wave of pain. I know this hospital. Not just because Deacon works here, but because Lauren was born here. I remember holding my tiny bundle for the first time. Her face was all screwed up, purple and angry at the world. I remember when the doctor tried to take her off me to check her over. Even minutes old, she put up a hell of a fight, clamping her tiny fingers around mine and screaming blue murder.

Be strong, Lauren. Be as strong as you know how to be.

"Can you tell me your name?" the doctor asks now. Her smile is a little too bright and she speaks at double speed, as if someone's hit fast forward.

"Isabel Frost."

"How are you feeling, Isabel? Any pain in your shoulders or abdomen?" Her hands prod and poke as she assesses my condition.

"No."

"Feel faint or dizzy?"

"My daughter's been kidnapped," I say. "I really don't know what I'm feeling right now. Where's that policewoman?"

The doctor glances briefly over her shoulder, like she's about to change lanes. "She's probably on the phone," she says. "Bear with me a little longer. I need to make sure you haven't done yourself any damage."

I grit my teeth as she continues her examination, the smile still plastered to her lips. I try to focus on her questions, but I keep seeing flashes of Lauren being shoved into the van. Panic overwhelms me.

The doctor finally lets go of me and washes her hands thoroughly in the sink. The soap dispenser squeaks as it emits a green substance, which she works up into lather. The lather swirls round and round in the sink, punctuated by a burping sound as it washes down the plughole.

I pull the phone out of my pocket, hoping it has miraculously mended itself, but it's still cracked and useless.

"Is that the right time?" I ask, pointing to the clock on the wall.

"It is," a nursing assistant says.

"Then Lauren has been missing for nearly an hour."

I think about how far Lauren could have got in that time and grip the side of the bed.

"Here, drink this," the nursing assistant urges, thrusting a cup of tea into my shaking hands. "It will make you feel better."

"Nothing will make me feel better," I correct her, as my vision blurs with tears. But I take a sip. It's far sweeter than I like, but I drink it anyway. They give you tea for everything, don't they? A bad day, a broken heart, a missing child …

Images assault me. Lauren, her face white and bloody. Lauren, her face crumpled with pain. Lauren, blue and lifeless. It's nothing I haven't imagined before. As a mother, you have a repertoire of awful images you store in your mind. The images of the most terrible things that could happen to your child. You imagine them as a preventative technique, in order to keep them safe. If you have thought of everything, then it can't possibly come true. As if picturing your child dead somehow protects them from actually dying. As if warning them about strangers will stop them from being taken ...

"There's another police officer here to see you," the nurse says, leading a round-faced man into the room. He has the front teeth of a beaver, but his smile is warm.

"Mrs Frost?" he says, nudging the glasses up his nose. "I'm DS Paul Swanley."

"Please," I say. "Call me Isabel." Now, of all times, I can't be doing with pomp and formality.

"Isabel then," he says.

I wonder vaguely about Kirsty, the police officer who came in with me. Is this bloke more senior?

He continues to smile. Not a big, gaping grin like the doctor, but a gentle, patient smile that conveys kindness and understanding. Empathy is all very well, but is he up to the job? Does he know enough to make the right decisions? Does he have enough clout? I'd feel better if he had a partner with him, an assistant even. Someone to make him seem important.

"Can you tell me why you were late to pick up your daughter?" he asks, scratching his forehead with the other end of his ballpoint pen.

"I was only a couple of minutes late," I say, guilt burning my cheeks. "I had to pop home to pick up her permission slip for the school trip. They weren't supposed to let her go without me."

If only I hadn't faffed about feeding Fluffy. He could have waited until we got back. And that blasted form that seemed so important. What's the use of it now?

"If only I'd been on time," I say, tears welling in my eyes. "No one would have been able to take her."

"So, you didn't ring the school office?" he asks.

"No, I didn't. Someone must have rung pretending to be me."

Swanley hands me a tissue and I pause to blow my nose. I

can barely see through the fog of tears, but I need to get it all out – everything I heard and saw. How else are they going to find her?

"Do you have a reason to think someone would take your daughter? Has anything like this ever happened before?" he asks.

I'm distracted by Deacon's arrival. I hear his voice before I see him, loud and resonating. My husband has a presence.

"Deacon!" I call out.

He rushes towards me and hugs me. His face feels cold against mine. He must have been out when he got the call.

"Isabel, what the hell?" he whispers in my ear. He grips me slightly too hard, as he struggles to maintain his composure.

I shake my head in a meaningless gesture. How can I even begin to explain?

I did this. I wasn't there to protect her. I promised her I always would be.

Deacon looks at Swanley, surveying his round face for answers. "What now? What's happening with the search?"

I don't know how he manages to sound so coherent when I know that the horror I feel in my own heart must be mirrored in his.

"We are looking for Lauren, I assure you, sir. We still have more questions for your wife, though. I think it would be best if you would both accompany me down to the station. If you're up to it, of course," he adds, looking at me.

"How are you feeling?" Deacon asks me, a deep frown etched across his face.

"I'm alright," I say. "Physically, at least."

He nods. "I'll go and have a word with your doctor. See if I can get you out of here."

Minutes later, he returns with the doctor in tow. There's a slight twitch at the side of her mouth, as if her muscles ache from smiling so much. She feels sorry for him; I can see it in her eyes.

"You need to take it easy," she warns me, like that's going to be possible.

She grabs a clipboard and scribbles her way through the paperwork. I'm not even sure she's really writing anything, her pen flies so fast. It must be the quickest discharge ever.

6

Deacon's royal blue Bentley is parked round the side, in one of the staff spaces. I'm bruised and battered, but I don't feel like I have any right to complain as Deacon sets off at his usual brisk pace, only turning to look for me when he realises that I'm not right behind him. I can't even begin to keep up. My legs feel like they're two different lengths.

When we reach the car, he gets in the driver's side and sits there waiting for me. In happier times, I remember him coming round to my side to open the door for me, ushering me in with exaggerated deference. Today, he can barely look at me as I shuffle inside.

"Sorry," I tell him, as I reach for my seatbelt. "I'm so sorry."

"Stop saying sorry," he says, a little sharply. "Concentrate on remembering as much as you can. That's the best way to help Lauren."

I watch him start the car. His jawline isn't as chiselled as it once was, and the bags under his eyes have become more pronounced with each passing year. But there's still something about him that excites me. I don't know if he still feels the same way about me. We're both so busy these days. There's no time for the long, meaningful conversations we once had. I miss sitting on the kitchen counter, clutching a glass of red and talking and laughing with him until the sun comes up. We never do that anymore. We haven't in a long time.

He keeps his eyes on the road as we drive across town. His silence scares me. He's too quiet. It feels unnatural. I don't feel like talking either. It's all I can do to keep it together. Any minute, I might lose my mind.

Lauren. My baby.

❄

My stomach lurches as we arrive at the police station.

This is for Lauren, I remind myself, as I ease out of the car. Once again, Deacon strides ahead, disappearing inside. A stray tear runs down my face as I scurry after him. I wipe it angrily away and take a moment to compose myself before I go inside.

Deacon is standing at the front desk. He looks at me quizzically, as if to say, 'What took you so long?' before continuing his conversation with the duty officer.

The station is staffed by the next generation: fresh faced and jovial. I can't believe how young some of them look. Are these the people who are going to find my daughter? I barely notice the arrival of Paul Swanley. He and Deacon have been in conversation for a good five minutes, but it's only when Swanley says my name that I tune in.

"Isabel?" he prompts. "Would you like to come with me?"

He leads me through the labyrinth of corridors. The walls are decorated with prisoners' artwork. Pictures painted from the perspective of a prison cell. The view from behind the bars. Who would want to look at such grim representations? They are intended as a warning. A reminder of what lies in store for those who transgress.

Swanley comes to a halt outside an interview room. I exhale. I don't know if he senses my unease or if he puts it down to nerves.

"Come in and take a seat," he says. "Can I get you anything? Cup of tea?"

"No thanks," I say, staring at a familiar stain on the wall. Every inch of this room is imprinted on my brain. It's a scary black vortex and I am afraid to step inside.

This is for you, Lauren, I tell myself as I stumble towards the table.

I don't want to sit, but my legs buckle beneath me, leaving me no choice.

"You sure you don't want that cup of tea?" Swanley asks, kindly.

"Quite sure," I say.

He reaches into his pocket and pulls out a pen with which to stir his own cloudy tea. I am mesmerised by the riptide this causes.

"Hey, where's Deacon?" I ask.

"He'll join us in a minute," Swanley says. "My colleague had a couple of forms for him to fill in."

Bleeding bureaucracy.

He looks at me, his face filled with compassion. "Tell me, what's she like, your daughter?"

"She's strong-willed," I say. "That's what worries me the most. She has her own mind. She'll make things difficult for the kidnapper."

Salty tears wet my cheeks as I think about what might happen to Lauren. Sometimes, to be strong, you have to stay quiet. You have to make out that you're not going to be any trouble. You have to be willing to do what's asked of you. I'm not sure I told her that.

He hands me more tissues. "Try not to dwell on the what ifs," he says. "That kind of thinking isn't going to help Lauren." He consults his notebook. "You described her as four foot five, Caucasian with a slim build. Green eyes, auburn hair and freckles. Is there anything you'd like to add to that? Any birthmarks?"

I shake my head.

"I'd like you to think about what she was wearing. Can you remember?"

"She had her school uniform on," I say, as I blot my eyes with a tissue. "Grey pinafore dress, with a green cardy and a white blouse."

I let out a loud, choked sob as I think about how sweet she looked this morning.

"What about shoes?" he asks.

"Black shoes," I say. "From Clarkes. Size thirteen. Same as half the girls in her class."

I'm overtaken by another surge of pain as I picture her sitting on the back step, polishing her shoes with Deacon. He makes her do it every Sunday night, and though she moans about it, I think she likes it. Time spent with me is ordinary and mundane. But every minute with Daddy is special.

I hiccup loudly as I swallow too much air.

"Take your time," he says, gently. "Was she wearing a coat?"

I nod. "One of the school ones. Green, with a hood. And she's wearing white tights. Even though they're supposed to be grey."

"That's good," he says. "Anything else unusual? Did she have any badges on her coat? Any stickers?"

"Not that I can think of," I say. "The school is strict about uniform. Badges and stickers are not allowed. She'd painted her nails pink, though. In highlighter pen. It might have washed off by now."

The school doesn't approve of individuality. Lauren got in trouble just last week for wearing purple nail polish on her toes. Nobody would have even known if she hadn't shown it off when they were changing for PE.

"Any earrings?"

"She doesn't have her ears pierced," I say. A bone of contention between Lauren and me. She wants to get them done for her birthday and I keep telling her no. She's too young.

"Was she wearing a hat? Gloves?"

"No, she refuses to wear them."

"Glasses?"

"No."

I glance at the door. All this time, talking. Shouldn't we be out searching? She could be miles away by now.

"Try not to worry," Swanley says. "We're doing our best to find her."

He doesn't say that they will find her. He can't promise that.

"So, what happens next?" I ask. I have a feeling he is stalling me, but I'm not sure why. I've only just met the man, but if I knew him, I'm sure I'd find some significance in the slight flush of his cheeks and the way he keeps adjusting his collar.

"I'm sorry," he murmurs, so quietly I'm not even sure he really said it.

Then the door opens and in he walks.

DS Penney.

This can't be happening.

If he's in charge, we'll never find her.

7

"I gather you know DCI Penney?" Swanley says, breaking the tense silence.

So, he's a DCI now. More important. More powerful.

Penney smiles at me, but it is not a friendly smile. More of a snarl wrapped around a grimace. He is thinner and greyer than I remember and age spots have tarnished his face. But I bet his breath still smells of anti-septic. I get the impression he finds criminals so abhorrent that he has to cleanse himself inside and out. That would explain the shininess of his buttons and the neatness of his shirt.

"I'll take it from here," he tells Swanley.

Swanley flashes me an apologetic smile and slinks out. Penney waits till the door closes behind him, then he strides across the room and takes a seat opposite me. His chair looks too small for him. He is short in the body, but his legs are long and bony, and the ends of his trousers ride up, revealing woolly socks underneath. The room is silent except for my own laboured breath, which grows louder as I wait for him to pounce. I should speak first. Time is of the essence.

"My daughter has been kidnapped," I state.

His eyes swivel in my direction.

"Do you know how dangerous it was to drive through those barriers?" he demands.

I remember his aggressive style, the way he bombarded me with questions, pushing me to confess.

"Under normal circumstances," I agree, but he won't let me finish.

"Do you have any idea how much damage you've caused?"

I stare at him with incredulity. It's irrelevant. Why can't he see that? If I don't get Lauren back, it will all be irrelevant.

"Luckily for you, the signal man further up the track saw what happened. He managed to contact the driver and told him to brake. If he hadn't done so, you wouldn't be here now."

He watches me intently. "You showed no thought for your own safety or that of the passengers on the train. Let me say again how lucky you are."

I fold my arms across my body.

Lucky?

"You will have to pay for the repair of the barriers," he says, triumphantly. "You're looking at at least ten grand."

"My daughter is missing," I break in, "and you're talking about the cost of the barriers?"

Arsehole!

"It's quite a cliché, isn't it?" he says. "Abducted from the school gates."

I stare at him.

"What the hell are you implying? Lauren has been kidnapped! What are you going to do to find her?"

Penney inhales through his thin, oval-shaped nostrils. "I'm going to give you a chance, Isabel. I want you to tell me now if you have done anything to endanger Lauren."

"What the hell do you mean? I love Lauren. I would never do anything to hurt her."

Angel Dust

I summon all the humility I can muster. "Please," I implore. "I need you to find her."

He continues to look at me. He was always a fan of long silences. He thinks if he remains quiet long enough, I'll blab.

"Where's my husband?" I ask.

"He's with my colleague – answering a few questions."

"You've separated us," I say. *Why didn't I realise before?* "You want to see if we tell the same story."

He neither confirms nor denies my accusation, just maintains the stony silence. I glance towards the door. Is it closed or locked?

"You're wasting time," I tell him. "Deacon doesn't know anything about what happened. He wasn't there. I was."

"Then why don't you tell me what happened?" he says.

"Fine by me."

We go back and forth over the details: my description of the van and its number plate, the location of where Lauren was taken, what I heard and saw.

"And you're absolutely sure you didn't ring the school and tell them Lauren could walk home?" he asks.

"There's no way," I say adamantly. "I would never allow her to walk home without me."

"Could your husband have rung?" he asks. "The receptionist doesn't remember whether the call came from a man or a woman."

"She doesn't remember? Are you kidding me?"

I catch the glint in his eye and I know that I have caught him at a lie. The school receptionist is a pernickety sort of person. She wouldn't forget whether it was a man or a woman who called. She probably made a detailed note of it, down to the time of the phone call and the precise words they used.

"Why would Deacon have called?" I ask. "He knows Lauren's not allowed to walk home by herself."

"Are you sure about that? Sometimes we avoid telling the truth in order to avoid conflict."

I shake my head. "Even if Deacon didn't agree with me, he wouldn't have gone over my head like that. He'd have known I'd arrive to pick her up. He'd have known I'd freak out."

"Hmm!"

Whatever it is Penney's thinking, he doesn't share it with me.

I've never thought much of his interview techniques. He and his old boss, Millrose, asked me such leading questions, all those years ago. They thought they knew what was going on better than I did.

I look at Penney now. How can he not believe me? Does he really think I would make this up?

"Please," I beg him, "whatever you think of me, you have to help Lauren. She's young and innocent. She doesn't deserve this."

"Doesn't deserve what, Isabel? Where is she?"

Oh, for goodness sake!

"I want someone else on her case," I tell him, pointedly. "You're not taking me seriously."

"On the contrary, Isabel. I'm taking this very seriously. I just want to make sure that your daughter is really missing."

"Of course she's really missing!"

There's a knock at the door and a young officer peers in. "Here are the notes you wanted, sir."

He hands Penney a file.

"Thank you, Clyde."

The young officer withdraws and I wait while Penney sifts through the papers in front of him, flipping through the pages with his dry fingers.

Are they about Lauren?

"In the last eight and a half years, how many times have you called 999 to report your daughter missing?" he asks me.

"I don't know," I stumble. "A few times, I suppose." The words come out as a whisper, but he seizes on them at once.

"Including today, I make it twelve," he tells me. "I know this because I've asked to be notified every time you come into contact with the police."

"Why would you do that?" I ask, but it's just as I suspected. He can't let it go.

"Twelve times is a bit excessive, don't you think?"

"I know how it looks," I falter.

When Lauren was eighteen months old, she went missing at a parent and toddler group. I turned to put my coat on and she was gone. I searched for five minutes without finding her. I was terrified someone had taken her or she'd managed to get out the door and might at that very minute be tottering into the road. I had everyone looking for her, but to no avail, so I rang the police, only to find her moments later, giggling behind the curtain.

Two years later, we were in the park and I got talking to another mum. We were laughing about something, I don't remember what, but when we looked over at the sandpit, both our children were gone. We spotted them ten minutes later, hiding behind the climbing frame, but I had already rung 999 by then. I felt like a fool, having to tell the call handler that the children were fine, but for those ten minutes I really thought someone had taken them. I was in hell.

And there were other incidents over the years, like the time we lost Lauren at the garden centre. I know I over-reacted, but what are the police for if you can't ring them in an emergency? And a missing child is the very worst kind of emergency.

"Was this time any different to all those other times?" Penney asks me.

"Yes," I say. "Definitely. Someone rang the school and impersonated me, and I saw the kidnapping with my own eyes!"

He looks down at his notes again. "You need to get your story straight, Isabel. You told one of my colleagues that you couldn't see the van's number plate, but you told another you did."

"At first, I couldn't see it," I say, annoyed. "And then I only saw part of it. I'm not making things up. I'm telling you what happened."

I've gone over the details hundreds, maybe thousands, of times in my head since it happened. My body may have reacted slowly, but my mind ran off at a million miles per hour and it's still going. I still see the scene, over and over. Only, the more times I tell it, the more blurred and confused it becomes.

"Why don't you believe me?" I ask.

He studies my face. "Is there anything you're not telling me?" he asks, avoiding the question.

I know what it is; he has a gut instinct about me. I felt the same way the first time I met Alicia. Something was off about her. I just didn't know what. But how can I convince him that I'm innocent, that he should be helping me, not finding fault?

"I've told you everything," I insist. "Honestly, I have."

"I hope so," he says, grimly, "for Lauren's sake."

I expect Penney to put me in a cell for the criminal damage I caused to the level crossing, but to my surprise, he tells me I'm free to go. Probably so he can have someone follow me. He thinks I'm hiding Lauren somewhere. I know he does.

I feel lightheaded as I emerge from the interview room. As much as I hated it in there, I felt like I was at the epicentre of the search for Lauren. Now there's just silence and nothingness. I can almost hear the static in the walls. The emptiness grates on me as Swanley escorts me back to the front desk, where Deacon is waiting for me.

"Ready?" he mutters when I reach him.

"Let's go," I say. I want to take his hand, but it doesn't feel right in front of these people. And anyway, I'm not sure how he'd respond.

Deacon's face is so closed that I have no idea what he's thinking. Is he blaming me or is he just thinking about Lauren? We walk side by side to the car, our bodies not quite touching, but not quite apart. I feel unsure of myself in a way I haven't since we first got together. The air is thick with tension, but neither of us is ready to talk about it. Neither of us says a word until we arrive home.

I watch as Deacon punches in the security code at our front door.

"It's today," I realise.

"What is?" he asks, turning to look at me.

"Her due date," I say. That's what we use as our security code, not her actual birthday, which is three weeks later. That would be too easy for an intruder to guess. But her original due date, that is significant only to us.

Deacon sighs and opens the door. "I thought you'd remembered something," he says, as he switches on the lights. He sinks down on the sofa and pulls me towards him.

"Are you sure you don't remember anything else?" he asks me, searching my eyes with his.

"No," I say, quietly. "I've told you everything."

His frown deepens as he clings to me a little more tightly. I squeeze him back, but then he stands up abruptly, pulling himself free.

"I'm going to make a post on Facebook," he says.

I swallow. "If I had known for one minute this would happen…"

"I know," he says, but he can't look at me. I can't look at me. I stride past the hall mirror, where Lauren and I stood side by side this morning.

This can't be happening.

❄

Our big, empty house is eerily silent. There is no Shy Boyz

playing on the Sonos. No flurry of activity as Lauren sets up an assault course on the stairs. No one asking every five minutes what we're having for dinner or raiding the cupboard for crackers and crisps. Fluffy peers out from the kitchen and I remember the time she put doll's shoes on his feet.

"Oh, Fluffy!" I say, beckoning him over.

He narrows his eyes at me. Perhaps he senses the tension in my voice. Whatever the reason, instead of coming over to comfort me, he escapes out the cat flap.

I kick off my shoes and look at the photos on the mantelpiece. Lauren stars in every picture. There's a large framed photo of the three of us, taken just a few weeks ago at Christmas, then Lauren on her first day at school, standing by our front door. She looks proud in her brand new school uniform, clutching her new green satchel. Then there's Lauren as a toddler, with her hair up in wispy little bunches. She didn't have much then, but she already had that twinkle in her eye. And finally, there's Lauren as a baby, cherubic and perfect, all eyelashes and pouty pink lips. I let out a weird noise. I don't want to cry anymore, but I can't help it. I wrap my arms around my own body, wishing more than ever that I could hold her in my arms and tell her how much I love her. How Mummy doesn't mean it when she gets cross and shouts at her. That all she wants is for her baby to come home.

I stand in front of the liquor cabinet. Deacon keeps a fancy bottle of Cognac in there. He's been saving it for a special occasion. I wrench it out and unscrew the cork. I pour a large measure into one of the best tulip glasses. I raise the glass and feel its warmth on my lips. The heat lingers on my tongue, then spreads to my stomach. Oblivion is so close I can taste it, but I set the glass down abruptly. I could drink the entire bottle, but it's not going to bring Lauren back.

I look into the study. Deacon is staring at the computer, not typing, just staring. I once accused him of being the strong silent type, but he said he wasn't quiet; it's just that I like to talk all the time. I don't know which of us is right, whether he's quiet or I'm a chatterbox, but right now I really wish he would just say something.

I want to go in and comfort him, but I'm so scared that he blames me. I have enough guilt of my own. I can't deal with his recriminations. Instead, I go back to the lounge and slump down on the sofa. I feel in my pocket for my phone, but it's not there. What happened to it? I had it when I arrived at the police station. I'm sure someone asked to see it, but they didn't give it back to me. Maybe they needed it as evidence. It was badly smashed up anyway, but I could have still used the SIM card.

The phone we use for our landline sits on the window sill, looking dusty and forlorn. Only last week, Deacon suggested we get it disconnected. I pick up the receiver and listen. It still has a dial tone and there are a few numbers programmed into it, Julio's for one. I ring him. I ought to tell him about Lauren; I don't want him to hear it from someone else.

Julio takes his time to pick up and when he does, he sounds like he's been sleeping.

"What's up?" he croaks.

"It's Lauren," I tell him, the words burning my throat. "She's gone missing."

I hear the alarm in his voice. "What do you mean, missing?"

"She was snatched from outside the school," I say. The words sound more frightening the more I say them. "Someone in a white van…"

"What? Have you rung the police?"

"Of course I have!"

"Did you get the registration?"

"TR6 something," I tell him. "That's all I saw."

"I'll drive around," he says. "Which way did it go?"

He no longer sounds grumpy and lethargic. He's my

helpful big brother. The one who was there for me after I had Lauren and wasn't sure how I was going to cope.

"I'm not sure, maybe towards Portsmouth and Southsea," I say. "But it was hours ago. She could be anywhere now."

"It's still worth a try," he says.

"Maybe," I say.

"Don't worry," he says. "We're going to find her."

I want to believe him, I really do. My head pounds with images. The bright flash of light. The muffled screams. I had my chance and I didn't save her. It might already be too late.

8

The doorbell was an ill-considered Christmas gift from Julio. It plays any kind of music you want. I liked the idea at first, but it soon got on my wick. Lauren loves it, though. She spends ages choosing the songs. That's one of hers playing now, some guff by Shy Boyz, her favourite boyband.

I get up and answer the door. It's a police officer. I can tell that's what she is, even though she's in grey trousers and a crisp white blouse.

"I'm Erin Calthwaite," she tells me. "I'm your family liaison officer. Can I come in?"

"Yes, of course."

She has the kind of face that would blend perfectly into a crowd.

"Is your husband home?" she asks. "I'd like to speak to both of you."

"I'll get him."

Her expression is calm. "Which way is the kitchen? I'll put the kettle on."

"Straight ahead," I say.

I go through to the study. Deacon has not embraced the

Kindle age. He has glass cabinets crammed with books and papers. Everything has to be in paperback, or preferably hardback, or it's not a book to him. The computer looks wrong in this room. He should really have an old-fashioned writing desk with parchment paper and a quill pen. And yet there he is, staring at a flat screen.

"Find Lauren Frost," I read over his shoulder. He must have just set the page up, and now he's sitting there, waiting for someone to respond.

"There's a family liaison officer to see us," I say, pretending not to notice the books on the floor. Four or five of them lie spread-eagled on the rug behind his chair. He must have swept them off the table or perhaps hurled them at the wall.

"Oh yes," he says. "They said they were going to send someone."

"Did they?" No one mentioned it to me. Or maybe they did and I didn't take it in.

"Did you ask to see his ID?" Deacon asks.

"It's a she," I tell him. "And no, I didn't think…"

He stands up, leaving the books stranded on the floor like flightless birds. Erin is waiting in the kitchen.

"Hi, I'm Deacon," he says, putting out his hand to shake. He's gone back into business mode. I wish I could do the same. It's easier to hide behind a professional exterior.

"Erin Calthwaite," she says. "How do you like your tea?"

"Plenty of sugar, please," he says. He doesn't ask about her ID. Does that mean he trusts her? Since the worst has already happened, I let it lie.

"How about you, Isabel?" she asks.

"I don't care," I say. What does it matter how I take my tea? Lauren is missing. Right now, I'm not even sure I want to live.

She pours the tea and brings it over to the table. "Why don't we all sit down?"

I do as she asks. I'm so tired; I just want this all to be over.

"My job is to assist the investigation team," she tells us. "But I'm also here to support you and keep you informed."

I wonder how much Penney has told her. How do they work together? Is he her boss? Does she want his job?

"Do you know if Sophia got away?" I ask. For all I know, Kate's tried to ring me. Since I haven't got my phone, I've no way of knowing.

"She's missing too," Deacon says. "Rhett called while we were at the police station."

My heart sinks a little further. I had all my hopes pinned on Sophia. Kate and Rhett must be as frantic as we are.

"At least Lauren's not alone," Deacon says. "I mean, of course it's bad about Sophia, but two heads are better than one, aren't they?"

I think of the two of them giggling in the back of the car. I'm not so sure.

"Now, the more I know, the easier it is to build a picture," she goes on. "I know you've already gone over some of this with DCI Penney, but if you don't mind, I have a few more questions for you."

Deacon and I exchange a look. I'm getting the impression that the police are incapable of sharing information with each other. Every new person we come into contact with wants to hear it all again.

"Tell me, was Lauren happy at home?"

"Of course," I say, automatically. "Very happy."

"And at school?"

"Yes, I think so."

Deacon clears his throat. "She tolerates school, rather than likes it, wouldn't you say?"

"She's going on a trip to Stratford-upon-Avon soon," I point out. "She's excited about that."

Erin jots all this down.

"Now, I want to see all your photos of Lauren," she says.

"I know you've already passed some on to my colleagues, but we need more. Any photos or videos from the last few years. In my experience, this can really help."

"Yes, yes, of course," Deacon says. He looks at me. "We've got loads, haven't we?"

I nod. In the age of iPhones and digital cameras, we take more every week.

"There are hundreds on my Facebook page," I supply.

"Does Lauren have a Facebook account?" Erin asks sharply.

"God, no," I say. "She's not quite nine!"

"Oh, you'd be surprised," she says. "I've come across kids as young as six on there."

"Well, not Lauren," I say, adamantly. "We keep a close eye on her internet use."

"So she doesn't use any social media? Instagram? Snapchat?"

"No." I shake my head adamantly.

"Does she have a phone?"

"Yes. But they're not allowed to take them to school. She only uses it to play games and text her friends."

"Can she access the internet on it?"

"No," I say. "Lauren isn't allowed to use the internet."

"What about for school? Homework?"

"Well, yes, but then she's supervised. The computer has safeguards. We're careful."

"So, what happens now?" Deacon interrupts.

"Her details have been circulated on the Police National Computer," Erin says. "Any police officer nationally or internationally can contact us if there's a sighting."

I think that's supposed to be reassuring, but internationally? How far does she think Lauren's gone?

I glance at Deacon, but he's staring down into his tea. "You think she might have been taken out of the country?" he asks.

"There's no reason to think that at this stage," she says. "It's more likely she's somewhere nearby."

For the next hour, she asks us a long list of questions about Lauren. More detailed than the questions Penney asked.

"OK, well I think I have a better picture of what sort of person Lauren is now," Erin says. "Next, I need you to think about anyone you or Lauren may have had contact with. How do you get along with the neighbours?"

"Not great," I admit.

It started years ago, when Lauren was tiny. We'd never seen much of the neighbours, they kept themselves to themselves, but on this occasion, their front door opened just as I was taking Lauren down to the beach.

I looked up and saw a huge Irish Wolfhound bounding towards us. Lauren broke free from my hand and ran up to pet him, shrieking, "Nice doggy," as she tugged at his fur with her tiny hands.

"Lauren, stop!" I cried in horror.

"It's OK, he's totally harmless," his owner, Hilary, assured me.

Not taking any chances, I plucked Lauren away, which set her off screaming.

"All the same, I'd rather you didn't let him off the lead right in front of our house," I said, eyeing the pile of dog mess neatly deposited outside our gate.

"Oh, that wasn't Monty," Hilary said, sounding aghast.

I didn't believe her. It was a very quiet street, more of a dirt track than a street, with just our two houses at this end. How many other dogs came out this way of a morning?

❋

"We don't really have much to do with them, do we?" Deacon says now. His face looks so sallow it scares me. I've never seen him look that way before, not even when he had a root canal. Not even when his mother died.

"No, not really," I agree. "For the most part they go about their business and we go about ours."

"Well write their names down anyway," Erin advises us. "In fact, I'd like you each to make a list of people you and Lauren know. Underline anyone you think might have a problem with either yourselves or Lauren."

"There's only one person I can think of," I say, immediately. "Jody McBride. She and her sister had a real vendetta against our family ten years ago."

"We haven't seen her since, though," Deacon objects. "Do you really think it's her?"

I stare at him. "Who else would take Lauren?"

"I don't know," he says. "I think we should keep an open mind."

"You said she had a sister?" Erin asks.

"Alicia," I say. "She died. But Jody … Jody could have done it. She's pretty twisted."

"Deacon's right," Erin says. "It's very important we don't rule anyone out at this stage, so please, both of you. Think hard and write down everyone you can think of. Everyone."

She produces a wodge of paper and some biros from her bag. We have nicer pens in the drawer, but I don't have the energy to get them. Deacon takes a sheet of paper and starts to write. I hear his pen moving over the page and I'm tempted to look. What is he writing? We don't have any other enemies. We get on with people. We're normal.

"Start by writing down the names of everyone you and Lauren have had contact with," Erin prompts me.

"What about Sophia?" Deacon asks. "It could be someone she knows."

"My colleague is talking to Sophia's parents, so you just concentrate on Lauren for now," Erin replies.

I begin to write, but I feel like I'm incriminating every

person I write down. I know it wasn't Pam, our cleaner, or Hilary next door. So why do I need to write their names down? It feels like a witch hunt.

Deacon is still writing. He's turned over the paper and he's still going. He always was good at tests. I try to think, but my brain is constipated. There are the other mums at the school gates. I see them regularly, but I don't have many friends there. I used to have Siobhán and Kate to hang round with, but then Siobhán moved down to London and Kate stopped coming when Sophia started walking herself to school. Now I stand by myself. Nobody even speaks to me, aside from the odd hello. I write them down. School mums. Lollipop lady. Teachers. Classroom assistants.

Who else?

"Did you write down judo club?" I ask Deacon.

"Lauren does judo?" Erin asks.

"Yes," says Deacon. "Every Thursday."

I watch as she digests this information.

No, she's not going to fight her way out of this, if that's what you're thinking.

I'm sure she only goes to please Deacon. Judo is really his thing, something he loved to do as a boy.

"Who else goes to judo?" Erin asks.

"Just a bunch of local kids, the sensei and a couple of parent helpers," Deacon says. "They're all CRB checked, and I stay and watch each time."

"Still, it wouldn't be hard for someone to slip in and watch, would it?" I speculate. "Everyone would assume they were with one of the kids."

"It's usually the same people there every week," Deacon says.

He turns back to his list and continues scribbling, but my mind is whirling. I never go to judo, so I don't know exactly how it is. All I know is that it's the one evening a week where I'm not the one watching Lauren.

I struggle to think of more people to add to the list. My mum was here for Christmas, but she's gone off on her travels again. The only other family I have round here is Julio. And Deacon only has Rhett and Kate. We're a tightknit family; we've kept it that way on purpose. I'm not great at making new friends these days. I used to be much more easy-going, but since the hell Alicia put us through, I've been more guarded. I don't invite new acquaintances to the house and I'm cautious about accepting invitations. I felt we should be more careful than other people, but all this time I hoped I was being paranoid.

"Finished," Deacon says, from across the table. I look up. He has as well. Two A4 sheets worth.

"Keep thinking," Erin says. "There are bound to be more. Write them down as they come to you."

Deacon heaves a sigh. Like me, he wants all this to be done with.

"I know this must be very hard on you both," she says, more softly. "But this is the most important thing you can do to help."

It doesn't feel like helping. It feels like dobbing people in. It takes me over an hour to complete my list. And once it's done, I'm worn ragged.

Erin looks from me to Deacon. "I need to talk to you about the next step," she says.

Deacon glances at me. "Which is?"

She looks me right in the eye. "If it's OK with you both, I'd like to have my team come and search the house."

9

I stare back at her. "What on earth is that going to achieve? Lauren wasn't taken from home; she was taken from school."

"It's standard practice," Erin says.

"Why do you need to search the house?" I persist. "What are you looking for?"

"Searching the home has been proven to help in investigations like this," Erin says. "It tells us things about the family we didn't already know. It helps us get a better sense of who you all are and what has happened."

"You want to know if we've done it, you mean," I say, my face reddening with rage. I look at Deacon. "Why aren't you saying anything?" I demand. "Are you just going to go along with this?"

His eyes meet mine. "It's not like we've got anything to hide, is it?"

"Of course not," I say quickly. "It'll be a waste of time, that's all."

I can't believe he's staying so calm about this. In searching our house, they're practically accusing us. My mind flips back to the last time the police searched my house. It was ten years ago, when I was having all that trouble with Alicia and Jody. I didn't think the police could possibly find anything, considering I was innocent. But they found Julio's then fiancé, Holly, unconscious in the garage. And since she was too severely injured to speak for herself, it was easy for them to pin it on me. Penney wanted me to be guilty.

"Are they bringing in dogs?" I ask, trying to pull myself together.

"Yes."

"Then I need to put my cat out," I say.

"I think it's best if you all go out while we do this," she says. "Is there somewhere you can go? A friend's house maybe."

"You want us out of the way, so we don't hinder the search," I say. "Or worse, you're planning to plant something."

"I can assure you, nobody's going to plant anything," Erin says, "despite what you may have seen on TV."

"Let's go to the shop," Deacon says quietly.

"Shop?" Erin queries.

"I recently opened my own boutique," I say, flatly. I was so insanely proud of owning my own business, and now it seems inconsequential.

Deacon turns to Erin. "How does this work? Will you give us a call when you're done?"

"I'm afraid we'll need your phones," she says. "Don't worry, we'll monitor them and make sure someone answers if there are any calls."

"Mine's still at the police station," I tell her.

Deacon hands his over.

"Thank you," she says. "We'll get it back to you as soon as we can. I assume you have a landline at the shop?"

"Yes," I say. I produce a business card from the drawer and hand it to her. "The number's on there."

Angel Dust

❄

FLUFFY YOWLS as I scoop him up and carry him to Deacon's car. We have a cat box in the loft, but he goes berserk if I try to put him in it. He'd think we were taking him to the vet. He looks out the window and meows loudly. I suppose I could have put him in the garden, but I didn't want to risk him running off at the sight of the dogs. I couldn't bear that right now, on top of everything else.

Fluffy's yowls grow louder as Deacon starts the car. A van pulls up and I get a glimpse of the search team, all kitted out in hooded white overalls and blue plastic gloves. They look scary, as if they expect to find chemical weapons or something. I feel like a criminal more than ever, and I am terrified for Lauren's life. What do they expect to find in our house? What do they think has happened to Lauren?

"It's just standard procedure," Deacon says, parroting the phrase Erin used.

"I know," I say, but it doesn't make me feel any better.

Any minute, they will be marching inside to poke through our things. I cringe as I think of the dirty laundry I left lying in a heap by our bed, but I don't have the energy to go up there and move it. Besides, that might look suspicious. And, of course, they'll be in Lauren's room, rifling through her drawers, looking through her most intimate things. She's only eight years old, but we all have our little secrets, no matter how petty they might be.

I still hide stuff from Deacon. Basic stuff, like I close the bathroom door when I go to the loo and I don't let him see me shave my legs. It's about keeping the romance alive, isn't it? A woman has to have her secrets, like the bottles of red wine I drink on a Thursday night while they're out at judo. Deacon knows I like a drink, but if I finish the entire bottle, I've taken to hiding it in the recycling bin. It's my guilty secret – that and the family-sized block of chocolate I eat for dinner if I can't be bothered to cook. It's human nature to keep a little something for yourself, isn't it?

The self we present to the world is what we want everybody to see. That's why I search out the perfect top, with the perfect skinny jeans and heels that make me feel like the person I pretend to be. I don't want anyone to know that underneath my make-up, the wrinkles are starting to show or that if I didn't dye my hair every six weeks, the greys would be visible.

❄

When we arrive at the shop, there's a man asleep in the doorway. For all I know, he sleeps there every night. I step over his sleeping form and unlock the door. Fluffy's eyes glow with bewilderment as we step inside. He leaps out of my arms and races for the comfort of the armchair. We have a man crèche next to the changing room so that bored husbands and boyfriends can sit and read their Screwfix catalogues while their other halves try on clothes. Fluffy clearly thinks this is for him.

The power-saving energy bulb takes it's time to come on.

"Are you sure there isn't anything else you remember?" Deacon asks me as we stand in the half light. "Anything at all that might help?"

I turn to face him. "Why do you keep asking me that? Don't you think I've been over this again and again in my head?"

"I know," he says. "But you were there and I wasn't. There must be something."

There is a buzzing in my ears. The light flickers, drawing my attention to a single silvery thread that hangs from the ceiling. I blow on it. It sways precariously, but it doesn't fall.

Deacon is still looking at me, waiting for me to conjure up

a miracle. "There will be witnesses and CCTV evidence," he says. "If she was abducted in broad daylight—"

"What do you mean 'if'?" I demand. "I was there! I saw it happen."

"I know," he says.

But his tone betrays him. The same tone he used when his mother told him she would be alright, three days before she died of heart failure. He knew how ill she was – he's a doctor after all. He knew it and she knew it, but neither one of them wanted to admit it.

He's convinced I'm holding out on him. Perhaps the police planted that idea in his head while I was stuck in the interview room with Penney.

I walk towards the window and look out at the endless grey ocean. There's something about water that draws you in. Much like fire, I suppose. I fantasise about running down the beach and diving in. The waves are walls of water, rough and unforgiving. I wouldn't have to wade out far before I reached the point of no return. One little walk and all my worries would be over.

It's not the first time this thought has occurred to me, but I've never contemplated it as seriously as I do now. If anything's happened to Lauren…

"What do you think they're looking for?" I ask.

"I don't know, but it's good that they're doing a search," he says. "It means they're taking this seriously."

"I hope so."

I think of Penney, and the expression on his face when he saw me in the interview room. Is he taking this seriously? Or does he still think I've hidden Lauren somewhere? That I'm the one he needs to investigate?

I pick Fluffy up from the armchair and settle down with him on my lap. His fur is soft and warm as I stroke the smoothness of his head. I have to remind myself not to hold him too close.

If I had my phone, I would be ringing round, asking people to join the search for Lauren. But without it, I don't know anyone's numbers. I can't even do that much. I replay the morning in my head. Bickering with Lauren. We didn't even say a proper goodbye. How can that be my parting memory?

Grief fills the room like deadly gas. Lauren can't be dead, I would feel it. This situation is temporary. I'll soon be holding her in my arms again. I have to believe that.

Pink streaks of sunset bleed through the grey sky like the lines on a pregnancy test. One for negative, two for positive. One line between life and nothingness. I remember holding that stick in my shaking hands, knowing that my life had changed forever.

Deacon looks up at me with his sad brown eyes.

"Tell me what you're thinking," he says.

"You think this is my fault," I say. "Because I was late."

"Don't do this," he says.

"Do what?"

"Don't make this all about you."

"I'm not!"

I stare at him indignantly, spoiling for a fight. He opens his mouth to say something more, but his attention is diverted by the ringing phone.

He snatches up the receiver. "Yes?"

I hold my breath, waiting in agony for him to spill the news.

Finally, he turns and looks at me, eyes glistening. "They've found Sophia."

10

"Tell me," I beg, as he sets down the phone. "She jumped out of the van," he says. "They found her in the road."

My throat runs dry. "Is she–?"

"She's OK," he says, quickly. "She has a suspected broken collarbone but other than that–"

"And Lauren?"

"No word. They're searching the surrounding area, but there's no sign of her as yet. Most likely, she stayed in the van."

I breathe out slowly, as if I were smoking a cigarette. What if Lauren is injured too, lying helpless in the road, blood pouring from her head? I try to block out the hideous image, but I can't. I look at Deacon and long for his strong arms around me, but he can't deal with this any better than I can. I feel as though we're imprisoned in separate cages, each trapped in our own private agony.

"I can't believe Sophia jumped," he says, shaking his head.

"Me neither."

I don't like the thought of her jumping from a moving van, but she made it. She's safe. Lauren could be too.

I don't get it. Lauren is the bold one, not Sophia. That time we took them ice skating, Lauren was the first to strike out onto the ice, while Sophia clutched the rail for dear life. And at the swimming pool, Lauren is the one who dives head-first into the deep end, while Sophia climbs daintily down the ladder. Lauren was the first to ride her bike without stabilisers, the first to learn to somersault on the trampoline. How could she lose her bravado now, when she needs it most? Was it because I wasn't there to cheer her on?

Is the kidnapper angry, I wonder, that Sophia's got away? Or secretly relieved, because it was Lauren he wanted all along? That's what I believe deep down. That's what my instinct tells me.

"We need to talk to Sophia," I say. "She can tell us exactly what happened."

"I don't think she's ready for visitors," Deacon says. "Rhett said he'd call us later."

"Which hospital is she in? Did he say?"

"St Edmonds."

That's not our local hospital. St Edmonds is bigger, closer to London.

London. Is that where the van was heading?

I think of my little girl, lost in the sprawling metropolis. How will we find her in a city of eight million strangers?

"We could drive down there," I say. "It's got to be better than waiting."

"I don't know if that's such a good idea," Deacon says. "She's been through a lot."

"I know she has, but what about Lauren?" I challenge. "We need to know what happened, the sooner the better. Every minute counts."

I think of those precious minutes I wasted, stopping off at home to grab Lauren's form. Every minute counts. If only I'd known that then. If only I could start the day over. I look at Deacon. He has an unreadable expression on his face.

Angel Dust

"OK," he eventually says. "We'll go down there. But I'm driving."

"Fine by me."

I don't want to drive anyway. I can't look for Lauren if I'm driving.

I pour a bowl of milk for Fluffy and leave him in the shop. I feel guilty leaving him all alone, but I don't know what else to do with him. He hates being in the car. I'd call Erin to ask if we can bring him home yet, but I don't want to tell her where we're going. I have a feeling the police would rather we leave the investigation to them, but I can't do that. Lauren is my daughter, and nobody loves her more than me. Nobody is more determined to find her.

We get into Deacon's car and I sit in the passenger seat with my head pressed against the window. The sun has sunk below the horizon, leaving behind a pale twilight. The surrounding streets look familiar, yet different, obscured by the hazy glow. I glance over at the speedometer. Deacon is driving well over the speed limit. He catches me looking.

"I just want to get there," he says.

"Me too." I want to squeeze his hand, but I'm not sure how he'll react and I don't want to put him off his driving. We'll talk later, after we've spoken to Sophia, once we know more about the person who took Lauren.

Deacon puts on some music – a macabre compilation of Christmas carols sung by a Welsh male voice choir. It's an odd choice for January, but I don't object. The Christmas imagery feels all wrong – rejoicing over the birth of a baby when our daughter is missing, and why must they sing about angels? I have always called Lauren 'Angel', but people also refer to the children they have lost as angels, don't they? I can't shake the image of Lauren, dressed all in white with little angel wings.

Fifteen miles later, a vast Victorian building emerges out of the gloom. I look up at its sharp, pointed steeple and tall, narrow windows and give an involuntary shudder. The hospital is set in a sprawling estate that includes a research park. Despite this, it's almost impossible to find a parking space.

"There's one!" Deacon cries, triumphantly. He reverses the car into the empty space and switches off the engine. The male voice choir stops abruptly. Often, we sit in the car and wait for a song to end before we get out. But today, the music doesn't matter.

I go to the machine and pay for our parking while Deacon strides ahead to find out where Sophia is. I meet him at the enquiry desk.

"She's not in A&E," he reports. "They've put her in a private room."

We take the lift up to the ward and find Rhett in the corridor, getting himself a drink of water from the dispenser. The two brothers hug awkwardly. Neither is prepared for this. We didn't even warn him we were coming. He's probably wondering what we're doing here, barging our way in.

"How is she?" Deacon asks.

"She's OK," Rhett says. "The police have asked her a few questions, but she's a bit out of it."

"Where is she?" I ask, looking up and down the hall.

"In there," he says, pointing to the room next door.

I peer in. Sophia lies propped up in bed with her right arm in a sling. Her normally immaculate ponytail hangs limply to one side. She's safe, but she's not quite right; I can tell. Kate sits by her side. They're watching *Charlie and the Chocolate Factory* on a large TV that hangs from the wall.

I knock softly, even though the door is half open.

"Oh, Isabel!" Kate says, when she sees me. She jumps up and gives me a big hug, as if she can squeeze away all the pain. If anyone knows what I'm going through, she does.

"Let me get you a chair," she says, and before I can protest, she has dragged one over, placing it on the other side of Lauren's bed.

"Thanks," I say, sitting down. "How are you feeling?" I ask Sophia.

"It's a nasty break," Kate says, when Sophia doesn't answer. "She's going to have an operation. They'll do it tonight if they can fit her in."

"Oh, Kate!" I'm so torn between her need to be comforted and my own desperate need to find Lauren.

"I really need the loo," she confesses. "Haven't been for hours."

"Why don't you go now?" I say. "I'll stay with Sophia."

"Would you?" she says.

She glances at her daughter. "I'll only be a minute, OK?"

Sophia tries to nod, but the movement is so painful, she winces.

"Don't try to move," Kate tells her. "You need to rest."

I watch until she's out of sight. Deacon is still with Rhett out in the corridor, talking about safe things like search routes and logistics. I listen to the sound of Kate's footsteps heading away and then I lean towards the bed. The police might not have got much out of Sophia, but I'm her auntie. I know her better than they do. Gently, I take her hand. It feels cold and clammy in mine, even in this warm room, with the radiator whacked up to the max.

"You've had a terrible time," I acknowledge.

Sophia meets my gaze. Her face lacks emotion. I remember her, aged four, howling uncontrollably over the loss of an ice-cream, which had been swiped from her hand by a seagull. But she has not taken in what has happened today. She does not yet know how to feel about it. I want to help her. I really do. If I can get her to open up, she will not only be helping Lauren, she'll be helping herself.

"Did you get a good look at the kidnapper?" I ask.

She looks down, focusing on a loose thread in her sleeve.

"Can I get you anything?" I ask. "I bet you'd like some ice-cream, wouldn't you?"

"Mum said I couldn't," she says with suspicion, "cos of the operation."

"Oh … right, well. She's probably right about that."

Dammit! I rattle my brain, more and more desperate.

"What about some Shopkins?" I say. "There's a new season out. I could drive to the shop and get you some."

"Won't it be closed now?" she says.

"In the morning then," I say.

She doesn't even break a smile.

"My Little Pony?" I say. "Littlest Pet Shop. There must be something you'd like?"

But Sophia is closed to bribes.

I hear the sound of footsteps in the corridor and wipe the sweat from my brow. Kate will be coming back any minute. I've got to get her talking before she clams up again.

I move closer. "What happened, Sophia?"

She bites her lip.

"Come on, you can tell me. It'll be better if you do."

I don't mean it as a threat, but with hindsight I can see how it could be taken as one.

"What is going on here?"

I spin round to find myself looking at two thickset nurses. From the expressions on their faces, they've clearly got the wrong idea.

"You're not supposed to be putting her under any stress," one of them say, sternly.

"I wasn't," I say, my face blazing. "I just wanted to ask her—"

Kate appears from behind them. She has an angry look on her face. "Isabel, the police have already spoken to her. She needs to rest now. I thought you understood."

I stare back at my best friend. "Lauren might be dead," I say, realising too late that I shouldn't have said this in front of Sophia.

I run out into the hall, hot tears streaking my cheeks.

Those bloody incessant tears. What does crying ever achieve? I concentrate on putting one foot in front of the other. I must have stood up too quickly, because now the walls are spinning around me, the floor rising up to meet my face.

"Isabel?"

Deacon takes me by the arm and stops me before I fall. It's the first real contact we've had in hours. He helps me into a sitting position.

"Put your head between your knees," he says.

But I just look at him, through a sea of tears.

"Let's go," I say. "I can't stand being here, doing nothing. Sophia is not going to tell us anything. We're no closer to finding Lauren."

"Leave it to the police," Kate calls after me. Her words are like a bullet through my heart.

I don't have faith in the police.

Lauren, my baby.

I feel like I'm bleeding inside. The longer Lauren is missing, the more I lose of myself.

I just want them all to go away, but it's several minutes before I find the strength to get back on my feet. And when I do, Deacon wraps his arms around me, and we stagger back to the car together. I'm the one doing all the blubbering, but I know he's hurting just as badly inside. It annoys me that he's able to hold it together so convincingly, while I'm a quivering mess.

We traipse back to the car and Deacon's music comes back on. We listen in painful silence all the way back to Queensbeach.

"We need to pick up Fluffy," I say, as we turn off the coast road.

"I know," Deacon says.

He pulls up in front of my shop and waits while I go in and get Fluffy. I find him sprawled out on the armchair, his bowl of milk tipped all over the floor. I don't even attempt to clean it up. I check the phone and find a voicemail from Erin, to let us know that the search is finished and we can come home. Then I pick up my cat and wrangle him into the back of the car.

❄

Erin is still loitering in the kitchen when we arrive home. Everything is reasonably tidy, but you can tell someone has been here. I set Fluffy down, and he runs straight for the cat flap, probably to relieve himself.

I start up the stairs to check on Lauren, before I remember she's not there. It feels so strange for her to be away from me at this time of night.

"Sit down," Erin says, as if we're in her house, not she in ours. "I wanted to ask you more about Jody McBride. Do you really feel she could be behind this?"

"It's possible." I glance at Deacon and he nods grimly.

Erin looks at her notes. "And the last contact either of you had with her was the day Alicia died?"

"Yes," Deacon says.

"Not quite," I say.

Deacon looks at me. "What are you talking about?"

I bite my lip. "There was a letter," I say.

"What letter?" he demands. "You never told me."

"I know," I admit. "But it was ten years ago, and there's been nothing since."

"Tell me about the letter," Erin says, her face serious but neutral.

"It was supposedly from Alicia," I explain, "but I didn't receive it until after she died. I'm not convinced Alicia wrote it. It might have been Jody pretending to be Alicia."

"I'm sorry, I'm confused," says Erin.

"That makes two of us," says Deacon. He's so angry, he looks like he might explode.

Angel Dust

"Did you keep a copy?" Erin asks.

I shake my head. "I wanted to be rid of it, so I burned it."

"You burned it?" Deacon says, incredulously.

After all we went through with the McBride sisters, I've been nervous of fire ever since. I even gave up smoking thanks to them.

"It seemed appropriate," I try to explain. "It felt really good to burn something of theirs."

"What was in this letter?" Erin asks. "Can you remember?"

"Just the usual ranting and raving," I say. "They were both crazy."

"Can you be more specific?" she asks.

"Afraid not."

She presses her lips together. "Well, if you remember anything, be sure to let me know."

❋

"What did the letter really say?" Deacon asks, after Erin leaves. "You must remember something."

"Of course, I do."

It's been ten years, but I remember every word. I grab a pen and notebook from the table. The eerie letter practically rewrites itself:

If you are reading this, you have probably already killed me.
I want you to know that I forgive you.
I have prayed for you, as you must pray for me.
Do not mourn me, for I am in a better place now.
I am with you and I will watch over you always.

Your friend forever,

Alicia

"She was a raving psychopath," I say, looking down at the note. "I'm not sorry she died. I only wish Jody had gone with her."

I look up at Deacon. He has a bitter look on his face.

"I can't believe you've kept this from me all these years!"

"I wanted us to be able to get on with our lives," I say, in a strangled voice.

"Well, look where that's got us!"

I sit with my head in my hands. I told myself it was all over, but deep down I never really believed it. Why else did I impose so many restrictions on Lauren?

"Where are you going?" I ask.

"A few of us are going to drive around and see if there's any sign of the van," he says. "It's a long shot, but at least we'll be doing something."

"Julio's already out there," I say. "Maybe you should give him a ring to make sure you're not covering the same ground."

"Yeah, maybe," he says, dismissively.

"I could join you," I add.

"No, someone needs to be here if she comes home," he says.

❄

Left alone, I curl up on the sofa. Fluffy is out on the prowl, so I sit, motionless, in front of the TV, well into the wee small hours. The screen glows and flickers, but I can't tell you what I watch. I reminisce about a younger Lauren skipping about the garden, singing to herself and dancing in the breeze. I think about the future too. I picture her graduation and her wedding day. I think of the children she might have had. Might still have.

She has to come home. She has to.

I hear the Bentley pull up and rush to the window, but Deacon is alone. He hugs himself tightly as he walks up the path to our door. He yanks off a piece of the ivy that creeps up the side of the house. It's a futile exercise – no matter how much he cuts it down, it always grows back stronger. Behind him, the sky has begun to turn orange. I used to think a sunrise was magical, but now I hate it because it means Lauren has been gone all night.

11

I didn't eat last night. My stomach rumbles angrily to remind me. I take a loaf out of the bread bin and stick two slices in the toaster. Deacon went straight to his study when he came home. He'd borrowed a laptop from a friend, so he could trawl the social media sites to appeal for information about Lauren. I feel guilty that I've done nothing but lie around and wait. I wish I had the energy to do more, but I feel so awful and every muscle in my body aches from the crash. My toast pops up and I decide not to make anything for Deacon. He'll come out when he's hungry. I get the sense that he wants to be alone.

I eat the toast plain, standing at the sink and staring out at the vast ocean beyond. Occasionally, I'll see a boat, but mostly it's just a huge empty space, filled with nothing but endless waves as far as the eye can see.

The door chimes. Shy Boyz again.

Lauren!

I drop my toast and run to the door. My hand shakes as I unlock it. But it's only Erin.

"Oh," I say, unable to hide my disappointment.

"Morning," she says, politely. From the look on her face,

we should be expecting her, though I don't remember her saying she was coming back this morning.

"I hope you managed to get some rest?" she enquires.

"Hardly," I say. I know I sound abrupt, but I can't help it.

She brushes past me, into the house and springs into action, making tea. She seems to have memorised where everything is, from the cups to the sugar bowl. Or perhaps she's done this so many times in so many houses that she's developed an instinct for it.

Deacon comes out of his study and accepts a mug from her, which makes me regret not making him one earlier. I'd rather he drank my tea than hers. There's a slice of toast left in the toaster. I offer it to him, but he rejects it with a wave of his hand.

"Can you tell us the latest?" he asks Erin. "How much money is being spent on the investigation? What's the budget?"

Deacon likes to deal in solid facts and figures.

"I can't tell you exactly from the top of my head," she says.

"Can you please ask?" he says. "I want to know."

"I'll find out," she promises him. "Now, we're hoping to work with Sophia to get a sketch of the kidnapper," she says. "Meanwhile, we're out interviewing any potential witnesses. We're also focusing on the vehicle. We have identified half a dozen white van owners with children at Lauren's school and they're all being questioned so that we can eliminate them from the investigation."

"What about the reward?" Deacon asks. "When's that going to be announced?"

"What's that?" I ask.

"We're going to offer a million-pound reward," he says, "for information that leads to Lauren's safe return."

"Where are we going to get a million pounds?" I ask. "I

mean, even if we sold the house, it wouldn't be worth that much."

We had the house valued a few years back and found that it was worth considerably less than we had hoped. We're too close to the ocean apparently, and with the rising sea levels in recent years, it's hard to get insurance.

"We'd find it," he says, shortly. "All that matters is that we get Lauren back."

I nod slowly. We'll do what we have to do. We can worry about the details later. The important thing is that we look like we could have a million pounds. No one needs to know that we don't really.

"We could announce it at the press conference later," Erin says. "Or we could wait a day or two and announce it then."

"Why wait?" Deacon asks.

Erin bites her lip. "Well, for one thing, it would reignite the press interest in the case if it starts to wane, but also I think it would give you time to think about whether you really want to offer such a big reward."

"Why not?" he says.

"Don't get me wrong, it might help us get more leads," she says. "But on the other hand, we'd also get more timewasters. We need to think about what's best."

"Well, what do you think?" I ask.

"It's really not for me to decide," she says. "You need to talk it over yourselves."

I glance at Deacon. What the hell is she for if she's not going to advise us on these matters?

"What about the press conference?" he asks. "Do we need to take part?"

"If you're up to it," she says. "Ideally, I'd like you to sit beside me and talk a bit about Lauren."

"What are we supposed to say?" I ask.

"Just tell people a bit about her and the effect her disappearance is having on you. Make it personal."

"Will it make any difference?" Deacon asks.

"It might. It could prompt people to call in."

I inhale. My face has been on TV before, and splashed all over the papers. During my trial, there was a whole horde of people who were convinced I was guilty. It's all died down now, and people seem to have forgotten about it, but if I go on TV again, they might all come crawling out of the woodwork.

"We have to do it," Deacon says, reading my thoughts. "If you don't take part, it will look odd, like you have something to hide."

"I'm not sure I'm the best person to do it."

"You're her mother," he says, firmly. "Don't worry, I'll be there. And so will Erin."

He smiles gratefully across the table and I wonder if we see two different sides to Erin. I view her with my natural mistrust of the police. But Deacon seems to find her presence comforting. Perhaps I should be glad she's here to lend the moral support that I can't give him.

Around mid-morning, the house phone rings. Its unexpected trill makes me jump. I get up from the sofa, where I was trying to rest, and rush towards it, but Deacon gets there first.

"It's your mum," he says. He hands it over without a word. I suppose he can't face small talk right now. I'm not sure I can either, but I'm glad to hear from her.

For the past few years, she has flitted from one exotic country to another, on an endless quest to 'find herself'. For the most part, I don't mind that she's so far out of reach, but there are times when I wish she was around. She was abroad for most of the time I was in prison, although she sent a strongly worded letter to the Prime Minister. But she never came to visit me during all those awful months inside, when visitors were all I had to look forward to. This is totally different, though. Mum adores Lauren. She'd do anything to help.

"Oh, darling, you must be wretched!" she says. I hear loud

bhangra music in the background. It sounds like she's calling from a bar.

"I just want her back," I say.

"Of course you do! What do you want me to do? I can hop on a plane tomorrow, if you like? I could be with you Thursday. Or definitely Friday."

Thursday? Friday? But all this will be over by then, surely. They'll have found Lauren, for better or worse. She'll be back home with me.

Won't she?

Mum is silent, waiting for my answer, and it's all I can do not to hang up.

❇

"She probably won't be here till Friday," I tell Deacon, flopping back down on the sofa.

"She's coming here? Do you think that's a good idea?" he asks.

"What do you mean? My mum loves Lauren!"

"I don't doubt it," he says. "I'm just not sure I can handle having her around right now."

"That's not fair!"

"Look, her heart's in the right place," he acknowledges, "but please, think about it. Do you really want her here?"

I squeeze my eyes shut. His own mother was a saint, always said the right thing, never put a foot wrong, but I never felt very comfortable around her. I never had a clue what she was thinking. I still don't even know if she liked me. Personally, I find that harder to bear than my mum's flakiness. It's what you grow up with, I suppose.

"I don't know," I admit. And I really don't.

❇

THE PRESS CONFERENCE is scheduled for that afternoon. Almost twenty-four hours since Lauren was taken.

"I know this is going to be difficult," Erin says, before we go in, "but this is the best way to catch all the journalists at once. We want to make headlines, and you taking part will have a huge impact."

"I hope you're right," I say, grimly.

I remember the press conference after my trial. My lawyer, Brian, took that one for me. I couldn't bear all those cameras and reporters pointing and staring at me. It irks me even more now, in my darkest hours, when all I want is to be alone. I have to remind myself that the press coverage is a good thing this time. We want all eyes on us because they might help us find Lauren.

"Remember, many of the people watching at home will be mums too, with children of their own," Erin says. "Seeing you will help them to feel empathy."

I nod and remind myself again that this is for Lauren.

"You might find it helps to know you are doing all that you can," she adds.

But am I?

I have never felt more out of control.

DCI Penney slithers into the seat at the end and there he sits, shuffling his papers. Shouldn't he be talking to us, updating us on the case?

"Maybe Lauren will see this," I whisper to Deacon, as we take our places at the long table. I think about that as I look out at all those cameras.

Lauren, I know you're out there. Don't be scared. Just do what you have to do to stay safe.

Penney's long legs swing back and forth as he tries to get comfortable. I glance in his direction and he wrinkles up his nose as if I smell of rotten eggs. I look at Erin instead. She smiles thinly, as if it pains her to offer me any comfort. I shuffle a little closer to Deacon and try not to cry.

The reporters sit in serried rows in front of us. Some look smart and glossy while others look like they've slept in their suits. I stare at their equipment, the cameras and booms. I shift in my seat as another group crowds in at the back. We were supposed to start ten minutes ago, but we've been delayed because one of the main news outlets is not here yet. Apparently, their reporter is notorious for turning up late, and it's not going down well with the other journalists. I really hope this won't affect how they cover the story. I feel their eyes on me as they wait. They watch me closely, searching my face for clues. But I have learnt from experience that you can tell nothing from a person's face. The most conniving people can look as innocent as they like, while perfectly normal people seem shifty.

"It's always the family," a shrew-like woman whispers.

I've thought the same myself in the past. I can remember discussing cases I knew nothing about. It always seems so simple from the outside.

"Is this your regular gig?" Deacon asks Erin, while we wait. "Acting as a family liaison?"

"Actually, no. This is my first time," she says. "But don't worry, I'm perfectly qualified. I've been with the police force for twenty-five years."

"That's a long time," he says, raising his eyebrows at me because, honestly, she doesn't look that old.

"So how come you're doing this now?" I ask.

I want her to tell me that there's something about this case that resonates with her, that she's worked on kidnapping cases before or she has a background in child protection.

"I was assigned to the case," she says.

I rub my tired eyes. Is it possible that she was chosen simply because she's a woman? I can picture it.

"We need a family liaison. It might get emotional. Send Calthwaite."

There's no more time to think about it because the absent reporter has finally arrived and we are given the go ahead. I sit and wait while Penney tells the assembled group about Lauren and gives out the details of the white van. Then it's my turn to say something.

Lights shine in my eyes. They're so bright, they make my eyes water. I have always hated public speaking. Always hated the sound of my own voice. I glance out into the crowd. There's a face I recognise. She's tall and angular, with wavy brown hair that brushes her shoulders. Her dead-straight nose gives her a fierce look. I'm sure I've seen her before. I just can't put my finger on it.

My mind goes blank, so I glance down at the notes in front of me.

"Lauren, I want you to come home. You're not in any trouble, no matter what. We miss you and we love you. We just want you to come home."

It comes out sounding robotic. I've never been big on public displays of affection. It's not done. And here I am, expected to turn on the waterworks to make it sound more convincing. I have cried so many tears, but I can't cry now, not on cue.

"Can you tell us a bit more about Lauren?" one of the reporters prompts.

I nod. There's so much to tell, it's hard to know where to start.

"Lauren loves playing with her teddy bears," I say, thinking of the hours she's spent setting up teddy bears' picnics, playing schools with them, teaching them all to read. I think of all the stuffed toys sitting around her room. She used to leave them all over the floor, but lately she's been better at keeping them tidy.

"She loves animals too." The words stick in my throat and I force myself to continue, ignoring the heat of my cheeks. Will they take my embarrassment for guilt? Even through the agony I'm facing, I haven't lost all my inhibitions. I am still English, after all.

"Everything from cats and dogs, down to tiny insects. She loves looking for crabs in the rock pools near where we live. She asked me once if she could put a crab on each ear and wear them as earrings."

There are some strange rumblings from the assembled press, who aren't sure if laughter is expected or even permitted. I exhale sharply. Somehow, I've lost the art of breathing while talking and I need to catch my breath before I can go on. I glance down at my notes again. The last bit, the most important bit …

"Lauren, if you are watching this, I want you to be brave. If you can get to a phone, dial 999 and the police will come and get you. Even if you don't know where you are, they will find you. And if you can't get away then just … just stay strong."

My bottom lip quivers and I feel Deacon's arm reach across to hold me steady.

"That's it, you've done it," he whispers.

"Well done," Erin says, more formally from the other side. Her tone is a bit patronising, but I appreciate the sentiment.

"Well, I think that went as well as could be expected," she says, once we get outside.

"Is that good or bad?" I ask, feeling an unpleasant breeze down my back.

"Good," she says, quickly. "Very good."

I'm not sure whether I believe her.

I go straight to bed when we get home. I cover myself with the duvet, and still I can't get warm. I try to stifle my sobs with the pillow, but they keep coming back up, louder and louder. No one comes up to check on me and I'm glad. I don't want to be comforted. I want to be left alone with my grief. I deserve grief, if nothing else. I taste its salty bitterness on my tongue and wish I could choke on it.

12

When I look outside, it has grown dark. How long was I asleep? Four hours? Five? How could I sleep so long when Lauren is missing?

The house is quiet. I hear Erin out in the garden, talking on her phone. How she can bear to spend so much time out there, I don't know. The branches hang with icy fingers and the grass is as solid as badly gelled hair, but some people are outdoors people. I suppose she's one of them.

Deacon is asleep in his study, his head resting on his desk. His laptop screen blinks when I nudge the mouse, revealing the pages he created for Lauren. I see there have been some replies. I scan them quickly. Dozens of messages of support but nothing solid. Nothing useful.

I decide to go up to Lauren's room. I haven't been in there yet, not since she's been gone. At first, I didn't want to disturb anything, but the search team has been and gone now. There's no reason not to go in.

I push open the door. It looks much as it was, a little tidier maybe. The search team must have taken her pyjamas – she always leaves them in a heap on the floor, no matter how many times I tell her to put them in the laundry basket. I wish they were still there. They would smell of her.

I'm always telling Pam not to tidy in here. Lauren is responsible for her own room, but I bet she does it anyway. Lauren has her wrapped around her little finger.

I look around, desperate for something to straighten or tidy, but there are no sweet wrappers, no old cups of juice or crisp packets lying around. Lauren is not here, and her empty bin attests to this.

I bend down and pull up the edge of the rug, but there's not even a sequin. The search team has been thorough. I sit down at the desk under her cabin bed. Her books lean haphazardly on the shelf and I flick through the titles before I straighten them. Half a dozen Secret Sevens and Famous Fives. The books I loved to read when I was her age. I make my way up the ladder and peer into her bed. There's a magazine lying on her pillow. I leaf through it and see that she has filled in the quiz pages and doodled her name on the back cover. I climb back down again and notice the teddies, sitting neatly in their cubbyholes. I pick up her favourite Care Bear. How did he get so dusty? I wonder. Come to think of it, when was the last time I actually saw her play with her bears? Has she grown out of them without me even noticing?

Erin is on her laptop at the kitchen table when I return downstairs.

"You managed to get some sleep then?" she asks me. It feels like an accusation.

"Yes," I say. "Is there any news?"

"Our officers have spoken with Sophia again," she says, gravely. "She's given a good description of the kidnapper. They'll send us through a picture shortly."

"Good."

"And DCI Penney has asked if you could go down to the station."

"Why?"

Angel Dust

"He'd like to go over your statement with you again."

"I thought I was supposed to go through this stuff with you."

"You are, for the most part, but he said he wanted to talk to you. I can give you a lift if you like."

"No, that's OK."

I don't like the thought of Erin ferrying me around, but I've forgotten about crashing the car. I don't even know how badly damaged it is. The police must have had it cleared away by now, but nobody's mentioned anything to me. I could ask Penney, but I'm worried that if I do, he might think to confiscate my licence.

"I'm taking your car," I call to Deacon as I pass his study.

He looks up and nods. He's too engrossed in his social media sites to ask where I'm going. I grab his keys from the kitchen counter and go outside to reacquaint myself with the Bentley. It's been a while since I last drove it and it handles very differently from my Picasso.

It makes sense that Penney wants to talk to me again, I tell myself, as I edge out of the driveway. If they've got Sophia to talk, then they'll have more information, things they need to check with me. Still, it's hard to stay calm as I arrive at the police station.

Paul Swanley comes to escort me to the interview room. He is friendly and talkative, as if I were here for a social event. I get the impression he's one of those people who have a naturally sunny disposition. I did too, once.

A young officer sets a plastic tray of tea and biscuits down in front of me. The mugs are mismatched and the tray looks like it was swiped from somebody's living room, as if the police force is too hard up to provide kitchenware.

"Thanks," I say, with feigned cheer.

"How are you coping?" asks Swanley, crossing one portly leg over the other.

I meet his gaze. How can I possibly answer that?

"I can't imagine what you're going through," he says, gruffly. "I've got a little girl myself."

I was hoping Swanley would hang around, but he beats a hasty retreat when Penney comes in. Penney closes the door behind him. I don't like that. I don't want to be alone with him. I wish Swanley were still here.

Penney sits down opposite me, just as he did all those years ago. He sits very upright, as if he has a rod up his back.

"Does your daughter eat sweets?" he asks.

"Of course," I say. "What kid doesn't?"

I feel like he's questioning my parenting skills. Yes, I let Lauren have sweets. Not every day but probably more than I should.

"Why do you ask?"

"There appear to be a few inconsistencies in your statement," he says.

"What inconsistencies?"

He leans back in his chair and rests his arms behind his head.

"You called the police a bit too early, it seems."

"What do you mean?"

"You made a pre-emptive phone call."

I shake my head. "I'm sorry, I still don't follow."

"According to Sophia, the girls were kidnapped at around half past three. Why, then, did you report Lauren missing at a quarter past three?"

"Sophia must have got the time wrong," I tell him.

"Ah, but her timeline has been verified by staff at the One Stop Shop. Do you know it?"

"Yes, of course."

The shop is ten minutes down the road from the school and on the opposite side of the street. I've been there hundreds of times to pick up a pint of milk or a packet of biscuits on my way home from the school run.

"Lauren and Sophia went to the shop to buy sweets,"

Penney tells me. "They bought a packet of Jelly Babies and a packet of Wine Gums. We have them on CCTV, leaving the shop at a quarter past three."

"It can't be them," I say, shaking my head.

"Sophia herself says they went to the shop," Penney counters.

I stare at him. "I'm sorry, I don't understand. How is that possible?"

"That's what I'd like you to tell me, Isabel. If your daughter wasn't missing until half past three, why did you crash your car into the barriers at a quarter past three?"

"I ... I don't know!"

I play it over again in my mind. Arriving at the school gates, the frantic dash, the scream, the flashes of green and grey. How could they have been at the shop?

"Perhaps they were let out of school early," I suggest.

"Not according to Lauren's teacher, Mrs Darley, or Sophia's teacher, Mrs Percival."

"Oh."

"Oh, indeed. I suggest we run through your statement once again and see if we can get to the bottom of this."

I nod my head. There must be a rational explanation for this. I know what I saw, but the more we talk about it, the more confused I become. My statement is just as I remember it and yet Penney's evidence contradicts it. Is he lying to trip me up? Is that what's going on here?

I clear my throat. "Lauren was deliberately targeted. You can't deny that. Someone rang the school and pretended to be me. If the receptionist had done her job properly, none of this would have happened. She should have called me back to double check."

"Why would she, though?" Penney reasons. "Parents ring reception all the time. How was she to know?"

"She just should have."

"Where do you really think Lauren is?" he asks me.

"I don't know! All I know is that she was taken."

"Have you ever been on medication for anxiety or depression?" he asks.

"How do you know that?" I ask. "My medical records are confidential."

"How long have you been on medication?" he presses.

"Since Lauren was two months old," I confess. "She … she had the most terrible colic – cried night and day. I needed something to help get me through."

"Did you ever think about harming yourself – or her?"

"No! Never!"

"You didn't stop taking the meds, though?"

"Not until about six months ago. I realised I didn't need them anymore. Probably hadn't for a while."

"Did you talk to your doctor about your decision to stop?"

"It didn't seem necessary. I know my own mind."

He slides a picture across the table to me. "Have a good look at this," he says.

"Who's this?" I ask. "Is he the kidnapper?"

"You tell me."

"I didn't get a look at him," I say, staring at the picture. It's an e-fit of a man with long dark hair. He looks rough around the edges. He has a lot of stubble and his hair looks lank and greasy. There's no kindness behind his wrinkled eyes and he has a slight smirk on his face.

"Have you ever seen this man?" Penney asks.

"No," I say.

He watches me closely. He doesn't believe me.

"Well, you let me know if you remember anything else," he finally says.

"That's it?"

"For now," he says.

He swallows his tea and shudders, as if it's cold.

I have an unsettled feeling in my stomach, as if I shouldn't leave yet. There must be more questions I should ask. I just don't know what they are. We have a dodgy timeline and now a suspect I don't know. None of this makes any sense. The kidnapping must have been premeditated because someone phoned the school. But I don't know this man. Why did he choose Lauren?

❋

"I'm sorry, darling, were you busy?" Mum asks when she rings that evening. Her phone calls often start off this way, as if she thinks calling her only daughter is some kind of intrusion.

"No," I say. I'd been eating beans on toast for dinner. It wasn't terribly appetising anyway.

I twist the phone cord around my finger, something I used to do a lot back in the nineties, before I had my first mobile phone.

"So, listen. I tried to book a flight, but it looks like I can't come out until next week now."

"Next week?" I say.

"I know, darling. I told them the situation, but they couldn't get me on a plane any sooner. They're all fully booked."

"Right," I say, grinding my teeth. "Well, I suppose we'll see you next week then."

"Lauren will be back home by then," she tells me. "You'll see."

"I hope so."

"I know so. Now why don't you go out and get some fresh air? You looked so pale on TV."

"I hardly think it matters."

"Appearances are important, Isabel. Haven't I always told you that?"

"Being here is important," I shoot back. "Is there really nothing you can do?"

"I was on the phone with the travel agent for hours," she says. "What do you want me to do?"

"I don't know. I have enough to worry about. You work it out." I slam the phone down, then instantly regret it.

"Are you alright?" Deacon asks.

Erin peeks over her laptop, listening. Always listening.

"Mum can't come till next week," I say with a sigh.

"Oh," he says. There is sympathy in his voice, but after what he said about her yesterday, I can't accept it. I pick up my plate and scrape my uneaten food into the bin. Deacon continues to plough through his dinner, chewing mechanically and staring at the ink smudge on the wall where a four-year-old Lauren left her handprint. Mum does not ring me back.

13

"Wassat?" I jerk awake, convinced that Shy Boyz are in our bedroom, serenading us. Of course, it's the doorbell.

"Lauren!" I say, groggily.

"No, it's probably Erin," Deacon says, reaching for his dressing gown.

The mercury has dropped overnight. There's frost on the ivy that winds its way up the front of our house and the ancient yew tree shivers in the breeze. The stairs creak loudly as I listen to Deacon's retreating steps. Then Erin's nasal voice drifts up to me and I flop back on my pillow. I try to go back to sleep, but unpleasant images run through my mind. I can't think of Lauren without thinking of all the awful things that might have happened to her. It infuriates me. Can't I at least be left with my memories?

I think of baby Lauren, swathed in the blanket we brought home from hospital. I don't think we were meant to keep it, but I couldn't help myself. Lauren had been wrapped in that blanket the first time I saw her. I felt like it was part of her. I had to have it. Lauren apparently agreed. For years she dragged that blankie around with her, until it was little more than a frayed cloth. And then I had to wean her off it with promises of sweets and the Care Bear she'd been begging me for.

Lauren's baby blanket still lines my underwear drawer. I pull it out and run my fingers along the flimsy material, touching the smooth satin strip she loved so much. When she comes home, I will give it back to her. I don't care how old she is. I was wrong; you're never too old for your blankie.

Fresh tears spring from my eyes as I dress, not caring whether anything matches. I catch a brief glimpse of my face in the mirror and I hardly recognise myself. My face is so grey and drawn.

Downstairs, I find Deacon and Erin working in tandem, slicing cheese and tomatoes and some fresh crusty baguette she must have brought with her. It feels wrong, the way she puts herself to work in our kitchen. And I resent the way she makes Deacon his tea the way he likes it, without even having to ask, as if she knows him better than I do.

"Has there been any news?" I ask.

"Lots of calls from the public," Erin says, "but there were bound to be, following the press conference."

"Did they announce the reward yet?" Deacon asks.

"We're announcing it this morning."

"Good," he says. "That ought to keep it in the news."

"What about the kidnapper?" I say. "Do we know who he is yet?"

"Not yet," she says. "Of course, I'll let you both know if that changes."

She's smiling, but I get the feeling she doesn't like being prompted. She thinks I'm trying to tell her how to do her job.

"Has anyone fed Fluffy?" I ask, as my cat strides towards me.

"Not yet," Deacon admits.

Poor Fluffy. Usually, he's the first to be fed, if only to get

Angel Dust

him out of the way while we make our own breakfast. I spoon out some Sheba while he mews appreciatively. Taking care of Fluffy makes me feel a little better. At least someone still needs me.

I join Deacon and Erin at the table, not because I'm hungry but because I don't like them sitting there alone. Erin takes a piece of bread and butters it with precision. She lifts it to her lips and takes a bite, chewing thoughtfully while Deacon talks about his Find Lauren campaign. The conversation feels stilted and functional. If Lauren were here, we would be having a lively debate about whether Elsa is tougher than Spiderman and I would have to remind her every two minutes to sit still and stop wiping jam on her skirt.

When we've finished eating, Erin clears away the breakfast things. She rinses each plate in turn, then stacks them meticulously in the dishwasher, so they all stand exactly the same distance apart. Once the dishwasher is running, she settles down with her laptop, taking over the kitchen table, as she did yesterday. Fluffy attempts to jump onto her lap a couple of times, until Deacon sends him outside. I resent this. Fluffy is a member of our family. He shouldn't be shut out because of Erin.

"I'm going out to get some milk," I say. There's a bottle in the freezer, but I need the fresh air. I'm feeling stifled with Erin permanently stationed in our kitchen. It's like we're at war and our house has been commandeered by the army.

"Would you like me to drive you?" she asks.

"No thanks," I tell her. "I can drive myself."

I glimpse the neighbours as I climb into the Bentley. Hilary has Dogface off the lead again. We make brief eye contact, which is rare. They know. The police must have spoken to them. I can't read her expression. Is it pity because Lauren is missing, or anger that I put their names on my list? I don't know her well enough to judge.

I switch the radio on while I wait for the windows to

defrost. I imagine Lauren in the back seat, pouting as one of my favourite songs comes on. I drive on autopilot, barely aware of my surroundings until I glance in the rear mirror. There is a white van behind me. Right behind me. Dangerously close.

Is it him? Has he come back to taunt me?

Why else would he drive so close? I can see him watching me in the mirror. His face is obscured under a navy baseball cap, but I can see that his thin lips are downcast and unsmiling. His tattooed arm hangs out the window, dangling a cigarette. He flashes his lights at me and my heart beats a little faster.

Should I pull over?

Then I see the explosion of blue lights. An ambulance is coming this way. I feel instantly guilty. The white van man was trying to warn me. He didn't mean anything sinister, but life is made up of millions of random events. How am I to know which ones are significant?

I pull into the hedge to let the ambulance speed by. The white van man sees his chance and overtakes too. I let him go. What difference does it make to me?

I park outside the One Stop Shop and go in. I can't miss the morning papers. Lauren's face beams back at me from several of the covers. It makes me shiver. How many times have I looked at papers like these and pitied the poor child who was missing? Pitied their parents because, chances were, they'd never see their kid again.

I pick up a few copies and an ice-cold bottle of milk. The Pakistani shopkeeper gives me the same polite smile he always does. If he recognises Lauren's picture on the cover, he doesn't say anything.

"Hey! I want a word with you!"

I turn around to see Julio's girlfriend, Nina. I really don't know what he sees in her – she has a face like a pound of smacked tripe.

Angel Dust

"Is it true?" she demands, sticking out her ample chest.

"Is what true?" I ask.

She narrows her eyes. "Is your brother a paedo?"

I step closer. "What are you talking about?" I hiss, keenly aware of all the eyes and ears around us. I am so angry I want to rip out her hair and shove it down her throat.

"The police came knocking this morning," she says. "They asked me some really weird questions."

"Like what?"

"Like whether Julio's ever shown an unhealthy interest in my kids."

I almost drop my bottle of milk. "What? But that's crazy!"

"Is it? He spends a lot of time on the PlayStation with my boy."

I inhale deeply. "Julio likes kids. The normal amount. And he doesn't have any of his own. That doesn't make him a perv."

She gets her face right up close to mine and glares at me through a web of mascara. "It better bloody not do or I'll garrotte him myself."

There's no arguing with hot-headed people like her. Julio describes her as 'passionate', but all I see is a bitch. I back away, knocking into some tins of Quality Street, which have been heavily discounted now that Christmas is over. I don't stop to straighten up the display, just walk as quickly as I can towards the door. The shopkeeper gives me a brief wave, seemingly oblivious to the confrontation as he chats on the phone in Urdu.

I keep walking and don't stop until I reach the car. To my relief, Nina doesn't follow. She stands in the shop doorway, her dragon breath forming a cloud in front of her face. I don't feel safe until I've put some distance between us.

Why are the police asking about Julio? I wonder. It must be because of me, because I put him on my list. But I had to put him on my list, didn't I? He's family and he babysits for

Lauren every once in a while, when Deacon and I fancy a night out. I know my brother didn't take her. He wouldn't dream of it, but I can't blame the police for investigating him. They have to rule him out. They have to rule us all out.

※

THE SHARK-NOSED WOMAN from the press conference is outside the house when I get home.

"How are you feeling today, Isabel?" she calls after me. She hops from one foot to the other, presumably to keep warm. "Has there been any news?"

I push past her. I'll talk to the press when I'm ready. I'm not even sure how much I'm allowed to tell them.

This isn't like before, I remind myself. We need them.

I have the reporters to thank for splashing Lauren's picture all over today's papers. Thousands of people will see those covers. Without them, there would be no way to spread the news, to get people looking at Lauren's picture and reporting anything suspicious. But I have a history with them, just as I do with the police. I'll never forget how they trashed me when I was on trial. I'll never forget the terrible things some of the tabloids wrote about me. Absolute fiction, all of it.

She trots after me, like a little dog. Mairead Osmond, that was her name. How could I forget? I once caught her snooping through my rubbish bin. Nosey cow.

"What can you tell us, Isabel?" she calls. "Is there a reason you don't want to talk?"

I don't reply. I don't even look at her. There's a policeman stationed outside my house, but he doesn't say a thing. I stride up the path to my house and shut myself inside.

"You alright?" Erin asks, as I bolt the door.

"I'm fine," I say, forcing myself not to scowl.

Once I've calmed down a little, I walk through the house, closing the curtains and blinds in every room until I'm sure no one can see in. I wouldn't put it past those sneaky tabloid types to come and peer at the contents of our living room or bathroom to add colour to their writing. Along the lines of 'Neglected child Lauren was forced to live on tinned spaghetti' or 'Missing Lauren's mum couldn't be bothered to clean her bathroom'. I've seen the way they do things. Anything to get an angle.

"Isabel?"

Deacon's face is set in a stony expression and there's a purposefulness to his stride. He takes my hand in his.

"What is it?" I ask.

He won't look at me.

"The police have taken Julio down to the station."

14

I sit down heavily, falling back against the sofa as if the floor has come away. The room spins around me, eventually coming to a halt, like a children's roundabout.

"There is no way Julio has taken Lauren," I say, as Deacon's face comes into view.

"No way," he backs me up.

"I mean, it would be ludicrous!" I burst out "He wouldn't hurt her in a thousand years."

"Course not."

I grip the arm of the sofa.

"They're wasting time. That's what bothers me. Every minute they spend on Julio is a minute they're not out catching the real kidnapper."

My mind flicks back to the last time I saw Julio. His strange behaviour. I got the feeling he was hiding something. But what? Not this, for sure.

Deacon looks at me. "I mean …"

"What?"

"No, it's nothing."

"What were you going to say?"

"Just leave it."

"I want to know," I spit.

"I told you, it's nothing." He enunciates incredibly clearly as though he were talking to a non-native English speaker.

I stare at him for a moment, challenging him to say something about my brother. Deacon has never liked Julio, never really trusted him, but he must know this wasn't him. He's not some kind of monster. I've seen the way he looks at Lauren, with love and envy. He wants what I've got, a child of his own. Perhaps that's why he puts up with Nina, because he enjoys playing stepdad to her kids. The next best thing if he can't have his own. My brother is a decent man. He doesn't deserve this.

"Are you alright?" Deacon asks me. "You've gone a bit green."

"I'm fine," I say, shortly. "I just need a minute."

"Right, well I'm going to check Facebook," he says.

I watch with a heavy heart as he stalks back to his study. His sanctuary. A minute later, I hear a loud thud. It sounds like a paperweight hitting the door.

What is happening to us?

And why is Penney interested in my brother? Is he using him to put pressure on me?

The room gradually ceases to spin. I get up from the sofa and flounder about, as if I've just got off a fairground ride. Fortunately for me, Erin is engrossed in her work. I do not want her to see me in this state. I am so weak, so useless. I should be doing something. Anything.

I stop in front of the bookshelf as if perusing the titles, but all the time I'm picturing myself handing Lauren over to Julio. All those times I left her with him so I could go out shopping or to the cinema. Those times Deacon and I went out for a cosy dinner at the Corner House. I fretted about silly things then, like whether Julio could cope with an explosive nappy.

As she got older, I'd worry about whether he'd feed her too many sweets or let her stay up after her bedtime. Was there something else I should have been worrying about all that time?

I pull myself together. I can't even think those things. I know my brother would never harm Lauren. Not even for a minute.

"Do you think I should go down the station?" I ask Erin, boldly. "Maybe I can help clear this up."

"I don't think that's necessary," she says, pecking away at her laptop. "Your brother will be out soon enough, if he's got nothing to hide."

Yeah, that's how I used to think it worked, before I was put on trial for a crime I didn't commit.

I thrum my fingers on the table. I'm full of pent-up energy and I don't know how to release it. My mind shifts back to the picture Penney showed me. The man with the long dark hair.

"Erin," I say, a bit too loudly.

She looks up. I can't see what she's been typing because of the way the screen is angled. I fight the urge to grab her laptop and run off with it.

"I was wondering if I could have a copy of Sophia's statement," I say.

She looks at me with a slightly pained expression, as though I've asked her to get me the private number for Downing Street.

"I want to know more about how Lauren was abducted," I explain. "I mean, I could get it from Sophia, but I don't want to make her go through it all again. You can understand that, can't you?"

"Of course, I will absolutely pass on your request," she says.

The word 'absolutely' catches in her throat.

"But?" I prompt.

"But the request might not be granted, Isabel. Not at this sensitive stage in the investigation."

"I just want to know what's happened to Lauren!"

"Of course you do. We all do."

Her hand delves into her jacket pocket. I watch with incredulity as she produces her phone. "Excuse me, I have to take this."

She goes out into the back garden. I spy on her from the kitchen window as she smokes a cigarette while she takes her fake phone call. The gall of that woman. What the hell is she here for if she's not going to share information?

Fluffy saunters up to her and winds his furry body around her legs. She looks down at him as if he's got fleas and steps away. I see now why Penney chose her for this role. It wasn't because she's a woman after all. It was because she's a bureaucrat first and a human being second.

I take a deep breath. This is all so infuriating. I feel more powerless than ever. I can't trust the police to find Lauren for me. I need to get out there and do something for myself. First things first; I need a phone. The police still have mine and I feel like a leper without one. I go upstairs and rummage through the guest room. Sure enough, I find an old iPhone in the dresser drawers. I think it must belong to my mum. She bought herself a new one for Christmas and must have left her old one behind. It looks a bit battered, but it should still work. As I plug the charger into the wall, I hear Shy Boyz chime.

Could it be?

I dash down the stairs, praying it's Lauren – there's been some mistake; she was just sleeping over at a friend's; she's going to tell me nothing happened to her, that that man never …

Erin has already answered the door.

"Someone here to see you," she tells me. "She's waiting in the lounge."

Not Lauren. Kate, then.

I don't have that many friends who'd just drop round. I feel bad about the way we left things at the hospital, but we've both had time to cool down now, at least I hope we have. I paste a smile on my face and hurry through to the lounge. But it's not Kate. It's Pam, our cleaner, waiting for me in the armchair, a pair of knitting needles poking out of her oversized handbag.

"I wish you'd rung me," she says. "It was such a shock to hear it on the news."

"I'm sorry," I say, though I don't really know why I'm apologising. "It all happened so fast. There wasn't time."

"Well, I don't suppose you want me in today," she says, pulling herself to her feet.

"Wait," I say. "Stay for a bit. I could use some company."

Pam is really much more than a cleaner. She's a grandmotherly influence in our lives. Always around to lend me a bit of advice – completely unsolicited most of the time, like when she tells me it's not good for Lauren to be an only child and am I absolutely sure I don't want another baby, before it's too late? She's infuriating, but she means well. She always has.

"I still can't get my head around the fact that she left school without me," I tell her. "She should have known I wouldn't ring to say she could walk home with Sophia."

"She would have been excited," she says. "Far be it for me to tell you how to raise your daughter, but you never gave her much rope, did you?"

"Rope?" I repeat.

"You wrapped her up in cotton wool, you know you did."

"You think I'm overprotective?" I ask.

Pam straightens the collar of her fussy blue blouse. "Like I said, far be it for me to judge. But I see other girls her age going about in twos and threes. Your Lauren was always with a grownup. Always. She was never let off the leash, so when she had the chance, she probably took that bit of freedom and ran with it."

"You think she rebelled?"

"This morning's paper said she was seen at the shop when she wasn't supposed to cross the road," she says.

"But Sophia was allowed to walk home alone all the time," I point out. "Why wasn't she more sensible?"

I've always thought Sophia was the mature one of the two, the more grownup influence.

"That's where a lot of parents get it wrong," Pam says. "They think the more sensible child will keep the other one in check, but it isn't like that. When two children get together, they usually go down to the lowest common denominator. It sounds to me like Sophia followed Lauren's lead, not the other way around."

I find myself nodding. "You know what, Pam? I think you might have something there."

"Well," she says, patting her huge handbag. "I won't keep you all day. If you don't want me to clean, I might as well go into town and do a bit of shopping. There are a few things I'd like to get in the sales."

"I'll give you a lift," I offer. Pam doesn't drive and I'm always horrified by how far she walks on her old, arthritic legs.

"You don't have to do that, dear," she says.

"It'll give me an excuse to get out," I say, thinking of the frost on the path. "I'll go crazy sitting around here all day."

I pick up Deacon's car keys from the bowl.

"Popping out again," I tell him, through the walls of his study. "I'm giving Pam a lift into town."

"He's not there," Erin tells me. "He said he was going for a walk."

"Oh right, thanks."

Pam and I walk past a group of reporters huddled in front of the house. I count at least two vans out there now, the crew members sipping from steaming polystyrene cups. Mairead Osmond blends almost perfectly into the background, kneeling down behind one of the vans, phone pressed against her ear.

Pam raises her eyebrows as I lead her towards the Bentley. I don't tell her I wrecked my car. I can just imagine what she'd say to that. She wraps her thick coat around her and snuggles into the passenger seat.

"You want to go right at the traffic lights," she tells me.

"I know."

"You need to get into the right lane," she adds, as if I've never driven before. But you can't argue with the Pams of this world. It's best to humour them.

The road is a little icy, but not enough to slow down the traffic. A couple of boy racers whizz past.

"I wonder which ditch they'll end up in," Pam says, cheerfully.

I drop her off at the market and then I pop into the phone shop to top up Mum's phone. The January sales are in full force with brightly coloured signs everywhere. I pass a department store window with 50% off designer handbags. What good are designer handbags to me now? Nor do I care about the new range of jeans in the department store window or the smell of iced buns at the baker's. Instead, I trudge back to the Bentley.

As I approach the car park, I realise I forgot to pay for my parking. I glance around, but there aren't any traffic wardens about. I don't even know if they have them here anymore. The council laid off a boatload of people while they were doing the beach renovation, so who knows?

I jump into the car, thinking I've got away with it. Then I notice the piece of paper on my windscreen.

Dammit! That's all I need.

I'm tempted to drive off and leave it fluttering in the wind, but it's blocking my view. I get out of the car and pull it out, but when I take a closer look, I see it's just an advert: *20% off a reading at QPC.*

What's QPC?

I look up at the building directly in front of me. *Queensbeach Psychic Centre*, the sign reads. It's one of those places I must have passed hundreds of times before but never noticed. If I had, I probably would have laughed at the idiots who were gullible enough to go in there. Well, today, I am one of those idiots.

15

I take a step towards the building, then stop myself and look around in embarrassment.

What on earth am I thinking?

I'm unravelling, coming undone. I'm an intelligent woman, not some sort of halfwit, but my legs have a mind of their own. I stride forward before I can think better of it, up the ramp and through a set of glass doors, into a sterile room that looks like a cross between a post-modern art gallery and a dentist's office. There are white walls, shiny marble floors and a brown mahogany desk. There's no other furniture, no posters, nothing.

"Have you got an appointment?" asks the woman behind the desk.

"I didn't know I needed one," I say.

Wouldn't a real psychic know I was coming?

"Is it urgent?" she asks.

"Yes," I say, swallowing my pride. "Yes, it is."

"What's your name?" she asks.

"Isabel Frost."

"Wait here for a moment," she says. "Madame Zeta will fit you in when she can."

Angel Dust

"How long's that likely to be?" I ask.

"About fifteen minutes or so."

"Do you have Wi-Fi?"

"Of course."

She points me towards another room with apple-green Bentwood chairs. There's no one else waiting and I can't help wondering if there are any other customers. Is this waiting lark just for show, to make the psychic appear more busy and important?

I sit down and scan the emails on my phone. I haven't missed much. I check the Find Lauren Facebook page and see that it's buzzing with responses. Lots of messages of support, but still no actual sightings. It's so frustrating. Someone must have seen something. Someone knows where she is.

"Isabel?"

I almost lose my bottle as I take in the middle-aged woman in blue jeans and a long-sleeved top from Gap. No headscarf or hoop earrings for this woman. But that's OK. She doesn't have to put on airs and graces if she's the real deal.

"I am Madame Zeta," she says. "Please come through."

In contrast to the sterile reception area, the psychic's room boasts Eastern promise. The four walls are draped with rich, heavy fabrics and the floor is a patchwork of rugs that feel soft and soothing underfoot.

"Please, make yourself comfortable," she says, waving her hand at the pile of beanbags on the floor.

I sit cross-legged, something I haven't done in years, and wait for her to speak. A stack of oversized cards lies face down on the floor beside her, but she doesn't consult them. Instead, she looks gravely into my eyes.

"You've lost someone very dear," she says. It's a statement, not a question. I feel a momentary shudder before I remind myself that most of the people who come here have probably lost someone, though not in the same circumstances as me. Normally, it's a family member who has died. A parent or a partner. But my Lauren isn't dead, she's missing. My grief is temporary.

"What do you want to know?" she asks.

"I want to know where my daughter is," I say, annoyed that she doesn't know this.

She lays her palms on the table and closes her eyes. The candles quiver like inverse tears, radiating yellow warmth around the room. Thin spirals of smoke rise up towards the ceiling. The place lacks ventilation and I wonder how she can work like this. It's a fire waiting to happen.

"I'm sensing a powerful female energy," she says at last. "Very strong."

She draws me in with her eyes.

I nod keenly.

"You're going to need all your strength to get through what's ahead," she tells me.

"Yes," I agree.

"Your daughter," she says, "is she a redhead like you?"

"Yes!" My heart flutters.

"That's good," she says. "It's true what they say, you know, about redheads having fiery personalities."

I don't see myself as particularly fiery, but Lauren is definitely spirited. Perhaps it skips a generation.

"You think that's a good thing?" I venture.

"Almost certainly," she says. "It means she will fight back."

"You think she should?" I ask.

I think of the awful man who took my daughter. I realise I'm picturing the White Van Man, with his thin, unsmiling lips and tattoos running up and down his arm. Someone who takes what he wants and doesn't give a damn who gets hurt. What good would it do Lauren to fight a man like that?

"Can you sense her at all?" I ask, desperately. "Can you tell if she's still alive?"

The psychic closes her eyes and tenses all her muscles, as if she's having a spasm. I wait for her to speak, but she looks as though she's in a trance.

"Is she there?" I whisper. I'm afraid to hear the answer.

"What would you tell your daughter if you could speak to her right now?" she asks.

She sits with her head forward, her hair hanging limply in front of her eyes. I long to brush it away. I smell her coconut shampoo in spite of all the incense. It's almost as if Lauren herself is in the room.

I swallow. "I want to tell her that I love her," I say. "But that won't bring her home, so I would ask her to describe where she is."

"I'd tell her not to worry. Daddy's put out a million-pound reward," a familiar voice breaks in.

The curtain is yanked back and I turn to see Deacon standing there.

"What are you doing?" I cry.

"You're wasting your time, Isabel. That woman is no more psychic than I am," he says.

I look helplessly from him to Madame Zeta.

"Deacon, this is really rude!"

"No, what's rude is conning desperate people out of their money."

"If you want to know what happened to your daughter, you need to ask your brother," Madame Zeta tells me.

"Ignore her," Deacon says, pulling me to my feet.

I shrug helplessly and follow him towards the door. There's no point trying to continue this now. The moment is shattered. My cheeks burn as we traipse through reception. Maybe I was bonkers to think a psychic would be of any help, but I'll never know now.

"What about her money?" I ask as we walk outside. "I didn't pay her."

"Here!" He rips a couple of notes from his wallet, but

instead of giving them to Madame Zeta, he bends down and feeds them down the drain.

"How can you waste money like that?" I gasp.

"What's the difference?" he says, nodding at the psychic, who is still watching us from the doorway.

"Deacon!"

"Don't worry, she'll be out here to grab her money the minute we're gone. That type always do. Don't feel sorry for her, Isabel. She's making money from our misery. You make me sick!" he shouts in her direction.

"How did you even know where I was?" I ask.

"I was in town, meeting some of the volunteers who've been out looking for Lauren. They've taken over the old scout hut in Pepper Street. I was on my way home when I spotted the Bentley parked here and I didn't think you'd stopped to buy cat food."

I glance at the vets next door. "I might have."

"Oh, please!"

I fumble in my handbag for the car keys and fling them at him. They clatter to his feet.

"That's alright, you can drive," he says, making no effort to pick them up.

"I don't feel like it," I say.

Angrily, I swoop down and pick up the keys, this time pressing them into his hands. He shrugs and takes them. I don't get into the car until he climbs in the driver's side.

"She's a charlatan," he says, referring to Madame Zeta. "She's probably seen you on TV. These people have no scruples. They'll say anything to make you believe them. You mustn't let yourself be fooled."

"Don't you think I know that?" I shoot back. "I just wanted her to give me some hope. Just for a minute, I needed someone to tell me she's OK."

"What good is false hope?" he asks.

"What good is thinking negatively?" I counter. "I need something to keep me going. We all do."

"Not a psychic," he says with derision.

All the way home, he goes on and on about the tricks psychics use, rummaging through people's private lives so they can shock them with the stunning accuracy of their visions. I turn my head away. Going to the psychic was my decision. I know it was a bit wacky, but it was none of his business. He can be so condescending at times, as if his way is the only way.

I close my eyes and Madame Zeta's words float back to me.

Ask your brother, she said.

Where did she get that from? Is it a load of guff, as Deacon seems to think, or could there be something to it? Does Julio really know something we don't?

16

Deacon pulls up near our house and undoes his seatbelt.

"Aren't you coming in?" he asks, when I make no move to follow.

"No," I say. "I think I'll pop round to Kate's."

"Good idea."

He hands me the car keys. Normally, he would lean over and kiss me goodbye, but not today.

All the way over to Kate's, I argue with him in my head, telling him what an arrogant bastard he is. I used to think his assertiveness was attractive, sexy even, but now he's gone too far. We're not living in the Dark Ages.

I wind down the window and take in a lungful of fresh, salty air. The cold stings the back of my throat.

It's been a rocky road since Alicia died. My life will never be as carefree as it once was. I envy other couples, who haven't been through what we have. It ought to have brought us closer together, but our experience taints the way we see things, each in our own individual way. Sometimes, I wonder if we'd still be together if it weren't for Lauren. Would he love me enough?

Angel Dust

❆

KATE'S HOUSE is in the middle of Moulescoomb Road. The area is very popular with families, as evidenced by the number of swing sets and trampolines in the gardens. But today the road is strangely quiet. School should be over for the day and yet there are no children playing in their front gardens. Even in January, there are usually a few kids outside, kicking a football about or digging up worms in the mud.

It's because of Lauren.

They've all heard what's happened, I suppose, and they're frightened it could happen to them. That's why everyone's hiding indoors.

I park the car and open the garden gate. Sophia's scooter leans neatly against the wall, alongside the knee pads I bought her for Christmas. I feel a pang as I remember the hurt look on Kate's face the last time I saw her. I was only trying to find my daughter. And she was only trying to protect hers. I know I was being insensitive, but she was too.

I ring the bell and wait. Kate looks out through the net curtains, then the door flies open and she hugs me tight. There are no words, no apologies or recriminations. She just pulls me inside.

"The paparazzi were out there this morning," she says as I stamp my boots on the mat.

"They're at mine too," I say.

I study her face. She's not wearing any make-up and her skin looks tired and dry.

"You look awful," I say.

"Thanks. You should see yourself."

It feels good to laugh. I'd almost forgotten.

"Is Sophia OK?" I ask.

"She will be," she says, leading me through to the living room. "See for yourself."

Sophia sits in the big pull-out armchair, her arm resting in its sling. She has a book in front of her. She always has a book in front of her. But I don't think she's really reading.

"How are you feeling?" I ask her.

"Better," she says, eyeing me with those solemn eyes of hers.

"What are you reading?" I ask.

"It's homework," she says. "We're doing the Fire of London."

Kate gives a helpless shrug. "She doesn't want to fall behind."

We settle down on the sofa. "She's going to be off for the rest of the week, at least," Kate tells me. "We don't want her to get jostled in the playground."

Being jostled would be the least of my concerns. If Lauren comes home – *when* Lauren comes home – I'm not sending her back to that school. How could I ever trust them again? If they hadn't let Lauren out, none of this would have happened.

"Sophia can't wait to go back," Kate says. "She's fed up of sitting around here with just me for company."

"Hasn't she had any friends over?" I ask.

"Robyn's been round, but she's at school most of the day."

"Yeah, of course."

"So, what's happening with the investigation? Do they have any leads?"

"They're questioning Julio," I say, "which we all know is a total waste of time."

"They think he's involved?" she says slowly, as if trying out the idea in her head.

"But of course he's not," I say, a bit annoyed that she's even thinking about it. I know he's not her favourite person – their marriage ended badly, after all – but even she has to know that Julio wouldn't do this.

Sophia looks up sharply. "It wasn't Julio!" she states.

"I know," I say, quickly. "And we don't have to talk about it if you don't want to," I add, glancing at Kate.

Angel Dust

"I want to," Sophia says. "Because the police didn't listen."

I lean closer.

"I told the policeman. I said the man looked a bit like Lauren's uncle. I didn't say it *was* him. There's a difference."

A crucial difference.

"He had the same kind of hair, long and black, and a bit bald on top. But he wasn't tanned, and he had bad teeth, really bad teeth – mank, they were, like a row of bombed houses, as Gran would say."

I glance at Kate again. "But the sketch the police made – that's accurate, right?"

"I didn't see him for that long. Mainly just the back of his head, because he was driving. But you couldn't miss the bad teeth. He totally had camel breath."

Shame you can't capture a smell in a picture.

"Just one other thing I was wondering ..." I glance at Kate. I don't want to push it. "But what did you and Lauren buy from the shop?"

"Sweets," she says. "Lauren's got them ... had them."

"Where did you get the money?"

Sophia looks down at her lap. "We found a quid in the street."

"What, on the way to the shop?"

"Yes."

"So, you were already on your way to the shop when you found it?"

"Yes ... no – we found it first, and then decided to go to the shop."

"Right."

I glance at Kate, but she seems to take her daughter at her word.

"They've given me the week off work," she breaks in. "I didn't even have to ask."

"That's good," I say. I feel like she's deliberately changing the subject, but I suppose she doesn't want me to put too much pressure on Sophia.

"Would you like a cup of tea?" she asks.

"You know me too well," I reply.

We both get up and head for the kitchenette. I've always felt so comfortable in this house. It's practically my second home. And yet today I feel like a stranger. It's as if Kate and I have only just struck up a friendship, and we're at that awkward, stilted stage, where we're still getting to know each other.

Kate boils the kettle while I get out the mugs. She makes one for Sophia too, and takes it out to her. Despite being nine years old, tea is all she drinks.

Kate and I hover in the kitchen, just as we've always done, raiding the biscuit tin as we sip our tea. I take a big gulp and the hot water scorches my mouth. The sensation is almost enjoyable. A physical sensation of pain, as opposed to the emotional one in my heart.

The conversation falls to trivial things, like the new bookshop café that's due to open in the village. We speculate about whether it will be a success or a failure, like its predecessors. I feel myself relax. It's easy to talk about anything other than Lauren. For a few minutes, I can believe that the clock has turned back and it's a week ago, when our lives were normal. Back then, I was preoccupied with things like whether the boutique was bringing in enough money, or whether I'd missed the deadline to send in my tax return – things that seemed important but weren't.

"Do you want another cup of tea?" Kate asks, after a bit.

"No, that's OK. I ought to get back."

"If you're sure …"

I poke my nose into the living room. "Hope you feel better," I say to Sophia, who immediately looks down at her book.

She's definitely not reading.

Angel Dust

The street is still eerily quiet as I plod back to my car. I wonder if it will stay like this until the kidnapper's caught. But what if the kidnapper's never caught? Will this be Lauren's legacy?

❄

WHEN I GET HOME, I find the picture of the kidnapper stuck to the fridge. It draws me in. He's looking at me, and yet he doesn't meet my gaze. His hair is long and lank. His smile reveals bad teeth, jagged and uneven. I can well imagine the camel breath Sophia described.

"He looks a little like Julio, doesn't he?" Deacon says. His breath is warm on my neck.

"Maybe if he didn't wash for a few years," I say.

But those dull eyes are never my brother's. They lack animation. Spark. He looks as though he doesn't care if he lives or dies.

Deacon must be having similar thoughts. I feel cold as he withdraws and mumbles something that sounds like, "Better get back to it."

His study door closes behind him and I am alone again, gazing at that horrible face.

I go upstairs and sit in Lauren's room again. I don't want to be downstairs because of Erin. It feels like she's always here these days. It's not my house anymore, it's hers.

I take out my phone and check my emails. There's a ParentMail from Lauren's school, which I ignore, and an email from a supplier that should have gone to my work account. Then I check my junk folder, and that's where I find a message from a woman called Caroline Dorking. Against my better instincts, I open it:

DEAR ISABEL,

You don't know me, but I understand how you feel, probably better than most. I was once in your place. When my Freddie went missing, my whole world fell apart ...

I READ ON. The email is full of kind words and support from this woman I have never met. I feel a little heartened, until I reach the bottom and realise who she is. I remember reading about Freddie in the papers. It was nine years ago, while I was pregnant with Lauren. Her boy was murdered by his uncle, this woman's brother. Does she see similarities between the two cases? Is that why she's contacted me? Does she think this will end the same way? Because I don't. I can't.

I pull my legs up to my chest and hug myself tightly, my body wracked with pain. I don't believe in telepathy, but I try it anyway. I picture my daughter's beautiful face, her long dark lashes and thick red hair, so like mine.

Lauren! Lauren! Come home. Just come home.

Shy Boyz taunt me from the poster on her wardrobe door, alongside this week's spelling list. I stare at the smiling faces she loves so much, and they stare back like they know something I don't. I yank the wardrobe door open. Lauren has stuck glow-in-the-dark stars all over the inside walls. I never noticed them before, but she was forever climbing in and shutting the door, making it into a little hidey-hole. At first, we told her not to do it, but, in the end, Deacon put a light inside, so she didn't have to sit in the dark. I fumble around. Here it is. I switch it on, and the space lights up, like a hidden room. All her dresses, trousers and skirts are lined up in a row with her bags and other accessories in a box below.

I spot the kimono my mum brought back from her trip to Japan. All Lauren's clothes face the same direction, all except the kimono. I take it down, and as I do, I feel a lump in the material. The pocket itself is empty, but there's a hole in the lining at the bottom. I push my hand through, and draw something out, about the size of one of those little packs of travel tissues. I hold it in front of me, unable to comprehend what I'm seeing. It's a wad of money. I count it. Seventy pounds in five- and ten-pound notes. Where did Lauren get so much cash?

"Isabel," Deacon calls up the stairs.

"What?" I turn sharply, as if I've been caught with my hand in the till.

"They're letting Julio go. He wants you to go and pick him up."

17

I run down the stairs and wave the wad of money in Erin's face.

"I found this in Lauren's wardrobe. Your search team missed it."

I don't mean to sound accusatory, but I'm filled with adrenaline. It has to mean something, doesn't it?

Erin examines it. "The search team is very thorough," she states, sounding puzzled.

"It was well hidden," I say, "in the lining of her pocket. I don't know where she got it. She normally spends all her pocket money."

"Could your mum have sent it?" she asks. "Or another relative?"

"Not very likely," I say, thinking of my mum's previous gifts. I've never known her to send money. She loves buying her knickknacks that she finds on her travels. Julio gives her money sometimes, but no more than a tenner, and he bought her that expensive drone for Christmas – largely, I suspect, because he wanted to play with it himself. But I doubt he would have given her money on top of that.

"We'll have to take this as evidence," Erin says curtly. She produces a little plastic bag and slips the money inside. "I hope you haven't handled it too much? We might need to have it analysed for prints."

"I suppose I have, a bit. I didn't mean to …"

"Maybe you should check with Deacon," she suggests. "Maybe he knows where she got the money from."

"I doubt it," I say, but I go and get him anyway.

I feel like I'm invading his privacy when I enter his study. We used to make a bit of a joke of it, that he had this private room. I never minded him being in here before. I felt like I could come in and out as I pleased. But it feels different now, as if this part of the house is off limits. As if he only comes in here to get away from us. Away from me.

"What's up?" he asks, as I loiter in the doorway.

"I found seventy pounds in Lauren's wardrobe," I tell him. "Any idea where she got it?"

His eyes narrow. "That's an awful lot," he says.

"I know."

"How many weeks would it have taken her to save up that much?" Erin asks, standing behind me.

"More than three months," Deacon says. "There's no way she saved it."

"How much pocket money does she get?"

"Five pounds a week," I say.

"That's pretty generous."

"It would still take her fourteen weeks to save up seventy pounds," Deacon says. "And saving has never been her forte."

"Someone must have given it to her," I say. The thought makes me uncomfortable.

Deacon looks at me. "Weren't you just off to get Julio?" he asks.

"Oh yeah, I forgot." I look at Erin. "I can take the money to the station with me," I offer.

"That's alright. I'll deal with it myself," she says.

I look at her, steely eyed. "I don't mind. I'm going there now."

"I'll deal with it," she says again. I feel a bit like a naughty schoolgirl, being put in my place. I glance at Deacon, but he's miles away. Does she think I'm going to tamper with it in some way? Why would I? I'm the one who found it, for crying out loud.

On the drive over to the police station, I can't stop thinking about that money. Could she have stolen it? I don't think Lauren would do a thing like that, but it doesn't make sense that an eight-year-old girl would have so much cash. And if someone gave it to her, then why didn't she tell me? That much money must have been a big deal to her, and yet she never breathed a word.

※

Julio is waiting outside on the street. I watch as he shifts from one foot to the other, blowing on his hands to keep warm. He could have waited inside, but I suppose he didn't want to. I should know how that feels. The walls inside that building seem to move closer the longer you're in there. I can't even begin to imagine how claustrophobic it would be to work there.

"Thank God that's over," he says, as I greet him. "You won't believe some of the questions they—"

"Shh! Wait till we're in the car," I warn him.

He looks at me, puzzled, but then he sees. Mairead Osmond leans nonchalantly against her car. Her beige mac is done up tightly against the cold and she has her phone clamped to her ear as always. This is what she is best at – blending in. She has a way of making herself inconspicuous, so people speak freely in front of her. It's only when you see all your secrets revealed in the morning papers that you realise she's struck again.

"I don't care what you write about me!" I yell, as we walk by.

I resist the impulse to bang on her windscreen. There's no point. It would take a lot more to rattle that snake.

"Hey, you brought the Bentley!" Julio says with delight when he sees the car.

I roll my eyes. "The only reason I'm driving Deacon's car is because I smashed mine," I tell him.

"Can I drive?" he asks, eagerly.

"No, you cannot."

"I'd be careful," he says.

"No way. Deacon would go nuts."

Begrudgingly, he hops into the passenger side and rants about the way the police hauled him in for questioning.

"You don't need to tell me what's fair," I mutter, but he isn't listening.

"Man, I've got thirty-eight missed calls from Nina," he says, scrolling through his phone.

I feel a twinge of sympathy. I doubt there's much of a future for him and Nina now, but no loss there. We don't need sour people like her in our lives. He'll forget her when the next one comes along. He always does.

"Why did the police want to question you?" I ask, as I start the car. "Did you speak to a lawyer?"

"No, it didn't come to that," he says.

I glance at him. I get the impression he isn't telling me everything.

"So, you've been cleared?"

"They didn't say so in as many words, but I haven't been charged with anything."

"Good. Maybe they can focus on the real kidnapper now. Have you seen the picture?"

"Yeah, he looks like my evil twin."

"That's exactly it."

I would laugh, if it weren't so awful.

I park in the only available space outside Julio's house. The day has lost its brightness, and the street is filled with shadows.

"Do you want a cuppa?" he asks.

"OK," I agree. I want to hear more about what the police said to him. Lord knows I'm not going to get it out of Erin.

The wind hits me as I open the car door. I wrap my scarf round my neck and stick my hands in my pockets as I trample down the path towards his house. The porch light comes on as we approach, illuminating a lump on the doorstep.

"Ugh, what's that?" he cries.

"Dog poo," I squeal, covering my mouth. It smells so vile I can almost taste it.

"It looks human," he says. "Jesus!" He spits on the ground as if hacking up phlegm will somehow take the smell away.

"Why would there be human poo on your doorstep?" I object.

"Why is there dog poo?" he reasons. "Shitting hell, it reeks!"

"Will you stop swearing?" I say, as he gets more and more worked up.

"How do you expect me to react?" he says, raising his voice even louder. "Some little gobshite has crapped on my doorstep!"

"It's probably some teenage twat with nothing better to do," I say.

I glance around, but there doesn't seem to be anyone about. No kids giggling in the bushes.

Julio is already doubling back to the gate to look. He looks up and down the street but doesn't find the culprit.

He lets out another stream of expletives and kicks a coke can across the lawn. "And that's not mine either," he says, referring to the can.

He glances around and looks almost disappointed when he doesn't find any other evidence lying about.

"I'll get the hose," I say. Anything to get away from that smell.

I let myself in through the back gate.

"Julio!" I shriek.

"What is it?"

"Look!"

I point at the bin. The word 'Nonce' has been painted on it in white letters.

I touch the paint lightly with my finger. It's dry. Whoever did this must have done it hours ago. Has the poo been there all this time too?

"Someone broke into your garden!" I say, glancing about.

I shudder as I remember Jody and Alicia getting into my garden and scaring the life out of me by appearing at my backdoor.

"No, it was bin day today," he says. "I put my bin out on the kerb last night. One of the neighbours must have wheeled it back in for me. They probably didn't even notice it had been vandalised."

I turn on the hose and have a go at washing the paint off, but it doesn't budge.

"Give me that," he says, and walks round to the front to tackle the poo.

"Do you still want that cup of tea?" he asks, when he's finished.

"Yeah, I suppose."

I suspect he'll hit the beer as soon as I've gone, and we haven't really had a chance to talk.

We go inside. His house looks about the same as it did the last time I was here. The pizza boxes are gone, but Indian takeaway containers sit on the kitchen counter, along with several empty bottles of Kingfisher. He makes two big mugs of tea and carries them out to the lounge, not caring that he's sloshed some down the side of the cup. I look around for the wicker coasters I bought him, but they're nowhere to be seen.

"Excuse the mess," he says, as I shift a pile of laundry off the small sofa. I can't tell if it's clean or dirty, so I heap it on top of his computer table.

"So, tell me what happened," I prompt, "from the beginning."

He shrugs. "I was woken up by the police hammering on the door," he says. "Scared the bejesus out of me. When I answered the door, they told me to get dressed because I was coming down the station. They took me in the back of a police car like I was a criminal, and when we got there, they told me they wanted to search my house. They were going to do it anyway, but it would be easier if I cooperated and gave them the key. Otherwise, they'd have to wait for a warrant."

"So you let them?" I ask.

"It's not like I had a choice. If I'd said no, I'd have looked guilty as sin. Besides, the only thing I had to hide was a little bag of weed in my bedside drawer. But no one's even mentioned it, so I think I'm off the hook for that."

"Who questioned you?" I ask.

"DCI Penney. I think I may have met him before."

"You have," I say, grimly.

I know for a fact that Penney questioned him all those years ago, when I was in trouble. I know because he taunted me with his statement afterwards. Alicia and Jody got him to say things to incriminate me. I try not to think about the way Julio betrayed me. I could stay angry forever, but I choose not to. I'd rather have a brother.

"What did Penney ask you?" I want to know.

"He wanted to confirm my alibi," he says. "And then he asked me all kinds of questions about whether I like children."

He spits on the vinyl floor.

"I wish you wouldn't do that," I say, but Julio reverts to adolescence when he's upset.

"You should have heard the crap he was saying to me," he says. "Can you imagine what it's like being asked all that shit?"

I swallow. "I've been having a terrible time too, you know. Lauren is missing. You can't imagine what I'm going through."

"Hey, I love Lauren too," he says, like it's a competition.

I'm about to argue, but then I realise how futile it is. Julio has a selfish streak, but he's always been good to Lauren.

"What else did Penney say?" I ask.

"He said they were taking my phone and computer, so if there was any evidence, they'd find it. But, of course, they won't. I'm not some kind of sicko."

"Of course not."

He gets up and sits down again, like he doesn't know where to put himself. "How could anyone even think that about me?"

He's working himself up into a rage again. Does he really think I need to listen to him ranting and raving about the injustice of it all? Still, my mind returns to the police sketch of the kidnapper. It's strange that he should resemble Julio.

※

DEACON IS in his dressing gown when I get home. His dark hair is slicked back the way I like it. He's finally taken a shower then. I watch him talking to Erin, drinking a cup of tea she must have made him. I know this because she's used the mug he gave me for Valentine's Day. The one we never use because it's got a large heart cut out in the middle that takes up half the cup.

"Has my brother's name been released to the press?" I ask, as I drop my bag down on the sofa.

She looks at me calmly. "No, Julio was questioned as part of standard procedures, to eliminate him from the enquiry."

"Then how did they know?" I ask. "Someone pooed on his doorstep and sprayed 'Nonce' on his bin."

"Didn't you say you had a run-in with his girlfriend earlier?" Deacon asks.

Nina.

I should have known she couldn't keep her trap shut.

※

THE SKY IS black with seagulls when I open the curtains on Wednesday morning. From my window, I see Erin picking her way along the beach towards our house. I wonder why she hasn't parked a bit closer, then I realise there must be reporters out the front, and like us, she wants to avoid them. Last night she suggested we send them out some pizzas to 'butter them up'.

"I'm not bribing the hacks," I told her.

"It's not a bribe," she argued. "They've been out there in all weathers. It doesn't hurt to keep them on your side."

"No," I said. "No way."

It still pisses me off. The awful things they wrote about me ten years ago. The awful things they're probably still writing about me now. I don't know. I haven't read any of it. Deacon's the one reading all the papers, keeping up to date with everything online. I'm staying out of it as far as I can. I need to keep my mind fresh for Lauren.

I throw on some jeans and a jumper and mooch downstairs to let Erin in, but Deacon is already in the kitchen. I'm not sure what time he came to bed or even if he came to bed. There's no routine anymore.

"What's the latest?" I demand, as Erin sets her bag down on the table.

For a moment, she remains silent. She looks troubled.

"What? What is it?"

"I need to show you something and I want you to tell me if it's Lauren's."

"What is it?"

"An item of clothing. It was found in a wooded area not far from where Sophia was found."

My stomach twists itself in knots.

They've found her clothing?

"Let's go to my study," Deacon says. He wants to deal with it, so I don't have to.

"I can do it," I say.

"I know," he says. He puts his hand on my shoulder. He wants to protect me, but I don't want to be protected.

He and Erin disappear into his study and shut the door. I wait outside, desperate for the truth.

A moment later, Deacon comes out. "I'm sorry," he says, "I need you to look."

"OK."

My stomach flutters as I go in. There's an item of clothing laid out on the table. It's in a clear plastic bag. Sterile. Untouchable. It's a child's vest. Not the whole vest, but enough that you can see what it used to be. It's torn and mottled with dark red blood. It looks so small and fragile. I swallow hard. There's a pile of similar vests in Lauren's underwear drawer. I remember stocking up on them at the end of the summer holidays. It had been an unusually hot summer, and the Met Office was warning that we were in for a Siberian winter as recompense. So I went to Filberts and piled my trolley with 70-denier tights, thick jumpers and four packs of winter vests. They were buy one get one free and I thought they were a bargain. I brought it all home and put it through the obligatory cycle through the washing machine, so they were fresh and clean, ready for Lauren to wear when the weather turned, which it did promptly and unforgivably over the August Bank Holiday. I settled into the cold, lip-chapping, skin-flaking autumn season, confident in the knowledge that my daughter was adequately kitted out for school.

"It's not hers," I manage. "It's not Lauren's."

"Are you sure?" Erin asks me. "Filberts own brand, age eight to nine?"

"Not hers," I repeat.

She wrinkles her brow. "Are you absolutely positive?"

She's worried I'm in denial.

"I'm sure," I tell her. "It's not hers."

Because Lauren refused to wear her vests. They remain in her top drawer, as white as the day I bought them. All of them. I try not to think about the real owner of the vest and what might have happened to them. There isn't room in my heart for more anguish. My whole being is consumed with the need to find my daughter.

I excuse myself and hurry to the bathroom. I shut myself inside and slide to the floor. My grief comes in wave after uncontrollable wave. The agony is as intense as any contraction I experienced giving birth.

"God, Lauren, where are you? Why are you doing this to me?"

I focus on breathing in through my mouth and out through my nose. I remember Deacon squeezing my hand, holding it tight as each consecutive contraction grew stronger. We were never closer than the day I gave birth to Lauren. We were never more in love, all three of us. I recall her screwed-up face, the infinite wait for her breath, and then the wonderful sound of her first cry. The best sound I ever heard.

"Hello, Lauren," I said as they placed her on my breast. "I'm your Mummy and I'm going to love you forever."

I rock back and forth, her beautiful face burned into my memory, until the spasms of fear subside.

18

Sophia and Lauren have been the best of friends since they were babies. No one else comes close, but lately they've been hanging around with Robyn Ritter. The Ritter's house is near Sophia's, at the other end of Moulescoomb Road. I've never been there before, but they have a distinctive garden, with a large wishing well in the middle.

I ring the bell and Robyn's mum, Cheryl, ushers me inside. I'm not sure if what she's wearing constitutes pyjamas or a tracksuit. Either way, she looks both warm and fashionable. Cheryl views me with undisguised curiosity. Lauren's kidnapping must be the talk of the playground. I picture her and all the other mums gossiping about it, mulling over the various theories they've read in the tabloids.

"How are you doing?" she asks, in her husky voice. "Holding it together?"

I fight back the ever-present tears.

"I'm OK," I lie. "If you don't mind, I'd like a quick word with Robyn."

"No problem, babe."

She leads me into the lounge, which is as immaculate as the garden. Her sideboard is crowded with Sylvanian Family figures, each one spaced exactly two centimetres from the next. Robyn and her baby sibling – I can't tell if it's a boy or a girl – sit at a small table, eating their dinner while *Danger Mouse* plays on the TV.

"Hello," I say as cheerfully as I can manage.

"Hi." Robyn's oval eyes dart towards me, then back to the TV.

"Robyn, Lauren's mum wants to talk to you," Cheryl says.

"OK." The response is automatic. Pre-programmed, like the way her hand lifts her fork and her mouth opens.

My legs ache from the effort of standing, so I perch on a nearby pouffe.

"Robyn, do you know – did Lauren or any of her friends ring the school to say she could walk home on Monday?"

Robyn shook her head.

"Are you sure?" I ask. "I need to know. You wouldn't be getting anyone into trouble."

"No," says Robyn. "She was gobsmacked when Mrs Darley said she could walk home. She wouldn't shut up about it."

I imagine how excited Lauren must have been. After our conversation that morning, it must have been the last thing she expected. I pause for a moment, wondering how to word my next question.

"Do you … do you know where Lauren might have got money from? I found some in her room."

Robyn swallows the last of her food and pushes her knife and fork to the twelve o'clock position.

"It's probably from the sweets," she says.

"Sweets?"

"They sell them at break time, at the back of the library."

"Who does?"

"Lauren and Sophia."

I narrow my eyes. "What kind of sweets?"

"Pick and mix," Robyn tells me. "They put them in little plastic bags, decorated with stickers and ribbons."

"Have you heard about this?" I ask Cheryl.

She shakes her head.

"They started selling them after Halloween," Robyn says. "They had a mega haul from trick or treating so they decided to sell them. And then they bought more with the money they made."

"Why didn't Lauren say anything?" I wonder. Her first business venture. I would have been proud.

"It's against the school rules," Robyn says. "They'll get in trouble if they're caught."

I suppose that makes sense.

"Thanks, Robyn, you've been very helpful," I tell her, getting to my feet. To my shame, I always thought Robyn was a bit gormless, but right now I'm so thankful she's honest. Why did it take Lauren going missing for me to find out what was going on in her life?

"I bet Kate didn't know either," I say to Cheryl as she shows me out.

Cheryl smiles affectionately. "Poor Kate. She thinks her kid's crap smells of rainbows."

"I beg your pardon?"

"You know what I mean. Sophia's a nice girl, but I don't think she's half as angelic as she makes out. Do you?"

I smile politely, but she's got it wrong. I've known Sophia since she was a baby. She was always mature for her age. I can't ever remember her being naughty. It used to infuriate me, actually. When they were in reception, Kate got nothing but good reports of Sophia, while I was forever being hauled in to hear about Lauren's misdemeanours: painting on the walls, putting sand in the flower pots, flooding the sinks.

I remember her reception teacher, Miss Bates, asking if she had behaved like this at nursery.

"Lauren didn't go to nursery," I'd told her.

I'd wanted to look after Lauren myself until she started school. I didn't trust anyone else to keep her safe.

"Oh, well perhaps that explains it," she had said.

"What do you mean?" I'd asked.

Miss Bates had licked her lips. "Lauren's an only child, isn't she? I think she's having a little difficulty adjusting from being the centre of attention to being one of a class of thirty."

"You think she's spoiled?"

"Not spoiled, no! She's still learning to share with other children. It's not something we are born with."

"Oh."

"But she will learn," she'd assured me.

"Yes, of course," I'd said with false cheer. All the same, I felt like I'd been slapped. I thought I'd been protecting my daughter, but instead I had created more problems for her. Problems of a different nature to the ones we were running away from. I didn't want Lauren to be the awkward child, the naughty one. I wanted her to be happy.

❄

THERE'S a brown envelope on the table when I get home. Letters of support have been trickling in, some of them containing money or cheques to go towards the Find Lauren campaign. But this one is addressed directly to me. I slice it open and my heart jerks as I pull out a photo of Lauren's class, with 'copyright' emblazoned across the front and an order form at the bottom. I stare at it. It's not a great picture of Lauren. She's sitting on the far right, slightly apart from the rest of her class, and she's scowling, her lips pressed together so you can't see her teeth. Under normal circumstances, I wouldn't buy this picture. But now it has a special significance, because it might be the last picture ever taken of her.

"It was school photograph day," I yell to Deacon.

He comes out of the study. "Let me see."

"She doesn't look very happy, does she?" I say.

"No," he says. "She doesn't. All the same, we should show this to Erin. It confirms what she was wearing, how she had her hair." He looks about. "Where is Erin?"

"Probably gone for a fag," I say, unable to keep the distain from my voice.

"It gives her a headache, sitting at her computer all day," he says.

I wonder how much they talk when I'm not around. Erin's never mentioned anything about headaches to me, but then we don't really chat. She's left her laptop open on the table. Subtly, I take a peek, but it's password protected. It's just as well, because Erin slips back in a moment later, reappearing as silently as a snake. She's forgotten to take her boots off and there are now muddy tracks on the floor. I shouldn't mind. If it were anyone else, I wouldn't give it a second thought. But the fact that Erin has done this annoys me. She should have more respect for our home.

I tell her about the photo and she nods slowly, as if she's thinking about something else.

"I'll have to send it down the station," she says, holding out her hand for the envelope.

I hold onto it.

"What if it gets lost?" I say, unreasonably, I know because it's just a proof. We can order copies.

"Don't worry. I'll see that it gets returned to you."

I glance at Deacon, but he's lost in his own thoughts again.

Reluctantly, I hand it over. Erin slips it in an envelope and bends her head over her laptop once more.

"Shouldn't we take it down the station straight away?" I ask.

"I'll be going there in a bit," she says. "I'll take it then."

In a bit? Where's her urgency?

It's so infuriating having to let someone else do the most important work in the world. Despite the fact that Erin's here to help us, there's a part of me that finds it so hard to trust her. Is she even handing over the evidence I give her, or pocketing it and throwing it away? I know my suspicions are unfounded, but I can't help it. I find it impossible to have confidence in the system.

※

I RING Kate and ask her if she knows about the girls' sweetshop.

"Yes, I know," she says quietly.

"As in you've known all along, or you've just found out?" I ask.

"Just found out," she says, but I don't know whether to believe her. Is she saying that because it's true or is it that she doesn't want to hurt my feelings? Her relationship with Sophia is different from mine and Lauren's. Sophia is more rational, more grown up. It's been easier for Kate to give her more 'rope' as Pam puts it. And I see now that that could be reciprocal. In return, Sophia tells her things. More than Lauren tells me, at any rate.

"Look, I wanted to talk to you," she says. "Can I come over?"

"Of course. Right now, if you like."

There's a pause. "I'll have to wait until Rhett gets home, so he can look after Sophia."

"OK, later then. I'll be home."

I set the phone down and leave it to charge. The house has fallen quiet. Too quiet.

"Deacon?" I call.

I peer into his study and he immediately minimises the tab he was looking at on his computer. He thinks he's being subtle, but I'm not stupid.

"I could really use a cup of tea," I hint.

"What did your last slave die of?" he mutters. Once, he would have got up and made me a cup of tea, but not now.

"Do you need any help?" I offer.

"Not really," he says, giving me a weak smile.

"OK, well let me know if you find anything," I tell him.

"Of course," he says.

Except he hasn't.

❄

Kate turns up an hour later. I take her upstairs. It's a bit of a teenage throwback, going up to my room

"Remember your Leo poster?" she says, flopping down on the bed.

"You were the one who loved Leo," I smile. "More than I did."

We used to spend hours in my bedroom, a different bedroom back then, getting ready to go out. We used to listen to the Network Chart Show and sing along, holding perfume bottles in front of our faces and pretending they were microphones. The air would be thick with hairspray and nail varnish, whereas now it's lightly scented with vanilla bean or whatever air freshener Pam has used. Teenage Isabel and Kate are long gone, but I still miss them. It was all about love and friendship at that age. Nothing was more important than going out on a Saturday night, a Friday night, hell, even a Wednesday night if we felt like it. Nights were rife with possibilities. We always thought we'd meet the men of our dreams. We were so optimistic, we never considered that we'd meet a string of posers who'd charm our pants off then dodge our calls until we finally got the message.

"I don't think you got the full story earlier," Kate says, sitting on my unmade bed. "I wanted to tell you what Sophia told the police."

I wait, intrigued.

"They were saving up for the Shy Boyz concert, her and Lauren. That's why they started the sweet business."

I remember now. That bloody concert. It was all Lauren went on about for weeks. She was determined that she was going to go, but I put my foot down. Eight years old was too young to be going to a pop concert. Especially one held in a crowded arena. Concerts were no longer the carefree activity they had been when I was young. There had been too many terrorist incidents for that.

"Sophia's allowed to go," she'd told me, sulkily. "It's not fair! You never let me do anything fun!"

Her words stung. I wasn't trying to be a stick in the mud. I was trying to protect her. But that was months ago. I thought it was all forgotten.

"How were they going to get there?" I ask, in horrified awe.

"Lauren was going to ask Julio to take them, apparently."

"Julio?"

"She was going to spring it on him, on the night of the concert. She thought he'd be cool about it."

I can see it now. Julio likes to play the cool uncle. I thought it was a good thing that he's so involved in Lauren's life. A trusted adult she could talk to, who wasn't her mum or dad. I didn't mind if she told him things. I thought he was keeping her safe. I think he did too.

"An older boy at school said he would sell them the tickets," Kate goes on.

The hairs on the back of my neck stand up. "What boy?"

"Rhodri Aaronson. He's in year five."

"I don't know him."

"Me either," she says. "But he told Sophia to come round to his house after school and he'd sell her the tickets. So when Mrs Darley said Lauren could walk home, they decided to go together."

My head spins. "So, they didn't just go to the One Stop. They went to this boy's house too?"

"Yes."

"Where does he live?"

"It's the farmhouse next to Damson's Field. The place with the ponies."

I nod in recognition. Those ponies have got out onto the road more times than I can remember. I don't know if the owners are negligent or if they have especially wilful ponies, but they're an accident waiting to happen.

"The girls went to the shop first," Kate says, "then onto Rhodri's house. Sophia was worried because they didn't have the money with them, but Lauren wanted to see the tickets before they handed over any cash. She wanted to make sure they were the real deal."

"And were they?"

"Who knows? When they got to Rhodri's house, he couldn't find the tickets, so they left. But when they reached the lane at the bottom, there was a car parked there. The driver wound down his window and offered them a lift."

So the girls weren't taken from outside the school, like I thought. I didn't witness the kidnapping at all. I was just being my usual paranoid self. The actual kidnapping took place at an entirely different location, at a different time, in a different vehicle. Everything I thought I knew was wrong.

"And they got in?" I ask. "Just like that?"

Would Lauren really do that? After everything we've taught her?

"Sophia told him they didn't take lifts from strangers," Kate says, "but Lauren said it was OK. She knew him."

"She knew him?" I repeat, incredulous.

Do I know him too?

❄

For the longest time, I stand in front of the fridge, staring at the suspect's picture. I still can't place him. He doesn't look the least bit familiar, apart from his passing resemblance to Julio. So how could Lauren know him? If he were someone from school, say a caretaker or a teaching assistant, Sophia would know him too. And if it were from outside school, Deacon or I should know him. Lauren isn't allowed out by herself, not even to walk down to the park. How did she meet this man? How could she know him well enough to get into his car when I've told her so many times not to accept a lift from anyone? And why would he take her from Damson's Field? Did he follow the girls all the way from the school?

Or was he late, like I was? If you don't do the school run regularly, you might not know how crazy it gets. Did he also get held up at the train tracks? What if my bashing down the barriers caused him to turn around and go a different way? Was it only luck that led him to Damson's Field?

No wonder Penney didn't believe me when there was so much contradictory evidence. How could a child be abducted at the gates without anybody else noticing? And then they found the CCTV footage from the One Stop shop. I got it wrong. I got it all so, so wrong.

I can see it now, some kid having a tantrum as they came out of school. It's a common enough occurrence. A lot of kids have had enough by the end of the long school day, and you often see one kicking off as their harassed-looking parents try in vain to load them into the car. The times I've had to shove Lauren in and battle with her to do up her seatbelt. Hell, even on the morning she disappeared, we got close to it. I hadn't really seen the child's face, I now realise. In my panic about Lauren, I assumed it was her. It sounded enough like her, but a lot of them have high-pitched, whiny voices. It doesn't help that they're all dressed the same.

19

It's a small group that assembles for judo on Thursday night.

"That's Rhodri," Kate says, pointing out a sturdy boy with pink cheeks.

"Do you think it would be alright if I go and talk to him?" I ask.

"Not without asking his mum first," she says. "You can't talk to a kid without permission."

"Why not?" I argue. "I only want to speak to him."

We hang about at the back of the hall. A few people glance at us, but we must look familiar enough not to raise any alarm. A couple of people wave – to Kate, rather than me. But that's better than being asked to leave.

"You want a sandwich?" Kate asks, holding out a Tupperware box.

Her response to stress is to push food onto people. It used to be wine in the old days, but she doesn't drink so much since she had Sophia.

"No thanks," I say, wrinkling up my nose at the egg mayonnaise.

We watch as the children gather round and begin their

lesson. They're all impressively quiet as they listen to what the sensei has to say. After a while, they break into small groups to try out an exercise, expressions of concentration etched across their faces.

"Well, I must say, this is different to what I'd pictured," I say. "I thought I'd be bored watching them fighting and fending each other off, but I've never seen such well-behaved children."

"It's like he's hypnotised them," Kate agrees, as the sensei starts to talk again, drawing them all back into his spell. "Hey, I wonder if he does babysitting?"

I start to laugh, but my laughter turns to tears as I remember that I no longer need a babysitter. Lauren is out there somewhere without me. If she's even still alive.

My baby. My angel.

Once I start crying again, I can't stop. Kate leads me outside and I soak her shoulder with my tears.

"I'm sorry," I gasp. "I'm sorry."

"Stop saying you're sorry," she says "You're upset. Of course you are."

She's crying too now, quietly, as if she's not sure she has the right.

"I miss her so much," I say.

"I know."

She wipes her sleeve across her face and I do the same. Two snivelling wretches. We get into her car and sit there for a moment, listening to Radio Queensbeach.

"Why do they always play so much bollocks?" she says, after a while.

"I don't know. Why do you listen to it?"

"Because every time I go to switch over, they play something good," she says, and reaches for the knob.

"Wait!" I say, as Shy Boyz come on.

"You see?"

"I don't even like them," I say. "But Lauren …" I fall silent

Angel Dust

as the DJ talks about Shy Boyz's upcoming gig.

"Oh, God," I say. "She really wanted to go."

Someone bangs on the car window, making us both jump. I turn to see a woman – owl-faced and weather worn.

"Wind down yer window," she barks.

I glance at Kate, but she nods, so I do.

"You don't know me," she says. "Only, my boy saw it all, you know."

I glance behind her and notice Rhodri, his cheeks even pinker than before.

"She was at our house. Both of them were."

"Go on," I say.

"Rhodri watched them when they walked off down the lane. He saw them get in that car, only he thought it was one of their dads picking them up."

"You saw him?" I ask. My eyes dart towards Rhodri.

"Yes," he says.

"We already spoke to the police," Rhodri's mum says. "But I thought you'd want to know."

"Thank you," I say. "Did you see what he looked like, Rhodri?"

"I remember he was driving a blue Hyundai," he says.

"Did you see him, though?" I press.

Rhodri frowns. "I saw a man with dark hair. I was keeping an eye on him because some folk feed the horses the wrong food, even though there's a sign up saying what they can have. But this bloke didn't even get out of the car. He sat there smoking until the girls walked down. I thought he must be Sophia's dad or something."

I think of Rhett – lovely, harmless Rhett. My business partner. My friend. It crosses my suspicious mind that he could have done this. But of course, he didn't. Sophia would have told us. And besides, Rhett wouldn't harm a fly. My mind is becoming demented, seeing evil in everything and everyone. Even now, I'm looking at Rhodri, wondering if this cherubic schoolboy was in on it. Maybe it was his dad. His uncle. The list of possibilities is endless.

❄

"I'D LIKE to see that list I made," I tell Erin, Friday morning. "Deacon's too. If Lauren knows the man who took her, one of us should too."

"What makes you think Lauren knew him?" Erin asks, watching my face.

You see? Always trying to trip me up.

"That's what Sophia said."

Her expression doesn't change.

I swallow my pride. "I was wrong about witnessing the kidnapping. Sophia was there. She ought to know."

"So you're changing your statement?" she asks.

"Yes, I suppose I am."

"I'll let Penney know."

I think she's trying to be helpful, but I feel annoyed. I'm not changing my story; I'm working with the facts I have to go on.

"Actually, I've been having a look through the list," Erin says, "and I wonder if you've included all of Lauren's friends?"

"I think I did," I say.

"Isn't there anyone else she played with, anyone she had round for tea?"

"She only ever had Sophia round," I say, "and sometimes Robyn."

"I got the impression that Robyn is more Sophia's friend," Deacon says, joining us at the table.

"What do you mean?" I say.

"Well, why does Robyn only come over when Sophia is here?" Deacon asks. "And Lauren never goes round to Robyn's."

I stare at him, wondering if it's true. I always thought Robyn was the outsider, that Lauren and Sophia's closeness was hard to break.

"Lauren doesn't make friends that easily," he says. "She's always had Sophia, but she's her cousin. I think Sophia's the one who brings other children into their social circle. I can't remember Lauren ever playing with anyone else, unless Sophia was there."

"What about judo?" I say. "She must have made friends there."

"Not really," Deacon says. "I've tried to get her to talk to the others, but she gets shy."

Shy? I've never thought of my daughter as shy. Not the way she stomps around, demanding her own way. I suppose I see a different side to her than the one she shows to the outside world. Maybe even a different one than she shows to Deacon. The longer she's missing, the less I feel I know her. *Knew her.*

"How did you get that hole in the bathroom sink?" Erin asks me as I push past her to get myself a drink.

"Which bathroom?" I ask, puzzled.

"The one on this floor."

"No idea. I didn't know there was a hole."

"Well, there is."

I go and have a look. Sure enough, there's a small black hole in the base of the sink. I hadn't even noticed it. There's also a crack running up the right-hand side. It looks like something heavy fell into it.

"Did you see it?" Erin asks, when I return.

"Yes," I say.

"When do you think that happened?"

"No idea," I say. "I've had more important things to worry about."

She holds my gaze for a little longer than I'm comfortable with.

"Have you ever had a social worker involved with your family?" she asks.

"No!" I say.

"Has there ever been any domestic abuse?" she asks, in the same tone that she might use to ask whether we've ever considered red curtains.

"No," I say, firmly. "You've already asked me all this. Why are you asking again?"

"We ask everyone," she says, her face a little too close for comfort.

"Right, well the answer's still no," I say, annoyed.

As I traipse back upstairs, it occurs to me that she might have seen the books lying around Deacon's study. Is she building some sort of picture of him as a violent man who can't control his temper? Because Deacon is not violent. He is perfectly stable. It's only the extremity of our situation that causes him to act differently. I wouldn't be too shocked if he did hurl something at the sink. But so what? I've felt like smashing a few things myself. Haven't we got a right to be angry? Poor Deacon, he appears so calm and collected on the outside, but underneath he's simmering, just below the boil.

❅

ERIN HAS MADE Deacon a cup of tea. Funny, she didn't offer to make one for me. It feels like an intentional snub. Pointedly, I make myself a cup of tea, banging around the kitchen as I do so. Erin doesn't look up from her laptop, but it still feels good to take my anger out on the draining board. I rattle the cutlery drawer loudly, and open and close the biscuit tin as noisily as I can. I drink so much tea my stomach hurts.

A little later, Deacon goes upstairs for a nap. I push open his study door and walk over to the computer. I jog the mouse. The Find Lauren Facebook page appears on the screen, but

Angel Dust

instead of the kind comments I saw last time, I am faced with vitriol:

You killed your daughter! someone has posted.

What have you done wiv her? another troll has written. Or maybe the same troll, using another name.

Ask your brother, another has typed.

Ask your brother. The very same thing the psychic said. Is this where she got her information?

Has Deacon seen these comments? No, surely not. He would have deleted them. I press the delete button and eradicate as much of the hate as I can. But a second later, another comment pops up. The trolls are online with me right now, tapping out spiteful comments.

I delete the message. It's not like it means anything. The internet is run by thirteen-year-olds, everybody knows that. I don't know why they have chosen us to pick on us, but they can't hurt us right now. Nothing can hurt more than our daughter being taken from us, and the only thing that can make it right is her return.

❄

"Where are you off to?" Erin asks, as I pull on my coat and boots.

Her question irritates me. What business of hers is it where I go?

"Just out for a walk," I say.

She gives me a long, troubled look as though she's worried I'm about to throw myself off the rocks or something.

"I won't be long," I tell her.

I slip out the door and walk briskly down the garden path. I used to come out here a lot before Lauren was born, but I also smoked back then. I'd forgotten how therapeutic it can be, strolling along without any particular purpose. Why don't I do this more often? I wonder. But as I reach the garden gate, I come face to face with Hilary from next door.

"I'm so sorry to hear about Lauren," she says gently.

"Thanks," I mumble.

I glance behind her. Her great beast of a hound is some yards back, investigating a sausage roll one of the reporters must have dropped in the road.

"Would you … err, would you like to come in for a cup of tea?" she asks.

I glance around. For a moment, I think she must be talking to someone else. But there's no one else out here. The reporters must be on a break. I hesitate. Most people offer tea to be polite. I'm well aware of the etiquette. They ask and you're supposed to politely decline. But something tells me she's not just being polite, that she really wants me to come in.

"Thanks," I say, hardly recognising my own voice. "That would be nice."

I follow her into her house. She stoops down to remove her boots and I follow suit. I've always been curious to see what her décor is like. You can tell a lot about a person just by seeing the neatness or otherwise of their hallway and the layout of their lounge.

Hilary's house is filled with antiques. I don't know how she manages to keep the dog and the antiques apart. Even Fluffy has broken the odd ornament of mine. And as for Lauren, she's a walking whirlwind. I put all the china out of her reach when she started to toddle, which she did at a precociously young nine months. I haven't moved it since.

The fireplace is not lit, but judging from the warmth that emanates from it, Hilary was burning logs earlier this morning. Monty trudges over and lies himself down, taking on the form of a large shaggy rug.

"Let's sit here, shall we?" Hilary says, wiping invisible crumbs off the table.

I take a seat and wait while she pours the tea. She makes it weak, almost grey. It makes me grimace, but some people like it like that.

"I suppose the police have been round?" I say. "They said they were going door to door."

I don't want her to know I put her on my list. That would be really awkward.

"You know, Philip was out with the search team that first night," she says.

"He was?" I say, a lump forming in my throat. All these years of judging these people for the most trivial reasons, and now, at our time of need, they want to help. I should feel guilty, but I don't have room inside me for any more guilt.

"Here," she says, thrusting a tin of biscuits towards me. "They're stem ginger. Homemade."

"Thanks," I say. Biscuits and tea are my main energy source these days. Much easier to keep down than proper meals.

"Is there anyone else who might have seen something?" I ask. "Didn't you have visitors staying last week?"

"Not since Christmas," she says.

"What about the caravan that was parked outside?" I say. "I thought it must belong to friends of yours?"

She looks at me curiously. "I thought it belonged to your brother."

"Julio?"

She furrows her brow. "Nice looking chap, with long dark hair?" she says. "I've seen him come and go from your place, often enough."

"That does sound like Julio," I agree, "but he doesn't have a caravan. Wouldn't be seen dead in one."

"Well, then why would someone park it there if they didn't know anyone who lives here?" she asks.

She's right. It's a dead-end road, just our two houses and a mud track that leads down to the cliffs.

A feeling of disquiet settles over me.

"When did you first see the caravan?" I ask.

"It was around Christmas, wasn't it?" she says.

"Wish I could remember," I say, trying to picture it. "It was gone by the time Lauren disappeared," I realise. "But I remember it being there in the morning. I had to get past it to take her to school. But it wasn't there when I came home. I don't suppose you saw it being driven away?"

She shakes her head. "I was out at a charity fundraiser that day, and Philip was at work."

I can't believe this.

That bloody caravan. Hidden in plain sight. It would have been so easy for the kidnapper to talk to Lauren while she played in the garden. He could speak to her through the fence. Even if I were watching from the kitchen window, I wouldn't know. And if he was staying in the caravan, he might have seemed like a neighbour to her.

20

Kids don't really get the concept of strangers, do they? A stranger can be someone you know. It can be a family friend. A stranger could be the person you waved hello to while I was concentrating on pulling out of the drive. A stranger could be the person walking past us at the beach, that day when we went to collect shells. He didn't have to go to her judo lessons or turn up at her school. He was right outside our door the whole time.

"Wait, does your brother have a dog?" Hilary asks.

"No," I say.

"This man – I saw him with a little Shih Tzu."

"Do you remember anything else about him?"

"She was brown and white," she says, still talking about the dog, I presume, "with chocolatey eyes. Adorable little thing. She came right up to Monty and nuzzled against him. Didn't seem the least bit scared."

"And the man – did you speak to him?" I ask.

"Well, I tried," she says, fingering her string of pearls. "I said, 'What a lovely dog,' but he just mumbled something and pulled her away. I thought perhaps he wasn't a people person."

"Lauren loves animals," I say, looking at Monty. I wonder if the Shih Tzu was in the car with them on the day she was taken. Sophia didn't mention a dog, or not to me at least, but there might have been one. What resistance would Lauren have against a kidnapper with an adorable dog?

※

"This could be significant," Erin says, when I tell her about the caravan.

She pulls out her phone and rings Penney. I hear her ask for him to be pulled out of his meeting and I feel a swell of excitement. Something is finally happening.

When Penney comes to the phone, I wait anxiously to hear what's going to happen. He seems to be doing most of the talking, despite this being our breakthrough.

"Well?" I say, as soon as Erin gets off the phone. "What's happening?"

"We've got a team looking at the CCTV footage to see if we can get the caravan or its driver on camera," she says. "It's likely the caravan was stolen, possibly the dog too, given that your daughter loves animals."

"So, the police would already be looking for them?" I ask.

"Maybe," she says.

"I doubt a stolen caravan or a missing dog were that high on the police agenda," Deacon says to me, "but now they've been linked to the kidnapping, they have more reason to look into it. They might have had the footage all along; it just didn't seem important before."

"I hope so," I say. God, I hope so.

"Can you remember the registration number of the caravan?" Erin asks us.

"No," I say. "It was just a bloody caravan."

"What about the make?"

Deacon and I look at each other helplessly. "It was white,"

is all I can come up with. "Not huge, but big enough for someone to sleep in. Maybe a couple of people. It looked kind of old but not so old that you'd think it had been abandoned."

"OK, well I'm going to speak to your neighbours again and see if they can remember anything else," Erin says, picking up her notebook and pen.

"Great," I say, trying to sound grateful.

But once she's gone we're back to waiting again, floating around the house like mournful ghosts.

"I can't believe how stupid we've been," Deacon says. "The caravan was right outside our house for days, maybe even weeks, and neither of us made a connection. We've been fools, bloody fools."

"But we're on the right track now," I say.

His mood puts the dampeners on my victory. I was so excited that we've finally given the police something to go on. We can't beat ourselves up about not realising before. It's a caravan and we live by the sea. Who really notices caravans in a place like Queensbeach?

Erin returns a couple of hours later. Deacon and I open the door together, neither of us able to wait any longer for her update.

"DCI Penney asked if you could pop down the station," she says to me. "He wants to look at some images with you, to help identify the caravan."

"OK."

"I can come too if you like," says Deacon.

"He said just Isabel, for now," Erin says. She tucks a strand of her mousey hair behind her ear.

"OK," I say, with a sigh. "I'll go now. But I really think he should speak to Deacon too. He might remember something I haven't."

❄

Once again, I sit in the interview room at the police station. I hear Penney's footsteps down the corridor. He has a distinctive gait – both light-footed and brisk, legs a good deal longer than they need to be. He enters noiselessly and takes a seat. The room is cold. Perhaps the heating is broken. I can almost see his breath.

"So, this caravan," he says. "You really didn't notice it before?"

"I noticed it," I say. "I just didn't think it was significant."

"I'm surprised by that," he says. "I thought you were vigilant?"

"Well, I missed it," I say. "I don't know what else to say."

Penney purses his lips in a way I've seen him do before. He wants to say something but he's holding back, checking himself.

"My colleague, Paul Swanley, will be along in a moment," he says at last. "I have something else to attend to."

I glance at the clock. Yeah, right. It's quarter to five on a Friday. I bet he's pissing off early to get a head start on the weekend. And while my Lauren is still out there. The thought angers me so much I bite down on my tongue. It hurts, but I don't mind. Sometimes you need pain.

Swanley arrives a few minutes later, armed with mugs of tea for us to drink while we scroll through the pictures.

"Can you point out the one which looks most like it?" Swanley asks, as he begins to click through different images of caravans.

"I'll try," I say.

But it's so hard. A white caravan is a white caravan. They all look about the same to me, just that some are a bit bigger than the others. Some have little awnings at the front. Some look more like trailers, while others are little homes. Did the kidnapper live in there? I wonder.

Swanley gives me the mouse and tells me to keep clicking through until I come to one that looks right.

Angel Dust

"Maybe this one," I say, pausing on an image.

He makes a note. "Keep clicking," he says.

I find several more that could have been the one. There are just so many, and memory is a funny thing. The more caravans I look at, the harder it is to remember what sort of caravan I'm looking for. The images blend together in my head. It reminds me of a slide show I was forced to sit through as a kid. Some friend of Mum's harping on about her caravan tour of the Yorkshire Dales.

"Do you remember if it had any stickers on it?" he asks. "Caravan club? National Trust?"

"I didn't really look," I say. "It felt rude to stare. There was someone staying there. I didn't want them to catch me peering in."

"And the curtains were always drawn?" he asks.

"I think so, yes."

"Can you remember what they looked like? What colour?"

I shake my head, ashamed of my own lack of observation.

"It's OK," he says, soothingly. "We'll go through the CCTV footage. Maybe you'll recognise it."

It's not an easy task. Some of the images are so grainy that it's impossible to say for sure if it's the right caravan. I'm disappointed that none of the images show the driver, either. I want to catch him so badly. It's a long, laborious task.

"That's it, done," he says at length.

I breathe a sigh of relief. I'm not sure how productive this session has been, but now we've finished I feel physically drained.

"It's alright, I know my way out," I say, as I stand up.

"I'll go with you," he insists.

We walk in silence back to the front desk, where there's a bit of friendly banter between the staff waiting to finish their shift:

"You going down the pub?" a young sergeant asks.

"Yeah, see you there," another replies.

"Just going for the one."

Of course, it's the weekend. How can Lauren still be missing? How much do the police get done on a Saturday and Sunday?

"Have a nice weekend," Swanley says to me, and then he covers his mouth with his hand. "I'm sorry, I don't know why I said that!"

"It's OK," I say. "It's just one of those things people say, isn't it?"

I'm about to leave when Penney and a couple of uniformed officers march in with someone who is clearly under arrest. A man with long dark hair and crooked teeth.

"That's him, isn't it?" I gasp. "That's the bastard who took Lauren!"

21

"That was him, wasn't it?" I demand, as the man is led away.

I know I'm getting excited, but if it is him, the nightmare could soon be over.

"Take a seat," says Swanley. "I'll find out what's happening."

"No – wait! If it is him, I want to sit in on the interview," I say.

"Sorry, that's not going to be possible."

"I don't have to be in the room," I argue. "I can watch from outside. You have that double-sided mirror thing, don't you? He wouldn't even know I'm there."

"I'm sorry," Swanley repeats. "It's not allowed."

"I have to know what's happening," I say, my voice breaking. "I won't interrupt anything, I promise. I need to know."

"Look – it's important that we do things by the book," he insists. "The minute we deviate from that, his lawyer will have a field day. Do you understand?"

"I suppose," I say. But I don't care about justice. All that matters is finding Lauren. I don't care about how.

I hang around the front desk until the duty sergeant has had enough of me.

"Will you please take a seat, madam?" he says.

Madam, indeed. No one ever calls you madam unless they're trying to sound polite but would actually rather you'd piss off. Still, I'm not here to get in his way. I flop down in one of the plastic chairs. I try to sit still, but it's impossible. My legs are too restless. I bounce to my feet again, pacing back and forth, stopping to read every notice on the walls.

I haven't rung Deacon, I realise. I've been so caught up in my own thoughts that I haven't even thought of him at all. I pull my phone from my pocket. My fingers feel like bananas as I find his number.

"They've arrested someone," I blurt out as soon as he picks up. "I saw him. He looks like the man in the picture."

"Really? Erin hasn't said anything." He sounds bemused.

"They probably haven't told her yet," I say.

I feel irritated that he relies on her so much. We don't even know if she's in the loop. She could know everything or she could know nothing. What if all kinds of stuff is happening behind the scenes and she has no idea? Or what if she's filtering how much we're allowed to know? It's maddening. We should be told first. I wonder how long it would have taken them to tell us about this arrest, had I not been here.

"Should I come down?" Deacon asks. "I could ask Erin to bring me."

"I'm not sure there's much point," I say. "They're not telling me anything."

"I still feel like I should be there."

"One minute," I say, as Paul Swanley comes out, wearing his coat. "I'll have to call you back."

I step right in front of him, blocking his path.

"What can you tell me?" I ask. I'm almost begging at this point.

Angel Dust

"There's not much to tell yet," he says, regretfully. "The suspect needs to sober up."

"He's drunk?"

"High, more likely," he says. "They won't get much sense out of him till he comes down."

"How long will that take?"

"I don't know," he says. "Could be hours. He should be alright by the morning."

The morning? How can we wait another night? I think of what might happen to Lauren in that time. She might be all alone, chained up in some cold, damp cellar. I think of little Freddie, the boy who was killed by his uncle. He was kept in a dark room for weeks before he died. The things that his uncle did to him ... I wish I had never heard about that case.

"You really should go home," Swanley says, softly. "It's going to get busy here tonight, what with the late-night boozers and such. Not a nice place to hang around."

I know he's right, but I'm still torn. I could wait here all night for nothing, but what if the suspect becomes lucid and starts talking? I'd want to know straight away.

"Look, I'm working tomorrow," Swanley says. "You can give me a call if you want."

He has a look in his eye that suggests that he's not really supposed to do this. I'm supposed to be going through Erin after all, but I think he feels sorry for me. He understands something of what I'm going through. Better than Erin does, anyway.

"Thank you," I say. "I'd appreciate that."

We trudge out to our cars, me to the Bentley, him to a battered old Fiesta. It feels weird that in my time of need, the person who has shown me the most compassion is a police officer, of all people. Just not the most senior one, unfortunately. What a shame Swanley wasn't chosen to be our liaison officer, instead of Erin. How much easier things might be.

❄

There's a police car coming out of my road as I return home. I park the Bentley and run up the path to the house. I find Deacon in the lounge. He has the curtains open, for a change, and I suspect he has been looking out.

"Has something happened?" I ask, setting down my handbag.

"They were doing something outside the house," he tells me. "Looking for tyre tracks."

Of course, the caravan must have left tracks of some sort. They should help the police to identify it.

"Didn't they already do all that?" I ask.

Days have passed now, and any evidence would be old, maybe even destroyed, given the number of reporters and other people we've had coming and going.

"I don't know," he says. "So much has happened, it's hard to keep track. Perhaps they decided to look again, now they know the tracks might be significant."

"Has Erin gone?" I ask, as I fling my coat over the back of the sofa.

"Just left," he says.

I glance at the clock. "It's a bit early for her," I comment.

Deacon shrugs. "Well, you know. It is Friday night."

I waste the evening as best as I can, taking a bath and watching nonsense on the telly. When I go up to bed, I toss and turn, constantly checking my phone for news. It's the worst Friday night I've ever spent. A conflict of exhaustion and alertness. My body wants to sleep, but my brain is wide awake. Images run through my mind. Such awful, terrible images. It's like a film that I don't want to see, except I can't switch it off.

Finally, I go downstairs to where Deacon sits slumped in his study.

"Surely, there's something you can give me?" I say, thinking of the prescription pad tucked into his doctor's bag.

"You know I can't," he says.

I can't believe he's being such a stickler for the rules. "These are not normal circumstances," I emphasise. "I just need a few sleeping pills to help me get through."

Deacon meets my eyes. There's still kindness in those eyes, hidden beneath a blanket of arrogance and grief.

"Not with your history," he says.

"My history?" I repeat. "Don't you mean our history?"

It's as if everything that's happened to us has only affected me.

"I was referring to your postnatal depression," Deacon clarifies.

"I didn't have postnatal depression," I argue. "It was the pressure of having Lauren on top of everything else we'd been through. I never would have had it otherwise. It wasn't my fault."

Deacon purses his lips. "No one's saying it was your fault. No one can help being depressed."

"It wasn't postnatal depression," I repeat firmly. "I could have coped fine if it weren't for what happened with Alicia and Jody."

❄

I SLEEP in Lauren's bed. It feels weird, climbing up the ladder into her world. The bed is big enough to accommodate me, but I'm aware of the low ceiling above my head. Lauren has never mentioned it, but to me it feels too low. I can't decide if I feel claustrophobic or cocooned. I pull the duvet over me and try to imagine what it must feel like to be Lauren, listening to all the sounds of the house. The radiator gurgles and I begin to understand why she's so obsessed with the idea of ghosts and monsters, lurking in the darkness. I think of all those times I told her there were no monsters. How wrong I was. They were there all the time, right outside the window. It was just that I couldn't see them, and she, with her child's imagination, could.

I nod off as the sun comes up. It's not a proper, deep sleep but a strange, shallow one in which I hear the sounds of the gulls squawking outside. I try to concentrate on the gentle lull of the ocean and in my dream, I picture Lauren in a rowing boat, floating further and further away from me. I dive into the water and swim until I reach the boat. She reaches out to me and I grip onto her, but then a big wave hits and I'm washed far away. The only thing I have left of her is a piece of material from her sleeve. She floats on over the horizon and I am powerless to save her.

22

I whack my head on the ceiling. Someone is moving about downstairs. I climb down Lauren's ladder and pad down the hall. My bedroom door is open. Deacon is sprawled out in the middle of the bed, so it's not him downstairs.

Could it be?

But when I lean over the bannisters, I see Erin's bag on the table and I realise with a heavy heart that it's her and not Lauren down there.

How did she get in? I wonder. Did Deacon give her a key? Would he do that without asking me? Without even mentioning it? Perhaps he didn't think it was important. Still, maybe Erin has news. I pull on my dressing gown. A lot could have happened overnight. Maybe that's why she's here so early on a Saturday morning. Maybe she has something to tell us.

I take the stairs two at a time, arriving in the kitchen so suddenly I make her jump.

"Good morning," she says, primly. "I hadn't realised anyone was up."

"Has anything happened?" I demand, not bothering to respond to her small talk.

"We've got a name," she says, plugging in her laptop. "The suspect calls himself Shane. Won't give a last name."

My spine tingles.

Could he be a McBride?

"Why was he arrested?" I ask. "Is there any evidence against him?"

"I can't comment on that – sorry," she says, back to her usual evasive style. I study her tight, thin lips. Is she being careful or does she really not know?

"Have they searched his house?" asks Deacon, rubbing his eyes as he walks into the kitchen.

"He's of no fixed abode," she says, unpacking her laptop.

"Homeless, you mean," I say. "There was a homeless man hanging around outside my shop the other day."

"He looked harmless," Deacon says.

"How do you know?" I ask.

He looks at me. "Didn't you see the state of him? I'd be amazed if that man was capable of driving a car."

"We'll check it out," Erin says, making a note.

"So, what now?" I ask.

"The suspect is still being questioned," she says. "If he knows anything, DCI Penney will get it out of him."

"I hope so."

I think of Penney's cold, determined face. There were moments when he was questioning me years ago that I felt like I was going to break, and I was bloody innocent! But if he can get a confession out of this man, then it will all be worth it. As long as this is the right man.

"Has he said anything about Lauren?" I ask. "Has he admitted anything?"

"Not yet."

"If he won't say where she is, can he at least tell us how she is?" I persist.

"My colleagues are handling it," Erin says, in that superior way of hers.

"But I'm her mum," I say. "If I could just talk to him …"

She looks at me with pity. "I'm sorry, but that's not possible. It's not appropriate."

"Who cares what's appropriate!" I burst out. "This is my daughter's life we're talking about!"

"Isabel," Deacon says, gently, "you need to cool down."

"Cool down?"

I'm so angry, I'm physically shaking. I storm up to the bedroom. Why is Deacon taking her side? He should be helping me fight my corner. We should be in this together. Instead, I feel like we're moving further and further apart.

He comes up a few minutes later.

"I know you're worried," he says.

"Worried?"

"Look, I am too," he says. His face is blotchy, I notice. "But it's not Erin's fault. Arguing with her isn't going to get us anywhere."

"Do you know what is?" I challenge.

"Do you?" he shoots back.

❄

I WAIT until nine and then I ring Paul Swanley, from the privacy of my room.

"What's happening?" I ask. "Erin hasn't told us anything."

"There's not a lot to tell, I'm afraid," Swanley says. "We've got the man sobered up, but he's playing silly buggers. Every time we try to interview him, he wants a drink, a fag, a burger. He's not answering any of our questions. We've got officers out making enquiries about him. We hope we might pick up more information that way, but for now, the man's refusing to talk, Isabel. I don't know what more I can tell you."

❄

I MOON ABOUT THE HOUSE, unable to do anything. Waiting is agony. Even more agony than before.

"Tell us what we can do," I demand of Erin. "There must be something."

"I'm sorry," she utters. "There really isn't much you can do to help right now."

Her response angers me. Family liaison, my arse. She's been about as useful as a chocolate teapot.

"Do you have kids?" I ask her.

"No," she says, looking down at her computer.

"Then how can you possibly know what we're going through?" I ask.

I know I sound spiteful, but I don't care.

"It's not for the lack of trying," she says, in a small voice.

I look up.

"I'm sorry," Deacon says. "She shouldn't have said that."

I glare at him, not because he's wrong but because it makes me feel worse.

I open my mouth, but words fail me. Erin goes back to her typing.

I can't believe I've got to this point, where I'm feeling sorry for her. Me, in the terrible position I'm in. But at least I've had my Lauren. For almost nine years, I've been a mum, and I didn't even know how lucky I was. I thought I knew, but I didn't really. You can't, until you have it so cruelly taken away.

All at once, my body feels impossibly heavy. I struggle to hold myself up, but it just folds in on itself and I drop to the floor like a sack of potatoes. I lie there, rocking back and forth as I wait for this latest wave of pain to subside. I miss her so much. If only someone could tell me if she's still alive. If we still have a chance.

Deacon kneels down beside me and awkwardly brushes the hair away from my face. I long for his warm hands to caress my back, but of course, Erin is still there, watching us.

Her shadow loom over us, preventing us from healing the growing rift between us. Preventing me from getting warm.

"Why don't you go and have a bath," Deacon murmurs in my ear. "You might feel a little better."

Erin gives an encouraging nod.

"Why don't you stop telling me what to do?" I snap.

"What? I was only—"

But I don't wait to hear what he was 'only' doing. I'm a grown woman. I do not need to be told what to do. I haul myself to my feet and walk gingerly towards the stairs, ignoring the black dots that dance before my eyes.

I climb the stairs and stand on the landing, panting like a bulldog. A part of me hopes that Deacon will come up after me, but when he doesn't, I go and run a bath despite myself.

I add a capful of the lavender bubble bath Mum got me for Christmas. When it doesn't have the desired effect, I add another capful, finally dumping the whole bottle in the bath. I end up filling it right up to the chain at the top. I peel off my clothes and step in. It's too warm, but I don't care. I lie back and close my eyes, listening to the rhythmic sound of the fan.

Mummy?

I hear Lauren's voice as if it were real. When she was little, she used to go nuts if I locked the bathroom door. She didn't like it. Couldn't stand the idea that she didn't have instant access to me.

Mummy, where are you? I need you!

"Isabel?"

I jerk my head up. Deacon is standing in the doorway.

"I thought you might like some tea."

He sets the peace offering down on the side of the bath.

"Thanks." I muster a smile.

"Don't lock the door," he says. "Just in case."

"I'm not going to bloody faint," I say.

"All the same."

He leaves the door ajar and heads back downstairs. I wonder if he's made a cup of tea for Erin, too.

❄

ALL DAY WE WAIT, but there's no news. The police still have the suspect in custody, but he has yet to tell them anything useful. It's bitterly disappointing to get so close and have it come to nothing.

I keep close to Erin, waiting to see if her phone rings, but it doesn't. She taps away at her computer, her face stoically neutral. If she has any information, she's not sharing it with us. With me.

"You can ring us at any time if there's an update," Deacon says, a bit too cheerfully, as Erin packs up her laptop for the night. "It's not like we really sleep."

"Do you need anything?" she asks.

"We just need Lauren," he says. Lines have formed around his eyes and mouth. He's ageing before my eyes. I don't want to think about my own appearance. I've barely glanced in a mirror. Getting Lauren back is all that matters now. No matter what the price, we'll pay it.

Once Erin leaves, the house grows colder, as if an extra person is needed to keep it warm. If Lauren were here, the two of us would huddle under a blanket, watching some crap on TV. She would still demand a bowl of ice-cream, no matter what the weather. I'd let her have it too. I'd let her have anything, if she would just come back.

Suddenly, the house phone trills. I grab it first.

"You've got to help me!"

"Julio? What's going on?"

"There's a mob outside my house. They're all chanting and throwing stuff, calling me a paedophile."

"Christ! Have you rung the police?"

"Five minutes ago." He's unable to hide the panic in his

voice. "They're still not here. I've locked myself in the bathroom. I don't know what else to do."

"Just stay where you are," I say. "We're coming to get you."

"What is it?" Deacon asks. From his excited face, I can tell he thinks it's Lauren.

"We have to go to Julio's," I tell him, setting down the phone. "He's under attack from a mob."

His face automatically droops. I understand the pain of dashed hopes, but I need him to get it together.

"We have to help him," I say.

"I'll go," he says, snatching the car keys. "You stay here."

I think of the sink, and the books scattered around his office. What if Deacon loses it with these people and gets himself in trouble?

"I'm coming too," I say. "He's my brother."

"No," Deacon says. "Let me handle this."

I'm not about to let Deacon 'handle' anything, but I know there's little point in arguing.

"I'll stay in the car," I promise. "I just want to make sure he's alright."

"I'd rather you stayed here," he says. "What if Lauren comes home?"

"I highly doubt Lauren will be returning this evening," I say, a little curtly. "And even if she did, they'd take her to the hospital or the police station first. She wouldn't be allowed to come straight home."

Deacon presses his lips together, but he can't force me to stay.

"Come on, let's go."

23

I'm a ball of nervous energy on the short drive over to Julio's. My eye keeps going to the clock on the dashboard, mindful of every minute that ticks by. As we turn into his street, the first thing I notice is that there are people standing on the lawns and in the street. Then, as we get nearer, I see his front window has been smashed in.

Over a dozen people are standing outside his door, chanting, "Paedo out! Get him out!" and yelling obscenities. I've never seen anything like it, not in Queensbeach. I don't know any of these people, which makes me wonder if they've come from out of town. Maybe somebody brought them here so they could do this. Some kind of rent-a-mob.

Deacon drives right past without stopping.

"What are you doing?" I cry.

"I'm not leaving the car here," he says. "It'll be wrecked. I'll park a bit further up the street."

"Drop me off first," I say, through clenched teeth.

"You should wait for me," he argues.

"No," I say. "There's no time."

I crane my neck. "Do you think he's still hiding inside?" I ask.

"Maybe," Deacon says, looking around for a suitable parking space. "But if they've got into his house, it's only a matter of time before they work out where he is and kick down the bathroom door."

"Oh, my God!" I scream, as I catch sight of Julio. "Look!"

They drag him down the driveway. Four or five of them, bashing his flailing body as he squirms like a wild animal.

"Christ!" Deacon swears. He parks haphazardly, the car half up the pavement, and we run into the midst of the baying mob.

"Stop it! Stop it!" I scream.

A couple of people look up, but the others will not be stopped. They continue dragging my brother along with no mercy as he kicks wildly with his arms and legs, his ponytail trailing in the mud. A couple of the younger mob members have their phones out, recording the whole thing.

"For God's sake, leave him alone," I yell. "He hasn't done anything! He's innocent!"

Nobody seems to care what I have to say. They must know who I am, if they're following Lauren's case, but it seems my word isn't worth squat.

They set Julio down in the middle of the road. The ringleader grinds his boot on his head, smushing his face down in a puddle.

"Get off him!" Deacon yells.

The bloke gives Julio's head one last grind with his boot, causing him to howl like a wounded animal. Then he and his friends step back onto the pavement.

Julio sits up, muddy water dripping from his hair, blood and grime running from his nose.

"You stay down until we're gone," the ringleader barks at him.

I glance at Deacon. There could be a car or bus along here any minute.

Deacon looks them over. "There's too many of them," he murmurs.

Julio starts to get up, but one of his assailants takes a running kick at him, knocking the wind right out of him. He falls back down into the road with a sickening thud. As I move towards him, I feel the wrath of the mob.

"Stay away!" an angry-looking woman warns me. "Unless you want a taste of what he's had? I've got kids, you know. We don't need this kind of scum around here."

"Poor kids," I spit, "having a Neanderthal like you for a mum."

The woman lunges at me. Her temper is as savage as her words. She grabs the lapel of my jacket and wrenches it off me. I swipe at one of her huge hoop earrings. I know how much that hurts. Out of the corner of my eye, I see Julio trying to sit up again, while Deacon attempts to fend off the mob. None of us hear the car approaching.

"Shit! Police!" someone yells.

I turn to see headlamps blazing. The police car has its siren on, but the battery has worn down and the noise it makes is distorted and muffled. Deacon acts quickly to pull Julio out of the road. I immediately stop clawing at the woman, and instead take a dive. She blinks in surprise as I lie twitching on the pavement, moaning and holding my stomach. She stands over me, unsure what to do, and I stay down until the police come to my aid.

"I want to press charges," I say, indignantly, as an officer hands me a wet cloth to dry the blood on my chin. "These people need to be made an example of."

The crowd has dispersed now, leaving behind just the most hardcore members of the group. I watch with satisfaction as they piss off the police and end up inside the police car.

"Are you sure you're alright?" Deacon asks me.

"I'm fine."

Julio sits at the side of the road, looking dazed.

Angel Dust

"Right," one of the police officers tells him. "You need to get your house boarded up, sir, until you can get the new windows put in. I can give you the number of a bloke I know, if you like. He's quite reasonable."

"Thanks," Julio mutters. His face is still red with rage. I think it's the humiliation that hurts the most, not the cuts and bruises. To be accused of what these people have accused him of – no one deserves that.

"I'd advise you to go to A&E to get yourself checked over," he tells Julio. "That's a nasty cut on your head."

"No thanks," says Julio. "I just want to go home."

"Why don't you stay with us for tonight?" I suggest. "You can't stay here by yourself – they might come back. And Deacon can take a look at that cut for you."

I glance at Deacon, hoping that he will back me up, but he bites his lip and says nothing. I know he and Julio are never going to be the best of friends, but Julio is my brother, for God's sake.

Julio wordlessly accepts and follows us back to the Bentley. As Deacon starts the car, I glance back at Julio and see that he's crying. I turn my head away and pretend not to notice. It's the least I can do.

Poor Julio. His reputation is ruined. And it's very hard to get a reputation back once it's lost. I should know. People are always hungry for gossip.

❄

"Any chance of a beer?" asks Julio, once Deacon's dressed his wound for him. He still looks terribly shaken.

"Course," Deacon says, going to the fridge. "Isabel? You want a glass of wine?"

"No," I say firmly. "If I start drinking now, I'll never stop."

Julio cracks open his beer. He doesn't look right. His eyes are red and raw.

"Do you think the police have got the right bloke?" he asks, unexpectedly. "This one they've got in custody?"

"I hope so," I say. "Who knows?"

Julio clears his throat. "I don't know if I should tell you this," he says, slowly.

Deacon looks at him. "What?"

"I didn't want to scare you but …"

"Go on," I urge. I glance at Deacon and pray he won't interrupt. I have a feeling my brother's about to share something important, and Julio isn't good at sharing. I don't want him to get spooked.

"The night before Lauren went missing, I went to Mustaffa's with Nina," he says. "We'd been drinking all night, and Nina started having a go at me about something. I can't remember what. She's always a bit mardy when she's drunk."

I can imagine.

"I told her to piss off and she went off in a strop. I think she expected me to go after her, but I didn't. I still had most of my pint left and I wasn't going to waste it."

I smile a little at the thought.

"While I was finishing my beer, she sent me half a dozen angry texts. I wasn't in the mood to deal with her, so I went back to the bar to get another. That's where I met this blonde. She smiled at me and offered to pay for my drink. And I thought, what does one beer matter? So, I let her."

I glance at Deacon. He's sitting a little apart from us, on the edge of the sofa. If I didn't know him so well, I would think he wasn't really listening.

"I suppose I should have eaten something cos that last beer went to my head. And this girl – she was really sweet. She offered to see me home. I staggered up the road with her. I must have been really hammered because I had to hang onto her to keep myself from falling over."

I give him a nod, encouraging him to continue.

"I crashed out when I got in, but when I woke up, she was

in the bed with me. My memory was a bit hazy, so at first, I thought it was Nina. Then I realised it wasn't and I felt really bad and told her she had to leave. She laughed as if I'd said something funny. My head was pounding, and I tried to get up, but I couldn't. She lay there, propped up on her elbow, staring at me. It had been dark at Mustaffa's, but in the cold light of day, I realised I knew her. Even with the blonde hair and the fake eyelashes, I should have realised."

I stare at him, dread bubbling up in my stomach.

"It was Jody."

Lauren: Three Months Earlier

"What do you want to play?" Uncle Julio asks.

I hug the stack of games.

"I want to play them all," I squeal.

Julio laughs. "OK, which one do you want to play first?"

I love the way he always asks me. He talks to me like we're both adults or maybe we're both kids – I'm not sure which. But I feel like he's on my level.

"This looks fun," I say, taking out Minecraft.

"You'll love it," he agrees.

He pops it on and I start to play. Soon, I'm lost inside a world of my own making. I love the little pixelated images. It's like being lost in a cartoon. Julio lolls on the sofa and talks to me while I play. He doesn't rush off to put on a load of washing or sit down at the table to do his taxes. He never seems as busy as Mum and Dad.

Later, he asks if I want to try *Star Wars*. It's a two-player game and we go nuts, shooting our weapons and destroying everything in our paths.

"How's the judo going?" he asks, reaching for his can of coke.

"It's OK," I say, taking a sip of mine.

"Just OK?" he says. "I thought you were kicking arse!"

I giggle. "I am," I say, "but it can be a bit boring sometimes. Sensei Ling won't tell us how to do any of the really gross stuff, like eye-gouging, and he keeps banging on about peace and respect, like we're still in Reception."

Julio rolls his eyes. "Sounds like a yawn," he says.

His phone beeps and he glances at it but continues playing. That's another great thing about Julio. He doesn't think his phone is more important than me. I bet that text was from Nina, but he continues to play the game as if it's no big deal. He'll answer it later. Right now, he's spending time with me.

"Hey, I'm getting hungry," I say, after a while, setting down my controller.

"What do you want to eat?"

"Can we get pizza?" I ask.

"Go ahead," he says.

I bounce over to the computer and log onto the delivery site we always use.

"Can I get ice-cream too?" I ask.

"Go for it!"

I scroll through the options and choose a small cheese pizza for myself and a medium spicy chicken for Julio, because I know what he likes. They're out of ice-cream, so I add mini doughnuts for dessert.

After I complete the order, I check my emails, but there's nothing new. I send an instant message to Sophia to see what she's doing, then I look at a couple of funny videos on YouTube. Fifteen minutes pass and Sophia still hasn't replied.

I bet she's gone round Robyn's.

My cheeks burn as I picture the two of them having fun without me. I'll have to think of something really amazing to do with Sophia. Something totally, utterly cool. And Robyn is not getting an invite.

Lauren: Five Days Ago

My shoes are all muddy from the road. I scrape some of it off onto the doorstep. I hear the sound of dogs barking, then Rhodri comes to the door. When he sees Sophia, his face lights up like the Blackpool Illuminations. Then he sees me.

"What are you doing here?" he asks me.

"We came for the tickets," I say, folding my arms.

"Right," he says. "Why don't you come in?"

"That's all right, we'll wait here," I say.

"Right."

"So, have you got them?" I ask.

"Of course – I'll go and get them."

He disappears upstairs.

"He's full of it," I say to Sophia. "I bet he hasn't got the tickets."

"Give him a minute," she says.

We wait and wait. Then Rhodri returns, empty handed.

"You never had them, did you?" I say.

"I did," he insists. "My brother must have nicked them. He's a right little tealeaf. Hey, do you want to come in for a drink while you're here?"

"Well ..." Sophia stalls.

"We have to get going," I say.

Rhodri's eyes narrow. "Who left your cage open?" he says. "I was talking to Sophia."

I give him the evil eye. "I'd love to stay and chat, but to be honest, I'd rather catch chicken pox again."

"I've got cherry coke," he says to Sophia. "You can have a can if you like."

"I am kind of thirsty," she says. Her voice sounds a bit funny. All high-pitched and sugary.

"Cool!" He disappears back inside.

"Why did you say yes?" I ask, crossly. "He's being such a turd!"

"I'm thirsty," she says. "Aren't you?"

"That's not the point." I scrape my shoes against the doorstep, but the mud doesn't come off.

Rhodri comes back with the can and gives it to Sophia. His hand lingers slightly as he gives it to her, then he leans in. It looks like he's about to kiss her.

"Ew, gross!" I screech, pulling her away. "Come on, we've got to go. We're going to be late."

Rhodri completely ignores me. "Enjoy the coke, Sophia. I'll see you at school tomorrow."

"See you then," she says, a goofy smile on her face. She's still looking back at him as we walk down the garden path.

Sophia opens the coke at the bottom of the lane. "Here, want some?"

"No thanks. Don't know where it's been."

She trails along behind me, dragging her school bag.

"We need to hurry up," I say, consulting my Minnie Mouse watch. If I'm late home, Mum's never going to trust me again.

"It'll be fine if we get a move on," she says, but I can tell from her face that she's worried too.

We hurry down the lane.

"Was that car there earlier?" she asks, pointing just ahead.

"Yeah, I think it was," I say. It seems a strange place to stop. There's only fields and ponies round here, besides the farmhouse where Rhodri and his family live.

A window winds down as we get closer. When I see who it is, I wave.

"Would you girls like a lift?" he asks. "It's going to get dark soon."

"No thanks," Sophia says curtly.

"It's OK," I tell her. "I know him."

His little dog yaps at me from the back seat and clambers up onto my lap when I sit down. His paws are all muddy, but I don't mind.

Angel Dust

Sophia is still standing in the road.

"Come on," I beckon. "You don't want to be late, do you?"

With a moment's hesitation, she gets in.

Dog turns to look at her and wags his tail.

"Oh, what a sweet dog!" she says, inching away. She's scared of dogs, even little ones.

"He's really friendly," I tell her. "You can pet him, if you like."

"No, that's OK," she says. "Hey!" she squeals, as the car starts to move. "I haven't done my seatbelt."

"Here, I'll help you." I reach across, but it's difficult with Dog on my lap.

"Got it!" Sophia says. She leans forward. "I live in Moulescoomb Road," she says. "You should probably drop me off first."

"Why don't you come to my house?" I say.

"Better not," she says. "Mum's expecting me."

"You can ring her from my house," I say.

"No, I don't think she'd like that," she says. "I'm supposed to go straight home."

We drive past the ponies, heading towards Thorne Road, where I do judo.

"Hey, my house is that way," Sophia tells the driver. "You'll have to turn around at the end of this one and go back."

"Don't worry, I know a shortcut," he says, with a sniff. He sounds like he's getting a cold.

There's a song playing on the radio. Sounds like country.

"Do you like Shy Boy—" I start to ask, when Sophia grabs my hand. "Ow!" I say, annoyed. "You nearly made me drop the dog."

I wait for her to say sorry, but she doesn't. She turns her head this way and that, like a horse that doesn't want to be ridden.

"Why are you acting so strange?" I ask.

"I think we're being kidnapped," she whispers.

"Don't be silly!" I say, but then I look out of the window and I notice all the green. We're leaving Queensbeach, going further and further out of our way.

"Kidnappers don't have dogs," I say, looking at the furry bundle on my lap. He rubs his wet doggy nose against me.

"Why not?" Sophia says.

"Because dog owners are nice people." I realise mid-sentence how stupid that sounds.

"We never should have got into the car," she snaps. "I had a bad feeling all along."

"Then why didn't you say something?"

"I didn't want to be rude."

I cuddle Dog a little closer. I can't understand what's happening. Why would he do this? Is he playing a joke on me? Any minute I expect him to turn around and shout, 'Surprise! I really had you going there, didn't I?'

"What are we going to do?" Sophia hisses.

"I don't know," I admit. For the first time in my life, I'm fresh out of ideas.

I look out at the telegraph wires and picture the energy that flows along them. If only I could use that energy to stop the car.

❋

"He was so nice to me before," I tell Sophia, thinking of our cosy chats over the garden fence. He was so talkative then, telling me funny stories about his childhood, but he's barely said a word since we got in the car. I'm not sure he even knows we're still here.

"I think he's gone crazy," I murmur.

"I think *we're* crazy for getting in the car," Sophia says, still sounding cross. "That's the last time I listen to you."

Angel Dust

"I wish you'd stop saying that and help me work out a plan," I say. "We have to do something."

"When the car stops, we'll scream as loud as we can," she says.

"What if there's no one around?" I say. "We don't even know where he's taking us. Or what he's going to do with us."

I notice the wetness on Sophia's cheeks and I feel really bad. I hate it when she cries, especially when it's my fault.

"My mum's going to be so worried!" she sobs.

"My mum's going to be even more worried," I say. "You know what she's like. And Daddy. They'll call the police as soon as they realise we're missing."

He looks at me in the mirror. "Why do you think we're in such a hurry?"

He flashes me one of his trademark grins, big and wide. He looks like it's all a big laugh, even as he takes us further and further away from home.

The roads are getting less windy, I notice, and more grey. I glance at the speed dial by the steering wheel. We're definitely going faster.

"We've got to get out of here," I whisper. I try to wind my window down, but it's locked. I wave at the other cars, but no one notices me, or if they do, they just think I'm saying hello.

"How?" Sophia asks. She pulls a thread from her cardigan and sucks on it.

"I don't know, but there are two of us and only one of him," I point out. "I don't think he's got a gun or anything."

"He's going to kill us!" she wails, proper hysterical now. "I don't want to die."

I feel like there's a lump of Play-Doh stuck in my throat, and it's all I can do to keep breathing. "Well, what are we going to do then?"

"We could offer him money," she suggests.

"We spent all our money on sweets," I remind her. "And the rest is at home."

"We could jump," she says.

"But we're going so fast – we might get killed," I argue. "And what if there's a car coming the other way?"

"We have to wait till the car slows down," she says. "At a traffic light or something."

"I don't know," I say. "It sounds dangerous."

"So is this," she reminds me. "We don't know where he's taking us – or what he plans to do with us when we get there."

We fall silent and stare glumly out of the window.

Maybe he's taking us to a party, I tell myself. A surprise party. And all our friends and family will be there.

But I don't really believe it.

"Any idea where we are?" she asks, a little later.

I shake my head, regretting a lifetime of sleeping in the car. That's what I usually do on long journeys. I go to sleep. Otherwise …

"I feel sick!" I say, triumphantly.

When I was little, I used to get car sick a lot. I know the power those words hold over grownups. No one wants you to be sick in their car. It's guaranteed to make them stop.

"I feel sick," I say again, louder.

Why isn't it working?

"I'm definitely going to be sick," I say, covering my mouth with my hand. In fact, I'm annoyed at my body for not being sick on cue. All those times I wished there was a way to stop it. And now, when I need it, my body refuses.

"Go for it," he says, with a sniff. "You'll find a plastic bag under the seat. Just don't get it on the dog or I'll have to wring its scrawny little neck."

My hand flies to my mouth. I can't believe he threatened Dog like that. Such a dear little dog – how could he even joke about it?

"He doesn't care," Sophia hisses, rather unnecessarily.

If he doesn't care if we're sick, then he certainly won't

care if we need the loo, which was my next idea. What do we have to do to get him to stop?

I go back to staring out the window. "Look, we're going through a tunnel."

It's dark in the tunnel. We can only see the lights ahead of us and the lights from other cars. We seem to be travelling impossibly fast. I wish the car would slow down a bit. My tummy hurts and I really do feel a bit sick now. I don't like the dark. What if there are ghosts out there?

The little dog whimpers and presses himself against me as the lights flicker. I feel a shiver down my spine. Animals can sense evil spirits, can't they? I squeeze my eyes shut until we're out the other side.

"There's a sign for Stowebridge," I tell Sophia, once my eyes get used to the light again. "Do you know where that is?"

She shakes her head.

"Pennington," she says, a few minutes later.

We continue reading the signs aloud, trying to work out where we are.

"Water's Edge," I say, as I spot a new sign up ahead.

"We're slowing down," she whispers, urgently. "I think we should do it now."

"What?"

"Jump."

I glance out the window. We're going slower than we were, but still too fast.

"Don't!" I hiss.

There's a loud, bleeping noise. Sophia has opened her door.

"We're going too fast!" I say.

The kidnapper shifts in his seat and stares at us. "What the hell do you think you're playing at?"

The car swerves in the road as he tries to grab Sophia's hand, but it's too late. I watch in horror as she leaps.

"Sophia!" I scream.

I look back through the rear window. She lies in a broken heap in the road, twisted and bloody like roadkill.

"Stop!" I scream.

"You want to die too?" His voice has gone a lot deeper. He turns round again and looks at me. His eyes are like two dark moons. "Well, do you?"

I force my head to shake from side to side.

"Well then, close that door and do as you're told from now on."

24

This is where he brings me. An empty car park in the dead of night. The only lights are the ones inside the car, and a sliver of the moon that shines through the trees. I wonder what's out there, lurking in the darkness.

Mum, I want to go home now.

There are no cars here, except ours. In front of us is a large shrub that lines the edge of the car park, obscuring whatever lies beyond. Is it a school? A field? If I had to guess, I'd say it was a park. But it doesn't make any sense. Why would he bring me to a park so late at night?

He kills the engine. There's no noise now, except for the sound of him sniffing.

"Do you have a cold?" I ask.

If I'm nice to him, maybe he'll let me go.

"My life is one long cold," he mutters, wiping his nose on his sleeve.

"Poor you."

"Like anyone cares. I'm going to stretch my legs."

"I need to stretch my legs too," I say.

"No, you need to stay in the car."

He turns to look at me again. There's something wrong with his face. He looks like a demon.

He gets out and locks me in. I watch the fiery red dot of his cigarette as he marches up and down to keep warm. Dog uncurls himself from my lap and gets up to investigate. I rub his back. Poor little thing, trapped in a car all day. It's not right. He doesn't deserve a dog.

I try every door and window, but they're all locked. I climb over the seat and fumble in the glovebox. There's a lighter. I stick it in my pocket. There's nothing else of use, just some empty food wrappers. Nothing that's going to get me out of this mess. I could bang on the window and call for help, but there's no one around to hear me. No one but him, and I've a feeling he won't be very nice if I start making trouble.

Still, I have to do something. I take a jelly baby from my bag and chew on it. Once it becomes sweet and mushy, I climb over to the driver's side and stick it in the hole where the key has to go.

Crap, he's coming back.

I scramble back into my seat, wishing there was something else I could do. There's a cold gust of air as he slides back in and closes the door.

"Dog needs the loo," I tell him.

Actually, Dog has already done a widdle on the floor, but he doesn't need to know that.

"He keeps parping," I lie. "I think he needs a poo."

To my surprise, the demon laughs.

"You smelly little git," he says to Dog.

It must have been the cigarette that's made him happy. I watch as he tries to pour his drink from a can into a plastic cup. It seems like an easy enough task, but he completely misses and howls when the wet liquid pours down his jeans. He laughs again, weeping like it's the funniest thing that ever happened.

"He really needs to go walkies," I say. "It won't take long."

Angel Dust

He isn't listening to a word I say. Instead, he stares into his cup as if it's the most fascinating thing he's ever seen.

"Who stole my drink?" he mutters.

The weirder he gets, the more I want out.

"Was it you?" he thunders. I'm not sure if he's talking to me or the dog.

"You're holding it," I remind him, but he doesn't seem to hear me. His eyes don't focus properly as he swipes this way and that, still looking for his drink. Then, all at once, he lurches sideways, slamming his head against the door. He stays in that position, his head pressed against the glass. His body twitches, so he can't be dead, but is he sleeping soundly enough that I can climb over him?

I clamber over the gear stick. He moans slightly as I climb across. He has his head right on the latch. The only way I can get out is to move him. I do so quickly. His head bobs about like an overinflated football. I pull the latch and he slumps sideways, his body hanging out the door.

I expect the cold air to wake him, but it doesn't. I climb over him. I don't want to touch him, but I have no choice. His shirt is gross and sweaty, and I smell his B.O. He looks so stupid, hanging out the door like that. If that's what cigarettes do to a person, I don't want to know.

I'm about to run when I hear a tiny yelp. Dog raises his paw at me.

"Come on!" I whisper. "You have to climb over him like I did."

Dog looks afraid. He trots from one side of the passenger seat to the other.

"Come on!" I say in frustration. "We have to go!"

Dog whimpers louder. He looks so tiny and alone.

I can't leave him here with that monster.

I take a deep breath and lean over him again to scoop up Dog in my arms. Dog thumps his tail and wriggles, making it difficult for me to pick him up, but at last I manage it. As I work my way out, I accidentally hit the steering wheel. The horn makes the most almighty racket. Not just a beep, like the one in Mum's car, but a whole tune.

He wakes up with a start and grabs my hand. His eyes are red and bloodshot. I don't think he even knows who I am. He looks more frightened than I am. I scream loudly and kick him where it hurts. I think about sticking my fingers in his eyes, but I can't go through with it. His eyes already look freaky enough.

He roars like a wild beast as I hold Dog under my arm and run into the night.

A set of stone steps looms ahead of me. I run down them, Dog wriggling to be set free.

"Not yet!" I say. "It's not safe yet."

But Dog doesn't understand. He claws at me, desperate for his freedom.

I glance behind me. It's hard to tell, but I think I can make out a figure moving through the darkness. I need to keep moving. Dog leaps from my grasp and runs ahead of me. I can't see him anymore, but I hear the clip of his paws and there's the occasional brush of his tail as he gets under my feet.

"Dog! Wait!" I try to scoop him up again, but he darts away.

"Come back!" I cry, but I can no longer hear his bell jingling.

I glance behind me, then take a sharp turn to the left. I follow the arch of trees, swaying and rustling in the wind. They seem to go on forever, lining whichever path I take. I have no idea where I'm going. And the further I go, the darker it seems to get. I pull my coat tighter around me. I wish I was wearing my new one, with its big fluffy hood. It's so much warmer than this one, but Robyn called me Red Riding Hood the last time I wore it, and I wasn't going to have her laugh at me.

I stop dead.
What was that?
I thought I heard footsteps on the path.
Is that him?
I pull his lighter from my pocket and flick it with my thumb until it makes an orangey glow. I check all around, but I can't see anyone, not even the dog. I walk on quickly, using the light to guide the way. The flame flickers as I move. Any minute, he will catch me. Any minute …
What's that?
A hissing noise. I shine the lighter to my left. It sounds like a goose or something. I try not to think about what else it could be. Who knows how many ghosts and witches live in these woods. More than ever, I wish I were safe in my own bed.

The ground become soft and swampy, and I realise I'm heading towards a pond, so I run in the opposite direction, running until my lungs scream for air. I hide behind a tree and wait for my breathing to return to normal. The tree feels big and strong. I wrap my arms around it and pretend it's my parents, come to take me home.

"Dog?" I whisper, but I don't dare call too loudly.

Dogs are clever, I remind myself. He'll be able to sniff me out, even if I can't see him.

I clump through some reeds. My feet are soaking wet and they squelch as I walk. I come to a fenced-off area. It looks like a tennis court. I step through the hedge that separates the tennis court from the rest of the park and find a small stone building, which turns out to be a toilet block. I try the door to the ladies, but it's locked. So is the men's. I walk around the concrete block until I come to a third door with a faded picture of a wheelchair on the front. I try the door and it gives way with a loud creak.

I fumble for the switch. For a moment, nothing happens and then there's a buzzing sound and the room lights up.

Quickly, I step inside and pull the door shut behind me. I pull the bolt across and lean against it, exhausted.

The toilet smells of sick and there's a big crack in the seat, but at least I'm safe. I wrap my coat around me and try to calm myself down, but I can't stop myself from shivering. My throat tightens as I remember Sophia, lying lifeless in the road. We should never have got in that car. I should have made him stop. It's all my fault.

What was that?

A noise. Like a ghost rattling its chains.

"Is someone there?" I whisper.

There's no reply, but I definitely heard something. Something scratches at the door.

"Dog!" I cry. I jump up and pull it open just enough to let in a small dog.

Or the grabbing hands of a stranger.

25

It's too dark to make sense of the shadows.

"Let go!" I shriek. "Let go!"

"Whatever's wrong?" a voice asks softly. Not him. Someone else. A woman.

I throw my arms around her neck and cry with relief.

"There's a man after me," I say, knowing that the words sound dramatic, even as they spill from my mouth. "I was kidnapped. I've got to get out of here before he comes back."

"I didn't see anyone." She sounds sympathetic, but I hear the doubt in her mind. No one ever listens to a child. "I thought you'd locked yourself in the loos," she says. "I noticed the light was on, which is what led me to you."

"What are you doing here?" I ask, curiously. "Do you live here?"

Only a witch would live in a place like this.

"Oh no," she says, laughing. A proper laugh, not a witch's cackle. "I'm taking a shortcut," she confesses. "On my way back from the pub."

By the light of her torch, I can make out her face. She looks at me fondly, like she knows me.

"Can I borrow your phone?" I ask. "I need to ring my mum."

"Haven't got my mobile," she says, regretfully. "But you can ring her from my house if you like. It's not far."

I hesitate. "He's still out there somewhere," I point out.

"Then I think it's best to keep moving," she says.

I'm not so sure, but I don't want to be left on my own again.

"My name's Jody," she says, as she takes my hand. Her hand is as cold as the night.

We walk briskly through the park, guided by her powerful torch. Minutes later, we reach the fence. I was so close and I had no idea. I take one last look, but there's no sign of him. There's no sign of Dog, either. I hope he's found somewhere safe to hide.

"How far is your house?" I ask, as we clamber over the fence and jump down onto the pavement.

"Just around the corner," she says.

"Good," I say, with a shiver. My teeth are chattering badly. There are few cars around at this time, and fewer people. I glance over my shoulder every so often to check that he's not following us, but I don't see anyone. The rest of the world has gone to bed.

Her house is a lot further than 'just around the corner', but I don't complain. She's helping me, after all.

"Look, a Tudor house," I say, pointing it out. "I've never seen one in the dark before."

"Let's see if we can spot anymore," she says.

We only find two more Tudor houses, but the search keeps us occupied for the last ten minutes of the walk and helps take my mind off the kidnapper. All the same, I keep looking round every so often to see if I can see him. I can't help thinking he must still be out there somewhere.

Jody leads me to a residential area, with rows of red-brick

houses, the kind most of my friends live in. Her house is just like all the others, with the same unremarkable red door.

❋

"Would you like something to drink?" she asks as she ushers me inside.

I nod, my teeth still chattering as I take off my wet shoes and socks and leave them by the door. She goes into the kitchen and returns with hot chocolate for us both and some biscuits.

"You can watch TV, if you like," she says.

"Thanks," I say.

I'm not normally allowed to stay up this late, but it's hard to enjoy it after the day I've had.

"Now, what's your mum's number?" she asks.

I tell her and she dials.

"She's not answering," she says. She holds the phone out to me so I can listen.

"Try again," I say.

She redials, but once again Mum doesn't pick up.

"What about your dad?" she asks.

"I don't know his number," I say. "I only know Mum's because she made me learn it."

"Perhaps they've gone to bed," she says. "It *is* rather late."

"Maybe," I say, feeling annoyed.

We stay up really late, but still we can't get Mum on the phone.

"I'm not sure what more I can do," Jody says. "I think maybe you should sleep here tonight. I have a spare room."

"OK," I say, but I can't help thinking that if we wait just a bit longer, Mum will call back.

Jody seems keen to take me up to bed, but I'm wide awake, terrifying images running through my mind.

"What do you think he would have done if I hadn't got away?" I ask. "Do you think he was going to kill me?"

I try to sound brave, but the wobble in my voice gives me away.

"Oh, Angel!" She uses my mum's nickname for me, though she can't know it. I usually get embarrassed when random grownups hug me, but since Mum isn't here, I let her. She strokes my hair, and for a moment, I pretend it's Mum, hugging me before I climb up the ladder to bed.

"You really should get some rest," she murmurs. "It's been a long day."

"How can I sleep?" I wail. "I want my mum. I want to go home!" I fold my arms and stamp my foot. Anger burns inside me. It really is too much. How dare Mum ignore me like this? Why doesn't she care? My feelings bubble up inside me until I'm howling on the floor like a baby. I'm so angry that I don't even care what she thinks of me. I'm barely even aware she's there. I remember what it was like when I was lost in that park, desperately trying to find somewhere to hide. And now my mum won't even answer the phone. Never in my life have I felt so alone, so unloved.

She kneels down beside me and puts her arms around me. I try not to mind that her nails are long and jagged.

"It's alright," she tells me. "It'll be alright."

"You don't know that," I wail. "You didn't see my cousin lying in the road. You don't know how bad it was."

"Tell me," she urges, squeezing me just a little too tightly. "I'm a good listener, I promise."

26

I jump back as if I've been bitten. "I knew it! Jody's got Lauren!"

I turn to look at Deacon. He's sitting with his head in his hands, his shoulders hunched over. He's so still, he could almost be asleep, but when he finally looks up, he glares at Julio with frightening intensity.

"How could you keep this to yourself?" he thunders.

"I didn't want to upset you," Julio says, backing away. "But I did tell the police. I called them the minute I heard Lauren was missing."

"Too late," Deacon spits. He gets up and walks over to the mantelpiece, examining our family photos as if he's never seen them before.

"I'm still trying to get my head around this," I admit. "What did Jody want with you? You said she wouldn't leave?"

"She wanted ... She wanted me to get her pregnant," Julio says, his face flushed.

I gasp. "What did you say?"

"I told her there was no way I would even consider it, not after the hell she put us all through. Can you imagine Jody as a mum? There's no way!"

"I take it she didn't react well to that?" I say.

"She flew into a rage, pulling stuff out of the drawers and throwing a glass of water over me. Then she started kicking me really hard in the groin. I thought I was going to be sick."

"So, you let her go?"

"I wasn't in any state to stop her," he says. "You wouldn't believe how strong she is. I had to go to A&E, it was that bad. That's why I've been off work."

"You should have said something," Deacon says. "If we had known Jody was back, we could have … we would have taken measures."

"You wouldn't give her a baby, so she took mine," I say, staring down at my hands. They are shaking uncontrollably.

Of course Jody is behind this. She's the only person I know who is twisted enough to take a child. But when I heard there was a male suspect, it threw me off the scent. I thought if Jody wanted to take Lauren, she'd do it herself. I never thought she'd get someone else to do her dirty work.

Deacon storms out of the room, to his study. A second later, we hear the sound of his door slamming and then the sound of breaking glass.

"Do you think he's alright?" Julio asks.

"Leave him," I say. "You don't want to mess with him while he's in this mood."

I don't know whether I'm more angry or perplexed. If he had only warned us, then all of this could have been prevented. I wouldn't have let Lauren out of my sight. I probably wouldn't have even sent her to school. The trouble with Julio is that he doesn't think. If he had even talked this over with someone, I bet we wouldn't be in this mess. But no, he kept it all to himself, until it was too late.

"Why couldn't this other bloke get her pregnant?" I wonder. "Sounds like he's her type."

"Who knows," Julio says. "Maybe he already tried."

Ten minutes later, Deacon comes back in. His fists are

clenched tightly and he refuses to look at Julio when he speaks to him.

"Jody's DNA must still be there in your house," he says.

"The police have searched my place," Julio tells him. "I don't know what they found. They didn't share the results with me."

"Erin never said a word," I say.

"Maybe she didn't know," Deacon says.

"Like that makes it any better," I say. "The police should have told us about Jody, even if Julio didn't."

I will my hands to stop shaking. "I'm going to ring Erin," I decide.

"It's late," Deacon warns. "She'll be in bed."

"I know it's late, but I want to know what's happening and I want to know now."

I take Erin's business card down from the fridge and dial. She answers on the third ring. She sounds sleepy. On edge. She said we could ring her anytime, but she clearly wasn't expecting this. I start talking the minute she answers the phone. I don't even bother with 'hello'. I know I must sound irate, but I can't help it. I'm in shock, and I want someone to blame, someone who isn't my brother.

"There's nothing more I can tell you tonight," she says, unable to mask the irritation in her voice.

"But wait, listen," I say. "If Jody's got Lauren, then the police need to be looking for fire. Jody is a pyromaniac."

"Anything else?" she says, with exaggerated patience. I can tell she just wants to go to bed. Hell, she might even have a lover, just waiting for her to hang up.

"I knew her younger sister, Alicia, better," I say. "She looks so much like her, they blend together in my head."

"How do you mean?"

I lean against the wall. "Alicia had this way about her, a knack of making people like her. Sometimes I felt like I was the only one who could see through her. They stalked me obsessively, the pair of them, and they were constantly starting fires. They weren't like normal people, Erin, there was something evil about them. And I don't even believe in evil," I add, imagining her sceptical expression.

There's a noise on her end of the phone, like she's trying to stifle a yawn. "Look, I've got a meeting with DCI Penney first thing tomorrow morning," she tells me. "I'll be round to see you straight after. Hopefully we'll know more then." She says it as if we're all in this together, but we're not. We're the victim's family and she's part of the investigating team. She's only going to tell us as much as she feels we need to know. My faith in the police is at breaking point.

Julio skulks upstairs to the guest bedroom. He knows well enough to stay out of Deacon's way. An unpleasant animosity spreads through the house. Our grief has turned septic.

"I don't want him here," Deacon says, as I'm about to go up to bed. "He can find somewhere else to stay tomorrow."

"We're not chucking him out," I say. "It's not safe for him to go home."

"He can go somewhere else then."

"Where? He's fallen out with Nina, and I wouldn't trust any of his friends as far as I could throw them."

"He's brought this on us," Deacon says.

I don't disagree. "I need him safe," I say. "I don't need anything else to worry about. And I can't believe you're doing this to me now, when I need my family."

He looks at me with cold fish eyes. "I'm not doing anything to you. This isn't about you. I always knew Julio was irresponsible. I didn't have him down for stupid." He says this in a loud voice, loud enough for Julio to hear.

"He's not stupid," I argue, weakly.

"Stop defending him," he says.

"I'm not," I say. "I'm as angry as you are."

"I've always had my doubts about him," he says. "And this proves it. He doesn't deserve to be a part of this family."

Angel Dust

❄

At nine o'clock the next morning, I pick up the phone and call the police station.

"Is Paul Swanley there?" I ask. I know it's early, but I want to nab him the minute he gets in.

"I'm sorry, Paul's not working today," answers the voice on the other end.

"Not working?" It hadn't even occurred to me. Of course, he's not. It's a Sunday, and he's been working all week.

"What is it regarding?" the woman asks.

I tell her I'm Lauren's mother, and her tone becomes sympathetic. "I could ask DCI Penney to give you a call," she says. "He'll be in later."

"No, that's alright," I say. Getting information out of Penney is like getting blood from a stone. I set the phone down and pace about the room, almost tripping over Fluffy in the process. Erin isn't here yet.

Is she even working today? I wonder. Or does she also take Sundays off?

❄

My Sunday mornings are normally spent loafing about in my dressing gown. Right about now, I should be flipping through clothing catalogues and watching DVDs with Lauren, while Deacon fries up eggs and hash browns, not crying my eyes out and clutching a picture of baby Lauren.

I hear Deacon's footsteps on the stairs and brace myself for the storm.

"Is he still here?" he asks, turning up the thermostat.

"Julio?" I say.

"Of course, Julio."

"Then yes. He had to sleep somewhere."

Angrily, I reach for my coat.

201

"Where are you going?" he asks. The smudges under his eyes look painted on. I can't believe how tired he looks. How defeated.

"I'm going for a walk," I say. "I need to clear my head."

"Wait – I'll come with you."

I meet his eyes. He's offering me an olive branch.

We don't say another word about Julio. Sometimes it's better to brush the problem under the carpet and hope it resolves itself. If Lauren is found today, Deacon might find it easier to forgive him. If she's found alive that is. And if she's not, well then, it's game over for all of us.

There's nobody else out, not Hilary and her giant hound, not even a single reporter.

"Where are they all?" I ask, looking around. The mud track in front of our house looks strangely desolate, as does the car park.

"It's still early," Deacon points out. "And some of them don't work weekends."

"I'm beginning to hate weekends," I mutter.

I hate the thought that no one's on the case. Annoying and intrusive as they were, those reporters were there to do a job, to keep Lauren in the spotlight.

Deacon takes my hand, the way he always used to. He's wearing the cashmere gloves I gave him for Christmas. They feel warm and snug against my bare fingers. We trudge down towards the beach and I remember how excited I was when I first moved in with him. Even though the beach was a bit desolate and unkempt, I still thought it was a magical place to live, and I couldn't imagine a nicer place to bring up a child.

"Maybe the reporters are outside the police station," I say, "waiting to hear if there's any news."

"Maybe," he says, but he doesn't sound convinced. I grind my boots into the damp sand. I can't believe they've lost interest in Lauren's case so quickly. What could be more important than a missing child?

We traipse along the empty beach. The wind flicks sand in our faces and my nose is cold and runny. I wish I had a hanky. I look out at the ocean. There are barely any boats on the horizon. The water is too choppy. I pick up a few pebbles and hurl them into the water. I've never been able to skim stones the way Deacon does, but it feels satisfying, nonetheless.

"Do you think Lauren was happy?" I ask.

"Of course she was," he says.

"But what about all the tantrums?" I ask. "And her lack of friends."

"That's a normal part of growing up."

"I don't know about that. Having no friends is rotten, no matter how old you are."

He picks up a stone and effortlessly skims the water.

"How do you do that?" I ask.

"It's all in the aim," he says. "You need to get it spinning in a straight line towards the water."

I pick up a stone and aim it as straight as I can, but it doesn't make any little hops.

"I don't get it," I say.

He reaches for another stone. We both watch as it bounces five times before disappearing under the water.

I take another stone myself and throw it into the sea. It falls into the water with a plop.

"How do you do it?" I wail.

Deacon rubs his eyes. "I can explain it to you, but I can't understand it for you."

"Why do you have to be like that?" I demand. "I just asked you a simple question."

"I was being funny," he says.

I fold my arms. "Yeah, well your sarcasm is only funny to you."

"You used to like it," he says, sounding hurt.

"I like it when you're funny," I say, "not when you're mean."

"I'm not trying to be mean."

He reaches for my hand again and I let it hang limply in his.

"I'm so tired of arguing," I say.

"Argumenting," he corrects me. This is a Lauren word.

This time, I muster a smile. "Remember when Lauren used to call cornflakes *fawncakes*?" I say.

"Remember when she ordered raspberry nipple ice-cream?" he snorts.

"I thought that was you."

He gives my hand a squeeze. "I do still love you," he says.

"Do you?"

"Of course I do."

I look into his eyes, so familiar, yet so distant. He still struggles to meet my gaze as if looking at me causes him pain.

"Then what's wrong?" I ask. "I mean, things weren't quite right, even before Lauren …"

"Lately, I've felt so empty," he says, "like the joy has been gradually seeping out of me. It isn't you. Really it isn't. I still love you."

I blink back tears.

If you love me, you shouldn't have to keep telling me.

"Is there anything I can do?" I finally say.

He squeezes my hand again, a little harder this time, almost reproachfully.

"You need to tell me things," he says. "No more lying."

"I don't lie!"

"You know what I mean. That letter from Alicia. It tells us Jody was still thinking about us. She might have gone away, but she hadn't forgotten."

"What about you?" I say. "You never tell me anything. When I ask you what goes on at judo, you're so vague. You never told me no one talks to Lauren. You never said she was a social pariah."

"I wouldn't go that far!"

"No, well what about her friendship with Sophia and Robyn? I could have done something."

"That's exactly why I didn't tell you. She's old enough to make her own mistakes."

"Is she?" I say. "I know she flounces about like a teenager, but she's still a little girl really."

"She's nearly nine," he says, "and growing fast."

"She's just a child," I say. "She still needs us."

He looks into my eyes. "Of course, she needs us. More than ever."

"My fingers are getting numb," I say, as a gust of wind blows my back.

"Mine too," he says. "Let's head back."

We clamber back up the cliff path. It's much harder to climb up than down and I have to stop halfway to catch my breath. I look down into the water below. There's no fence here, nothing to stop you falling off the edge if you get too near. Instant oblivion awaits down there as opposed to the slow, drawn-out reality we're living up here. But I can't do it. Not until I know for sure.

"Hey, what's that?" Deacon asks, pointing down at the cliffs below.

At first, I can't see what he's talking about, but as I follow his finger, I notice the white object, floating in the water.

"Do you think …?"

"That looks like a caravan," I say, unable to take my eyes off it. The whole thing has been smashed to smithereens.

27

I feel the ground move beneath my feet and I have to hang onto Deacon to stop myself from falling. The broken caravan is off-white, like the one that was outside our house. It's also some sixty feet below us. No way we can climb down there.

Deacon pulls out his phone and rings Erin.

"The police are on their way," he tells me.

I stare down at the rocks, trying to figure out the best way down, but it's impossible without ropes or proper equipment. Most of it is under water, with only the roof and a section of the window visible beneath the waves. There's seaweed hanging off the window, and a couple of seagulls swoop down and take a rest on top of it.

"There must be some way down," I say. Lauren could be down there, trapped in the half-submerged caravan, and there's not a thing we can do, except wait. Logically, I know this isn't likely – the last we knew of Lauren, she was on the road to London; it wouldn't make sense for her to turn up now in the wreck of a broken caravan – and yet I can't get the possibility out of my head. I just need someone to tell me she's not down there. I need to know for sure, before my aching heart explodes with pain.

"No, we have to wait," Deacon says, motioning for me to sit down on the ground. "There's no point risking ourselves for this. The police will be here soon enough. They'll know how to get to it."

"How long do you think it's been down there?" I ask, unable to take my eyes off it. I can't even be certain that it's our caravan, though it seems too much of a coincidence for it not to be. Why else would it be down there?

"It's probably been there the entire time Lauren's been missing," he says. "It's not like anyone really comes this way."

I shake my head. "I can't understand how we all missed it." Because we all did: me, Deacon, Hilary and Phillip, all those reporters and police who have been milling around. It makes me wonder what else we've all missed. What else has been going on right under our noses?

"It's a good thing," Deacon tries to reassure me. "Now that we know it's there, it's evidence."

I nod, but my breath feels ragged and fast.

He sits down beside me and we wait. I watch as a large wave comes in and knocks the wreck about. "It'll be washed out to sea," I fret.

"I doubt it," Deacon says. His calmness irritates me.

I glance at the time on my phone. "Oh, come on," I mutter impatiently. We're waiting again. Our whole existence is about waiting.

❄

THE EMERGENCY VEHICLES pull up as close as they dare. Deacon goes to greet them and brings them over to the wreck. Within minutes, Erin arrives in her little blue Corsa. I'm impressed that she got here so quickly but annoyed when she urges us back to the house. I want to know what's happening.

If we go inside, I'll have to hang about, waiting for her to update us.

"How do you think it happened?" Deacon asks her. "Do you think the kidnapper pushed the caravan over the cliff to get rid of it?"

"Can't say for sure," she says, "but it looks that way. We'll have a better idea when we've been down there to have a look."

"What do you think?" I ask Deacon in an undertone. "Should we hang around and see what they find?"

He shakes his head. "This is going to take a while. I reckon we should head back for a bit. We can come and take another look when things have got going."

"OK."

Reluctantly, I let him hoist me to my feet, and the two of us trek back to the house. I'd forgotten how cold I was. I only notice when the central heating hits me. I stand in front of the radiator, but still I can't get warm.

"You want some parsnip soup?" Deacon asks, pulling off his scarf.

"That would be great," I say.

We eat our soup with hunks of wholemeal bread. I enjoy the warm feeling in my tummy, and I enjoy the fact that it's just us for a change. We sit close together at the table, and I enjoy the closeness between us.

Once we've finished eating, Deacon returns to the cliff to see if he can find anything out. I have just finished stacking the bowls in the dishwasher, when I notice Mairead Osmond lurking outside, just below the window. She's scribbling in that little notebook of hers. I wonder what she's doing at the house, when all the action is going on at the cliff.

I open the door and step out into the cold. She's so engrossed in what she's doing that she doesn't even hear me approach, not until I swoop down and grab her notebook.

"Hey!" she squeals, as I run back towards the house. "Give

that back!"

Ignoring her indignant cries, I run back inside and lock the door. If Deacon or Erin were around, they would intervene for sure, but luckily for me, they're both down at the cliffs. I race upstairs and flop down on the bed, but when I open up the notebook, I'm faced with page after page of illegible scrawl. Mairead has written everything in shorthand. I can't read a word.

※

I RATTLE MY BRAINS, but I can't think of anyone I know who can read shorthand. Hardly anyone has a secretary anymore.

Mairead pounds at the door. She wants her book back and she's not going to give up until I hand it over. I race downstairs to Deacon's office and scan the pages, one at a time. I will have to find someone to transcribe them on the internet. Mairead rings the doorbell again and again till the Shy Boyz drive me crazy.

I go to the door and thrust the book back into her arms.

"You can have it back," I say.

She looks almost amused. But, then again, this is just a job for her. Her daughter isn't missing. Once she's gone, I post an advert on a job site for someone to transcribe the notes. I offer a ridiculous amount of money, so it's hardly surprising that I get three instant offers. I pick the one whose CV looks the best. I just hope after all this effort that Mairead is as resourceful as I think she is.

※

A LITTLE LATER, Deacon returns from the wreck site to report that police divers have arrived.

"It looks like they're planning to take the whole thing away," he says.

"There's no sign of anyone down there, then?" I ask.

"No, thank heavens," he says. "But it might still be useful."

I go upstairs to check on Julio. When I push open the door to his room, I see him curled up in a foetal position, sleeping the deep sleep of someone who has tossed and turned all night. He clutches the duvet tightly as if he's afraid to let go. Julio is suffering, I can see that. I swallow my resentment and leave him be.

The house is unnaturally quiet. I curse the fact that it's Sunday. How much easier it would be if I could call Swanley and find out if there have been any developments down at the station. I'm so impatient for an update that I consider ringing Penney. But no, he would just tell me to go through Erin, wouldn't he? And besides, I don't want to interrupt him. If he's in work today, then I want him to do what he's there for, to work on Lauren's case.

Deacon retreats to his study and I while the time away until Erin returns.

"Can you both come into the kitchen for a moment?" she calls, placing her bag on the table. She doesn't have to ask us twice. I'm practically holding my breath as I wait for her to speak.

"Things have progressed somewhat," she reports. "In addition to the discovery of the caravan, we've established that the suspect's name is Shane O'Leary and he has now admitted abducting both Lauren and Sophia."

I can hardly believe it. I thought the bastard was never going to break.

"Has he hurt her?" I want to know. "Just tell me! What has he done with her?"

Deacon places his hand on top of mine and we both look anxiously at Erin.

She scratches her chin. "He said he drove Lauren to London and left her at a place called Passmore Park, at around ten p.m. on Monday."

I shudder at the thought of my little girl, abandoned so late at night. But if he let her go, then why didn't she come home?

"Is she—?"

"We still have to verify his story," Erin says. "He said when Sophia escaped, he decided she was more trouble than she was worth, and he didn't bother to pursue her. He has refused to give us any kind of motive, other than he thought it would be a laugh. He said the plan was to take the girls on a joyride to London, to give their middle-class parents a fright."

"So, he hasn't admitted to working with Jody?" I ask.

"No and we don't yet have anything to link the two of them."

"Why did it take him so long to confess?" Deacon asks.

"Sometimes it does," she says.

"So you can't tell us anything about where Lauren is now?" I ask.

"I'm afraid not. We're still working on the theory that Jody McBride has her."

"Isn't there anything you can tell us?" I plead. "Anything at all?"

"Nothing, except that Shane O'Leary had some unusual drugs on him when we brought him in."

"What kind of drugs?" Deacon asks.

"Angel Dust."

"What's that?" I ask.

"Freakiest stuff this side of Glasgow," Deacon mutters.

"So, what about this park?" I say. "Has anyone checked it out?"

"We have officers down there now," she says. "Our colleagues from the Met are conducting a thorough search and going door to door in the area."

"What I don't get," Deacon says, "is how come the suspect is talking all of a sudden? Why now, when he wouldn't say anything before?"

"He boasted about it to a cellmate," Erin says. "Unfortunately for him, that cellmate was a grass."

I never thought I'd be grateful to Penney, but right now I am. I bet it was his idea to stick a grass in with the kidnapper. Who gives a toss about the ethics? I want my daughter back.

I hear a noise behind me and turn to see Julio, starkers aside from his boxers. Deacon refuses to look in his direction.

"You want some tea?" I say.

"Any beer left?" he asks, with a weak smile.

"Not a drop," I say, putting on the kettle. I don't know if it's true or not, but beer is not going to help him.

Erin watches him surreptitiously.

"Have you met Erin Calthwaite?" I ask.

"No, I don't believe I have," Julio says, flashing her a charming smile. I doubt he even knows he's doing it. Flirting is an automatic response for him.

"Erin is our family liaison officer," I inform him. "Police," I emphasise.

Julio's smile wanes. He digs through the cupboard for a box of Lauren's cereal and pours himself a huge bowlful. I bite my lip. When she comes home, I'll buy her another box. I'll buy her another ten boxes. What does it matter?

I head upstairs and grab a warm jumper from my bedroom. Then I drift across the hall to Lauren's room. I sit down in her chair and flip through her notebook, looking at her childish scrawl. She has drawn the Shy Boyz logo over and over again. I'm wondering for the millionth time what she sees in them, when I feel an unexpected vibration in my pocket. I pull out my phone.

"Hello?"

"Isabel?" says a breathy voice.

"Who is this?" I ask.

"This is Madame Zeta," she says. "I wouldn't have bothered you, but I've been having a vision I can't ignore."

28

If I were Deacon, I would have sworn at her and hung up, but something compels me to stay on the line.

"Go on," I say, hating myself for the tingly feeling of anticipation that washes over me. She's almost certainly a phony, but I want so much to believe her.

"I see her, sucking on a strand of hair," she says.

"Are you talking about Lauren?" I ask.

"I think so," she replies. "Having never met her, it's hard to tell."

"What is she wearing?" I ask. It's not even a good question. If she's seen the news, she'll know that Lauren was wearing her school uniform.

"I see pink jeans and a Shy Boyz sweatshirt."

Lauren has those clothes in her wardrobe.

I rise from my chair, the phone still pressed to my cheek. I open the wardrobe door and rummage through her things. I can't find her pink jeans. Her Shy Boyz sweatshirt is missing too.

But how? Did Lauren have them with her? Why would she have taken them to school?

"Where are you getting this from?" I ask.

My mind conjures up an image of Deacon's study. To the right of his computer sits a slightly cracked mug with a picture of Lauren on the beach. And next to that is a pile of invoices, dozens of them, from all the different private investigators he has out looking for Lauren. So many people trying to help, and even with the reward, they haven't got us anywhere.

"Are you alone?" she asks.

"I am," I say. Lauren's room overlooks the rocks, and there are still people milling around out there. Perhaps that's what the psychic can hear.

"Good," she says. "It's getting clearer."

"Where is she?" I ask. "What can you see?"

"I see a child's bedroom," she says. "With a small window and a bed. The door is open."

"Then why doesn't she escape?"

"She's made herself at home," she says, inhaling deeply. I suspect she might be smoking. "She's settling in really well. So well, she's starting to forget who she really is."

I start to edge towards the landing. Erin is downstairs. Maybe I should put the phone on loudspeaker so she can hear too.

"I know what you're thinking," Madame Zeta breaks in. "But if you tell the police about this phone call, there will be no more visions. You'll lose the link, do you understand?"

I nod, even though she can't see me.

"Or the visions might take a turn for the worse," she threatens.

"What do you mean, worse?" I ask. Her tone makes me wonder if this is coming directly from Jody.

"I see fire," she says. "Lots of fire. The more I think about the police, the more fire I see."

"The police know she's missing," I say. "They're already looking for her."

"Still, I think it's best we keep the visions between the two of us," she says.

"I won't tell the police," I say. I haven't decided whether I will or not yet, but words are cheap.

"Good," she says. "We wouldn't want anyone to be hurt."

She's relishing the role, I can tell. For once she must feel like a real psychic.

"So, what happens now?" I ask.

"You've already had a week," she says. "I sense your time is nearly up."

"What do you mean?"

My heart beats too fast.

"I reckon you've got one more day," she says. "One more day and that's it."

"Then what?" I cry. "Just tell me what I have to do!"

"What are you willing to do to get her back?"

"Anything! What do you want?"

"It's not me you should be asking."

"Tell Jody to call me. I want to speak to her direct."

But she has already gone.

I'm frozen by indecision. In films, I always scream at the victim's family to call the police right away. Things inevitably go wrong when you don't. But in real life, the risk is far greater. Which course of action is really the most dangerous? Telling the police or not telling them? What if Jody has someone spying on me at this very moment? What if she has somehow bugged the house? How can I possibly know?

I think of Paul Swanley again. Curse him for having the day off. The one policeman I trust. What if Madame Zeta calls back?

I march purposefully down the stairs, towards the kitchen, where Erin is stationed. But when she looks up from the table, my resolve melts away. There's something about her that makes me wary.

"Are you OK?" she asks, in that superior way of hers.

I nod and pour myself a glass of water, as casually as I

can. Then I go and see Deacon in his study. I shut the door behind me.

"I've had a phone call," I tell him in a low voice. "It was from the psychic, but I think Jody might have put her up to it."

"What did she say?" he asks, his face noticeably paler.

"She said she'd had a vision of Lauren wearing her Shy Boyz jumper and her pink jeans, and when I checked her wardrobe, those clothes were missing. I think it's Jody, feeding her the lines."

"Right, we have to tell Erin," he says.

"She said no police."

His face is firm. "We have to. The police know how to handle this stuff. If the psychic really does know something, they'll get it out of her."

"I wouldn't be so sure," I say, remembering how long it took them to get the kidnapper to talk. "What if Jody finds out? She might do something to Lauren."

Deacon rests his face on his knuckles. "We should tell Erin," he says again, but he sounds less certain.

"I don't know," I say, shaking my head. "I just don't want to make things any worse."

We are both silent for a few minutes, thinking.

"She hasn't asked for anything, the psychic?" he says.

"No. I think she wanted to wind me up. She said we were running out of time." I pause. "I didn't even plan to go to that psychic. It was a spontaneous decision."

"So why did you?" he asks.

"I just happened to park outside the building. No, wait …" I think back. "There was a leaflet on the windscreen. I thought I'd got a ticket, but it was an ad."

"Jody could have placed it there," he says. "Or had someone else do it. At the very least, she could have seen you go in."

I remember how the receptionist made me wait, even though I was the only customer. She could have been doing anything in that time, googling me, finding out who I was, even talking to Jody.

"I'd know if someone was following me," I say.

"There might well be people following you," he says. "What about those reporters outside?"

"What about the police?" I shoot back. "I can't take a widdle without Erin knowing about it. How do we know she's not in on it?"

"I hardly think it's Erin," he says.

"Well, right now, I don't trust anyone," I say, "which is why I think we should stay quiet."

Deacon folds his arms. "I don't agree," he says. "I think we're wasting valuable time."

"Please don't say anything yet," I say. "Give me a chance to think about it."

"We may not have time," he argues.

There's a stubborn silence. I can see his point of view, and yet I'm nervous.

"If she calls back, I can record the phone call," I say.

"The police can do better than that," he argues. "They could go round there and arrest her."

"But what if that doesn't get us anywhere?" I say. "Madame Zeta might not know anything about where Lauren is actually being held. Jody might have just told her what to say. And if she finds out the police have been, she might take it out on Lauren."

My eyes fill with tears at the thought.

Deacon stares out the window, his face dark and troubled.

"We could go round there," he finally says. "Talk to the psychic face to face."

I mull it over. She didn't say we couldn't talk. It's not the same as calling the police.

"OK," I say. "Let's try it."

"And we can tell Erin the clothes are missing. She doesn't have to know how we found out."

"OK."

※

Erin looks up expectantly when we emerge from the study.

"We're going for a drive," Deacon tells her.

"Do you want me to come?" she asks.

She wants to keep an eye on us.

"No, I'd rather there was someone home," I say, firmly. "Just in case."

"Are you sure? It's really no trouble."

"We're fine," I tell her firmly. "I'm sure you have plenty of work to do, finding Lauren."

I look at her pointedly and she meets my gaze. There is no expression in her eyes. I have absolutely no idea what she's thinking.

As we climb into the Bentley, I feel a little excited. I'm not sure what we're going to say to Madame Zeta, but Deacon is good at this type of thing. Maybe he can get some sense out of the woman.

Deacon drives, but he lets me choose the music. I put on Foo Fighters because he likes them, and they don't drive me nuts like some of the stuff he likes.

The town car park is half empty, it being Sunday. The shops are starting to close and people are heading back home for the evening. Deacon leads the way, striding up the ramp towards the psychic centre.

"It's closed," he says, bitterly.

I stare at the darkened building. All the lights are off and the blinds drawn. Of course, it's closed. it's a bloody Sunday.

I stare at the door, willing it to open. "She could have called from her mobile," I realise. "The number was blocked. She could have been anywhere. Anywhere at all." I stare at him in despair. "What shall we do?" I ask.

"There's not much we can do," he says. "The door's locked and the building's alarmed."

We check every window. If only they'd left one open, even a little bit. We could climb in and check their computers, go through their files. But everything looks secure.

"We'll have to come back tomorrow," I say, unhappily.

"The police could get in now," Deacon says.

"Even they would need a warrant," I point out. "I'm not sure it would be that easy at this time on a Sunday."

"Perhaps this was Jody's plan all along," he says. "Leading us here on a wild goose chase, knowing we wouldn't be able to find anything."

"Just like her," I say.

I bet she thrives on the anguish she's causing.

"How did she get the clothes?" I ask, as we walk back towards the car. "Her Shy Boyz sweatshirt and pink jeans."

"Who else has had access to Lauren's room?" he asks.

"Erin," I say.

"Oh, come on! Who else?"

"No one," I insist. "Really, it's just you and me." I look at him, a cold feeling creeping over me. "And Pam."

"Pam has nothing to do with this," he says.

"How do you know?"

"Are you serious?"

He's right. Pam is a good person. I checked her references when I took her on. I was very careful. And yet, I picture her sneaking Lauren's favourite clothes out of her wardrobe. How else did Lauren come to be wearing her pink jeans and Shy Boyz sweatshirt? It wasn't like she knew she was going to be kidnapped. And it would have been so easy for Pam to take them. Was that why she came to see me that day? So she could pop up and grab some of Lauren's things? Something to calm her down, perhaps, to stem the tide of hysteria?

I picture her reporting back to Jody, telling her everything she saw, telling her about the policewoman stationed in my kitchen, and anything else Jody wanted to know.

※

"Erin," I say as soon as we get home. "Have you talked to my cleaning lady, Pam?"

"Do you have a reason to suspect Pam?" Erin asks, her brow furrowed.

"Well, not exactly," I say, "but she was here the other day. It got me thinking."

"Thinking what?"

"I don't know – just that she had access to Lauren. To us."

Erin studies my face as if trying to work out what I'm talking about.

"Pam's name is on the list," she says. "She'll be getting a visit."

Pam is semi-retired now. She isn't taking on any new clients. She cleans for us and two other families. That's it. I thought it was because she enjoyed being around us. There's a heaviness in my chest as I remember the early days when I'd been up all night with Lauren. Deacon had gone off to work and left me, weepy and tired – too tired to deal with our screaming baby. And then Pam arrived.

"I'll watch the little mite," she'd said, and sent me upstairs for a nap. I was so tired that I was too weak to refuse her help. When I came back downstairs, not only was Lauren sleeping contentedly in her Moses basket, but Pam had cleaned the kitchen and hoovered the carpets as well. Apparently, it was the sound of the hoover that had put Lauren to sleep.

"It sounds the same as your uterus," Pam had told me. "Babies find it very soothing."

She was always full of useful tips like that, even though she didn't have any children of her own. She'd helped to raise plenty and most of her advice was sound. Dear, kind Pam. I picture her cradling baby Lauren, and I feel utterly sick.

Lauren: The Morning After

Yellow ducks dangle from a mobile on the ceiling and there is music, high and sweet, the same tune ice-cream vans play to bring the children out onto the street. I stretch and yawn, wondering how it got there. Then I realise the bed is wet.

"Mum?"

I feel silly for calling out because I know she isn't there. Because this isn't my bed. And this isn't my home.

I inspect the damage. The sheets are drenched. My clothes too. I tiptoe out of my room and into the bathroom next door. It has a round bathtub with taps in the middle. There are more yellow ducks lined up along the bath, all in a row. Their mouths are red like they're wearing lipstick. Their eyes are red, too.

I step out of my wet things and wrap a towel around me to keep warm. Then I stand at the sink, scrubbing my sheets and clothes with soap and warm water. I empty the sink and rinse the clothes under the cold tap, then I sneak back to my room and hang them on the radiator. It isn't warm like the one at home, but I don't know what else to do.

I check the chest of drawers for spare clothes, but they are all empty. Then I remember that I have my jeans in my school bag, along with my Shy Boyz top. I brought them in to show Sophia and Robyn when we were planning what to wear to Stratford-upon-Avon. I unzip the bag and pull them out. It's amazing how much better I feel once I'm warm and dry again. I try to turn the mattress like I've seen Mum do, but it's really heavy. I really hope Jody won't be cross.

I haven't heard a peep out of her yet. Maybe this is a good time to leave. I shove my wet things in my bag and pad softly downstairs. The TV is on, showing ad after ad, but there is no one about. Jody must have forgotten to turn it off last night. I try the front door, but it's locked. The backdoor too. I look on the kitchen worktops and hunt around in the drawers, but I can't find any keys. Perhaps she keeps them in her handbag, but I can't see that either. I plop down in front of the TV and wait.

My tummy rumbles. I'm hungry. I head back into the kitchen and open the cupboard. There's a packet of cereal there. Not any old cereal: Shy Boyz flakes. Guiltily, I reach for the box and peer inside. The wheaty bites glitter like jewels in the desert. I reach in and grab a handful. They are more delicious than I imagined. So, so sweet. I grab another handful, hoovering them up like I've never been fed. Shy Boyz flakes! What are the chances?

I hear her uneven footsteps coming down the stairs. She seems like a cool lady, but she might not be too happy about me helping myself to her cereal, especially one as amazing as this. I shove the box back where I found it and wipe the crumbs from my mouth. I realise too late that there are also crumbs all over the floor, but there's not much I can do about that now. I run back into the lounge and dive for the sofa. I pretend I've been there all along.

Jody is dressed in a long flowing robe. Her frizzy hair hangs down her back, fraying to a point at the ends. She stares at me for a long time without speaking. I stare back, waiting for her to speak. This is worse than the time I hit Mrs Darley in the face with my ball. Why doesn't she say something?

"How did you sleep?" she finally asks.

I shrug, unable to open my mouth due to the amount of cereal still in there.

"I tried calling your mum again," she says. "I've left a message so I'm sure she'll ring back when she wakes up."

"What time is it?" I ask.

"Quarter past nine."

"I'll be late for school," I say. "Maybe I should catch a

bus." The roads were full of them yesterday. Red London buses. One of them must be going my way.

"Not by yourself," she says. "It's not safe. That man might still be out there."

I think of him and shudder.

"Do you think he's still looking for me?"

"Who knows?" she says.

"But why? What does he want with me?"

Dread washes over me as I remember Sophia's crumpled body lying in the road.

Jody places an arm around my shoulder. She's wearing a lot of jewellery and her sharp rings dig into the flesh of my shoulder. Still, it would be rude to pull away.

"Why don't you put on a DVD?" she says, releasing her grip. "I've got a bunch of them in the TV drawer."

I open the drawer and peer inside.

"You've got Shy Boyz on Tour!" I shriek. I lift the shiny round disk out of its case and marvel at the gold lettering. Gently, I slip it into the machine, careful not to scratch the surface. Instantly, the screen comes alive.

I watch the DVD all the way through, then I watch all the DVD extras. There are interviews with the Boyz in their private dressing room, and a segment on the fans, screaming how much they love them.

"I'm going to meet them when I go to the concert," I tell to Jody. "Do you think they'll pick me to go backstage?"

"I'm sure they will," she says. "If you want it badly enough."

I nod, because I really do.

"Do you think they'll recognise me from the pictures I sent them?"

"I hope so," she says with a smile. "Otherwise, you'll have to make them notice you."

"How do I do that?" I ask.

"You could climb up on someone's shoulders and hold up

a banner," she suggests. "Or else, shout the loudest. There are always ways to get noticed, if you want it badly enough."

※

Jody makes me a ham sandwich for lunch and sprinkles the plate with salt and vinegar crisps. I look around for a table to sit at, but she doesn't have one. I choose another DVD, this time a Disney princess film, and settle in front of the TV.

"This is really nice," I say. "I wish my mum would let me eat in front of the TV." I look down and see that I've scattered crumbs everywhere. "Do you have a dustpan and brush?" I ask.

She laughs. "Don't worry about it. I was going to run the hoover round later anyway."

"Mum always makes me clean up my own mess," I say.

"Well, I'm not your mum."

I go to the window and draw back the curtains, careful not to touch the delicate spiderweb hanging there. The grass is tall and frosty and there are patches of wildflowers that bloom wherever they fancy. A row of toadstools has sprung up under the shade of a large oak tree. It looks like a tiny fairy village.

"Can I go outside?" I ask.

She frowns. "I don't think that's a good idea. It's not really safe out there."

"What do you mean?" I ask.

A strange look flickers across her face. "There are landmines," she says. "They've been there since the Second World War."

"We did the Second World War at school last year," I say, with a vague recollection of fighting and poppies and long, dull poems.

"Well then, you'll know all about landmines," she says. "They're very dangerous. They can blow up in your face if you step on them."

"Oh," I say. "It looks like such a pretty garden."

"Yeah, it's a shame."

She plonks herself down on the sofa and pulls out a box of sewing things from under the seat. She flips it open and I stare at the rows of needles in various sizes. She pulls one out and its sharp point glimmers under the lamp.

"Tell me about school," she says, as she selects a reel of blue cotton.

"Do we have to talk about school?" I groan. "It's really boring."

"But you must have friends there?"

"My cousin Sophia is my best friend, but she's not in my class," I say. "I'm in Saffron. She's in Violet, with Robyn." I pull a face as I say Robyn's name.

"What strange names your classes have," she comments, as she begins to sew. "So, is Robyn your friend?"

"Not really," I say, "but Sophia really likes her, so the three of us have to hang round together."

"Why don't you like Robyn?" she asks.

"She's such a know-it-all," I say. "She thinks she knows best about everything. She even thinks she knows Sophia better than me. Sophia liked her birthday present more than mine, but that was only because Robyn's mum spent more than mine did. My mum only gave me a lousy fiver. What was I supposed to buy with that?" I sigh. "Robyn likes reading, like Sophia does. They're always going on about books. It's such a bore. We always end up doing what Robyn wants to do. It's so much better when it's just Sophia and me."

"What if something were to happen to Robyn?" she asks. "Would that make things better for you?"

"What, like if she moved away or something?" I ask.

"Something," she says, with a smile.

"That would be great," I say.

I watch as her needle zooms in and out of the fabric. She's

utterly fearless, as though it has never occurred to her that she might prick herself.

"You're really good at that," I say.

"I've had a lot of practise," she replies, without even looking up.

"Could you teach me?" I ask, feeling a little shy.

❇

"I wet the bed," I confess to Jody a little later.

"We all do sometimes," she says.

I narrow my eyes. Grownups don't wet the bed. I haven't done it myself in a long time. It was because I was sleeping in a strange bed, away from home.

"Shall I put the sheets in the washing machine?" I ask.

That's what Mum used to do when I was little.

"If you like," she says.

So I go drag them down the stairs to the kitchen, where I stuff them into the machine. I don't know how much powder to put in, but Jody doesn't seem to care. I remember Mum carefully measuring it out at home. It always seemed important not to put too much in.

I get the machine working and watch proudly as the sheets whiz around. There seem to be an awful lot of bubbles in there, but if Jody doesn't mind, then nor should I.

"Have you got any more clothes I can wear?" I ask.

"Have a look in my room," she says, and she goes into the lounge and takes up her needlework.

It feels wrong, digging around her room. I find clean underwear in the drawer and a pair of long black socks that come all the way up to my thighs. I pull on an old, long t-shirt that comes down past my knees. I don't really need anything else, but I have a look around anyway. At the bottom of her wardrobe, there's a box of old toys. I spot a blonde-haired doll and lift it out. It has a grubby face and its hair is frayed at the ends like Jody's. It smells funny, like it's been to a bonfire. I put it back and take out an old blue teddy bear instead. His tummy has a large rip in it and his stuffing is hanging out. I wonder why Jody hasn't mended it when she's so good at sewing. He looks so sad I decide to call him Gloomy.

Gloomy and I sit and watch the street from my bedroom. It's funny how quickly I've come to think of this room as my own when I'm only borrowing it. The street below is so quiet. I see people getting in and out of their cars. There's a quick, muttered hello if two cars arrive at once, but then the people go straight back inside their houses. I haven't seen any kids playing outside, apart from one boy, who rides up and down and does wheelies in the middle of the street. He looks a bit of a prat. He catches my eye and pulls a face at me, sticking out his tongue and rolling his eyes. Boys my age are so gross. I hear his mum calling him in and then it all goes quiet.

A lone figure slopes along the street, stopping to peer into a couple of car windows as if he's forgotten which car is his. I see him try the handle of one of the cars, but then he walks on quickly. He has slicked-back hair and faded blue jeans hang from his skinny waist.

I freeze. It can't be.

"Jody!" I scream. "Jody!"

I barrel down the stairs and into the lounge, where she sits calmly with her needlework.

"Careful," she says, setting her sewing aside.

"He's found me!" I gasp, clinging to her for my life.

She's not warm or soft like Mum, but she slips her arm around me and I instantly feel safer.

"Where?" she asks.

"Outside," I say. "I saw him out in the road."

"Are you sure it was the same man? Can you describe him to me?"

"He was tall and thin … with black hair. Quick, Jody! He's coming to get me."

"Wait here."

She peels my arms from her waist and pulls herself into a standing position. I watch as she pulls the curtains across the window and checks that the doors are locked.

"Don't you have an alarm?" I ask.

"No. I've never needed one."

"What if he smashes a window or something?"

"I've got double glazing," she says. "It's very hard to smash, but you better stay out of sight just in case."

I get down low and hug my knees.

"How did he find me?"

"I don't know – I suppose he could have followed us."

"What are we going to do?" I ask. "He's going to get me."

"I won't let him," she says. "You'll be fine, just as long as you keep away from the windows."

"What if he comes round the back?"

"Then he'll probably step on a landmine," she says with a smile.

I wasn't really sure whether to believe her before about the landmines, but now I hope it's true.

29

Footsteps are like footprints. Everyone's are different. Jody's are uneven; she stumbles along the corridor, like a toddler who's just learnt to walk.

"How did you sleep?" she asks, when she comes into the nursery.

"Like a log," I reply. Then I reconsider. "Like a forest of logs."

"Like a log fire," she joins in with a smile. She sets a mug of hot chocolate down on the chest of drawers next to me.

Actually, I lay awake for some time, listening to the noises out on the street. In the end, I had to get up to check the window at least three times, but I couldn't see anybody down there.

"Why do you have a nursery?" I ask. "Are you going to have a baby?"

She doesn't look like she is. When Robyn's mum was up the duff, her belly looked like a space hopper.

"The nursery came with the house," she says.

"Oh. Do you want a baby?"

"I always wanted a child of my own," she says. "But it never worked out for me."

"Why not?"

"Because I never had a partner I could trust. I loved a man once … but he betrayed me. There hasn't been anyone like him since."

"Do you feel sad?" I ask.

"I don't feel much of anything anymore," she says, pressing her lips together.

"I like how you answer my questions," I say. "Most grownups don't want to talk, not about anything interesting, anyway."

"Well I'm not most grownups," she says with a smile.

"I always wanted a brother or sister," I venture, "but Mum doesn't want another baby."

She raises an eyebrow. "Why not?"

"If she had a baby, she wouldn't be able to work in her shop," I explain. "And that would make her sad again, like she was when I was a baby."

"I had no idea."

She has a weird look on her face, and I feel like I've said too much.

"Can you try her again?" I plead. I can't believe she's still not answering.

"I'll try." She takes her phone from her pocket and I watch as she redials my number. She puts it on speakerphone, so I can hear too, but it just rings and rings.

"Don't you think it's strange that she's not answering the phone, when I'm missing?" I ask, my eyes watering.

"I don't know," she says. "Maybe she needs a break."

❄

Despite Jody's warnings to stay away from the windows, I spend a lot of time peering out, watching to see if he comes back. I don't understand why Mum isn't answering the phone or why the police haven't come. Daddy always says the police are there to help if you're in trouble, but they don't seem to care about me.

"The police are too busy to come out," Jody explains. "There's a lot of crime in London. They have to prioritise."

"What does prioritise mean?" I ask.

"They have to decide which problems are the most urgent," she says.

"Then why don't they prioritise me?"

She gives me a squeeze. "Hey, you're OK here with me, aren't you?"

"I suppose, but what about Mum? Can we ring her again?"

"I just did but no luck, I'm afraid. Try not to worry, Angel. It will all sort itself out."

She takes a cigarette from her pocket and pops it into her mouth. I try not to mind that she smokes indoors, even though it smells like burnt worms.

"Here, do you want to try?" she asks.

"No thanks," I say. "Cigarettes are a fire hazard."

"Suit yourself."

We spend the day watching a Wallace and Gromit DVD. The same one I watched at Christmas. I remember snuggling up between Mum and Dad, our bellies full from Christmas lunch. Jody is kind and all, but I miss home so much. I wish I were back there now. I wish they would answer the phone.

❄

"WHAT'S FOR DINNER?" I ask later.

"Don't care," she says.

"We could order a pizza," I suggest, hopefully. "Then you wouldn't have to cook."

She hesitates.

"Please?" I beg. "I'm really hungry for pizza."

"Oh, alright then," she says, taking out her phone.

I give her a big hug. "Thank you!"

I go upstairs to the nursery and again, watch from the window. Nobody hangs around for very long in this neighbourhood. They all dash about, as if they've left the soup on the stove. It seems like forever until I hear the roar of an engine, and then the pizza man zooms into the street, like Darth Vader on a moped. I fly down the stairs, desperate to reach him.

Jody's already at the door, throwing back her head and laughing at something he says. I jump up and down behind her to attract his attention, but he only has eyes for her.

"I don't live here," I say, boldly.

Jody laughs. "I found her at the zoo," she says.

"I want to go home now," I say, hoping Darth Vader will offer to take me on his moped.

They both laugh, as though everything I say is a joke.

"I was kidnapped," I tell him. "I'm waiting here till my family come and get me."

He nods earnestly, but he thinks I'm playing a game. "Enjoy your pizza," he says. "The ice-cream's on the house."

"That's really generous of you," Jody says, and she blinks at him under her lashes.

She closes the door and places her hands on her hips. I have a feeling I've done something wrong.

"Maybe you shouldn't tell people who you are," she says, her face hard.

"Why not?"

"The kidnapper is still out there, remember? You don't want him to find you, do you?"

"No," I say, swallowing. "Of course not. But I do still need to go home."

"I know," she says. "I'm working on it."

She carries the pizza box over to the sofa and opens it up. "There's no pepperoni!" she cries. She sounds really upset.

"It still looks yummy," I say.

Angel Dust

Her eyes bulge. They look like they could pop right out of her head.

"It's no good!" she screams. She shoves the pizza back in the box and marches off to the kitchen with it. I follow close behind. For a horrible moment, I think she's going to dump it in the bin. Instead, she places it on the floor and jumps up and down on it.

"Stupid, stupid pizza!"

"Stop! Please stop!"

Sticky, red tomato sauce splats like blood, all over the floor. It's in my hair and on my nose and all over the kitchen counters. I shrink back as she kicks out at the kitchen cupboards. She swears and spits and hisses like a goose. I slip into the lounge and hide behind the curtains. What's wrong with her? Why doesn't she just call the pizza company and ask them to bring the correct pizza? I would suggest it, but she's so angry I don't dare come out of my hiding place. I just wish with all my heart that I hadn't made her order that stupid pizza.

Finally, I hear her stumble upstairs, her step as uneven as always. It's only once she's gone that I realise I was holding my breath. I want to go home now. I wish Mum would come and get me. Is she ever going to come?

My tummy roars like a lion and I think of the ruined pizza. I sneak back into the kitchen and find the box, still lying on the floor. Slowly, I lift the lid. The pizza is all squidgy and there is sauce everywhere. I break off a piece and take a little bite. It's a bit flat, but it still tastes good. I stuff another piece into my mouth and then another, chewing fast until the lion's gone, then I pick up the box and dump it in the bin.

30

"Come on, get your coat on," Jody tells me, zipping her legs into a pair of tall leather boots.

"Are you taking me home?" I ask, hopefully.

"Better," she says.

It's dark out, like the night I arrived. There are lights on in one or two of the houses, but the rest are in darkness.

"Can you see him?" I ask, as we get in the car. She lets me sit in the front. I've never sat in the front in my whole life, but my excitement is marred by the thought that *he* might be out there watching us.

She glances quickly around. "No," she says. "But don't worry. I've locked the car doors."

"Why don't you wear your seatbelt?" I ask, as she starts the car.

"What will be will be," she says. "Who am I to argue with the hands of fate?"

I think of my parents and pull my seatbelt across my body, but then I glance at Jody and I decide not to do it up. She hasn't said anything about yesterday's pizza incident, so I haven't either. Maybe she feels embarrassed, like I do after a really big tantrum.

"Hooray!" I squeal, as she parks outside a restaurant. I've been to a McDonalds before. We have one in Queensbeach. Daddy doesn't like it much, but Mum and I go there some Friday afternoons after school. Mum says she likes the coffee, but she always orders something naughty, like ice-cream or fries.

Jody pays for our food and steers me towards a table. Nobody gives us a second glance as I pull a green action figure out of my Happy Meal.

"Do you like it?" she asks.

Actually, I only like the pink action figures, but I don't tell her that. It feels good to be out of the house.

"One moment," she says. "I think I just saw a friend of mine."

I look around, hoping to see someone *I* know, someone who can take me home.

I munch on my fries while Jody talks to her friend. He must be rich because he has a mobile phone in one hand and another one sticking out of his pocket. She murmurs something to him and I see them hug. She bats her eyes at him like she did with the pizza man. I wonder if he's her boyfriend. A few minutes later, she returns to our table, looking pleased with herself.

"Come on, eat up," she says. "We've got plans for the evening."

"Are we going to the cinema?" I ask. If Mum and Dad take me out in the evening, that's usually where we go.

Jody laughs. "You'll see."

We walk up the street a little way. Some of the shops are still open, including the tourist shop on the corner. I stop to look at the t-shirts and snow globes in the window.

"Wow, look – an electric pencil sharpener!" I cry. Robyn has one, but she never lets me use it.

"You want it?" she asks.

"Yes! Yes – I've always wanted one!"

"Then you shall have it!"

I feel like I've won the lottery as she leads me inside. The shop is crowded, and no one gives me a second look as I follow Jody over to the counter. Not only does she buy me the electric pencil sharpener but also a new pack of pencils and a notepad to draw on.

"Thank you so much!" I squeal. "I can't wait to get home and try it."

"All in good time," she says. "There's something else I want to show you first."

We return to the car and Jody weaves through the heavy traffic. I see big London buses, ferrying people to all sides of the city. There are black taxis too and I wonder how much it would cost to take one home. Taxis are very expensive. Mum told me so on our last trip to London, when I was tired of waiting for the train.

"We're not made of money," she said.

"Of course not," I replied. "We're made of blood and bones."

Mum laughed at that. I wish she would laugh more often.

"This place is a rabbit warren," Jody says as she turns through a series of small streets.

I look out the window, but I don't spot any rabbits. I see tall buildings in dull shades of brown and grey, with murky windows that need cleaning.

"If your mum doesn't come and get you, I can train you up as my apprentice," she says.

"My mum will come and get me," I tell her. Then a moment later: "What's an apprentice?"

"It means you work for me, for my business."

"Doing what? Sewing?"

Jody snorts. "You'll see."

She parks the car and I let go of my seatbelt.

"Pass me my bag, will you?" she says.

I reach over and pick up the large canvas bag from the back seat. It looks a bit like the one Mum takes to the gym.

"Are we going swimming?" I ask.

"Guess again," she says.

She fishes about in the bag and pulls out some thin plastic gloves.

"Here, put these on," she says, handing me a pair.

"What are they for?" I ask.

"So we don't leave fingerprints."

I put on the gloves and she pulls a balaclava over my head. The wool feels itchy against my skin.

Sleet splatters the pavement as she pulls me down a dark alley full of overflowing bins.

"I can't see where I'm going," I say, peering out through the tiny eye slits.

"Shh!" she hisses. "Keep it down."

She bends down and produces a big metal thing from her bag, which she uses to open the window.

I expect to hear a burglar alarm go off, but it doesn't.

"The security is second to none," she chuckles.

"What if there's a silent alarm?" I ask. Dad told me about those once. They have them in places like banks, so the burglars won't know if the staff press the alarm.

"That's the chance we take," she says. "Don't worry, I do it all the time."

"I'm not going in there," I say. I know right from wrong, and this is definitely wrong.

"Come on, it'll be fun."

"I don't want to."

"It won't take long," she says. "Come on. Didn't I buy you that fancy pencil sharpener you wanted?"

"Yeah …"

"So, don't you think you ought to return the favour?"

I hear something rattling behind me. I turn sharply, but I

don't see anything. The rattling continues, like a ghost clanking its chain.

"Let's be quick," I relent.

"Good girl."

She hoists me up onto her shoulders.

"Man, you're heavy," she complains.

"I am not," I hiss back. "I'm a very nice size."

"If you fall, it's going to hurt," she warns, as I reach the window.

The ledge is narrow and slippery, making it difficult to get a grip, but somehow, I manage to pull myself up. The window is slightly ajar. I push it hard and it opens wider, enough for me to wriggle inside.

"Give me another push," I call down. Jody does as I ask and I vault into the building, landing in a heap on the floor.

"Ow!" I cry.

"Are you alright?"

"I'm OK," I call back.

It's hard to make anything out in the darkness. The room is alive, filled with pipes and things that gurgle and whirr. A scream escapes my throat as a ghost flies right out in front of me.

"What is it?" she calls from the window.

"It's … nothing," I say. The ghost has become a curtain, fluttering in the breeze.

"Good – then go and find the side door."

I feel in my pocket for the lighter. His lighter. I'm not going to forget where it came from. I flick it on and use its light to find my way along the corridor. My spine tingles at every creak and hiss. How can an empty building be so noisy? Something scampers past me.

What was that?

I shine the light around, but I can't see anything.

"Where are you, little mousy?" I call, but it doesn't come out of its hiding place.

I feel my way down the hall, until I find the door she mentioned.

"Good girl," she says, as I help her inside. She puts her hand up and gives me a high five.

I imagine what my parents would say if they could see me now. Mum would shake her head at me and say, 'If your friends jumped off the roof, would you do it too?' She says that all the time.

Jody carries a lantern. It shines brightly enough that I don't need to use the lighter anymore.

"Why don't we switch the lights on?" I ask.

"Then it would be obvious to anyone driving past that we were in here."

"Right," I say. "But why are we in here?"

We walk down the corridor. She seems to know exactly where she's going. She leads me to a large room, with lots of seats and a stage area. It looks like the sort of place where they give assemblies. She hops up onto the stage and sits there for a moment.

"Take a picture," she says.

"I don't have a camera," I tell her.

"Oh, right."

She hands me her phone. I point it at her and click.

"All done," I say.

I slip the phone into my pocket.

We wander into another room that looks a bit like Dad's study, with a large wooden desk and a computer.

"Let's get to work," she says. She pulls something out of her jacket pocket. It's a lighter, the same kind as mine.

"Can you see any paper?" she asks.

"There's some over there," I say, pointing to a tray that sits on top of a filing cabinet.

"Good."

She walks over to it and holds her lighter over the papers.

"Careful, it'll catch light," I warn her.

She laughs like this is the funniest thing she's ever heard.

It smells OK at first, a bit like a bonfire, but then the fire catches the plastic tray underneath and the smell becomes vile. I cover my mouth with my hand. Years of fire safety instructions ring in my ears.

I must not breathe in the fumes.

I stare at the smouldering pile. I should jump on it and put it out with my foot, but I'm scared. What if I burn myself? Every vein in my body reminds me I'm alive. Yet I can barely move. My knees knock against each other.

"Oh, look at that!" she says.

There's a wig sitting on a stand. A cloud of curly white hair. She laughs and places it on her head.

"What do you think?" she asks.

"You look like a sheep," I say. Normally I enjoy dressing up, but not here. Not now. "Do the people whose building this is like dressing up?" I ask.

"They certainly do," she says, removing the wig again. "Jeez, that's scratchy, but it will go up nicely. Here, you do it." She holds out her lighter.

"No, I can't," I say.

"You can," she says. "There's nothing so liberating as the feeling of starting a fire."

"What does liberating mean?"

"Freeing."

"Why?" I ask.

"Look, you won't get into trouble," she says, impatiently. "If we're caught, you can say it was me. I don't tell tales."

"Fire is dangerous," I tell her.

"Life is dangerous," she says. "Come on, live a little."

I look at the lighter, and then at her. I thought it was just my family who were obsessed with fire.

I've made her cross. She flicks the lighter at the wig and it catches light too. It smells even more foul than the tray.

I cough and edge away. There's a suit hanging from the

Angel Dust

back of the door, wrapped up in plastic, like the ones Mum brings home from the dry cleaners.

"Set light to it," she says, offering me the lighter again.

"No."

I wish I could take the lighter and run off with it, so she can't start any more fires, but to do that my body would have to cooperate, and instead it's gone limp.

She sighs and sets the fire herself. The plastic burns rapidly. Within seconds, flames are licking the back of the door.

"Time to go," she says, looking at her work in satisfaction. Three separate fires, all smouldering away. But she doesn't stop there; she walks over to the window and sets fire to both curtains.

"Curtains are always good," she tells me with a smile, as the heavy fabric smoulders.

I can only cough in reply. I keep coughing all the way back to Jody's house.

Am I a criminal now?

31

Jody makes Pop Tarts for breakfast. They smell amazing, like toasted marshmallows, and taste hot and sweet on my tongue. And yet, I'm unable to manage more than a few bites before I have a nagging feeling in my tummy. I can't believe how long I've been here. I'm starting to lose track of the days. Even Goldilocks only stayed one night. I want to go back to my old life, even if I have to eat boring toast and cereal for breakfast, even if I have to do my homework and brush my teeth, even if I have to sit next to Robyn at lunch, while she and Sophia go on and on about Harry Potter.

"Do you think I'll be going home today?" I ask.

Jody puts a rolled-up cigarette in her mouth and lights it.

"The school trip is next week," I tell her. "We're going to Stratford-upon-Avon to see the big theatre."

"Well, you don't have to go now," she says.

"But I want to," I say. "I've been looking forward to it." My bottom lip trembles. If I'm not there, Sophia will be partners with Robyn, if Sophia's still going. I remember the last time I saw her, how bad she looked.

I don't even know if Sophia's still alive.

Angel Dust

"Are you crying?" Jody seems startled. "Why would you cry about school?"

I turn my head away. I want to go, even though I haven't done my spellings. I want it to be a normal day.

❄

JODY SETTLES DOWN on the sofa after breakfast and takes up her sewing. She stitches effortlessly, the needle zooming in and out of the fabric. She seems quite absorbed, until something catches her attention on the news.

"Look at this," she squeals in excitement. She grabs the remote and turns it up. I blink at the footage of the burning building. It's as black as soot.

"Was anybody hurt?" I ask.

"They had to evacuate the street!" she says, in delight. She sets her sewing to one side and watches intently.

"Can we watch the Shy Boyz DVD again?" I ask.

"Later," she says, brushing me away.

"I want to watch it now!"

She pauses the TV. "Be a darling and start on the dishes, will you?"

"Why do I have to do them?"

"Because I asked you to."

I stick out my bottom lip. I hate washing up. It's really boring. And she doesn't even have a dishwasher.

"But it's not fair!"

She gives me this look that tells me she won't take any nonsense from me, so I do the dishes, but I don't do them well. I deliberately use too much Fairy Liquid, and I don't rinse them, so the draining board is full of soap suds. When I've finished, I find her loafing about on the sofa, staring up at the ceiling. Not really staring, because she's not exactly looking at anything. Her eyes blink and her chest rises, but when I wave my hand in front of her face, there's no response. It's like she's turned into a life-sized doll.

"Jody?" I say, nervously.

It's really weird, the way she just lies there.

"Are you ill?" I ask.

I give her a shake, but she remains a zombie. Maybe it's the stress of looking after me. Mum always looks knackered too. Once, when she wasn't feeling well, I asked her why she looked so old and tired. I remember how she glared at me.

"It's because of all the grief you put me through," she snapped. "If you would just behave yourself, I'd be fine. It's you who's given me all my grey hairs, you know."

I remember crying up in my room, my face buried in the pillow, so no one would hear. I didn't mean to be naughty or cause her to worry. I love her so much. Is Mum missing me right now? Or is she happy that she's got a chance to rest? I picture her sitting at the kitchen table with one of her magazines, laughing to herself as she does the crossword, and I feel a big lump in my throat. Why did she have me if she didn't want me around? And what about Daddy? Doesn't he want me either?

I go up to my room and find the stationery Jody gave me. I stick a red pencil in the electric sharpener. It makes a gentle humming noise as it sharpens it to a perfect point. I like the curly whirly pencil shavings. They come out in one piece, like the way Daddy peels his apples. I choose a yellow pencil and sharpen that too.

Once they're all done, I hesitate, not wanting to spoil the perfect white paper. I don't plan what I'm going to draw, but the first thing that pops into my mind is a rainbow. I'm really pleased with it – the colours blend beautifully. When it's finished, I take it downstairs to show Jody, but she's asleep on the sofa. I shake her, but she doesn't wake up. She smiles to herself and drools a little. She must be very tired.

I grab a bowl of cereal from the kitchen and bounce back

upstairs. I draw for hours, lost in my own little world. I draw all the people I miss: Mum and Dad and Fluffy. I don't draw Sophia, because thinking about her makes me sad.

It's dark by the time Jody finally comes up to check on me.

"What are you doing up here?" she asks, leaning heavily on the door. Her eyes are filled with little red cobwebs.

"Drawing," I say. I point to the pictures pinned to the walls. "Do you like them?"

She looks at my artwork.

"That's your mum, isn't it?"

"Yes," I say, proudly.

"You should do one of me," she says. "I'm sort of your mum now."

"You're not my mum!" I laugh. "You're nothing like my mum!"

She looms over me. Her face has gone from pale to purple. Her nose twitches and her eyes bulge. She raises her hand, as if to brush the hair from my eyes, but it comes down sharply as she slaps me across the face. It's so unexpected that I scream.

"What was that for?" I yelp.

I stroke my burning cheek.

She gives me a look that would curdle milk. I'm ready for her to attack again, but what she does is much worse. She rips one of my pictures off the wall and tears it to shreds.

"Stop! Stop!" I cry, but she keeps going until all my work is destroyed. I can't believe this is the same person who has looked after me all week, who took me into her home.

I was wrong. I'm not Goldilocks. I'm Gretel, trapped inside the witch's house.

❄

"That's it, I'm leaving!" I tell her.

I grab the pencils and the pencil sharpener and shove

them into my bag. She said I could have them, so I'm taking them. I stomp down the stairs and put on my shoes and coat.

The door is locked.

"Let me out!" I scream. "Let me out!"

She staggers down the stairs after me.

"I want the keys," I say.

She shows me her empty hands.

"Where are they?"

She laughs, like she's just heard the best joke of her life.

I stamp my foot. "Give me the keys! I want to go home!"

She shakes her head. "You're not going anywhere, Angel. Not till I've got what I want from your mummy."

"What are you talking about?"

She leans down, so her face is level with mine. "The man who took you? He's a friend of mine," she tells me. "I can call him right now if you want."

"You evil witch!"

Furiously, I grab her hand and jam her little finger into the electric pencil sharpener. Blood spurts out. It must hurt, but she doesn't make a sound. I use her moment of confusion to push past her. I can't open a locked door, but there must be another way. I dart into the kitchen and hide in the tiny space between the fridge and the wall. I hear her open the cupboard under the stairs and mutter to herself as she rummages among the junk in there. She hasn't worked out where I am yet. I peer around the corner and see her chuck a pile of coats out into the hallway. She still thinks I'm in the cupboard. I nip back behind the fridge and stay there while I think about what to do next. My hiding place is good, but it's not great. Sooner or later, she will find me.

Robyn Ritter's words drift into my head: "The secret to winning hide and seek is to keep moving, Lauren. You're never going to win if you stay still."

I wanted to prove her wrong, but Robyn always won,

every time we played. It's only now that I can admit she was right. I need to keep moving.

As quietly as I can, I dart out of my hiding place and into the corridor. I steal right past her and up the stairs. I'm about halfway up when she comes out of the cupboard and looks around, trying to work out where I've gone. She only has to look up and she'll see me, crouched down as low as I can go.

My breath roars in my ears. She takes a couple of steps to the right, then changes her mind and goes left, to the kitchen. I shoot up the stairs. Instead of going into my room, I head into hers. I open the wardrobe and climb inside, hiding behind her long dresses and boots. How long can I keep doing this – flitting from one hiding place to another, like a crab scuttling under the rocks?

A while later, I slide the door open. I'm hot from hiding among all the clothes. I sneak downstairs again. The front door is still locked, so I creep into the kitchen and open the cupboard next to the sink. Part of the cupboard is concealed behind the cooker and it looks big enough for me to crawl into. The trouble is, all the pots and pans that are in the way. As quietly as I can, I remove the largest pans and place them on the floor. Once I've made enough space, I slide into the cupboard, then begin the tricky business of pulling all the pots and pans back in.

I hear her stumbling about the house. She walked a little unevenly before, but now she's really wobbly. I grab the last pan and pull the cupboard door shut. I watch her through a crack in the cupboard as she comes in. It's a good hiding place but not great. She only has to open the cupboard and she will see me.

Instead, she opens the fridge and stands there, so close her head is practically inside it. A strong smell of cheese wafts into the room.

"I know every inch of this house, Lauren," she says. "You can't hide from me."

I wait for her to open my cupboard, but instead, she opens the tea cupboard above. There is the sound of a cup smashing against the floor, then another and another. She rattles the cutlery drawer and I hear knives and forks falling out. Then she kicks the washing machine and pulls the door off its hinges as she wrenches wet sheets out onto the floor.

"What have you done?"

I'm not sure if she's yelling at me, or herself. She opens and closes the cupboard doors, slamming them again and again.

I feel the urge to sneeze. I pinch my nose and cover my mouth, willing it away. Achoo! Achoo! Achoo! Achoo! Achoo! Achoo! I sneeze violently, again and again, at least six in a row. I wait for her come at me, but she's still taking out her anger on the washing machine. How is it possible she hasn't heard me? I was so loud.

She wears herself out after a while, but all the same, I wait a little before I creep out of my hiding place. There's no sign of her. She's not in the lounge either, so I think she might have gone up to bed. I go back into the kitchen and hoist myself up into the sink. I haven't had a wee in hours and I don't dare go upstairs to the bathroom. I squat uncomfortably, knowing that any minute she could reappear. I finish my business and sneak out into the corridor, into the cupboard under the stairs that she searched so thoroughly. I don't know how long I sleep there in the darkness.

Isabel

There's a second when I wake up where I forget what's happened and I wonder instead why Deacon is up before me. Then I look across at the doorway and I remember. My whole body sags as I think of Lauren. I sink my feet into my slippers and cross the room to pull my dressing gown down from its hook on the back of the door. As I tie the cord around my waist, the wind ruffles the curtain, exposing a glimpse of the outside world. The window ledge is covered with an inch of sparkling white snow and tiny flakes flutter like feathers against the glass. This is unexpected. I had no inkling it was going to snow today. I picture Lauren at a window somewhere, looking out at the fragile white crystals.

I hope it's snowing where you are, Lauren. I hope you're seeing this.

I shuffle onto the landing and down the stairs.

"Deacon, it's snowing!" I call. "Have you–"

Deacon is standing by the kitchen window. I don't know if he was there already, or if my words drew him towards the curtains.

"The investigation will be hampered," he says, grimly. "Everything stops when it snows. Everything." His eyes are wide and frightened.

I wish I could stop being me for a few minutes. I wish I could be Lauren instead. I must have spoken those last few thoughts out loud because my voice breaks. My eyes well up and more unwanted tears line the rims of my eyes. Deacon moves closer, but even the warmth of his hands brings little comfort.

Where is she?

I tremble as a fresh wave of grief hits me. I break away and stagger towards the bathroom. My breath flows too fast, in and out of my body. I lean over the sink, wheezing like a punctured balloon. My heart hammers to be let out of its cage.

"Are you OK?" he calls through the closed door.

"I'm …" Even finding an answer feels like an effort. "Just give me a minute, OK?"

❄

WHEN I EMERGE, he's outside shovelling snow from the path. I can only imagine he's doing this for Erin, since we aren't expecting anyone else.

A fresh burst of Shy Boyz sounds. I open the door to Julio's girlfriend, Nina. She's crying. Not crocodile tears but real ugly tears. Mascara streaks down her cheeks and orange foundation drips from her chin. She's wearing a thick faux-fur jacket, but she looks freezing all the same. I usher her inside and close the door.

"Julio!" I yell at the top of my lungs.

My brother skulks down the stairs. He's wearing the same boxers he had on yesterday. His nipples stick out offensively from his stubbly chest.

"Nina's here," I hiss.

He has his arms folded. His demeanour is hostile.

"I got your message," she says, in an unusually soft tone. "Please don't go."

"What do you care?" he says.

Her shoulders shudder. "I wasn't thinking," she gulps. "It was the police. They confused me with all the things they said. All the questions. I didn't think. I'm sorry. I really love you."

"I loved you too," he says.

"You're still leaving?" her voice quakes.

"I have to," he says. "I can't stay here with things the way they are."

"I can't believe you're leaving me like this." She's bawling now, properly wailing, like a toddler having a tantrum.

"Sorry."

He slopes off back upstairs, leaving me to deal with her. While I'm looking around for a box of tissues, she perches on the kitchen table, as if that's a perfectly normal place to sit. I lick my lips, unsure how to get rid of her. I don't even like the woman, but I can't exactly throw her out in this state. She fumbles in her pocket and produces a pack of cigarettes. She's just about to light one when Shy Boyz chime again.

"I'd better get that," I say, urgently.

Angel Dust

I jump up and open the door for Erin.

"What's all this?" she asks, peering at Nina, who is snivelling too hard to light her fag.

"I was just leaving," she sniffs, her face still red and puffy.

I don't say anything as she hops down from the table.

I watch with a mixture of sympathy and relief, as she disappears out into the snow.

I never liked her, I remind myself. This, at least, is for the best.

❄

ERIN SETS about making tea and warming some croissants in the oven. I go back upstairs and knock on the guest room door.

"She's gone," I tell Julio. "Maybe you should call her to smooth things over. She was in a right state."

He grunts.

"Why is it so cold in here?" I ask, as a sharp wind rattles around the room.

The window is wide open and ice from the ledge drips onto the radiator. I shiver and pull it shut.

"What you said about leaving – was that for Nina's benefit?" I ask.

"No," he says, turning to look at me. "I've decided to go to Alicante. I'll stay with Dad for a bit."

"Are you sure?" I ask.

"Yeah, I think it's for the best. I fly out this afternoon."

"What about your job?"

"I rang Gerry this morning and he told me not to show my face at work. He doesn't want his garage tarnished."

"Charming."

"Yeah, he's all heart."

"Are you even allowed to leave the country?" I ask. "I mean, what about the police?"

"I'm not a person of interest anymore," he reminds me. "It was O'Leary they were after."

"I know, I thought—"

"I'm a free man," he insists. "There's no reason I should be made to stay here and suffer further humiliation."

"What about me?" I ask. "Don't I count for anything?"

He looks perplexed. I don't think it even occurred to him how this might affect me, how I might need him, even if he can be a total gobshite.

"I've already booked my ticket," he says with finality. "I fly out this afternoon."

"That soon?" I say, unable to keep the hurt from my voice. "What about Lauren?"

"I love Lauren, you know I do, but my being here won't change a thing." He looks down at a speck of dirt on the floor. "I'll book a flight back as soon as she's home," he promises.

I narrow my eyes. "You don't think she's coming back, do you?"

"Of course I do!"

The more brightly he says it, the less I believe him.

"Don't go," I say, but he's already running through the practicalities in his head.

"I'll have to pop back home and pick up some of my stuff. Maybe Deacon will come with me."

"I wouldn't count on it. He's still really angry with you." My voice drops. "If I'm honest, I am too. I still can't believe you didn't tell us about Jody. You could have prevented the whole thing."

"It's not my fault," he says, defensively. "You can't blame it all on me."

"Not all," I say. "But some. When are you going to start taking a bit of responsibility?"

I feel my face turning red and I wish I hadn't started this argument. Here I am, trying to persuade him to stay, and instead, I'm practically pushing him out the door. I swallow my pride.

"I really wish you would stay," I say.

"I wish I could too," he says, "but it will be better this way."

"Better for who?"

Before I can say anything more, his phone pings and he turns his attention to the message. Self-preservation has kicked in, and the kinder, more thoughtful Julio has gone. I leave him to it and trudge downstairs to hot tea and croissants.

"I suppose you'll be pleased," I say, when I tell Deacon about Julio's plans.

"No, not entirely," he says. "I know this is tough on you."

His eyes flit to the window, where snowflakes scatter like desiccated coconut in the wind.

"I doubt the trains are running," he says.

Erin nods. "There's a good few inches of snow out there," she says.

"I could drive him," I say.

"Do you think that's wise?" Deacon asks.

"It'll give me something to do," I say.

"We could take my car," Julio says. We all look up to see him standing in the doorway. He walks over to the fridge and pours himself a tall glass of orange juice. "You might as well look after it for me while I'm away. You'll need something to drive while yours is being fixed."

"Could do," I say. "But don't I need insurance?"

"I'll sort it," he says. "Won't take long."

I see the tension in Deacon's face as Julio makes the arrangements.

"I'll be fine," I reassure him. "The drive will do me good."

He nods, knowing that he can't stop me.

"I can't just sit around," I explain. "The waiting is driving me crazy."

"It's driving us both crazy," he says, with so much sadness I almost reconsider.

"Shall we go round to the psychic centre first?" I ask in an undertone. "See what we can find out?"

"I've already been," he replies. "It's still closed, probably on account of the snow."

"Oh."

I wish there were something else I could suggest, some other useful avenue Deacon could explore. Nothing is worse than the endless waiting we've both had to endure, but it's been a week now and our chances of getting Lauren back diminish with every passing hour. I know it and he knows it. This is our life now.

32

Piles of muddy slush line the sides of the country roads, indicating that a plough has been through. I drive cautiously past hundreds of acres of fields, where grubby sheep huddle together against the bitter chill. Once we reach the motorway, the roads become less white and more slippery, and the traffic moves slowly until we approach London.

"I think you can turn them off now," Julio says, breaking the silence.

"What?"

"The windscreen wipers. They're screeching like bloody weasels."

Now that he has pointed it out to me, I'm hyper aware of them, see-sawing back and forth. I switch them off and concentrate on overtaking a caravan. I've always found caravans annoying, but now I look at them with unconcealed rage.

"Why do you think Jody's done this, after all these years?" I ask. "I mean, why now?"

"Who knows?" he says. "We don't know what she's been up to. Maybe she's been abroad all this time and only just got back. Maybe she found an old photo. Something must have jogged her memory and reminded her of our existence."

"I wish I knew what," I say.

"You know what this is really about?" he says, bluntly. "This is revenge for Alicia's death."

"But Jody is the one who killed Alicia," I point out. "And it was an accident. Alicia was as much to blame as any of us."

I recall the moment Jody tossed her sister a fag, igniting the fuel drizzled around the cabin. We were lucky we didn't all die that day. Incredibly lucky.

"Deacon didn't save her," he reminds me.

"He did his best," I say. "And a damned sight more than she deserved."

"Jody might not see it that way."

"Then why has she left us alone all these years? And why come after you again? You weren't even there."

"Nor was Lauren," he says. "She wasn't even born then. That's the McBrides for you, though, isn't it?" he says. "Waiting is their forte. They've always played the long game."

We fall silent as I concentrate on my driving once more. They've closed one of the side roads, due to the weather, and it's caused a tailback.

"Tell me more about your encounter with Jody," I say, while we wait behind a horse van.

"What do you want to know?" he asks, fiddling with the radio.

"Do you think she's changed at all, or is she the same as she always was?"

"She's still crazy, if that's what you mean."

"But you went out with her once. You must have some insight. What makes her tick?"

He thinks for a minute. "She drank a lot," he says. "Smoked too. She'd have anything going."

"She went to rehab, though, didn't she?" I say. I seem to

remember Holly dug up that information about her, years ago.

"Maybe," he says. "I don't know anything about that. If you ask me, she's still on something. You can tell from the craziness in her eyes." He thinks for a moment. "She still has that slightly fishy breath she used to have."

I pull a face. "What do you mean, fishy?"

"I think it's from the drug she takes. Angel Dust."

"Angel Dust?" I dart a glance at him. "That's what the kidnapper had on him when he was arrested."

"It was always her drug of choice," he says. "She's still on it, I reckon."

"Great! That's just great."

Is Jody high right now? Is she off her head while she's in charge of my daughter?

"Watch it, that's our turn coming up," he warns me.

"What? Oh yeah, so it is."

I see the junction and hit the brakes, skidding slightly as I approach the turning.

"Nice driving," Julio mutters. "I'm surprised they didn't take your licence off you after what you did."

"What?"

"Ramming the train barriers. I still can't believe you did that."

"You don't know what it was like."

"Roundabout coming up," he warns. "You want to go straight, and then take a right."

I force myself to concentrate on the road. I have never driven into this part of London before. I don't much care for all the honking of horns. City driving seems to bring out the worst in everyone. They're all like animals, fighting for survival. There's so much testosterone in the air, I can almost smell it.

Julio stops talking so I can concentrate on the road, apart

from every now and then, when he tells me I've done something wrong.

"Really, you're the world's worst backseat driver," I complain. "I don't know why you didn't just drive yourself."

"What, and miss out on your terrific company?" He's grinning as he says this.

"You like backseat driving, don't you?"

"I can't help it. Cars are my thing. Like clothes are your thing."

"Used to be," I say. I consider myself more of a mother than anything else these days. My entire identity is tied up with Lauren. I don't know who I am without her.

"Drop me here," Julio says, as we arrive at London City Airport. It's nowhere near as manic as Gatwick or Heathrow and easier to find a space.

"You're late," I say, glancing at the clock.

"That's OK, so is the flight. I checked on my phone."

"Do you want me to come in with you?" I offer.

"No, you should go back home," he says. "It might start to snow again."

"I suppose."

He masks his feelings by hugging me a bit too hard. I expect him to say something about Lauren, but he doesn't. I know she must still be very much on his mind, but perhaps he finds it hard to put those thoughts into words. I wait while he grabs his cases from the boot and wheels them towards the entrance. I wonder when I'll see him again.

He's a grown man, I remind myself. He'll be fine. He's better off away from all this. Away from us. I turn my attention to the sat-nav, and programme in the route I need next. If I head back now, I'll be home by mid-afternoon, but I'm not planning to go home. Not yet, anyway. I'm going to do what I came here to do. I'm going to look for Lauren.

❄

Passmore Park is bigger than I imagined. There's something incongruous about the miles of frosty grass and trees, amidst a sooty backdrop of long-defunct factories and crumbling blocks of flats, dozens of storeys high. I can see from the state of the place that this is not an affluent area. Certainly not the place to take a young girl late at night. I imagine Lauren, tired and scared. As a child, you tend to trust women implicitly. It's men you're warned to be wary of. Women are your teachers, your mother, your aunt. How poorly I've prepared her. I bet she thought it was all over when that bastard abandoned her in the park, but if Jody was here, waiting for her, she would have run straight into her arms.

A crazy part of me thinks that maybe, just maybe, Lauren is still here, hiding up a tree or somewhere. Even if the place is swarming with police, there might be something they've missed. Something only a mother would know.

To my disappointment, the park is extremely quiet. I expect to see posters up on all the trees or gates, but there's nothing about Lauren anywhere, aside from one small leaflet on the noticeboard.

They're not even trying.

Erin warned me that if there were any witnesses in the park in the dead of night, they were probably up to no good and would be reluctant to come forward, but I still hold out hope that someone was there, someone with a conscience, who might have vital information. They might not be willing to talk to the police, but they might talk to me.

I try to picture that night. It would have been dark and scary, with owls hooting overhead. Would there have been any light? I wonder. Or would it have been pitch black? If so, how would Lauren know where to go? I read on a missing persons website that children typically walk downhill when they wander off, so I follow the path downwards until I come to a lake. I stare into the still waters. There are icy patches in the middle, with ducks perched on top.

Is this where you ended up, Lauren?

There are a few men, dressed in drab greens and browns, stationed along the bank. Each one sits alone, in a camping chair or stall, armed with a fishing rod. I wonder how long they fish each day. Some people do it all night, don't they? Were any of them around when Lauren was here?

I walk towards the first one and try to catch his eye, but he gazes intently into the water and obviously doesn't want to be spoken to. I traipse around the lake. None of them seem to have caught any fish. They sit there, idly gazing into the water. They seem to enjoy the tranquillity. I watch as one of them unscrews the cap on his flask. A spurt of vapour escapes as he takes a tentative sip.

"Have you seen a little girl wandering around here?" I ask him.

He looks startled at being spoken to.

"How old?" he asks.

"Eight," I say. "Nearly nine."

The man swallows his drink. "Have you tried the swings?" he asks.

I get a similar response from each of the anglers. None of them is the chatty sort. They all give me short, sharp answers designed to get rid of me as quickly as possible. I'm imposing on their leisure time, I get that, but surely Lauren's disappearance gives me the right?

"I don't know nothing about children," the last of them tells me, crossly. "I'm here to fish." Then, like all the others before him, he points me towards the swings.

❄

THE CHILDREN'S swings are just beyond the lake. Would Lauren come here if she were alone and scared? I try to picture how it would look at night and I feel less certain. The slide would be shiny and cold. As for the swings, one of them has been pushed over the top, while the other one moves back and forth by itself. I wonder how long it remains swinging like this after a child has deserted it.

There are no children here now, perhaps because of the cold weather, but a bucket lies in the frosty sandpit and a teddy bear sits propped up on a bench, in the hope that its owner will return.

The climbing frame looks sturdy. I take a good look underneath, but there are no signs of my daughter, nothing to tell me she has been here.

A jogger lops past, headphones clamped to her sweaty head, though I can still hear the thud, thud, thud of the bass. What are those headphones really for? Another attempt to blank out the world. People wear them not just so that they can listen to their music, but also as an excuse not to have to interact with anyone. It occurs to me that everybody in this park is here to get away from other people. They make the worst kind of witnesses, locked away in their private worlds. Only the dogs appear to notice anything, not their owners, who trail behind them in a trance. If there are any clues to be found here, if there's a body … the dogs will be the ones who find it. I just hope their owners pay attention when they do.

The heavy gate creaks as I leave the swings and walk towards the toilets. The old brick building is the only real shelter I've found in the entire park. The ladies loos are dark and dingy, the brickwork crumbly. I check inside each cubicle. The toilet seats are cracked and covered with cobwebs. There are no windows and the walls are cold and grimy, but if you were alone and afraid, you could shut yourself inside one of these. If only Lauren had done that then she might have been saved.

I wrinkle my nose at the bin, overflowing with paper towels. A dirty syringe lies on the floor beside it.

Please, Lauren, tell me you didn't touch it.

I peek into the men's next door.

"Hello?" I call. "Is anybody in there?"

There's no response, so I venture inside. It looks even worse than the ladies. Broken bottles litter the sink and there are empty cigarette packets and coke cans scattered around the floor where the bin should be. Once again, there are no signs that Lauren or her kidnapper were here.

I leave the park with a greater sense of trepidation than when I entered. I was so sure I would find something, some sign that Lauren had been here, but there's nothing. Nothing but a miserable park full of unhelpful people. What if there's nothing left to find?

※

I STAND OUTSIDE THE GATE, uncertain of my next move. I spot a small café across the road. My fingers tingle with cold, so the thought of a hot drink appeals.

The bell jingles merrily as I go in. I take a leaflet from my bag and hand it to the middle-aged waitress who greets me.

"Have you seen this little girl?" I ask.

Her eyes fill with concern. "Is that your daughter?" she asks.

"Yes," I say. "Have you seen her?"

She shakes her head and instead leads me to a table. I sit down and stare unseeing at the menu. After a while, she brings me a cup of tea without my even asking.

"Do you want me to call someone?" she asks.

"No," I say.

I swallow down the tea and the warmth radiates through my body. I check my phone, but there are no updates from Julio, nor missed calls from Deacon or Madame Zeta. I finish my tea and trudge over to the till. The waitress who served me is now stationed there. She meets my eyes as I pull out my purse.

"No, that's OK," she says.

Angel Dust

"Thank you," I manage. Even this small kindness brings tears to my eyes. I leave a pile of Lauren's leaflets with her.

Once I reach my car, I don't know what to do next. I take a look at the sat-nav and set a course for home. Tears blur my eyes as I drive, but I press on regardless, past all the unfamiliar shops and houses, the buses and the noise. Ten minutes later, I realise I'm going the wrong way.

The heartless traffic rushes past me like dodgems. I force myself to concentrate. These are not the kinds of roads I'm used to. These are not my kind of people. Everybody seems so impatient to get to where they're going. What's so urgent in their lives that they need to behave this way? Whatever it is, it can't be worse than losing your only daughter.

Since I don't know where I'm going, I decide to drive back towards the airport. It may not be the most direct route home, but at least it's well signposted.

As I approach London City, I notice a sign for Gallion's Reach retail park.

Gallion's Reach. Why does that ring a bell?

Of course! My friend Siobhán lives round here. If only I had my normal phone, I could ring her, but all I know is the name of her shop – Blades. I enter it into the sat-nav, but nothing comes up. Too new, I suppose. I park the car and go into the nearest shop, which happens to be a B&Q.

"Excuse me," I say. "Do you happen to know where Blades is? It's a hairdressing salon."

The bald man at the counter shakes his head and glowers at me. He does not appreciate my expectation that he would know the location of a hairdressers. Luckily, one of the other customers pipes up.

"Blades? It's on the High Street. Not a bad place, when she's not in a paddy."

I thank her and return to the car. I just hope I can find the High Street without getting lost again.

❄

Siobhán crouches down, snipping an old lady's hair so it sits perfectly on her collar. It never ceases to amaze me how much time some old biddies spend at the hairdressers. It must be the company they crave, because their choice of hairdos never seems to change.

As Siobhán straightens up, I catch her eye in the mirror. She spins round, wielding the scissors in the air.

"Isabel! What the Donald Duck are you doing here?"

She's been talking this way since she had children. She used to swear like a brickie before.

"I was in the area," I say. My cheeks grow warm as the old lady stares at me in the mirror.

Of course she knows. Everybody knows.

"I saw you on the news," Siobhán says. "I would have rung you, but I didn't think there was much I could say."

Her honesty is refreshing. Siobhán is the least complicated person I know. Whatever's on her mind, she just comes out and says it. Kate thinks she's too blunt, but I like it. Sometimes I wish I could be more like her. It's so exhausting, all these games we play to avoid offending anyone.

"So, what's the latest?" she asks, as she helps her customer out of her gown. The old lady fishes a tenner out of her purse but doesn't make any attempt to leave. Instead, she stands by the mirror admiring her blue rinse, and, most probably, listening.

"I think Lauren's in East London somewhere," I tell Siobhán. "The police think she was dumped in Passmore Park, but the trail goes cold after that."

"Do you have anything else to go on?" she asks.

I think for a moment. "The woman who took her might be on a drug called Angel Dust."

Siobhán whistles. "Angel Dust? That's an acquired taste.

Angel Dust

Dunno where you'd even get that. It's about as rare as rocking horse shit."

"Then where should I start?"

"Camden," the old lady says. "Under the bridge. That's where they all go these days. You want to ask one of those Rasta fellas."

"I thought they just sold cannabis," I say.

"They sell whatever you want," she says. "Bennies, dolphin, dynamite. You name it."

"Even Angel Dust?" I ask.

"Yeah, maybe," she says, giving herself one last glance in the mirror.

I look at Siobhán, who shrugs.

"You think she knows what she's talking about?" I ask, once the old bird's gone.

"She ought to," Siobhán says. "She's lived round here all her life."

"So, you think I should go there?"

"Not by yourself," she says. "If you give me a few minutes, I'll come with you."

"What about the shop?" I ask, as she takes a broom and sweeps the blue hair from the floor.

"I'll close early," she says.

"You don't have to do that," I object, weakly.

"Yes, I do. You'll cock it up. You look like an undercover cop."

She disposes of the hair, then pulls on a long black hoodie, dressing down her outfit in an instant.

"Haven't you got any appointments this afternoon?" I ask.

She smirks. "I don't do appointments," she says. "This is a walk-in clinic."

She really does see it that way, as though she's dishing out aid to those in need. I bet there's plenty of unwarranted advice to go with the haircuts. Siobhán always enjoys the opportunity to speak her mind. She loves telling people what to do. I'm sure that's the primary reason she became a hairdresser. And a mother.

She scribbles a note for her customers and sticks it on the door:

Gone to buy drugs, it reads. Back tomorrow.

33

"Leave the designer handbag in the boot," Siobhán advises, as we walk towards Julio's car. "It makes you look like you've got money." She glances down at my Karen Millen boots. "I don't suppose you've got a pair of trainers?"

"No," I say.

"Never mind then."

She walks round to the driver's side. "I'll drive."

"What about the insurance?" I object.

"Don't get your knickers in a twist. It's not like I'm going to crash it."

"But what about the other drivers? One of them could crash into you."

"Not the way I drive," she boasts, running a hand through her short, bleached hair. Her haircut is as blunt as her manner, and about as short as you can go without being bald.

I should insist, but frankly it will be nice to have Siobhán drive. She's used to these roads and I'm not.

"Do you want me to programme the sat-nav?" I ask.

"Don't need it," she says, with confidence.

She tears away before I've even fastened my seatbelt. I

hang onto the door handle as she weaves round other cars, honking the horn. She always was a speed freak, but moving down to London has made her worse. I, personally, have only sounded the horn a couple of times in all the years I've been driving. She seems to do it as a matter of course.

"You must have been a taxi driver in a previous life," I say, in awe.

She shrugs. "Once you can drive here, you can drive anywhere," she replies, without taking her eyes off the road. "Hey, is that your phone?"

I feel in my pocket. I hadn't even felt it vibrate.

"It's Deacon," I say, looking at the display. I press it to my ear.

"Hi," he says. "Are you still at the airport?"

"No, I dropped Julio off a while ago," I tell him, "but then I remembered Siobhán lives round here, so I'm with her now."

I don't tell him what we're up to. He'll only worry.

"Siobhán?" he says, absently. "The one who gave the mayor a wedgie?"

"One and the same." But I can't even break a smile.

"Is there much snow?" he asks.

"It's not too bad," I say with a glance out the window. The sun has melted most of it, turning the roads brown and slushy. It seems a real waste. Snowy days are such a rarity and I never got to share it with Lauren. We never even got to build a snowman.

"Is Erin there?" I ask.

"Yeah. Do you want to speak to her?"

"No! I just …"

I just don't like you spending time with her.

"Let me know if there's any news," I say.

"Actually …" he begins.

I clutch the phone tighter. "Actually what?"

"I told Erin," he blurts out, "about the psychic. I know we

said we wouldn't, but I thought it was for the best."

"God, Deacon! What have you done?"

"It seemed like the right thing to do," he says. "I couldn't bear to do nothing."

"You'd better be right," I say, "because if you're not …"

I can't block the visions from my mind. The idea that Lauren might be in even worse danger.

"What did Erin say?" I ask.

"That's the thing," he says. "She rang Penney and he sent a couple of plain clothes detectives round to the psychic centre, but there was nothing there."

"It was still closed?"

"Not just closed. Closed down. There were no signs, nothing but an empty office building. Even the sheets had been taken off the walls. It was an empty office block, just like any other."

"That can't be!"

"The entire Psychic Centre was set up just for you. It's not real. It never really existed. They didn't even rent the office. The letting agent said it's stood empty for months."

I can't believe it. The signs. The leaflets. Why go to all that trouble?

"Now I've got Penney on my case," he says. "He must think I'm bloody bonkers."

"So, what are we going to do?" I ask.

"I don't know. It's just another dead end."

He sounds truly lost.

"God, I feel like such a fool. I bet Jody had a big laugh at our expense."

All day, I've been anticipating another call from this Madame Zeta, hoping that she was going to lead me in the right direction. I know she was toying with me, but her information was credible. If she has any idea the police are onto her, then that's the last we'll hear from her.

"Let me know if you hear anything else," I say with a sigh.

"I will," he says. "And you be careful in London."
If only he knew what I was really up to.
"I'll see you later," I say.
"Later," he echoes.
Why didn't I say I love you? But he's already gone. He didn't say I love you either.

※

CAMDEN LOCK IS BUZZING with activity, despite the weather.

"We might need money," Siobhán says, so I draw £200 at the cashpoint. I left my bag in the car as per her advice, so I stash half of the cash in my boots and the other half in my bra because that's what they do in the films. In reality, it's bloody uncomfortable. I never realised money was so cold and scratchy. We plod on, past a row of trendy-looking charity shops, towards the busier end of the street.

"Do you think he's a drug dealer?" I ask Siobhán, spotting a likely lad by the bridge. He's a Rasta, like the old lady said, with a colourful hat and dreads. His eyes have the sheepish quality of a person who has recently smoked a joint.

We stand in a shop doorway and observe him for a few minutes. People cluster round him, talking and laughing like they're old friends. If I didn't know better, I'd think he was very popular. But if you watch carefully, you can see money change hands.

I have always hated drug dealers. Who do these people think they are, hanging around the streets, messing up people's lives? Why can't they find a real job? I worked for years in a low-budget supermarket on crappy wages, not because I liked it, but because it felt like the best of the choices I had at the time. I bet this man doesn't even know what real work is. He took the easy option rather than haul himself down the Job Centre.

We wait a few more minutes for the crowd to die down,

and then we move closer. I'm aware of him unbuttoning my blouse with his eyes.

"You've got to stop looking at him like that," Siobhán murmurs in my ear.

"Like what?"

"All pissed off."

"I'm not."

"You are. You've got a face on you like Mary Whitehouse. You've got to lose the attitude or we're not going to get anywhere."

I attempt to adopt a more neutral expression, but it still irks me, the way his eyes flit over me, deciding if I'm attractive enough to look at. One of his companions says something to him, and they both laugh. Their casual mirth riles me. How dare they be happy? These vile, despicable people.

We're standing right in front of him now. He can't help but acknowledge us.

"What d'ya want?" he asks, in a slow drawl. Maybe he thinks he's speaking normally, but his speech is painstakingly slow.

I look at the growth on his top lip. He might be sixteen, he might be twenty-six. It's impossible to tell. He has long eyelashes for a man and a few delicate fragments of snow have got caught in them, making him look quite handsome. Shame his eyes are more glazed than a jam doughnut.

I wonder if his mum knows he's out here.

Maybe she's worried as hell about what her son's doing with his life. I push the thought away as I try to concentrate on looking casual. He's looking at me, expecting me to say something.

"Do you know where I can get some Angel Dust?" I ask, boldly. Even to my own ears, the request sounds too formal. I try to look like I know what I'm doing, but I don't even know what unit Angel Dust comes in. Is it a block or a bag?

"Ain't got none of that," he says. "Tell you what, you want

some Squirrel? I've got a special price for you today."

He's openly mocking me. I bet there's no such drug as Squirrel.

"I don't actually want to buy Angel Dust," I admit. "I just want to know who sells it."

"He's staring at you like you've got three tits," Siobhán mutters under her breath.

"I'll pay for the information," I say.

He wrinkles up his nose. "What are you, a copper?"

His face takes on an aggressive look. I'm not sure if he's angry or afraid. Once again, I get a glimpse of the little boy inside him, the one who wonders where this is all going to end.

"My eight-year-old daughter was kidnapped," I say, hoping the gravity of my words will get through to him. "I believe the people who took her take Angel Dust."

I press Lauren's picture towards him, even though I can't bear to see his filthy fingers all over it.

"Ain't never seen her," he grunts.

"What about her?"

I bring up an old picture of Jody on my phone. I downloaded it off Facebook this morning. It's years out of date, but the resemblance should still be there. He shakes his head without really looking at it. It doesn't matter whether he knows her or not. He isn't interested in helping.

"Come on," says Siobhán. "We're wasting our time here."

We walk over the bridge, looking for another dealer. We find one in the alleyway next to McDonald's. This kid is younger than the first, definitely ought to be in school, but he has the look alright, from the shifty eyes to the exaggerated swagger.

"What you after?" he asks, as we approach. "You want some coke?"

I'm so thirsty, I almost accept, then I realise he means cocaine.

He studies my face. "What gets you off? I got weed, K, Mandy?"

"Do you sell Dust?" I ask.

His laid-back demeanour disintegrates and he squares up to me, his eyes burning with fury.

"I don't sell dust."

"She means Angel Dust," Siobhán says quickly. "He thinks you're insulting his wares," she explains to me.

His young eyes bulge. "Angel Dust? That's hardcore, bitch!"

"Do you have any?" I ask.

"No," he says. "I don't mess with that shite. You want some E?"

"No," I say. I take out the pictures of Lauren and Jody and ask if he recognises either of them.

"I can't say I do," he says, "but give me your number and I'll let you know what I can find out."

He hands me his phone and waits impatiently as I key my number in. I know I should probably give him a false number, but you never know. He might be useful.

There, I've gone and given my number to a child drug dealer.

I thank him and watch as he tucks the phone into his back pocket, then pulls another one out of his jacket. An old man approaches him at that moment. I step back to let him make his transaction.

We find a couple more dealers in Camden, neither of whom have any Angel Dust, though they're both willing to source it for us at an extortionate cost. I tell them we'll be back if we can't find any. I'm lying. As Siobhán puts it, "If they don't flog the stuff, then they won't know Jody."

After that, we head to Tower Hamlets, which Siobhán assures me is rife with drugs.

"I reckon we'll find them hanging around the Tube stations," she says. "You see them all the time."

Sure enough, we find a couple of dealers near Lewisham

Station, but no one sells Angel Dust.

We try a few other stations. The dealers are fairly easy to find, hanging about in dark alleyways or under bridges, like trolls. It's not much of an advert for their lifestyle. As our luck starts to run out, we venture further from the stations, into neighbourhoods I would never normally enter. I try not to stare at the beaten-up cars and discarded sofas littering the grass. I feel eyes upon us as we pass a particularly depressing block of flats, with the words *Dog's Home* sprayed across it.

"Look at the state of this place," Siobhán says.

"Let's keep moving," I say.

"Wait," she says.

We watch as a group of young people disappears inside the flats. A moment later, a couple of others come out.

"I reckon someone's dealing in there," she says "Look at their eyes. They are definitely high."

As if to illustrate her point, a couple of girls stagger out. One of them giggles like crazy, while the other is totally morose. I wonder if they've taken the same drug to elicit such opposite effects.

"Shall we go in?" Siobhán asks.

I waver. Approaching dealers on a street corner is one thing, but entering their lair?

"Come on," she says. "I reckon this might be the kind of dealer we're after – someone with more than a few pills and roll-ups in their pocket."

A couple of student types cross the lawn, achingly casual in their distressed denim and heavy boots. Siobhán catches my eye and we follow them towards the building. One of them holds the door open for us and we step inside. We follow them as they clump up the stairs to flat 6. The door has been left slightly ajar. One of them knocks and they step inside.

This is a bad idea.

"Come on," I whisper.

I turn to leave, but Siobhán has disappeared inside.

34

"Siobhán!" I hiss, but she doesn't come back. I have no choice but to follow her inside, even though every instinct is screaming at me to run away. Siobhán is my friend and she's doing this for me. I have to follow.

The kitchen floor is covered with sheets of newspaper. I walk quickly across them to catch up with Siobhán. She doesn't look round. I don't think it's even occurred to her that I might not follow.

I can still make out the students ahead of us. Their playful banter has died down, which suggests to me that they might be nervous. We follow them down a carpeted hallway. The carpet is sticky with what smells like beer and old bits of chewing gum. It reminds me of a game I used to distract Lauren with when she'd had enough of walking: Bird poo or chewing gum? it was called. We became experts at identifying the various blobs on the pavement.

The hallway leads us around the corner, into an ordinary living room. The dealer, a man with a severe number-one haircut, has the TV on in the background, a bit too loud for my liking, but it's his house, I suppose.

I try not to stare at his synthetic tracksuit, which he wears open in the front, despite the coldness of the house. Ginger hairs sprout from his chest, on top of which he wears a solid gold chain, the kind of thing you would wear for Halloween if you were going as a chav.

The students put in their order.

"Do you have change for a twenty?" one of them asks, politely. His voice is really posh, public school, I would say.

"Piss off," the dealer says.

Reluctantly, the student hands over the money and the dealer hands him a tiny bag of white powder.

"Don't forget to tell your friends," he says with a greedy smile. I can see the pound signs in his eyes.

The students thank him with one voice and back away.

"Wait, take a DVD," the dealer barks, shoving a copy of *The Fast and The Furious* into their hands.

The students mutter apologies and flee.

Siobhán leans down to stroke a small Staffie, who is curled up under the table.

"No petting," the dealer says, his eyes coming to rest on us. "What are you supposed to be, anyhow?" he asks.

I swallow. "What do you mean?"

"Well, you look like a bloody social worker," he says, jabbing his finger at me. "And I don't know what you are," he says, eyeing Siobhán, "but I look forward to finding out."

"You wish," she says, boldly.

"I'm not a social worker," I object.

"Then you won't mind having a swig of this," he says, taking a bottle from the TV cabinet.

He pours some of the clear liquid into a couple of shot glasses and pushes them towards us.

"What's in this?" Siobhán asks, sniffing it.

"Granddad's Poitin," he says, with a nasty smile. "Give it a try."

I glance at Siobhán, who shrugs and necks it. Her face

immediately takes on a reddish hue, but she looks OK. "Not bad," she says.

"Now you," he says, directing his attention to me.

"I'm driving," I object.

"My house, my rules," he says.

Tentatively, I lift the glass to my lips. It smells vile. Potent as cleaning fluid.

"Go on," he says. "Down the hatch."

I take a swig and struggle to swallow it down.

"What's wrong with you?" he asks.

"She's a bit of a lightweight," Siobhán laughs, nudging me in the ribs.

It's not even true. I can drink red wine with the best of them. But this stuff … this is something else.

"Now, what was it you wanted?" he asks.

"I want to ask you a question," I say.

He puts his hand up. "Manners."

I look at him blankly.

"First you have to buy something," he says.

"It's about my little girl," I tell him. "She's been kidnapped."

He concentrates on rolling a joint as if we weren't even there.

"I'll buy some weed," Siobhán says, handing over a tenner.

I don't know if Siobhán really smokes weed or if she's just being a mate, but he hands her a little bag and she tucks it into her pocket.

"I want to know where you'd have to go to buy Angel Dust," I tell him, "because the woman who took my daughter – we think that's what she's on."

"She probably buys it online," he says, rubbing his nose. "Don't know anyone who sells it round here."

"Right," I say, feeling foolish. Of course. Why didn't I think of that?

"Can I show you her picture?" I say, bringing it up on my phone.

He looks momentarily at the decades-old picture of Jody and the more recent one of Lauren, but his face shows no response.

"Shite phone," he comments. "Not even worth stealing."

I accidentally catch his eye and wish I hadn't. He's no amateur drug dealer, despite the shoddiness of his flat. This man is the real thing, hardened and dangerous. The kind of person who would punch you as soon as look at you. The kind of person who thinks he's doing you a favour by letting you walk out alive. I glance at Siobhán, but she shows no fear. She's looking at his fish tank, a large rectangular tank that fills the whole left side of his wall. There are little fish swimming inside and a treasure chest at the bottom. Half the fish are dead, floating at the top of the tank. Perhaps he doesn't care. Perhaps he's the one who killed them.

THE MINUTE WE STEP OUTSIDE, the alcohol bubbles inside me and I vomit into the flowerbeds.

"It wasn't that grim," Siobhán says, producing a wad of tissues from her pocket.

"It was!" I argue, wiping my mouth. "Christ, that stuff was rancid!"

As I stand there recovering my composure, my phone buzzes. I glance at it. I don't recognise the number.

"Hello?" I say.

"It's Grant," a voice says.

"Grant?" I repeat. Then I realise I'm talking to the child drug dealer.

"Meet me by the ticket barriers at Elephant and Castle," he tells me. "I have some information for you."

"Can't you tell me over the phone?" I ask.

"I don't discuss nothing over the phone," he tells me.

Why do you have two phones then?
"What time do you want to meet?" I ask.
"Two thirty," he says. "Be there."
I don't much care for his tone, but he hangs up before I can answer.
"He probably wants to mug you," Siobhán says.
"Yeah, probably. Can we even get there in time?" I ask.
She consults her phone. "You can, but I wouldn't advise it. I can't come. I need to pick the boys up from school and it's in the opposite direction. Why don't you call it a day and head back home?"
"Yeah, I suppose," I say. I feel like I'll have failed Lauren if I go back now.
We return to the car and Siobhán weaves her way through the traffic once again, parking in the tiniest of spaces outside her shop.
"How am I supposed to get the car out of here?" I object.
"It's easy," she says with a laugh. "You have to shunt the cars on either side. Do it gently, mind. You don't want to make a dent."
I'm about to ask her to move it out for me when the car behind drives off. Instantly, she rolls the car back a bit. Just as well because, a moment later, there's another car trying to park behind.
"You *are* going home?" she asks, as we say goodbye.
"Course," I lie.
"Don't be a muppet," she warns. "It won't help Lauren if you get yourself mugged."
"I know," I say, wearily. "I know."

❄

Getting to Elephant and Castle is a mission. If you drive like Siobhán, there's plenty of time, but I'm not used to these roads. And finding a place to park is something else.

"What would Siobhán do?" I ask myself, then I spot a row of private spaces, prime real estate, right at the front of the car park. I park in the nearest one. I won't be long, and who cares about a ticket anyway? What does it matter in the grand scheme of things?

The station is cold and breezy, crammed with commuters. There are staff stationed near the ticket barriers where I'm supposed to meet Grant. I find their presence reassuring, even if they're a bit surly. I pace about, waiting and waiting. Half an hour slips by, but there's no sign of the child drug dealer. He's not coming, the arrogant little berk.

What did you expect?

I try ringing him on my mobile but fail to get through. I might have waited even longer, but it's freaking freezing. I buy a cup of tea in a cardboard cup and carry it towards the car park. It isn't that far, but I'm thoroughly fed up by the time I get there. The hot tea scorches my tongue and burns whichever hand I use to carry it. In the end, I give it to a homeless man, figuring I'll be warm enough once I reach the car. I silently berate myself for not making a note of where I parked. I thought it was up this end, but maybe it was on the other side.

As I walk across the car park, an Audi screeches to a halt in front of me, and the passenger door flings open.

"Get in," a voice hisses.

It's Grant.

Suddenly, this all feels like a very bad idea.

"Can't you just tell me what you know?" I ask.

He furrows his eyebrows. "Get in or I'm not telling you squat. I'm not hanging round here for the cops to nick me."

I look into his childlike eyes and wonder if the car's even his. He doesn't look old enough to have his licence, let alone such a nice car.

"If you want me to help, you have to trust me," he says.

Not that easy. In my world, the words 'drug dealer' and 'trust' do not go together.

He's heard about Deacon's reward, a little voice tells me. He's after the money.

"Wait a minute," I say, as my phone buzzes. "It might be the kidnapper."

I hold the phone to my ear and pretend there's someone on the line.

"Hello? Yes," I say, watching Grant out of the corner of my eye.

"Well, are you coming?" he asks, impatiently. I catch a glint of metal in his jacket pocket.

"Was that a police car?" I say, looking behind him.

"Where?" He looks around.

I don't wait for his reply.

35

I duck down behind a parked car and watch as the Audi cruises the car park. When he doesn't find me, he waits at the exit, not caring that he's blocking the way for other drivers. A moment later, another young lad jogs over. Grant tells him to get in the car and they both sit there, their eyes scanning the car park, trying to figure out where I've gone.

I stay down low and scan the email that made my phone buzz. It's from the guy I paid to transcribe Mairead's notebook. I scan through the notes as quickly as I can. A lot of it is irrelevant. *John 5 p.m. Beefeater. Check out tyre tracks. Make? Get an address for Nina. Ask Dog Lady about missing washing line.* I scan down, down, down, looking for anything that might be remotely useful:

Callum and Mel, 8.00, Wetherspoons. See Deacon's Dry Cleaners about any missing clothes/stains. Where is Isabel's mum? India? Pakistan? How long has she been there? Check out Fluffy's vet, Portdown Road. Who are Lauren's friends? Lunch with Mike. Golf on Tues. Bin schedule, every other Weds. Supermarket delivery – Saturday after Christmas. What day did the Christmas tree come down?

So much bloody nonsense, I'm annoyed with myself for bothering. Then, right at the bottom, I find it. The clue I'd been hoping for:

Jody McBride. Check out childhood home. Cold Bath Lane, Cubitt Town.

I glance up again. The Audi is still sitting there, waiting. Grant has found out about the reward. Why else would he go to so much trouble? He isn't here to help me, I'm certain of that now, but he must be a bit of a dimwit. Does he think I'd have that much money on me? Or that I would be able to draw it all out of the bank in one go?

His car door opens and he clambers out. For heaven's sake, why won't he leave me alone? His friend also gets out and walks round to the driver's side. He looks happy about that. I'm guessing he's too young to drive. Grant is running about on foot now, up and down each row, checking behind each car. He's coming for me, and I don't know where to go.

He's close. If I'm lucky, he'll run past too fast and miss me. He seems the impatient sort, too impatient to be thorough. My best bet is to stay where I am and keep still. It's quite dark down here, so I might be alright if I don't do anything stupid, like sneeze.

My phone vibrates. He's bloody ringing me! Good job I kept it on silent. I grab the phone from my pocket and switch it off. Grant is only a few cars away from me. I see him looking around, listening.

There's a loud honking from the entrance as a car beeps at Grant's mate to move.

"Out of the flaming way!" a man yells, sticking his head out of his car. Grant turns, distracted. His mate gives the bloke the finger, which angers him all the more. I watch as he gets out of his car and lumbers towards them. This bloke is built like a brick shithouse.

"What are you waiting for? I told you to move it!" he bellows.

He bangs on the window with huge fists and fragments of glass rain down like tiny crystals. He reaches in through the broken window and shakes the terrified teenager by the shoulders.

In other circumstances, I would blanch at this scene, but today the bully is on my side. The teenager whimpers and yelps for Grant. To give Grant his credit, he returns to the car, despite the fact that the big bloke is still there. They square up to each other, which is ridiculous because the aggressor is twice Grant's size. Then, to my disappointment, he backs down and returns to his car. I watch as Grant and the other boy switch places and drive through the barrier, their new friend ramming them with his car, like an over-amorous dog. I take the chance to leg it down the row and up the next one, where I thankfully find the car. I keep my head down as I start the engine and join the queue waiting to leave. I can't see Grant's car, but I'm not taking any chances.

I drive like a Londoner and don't look back until I'm a couple of miles down the road, by which time I have no idea where I am. My phone vibrates again as I pull into the petrol station. Grant has left me an irate message, swearing and threatening me with every name under the sun. I wish I could forward it to his mum.

I delete the hateful message and programme the sat-nav to take me to Cold Bath Lane, Cubitt Town. I feel a slight flutter in my tummy as I type in the address. Someone in Cold Bath Lane might well remember Jody. They might even know where she's living now.

I drive through the grey streets. The slush is melting away now, though there's still evidence of the snow on the tops of the cars and in the branches of the trees. The streets are strangely formulaic: every few buildings there is a takeaway or an off-licence and every once in a while, a grocery shop. People crowd the pavements, texting on their phones and chatting to one another while they wait for their buses. Few look adequately dressed for the weather, especially the teenagers in their thin t-shirts and leggings. Oh, to be so young and cool that you don't feel the cold!

I don't know exactly what I'm going to do when I reach Cold Bath Lane. Mairead would probably go door to door, but I've no experience of that. Are people really going to tell me anything? I've got Lauren's leaflets tucked away in my bag. I could hand those out, use them to convince people that I'm not a Nottingham Knocker, but I wish I had Mairead's training. Reporters have a knack for this kind of thing, a way of finding out the things you least want them to know. I wish I'd paid more attention to the ones hanging around on my doorstep.

The sat-nav keeps directing me to drive around in circles. I take the next turn off, to see if it will try to make me go back again. It doesn't. This time it indicates that I should follow the road straight ahead. I try to read the road names as I pass, then the blasted sat-nav tells me to turn around again. The damn thing has no better idea than I do.

There's a group of teenagers hanging about on the corner of the next turning. They're completely blocking the sign, literally sitting on it, but I trust my instinct and take the turn anyway, following the road round, into a private cul-de-sac. I know I'm in the right place when I see the smoke rising in the sky.

36

I follow the smoke down a side road, and there I see the source of the fire. It's coming from a modest detached house, not unlike the one I grew up in. Angry black smoke billows from the roof.

"Lauren!" I scream.

Has Lauren been held in Jody's childhood home all this time?

I feel my heart race as I run up to the door, but the smoke is so strong it stings my eyes. I pull out my phone and dial 999.

"Emergency. Which service?"

"Fire!" I say.

I'm immediately connected to the fire service. I recite the address and postcode from memory, something I would never normally be able to do.

"The fire brigade is on the way," the operator tells me.

"I need the police too," I tell her. "I think my daughter's inside the house. She was kidnapped."

"Kidnapped?" she repeats.

"Yes," I say, wishing I hadn't mentioned this last bit of information. I don't want her to think this is a prank call.

"Her name is Lauren Frost. The police have been looking for her."

"I want you to stay on the phone," she tells me, "and whatever you do, do not attempt to go into the house, do you understand?"

"Yes," I say. I'm well aware of the dangers.

I walk round the side of the building, looking for a way in. With the phone still pressed against my ear, I try to gain access to the back of the house, but the metal gate is hot, and flaming tiles rain from the roof.

"Lauren?" I call.

There's no movement from inside the house. She could be up there, at the window. I'd have no way of knowing.

"Lauren, can you bang on the window?" I yell. If only she would make some noise. At least then I would know if she was in there.

"Lauren!" I shout louder.

The smell of smoke surrounds me. The air is thick with it and my eyes feel like I've been peeling onions.

Nobody comes out of the other houses, not a soul, but there are a number of cars parked outside them. Surely somebody's home?

"Fire!" I shriek, into the empty street. I see a curtain twitch across the road. "Fire!" I shriek again, at the top of my lungs. The curtain stops twitching. Whoever's in there does not want to be involved. The silence is deafening. I suppose that's London for you. Everyone keeps themselves to themselves.

I find a window round the side and kick it repeatedly. When that doesn't work, I look around for a tool and spy a scooter abandoned on the grass.

"That'll do," I mutter to myself. I pick it up and charge at the window, using it as a battering ram. Still, the glass refuses to shatter. I have to find another way in. I circle the house again, my cough growing worse as I breathe in more fumes.

"Lauren!" I call. "Lauren! Are you in there?"

She knows to stay low, I remind myself. She knows to close

the doors. I think of all the practises we did. She'd get herself to the nearest door or window, but what if she couldn't get out? She would make noise to attract attention. I ought to be able to hear her, unless she's been overcome by the smoke.

I listen for a moment, but I can't hear anything. No Lauren, calling my name.

"Somebody help!" I scream at the rest of the neighbourhood. Why will nobody help us? They all stay obstinately inside their houses.

The fire brigade is on the way, but I can't wait. I continue to ram the window with the scooter until it finally shatters. It isn't a clean break. There are sharp, jagged pieces of glass everywhere. A knife-shaped piece slashes my leg as it falls, but I barely feel the pain. I need to get inside that house. I need to save Lauren.

Gingerly, I climb through the gap I've made, gritting my teeth as the remaining glass grazes my skin. A cloud of smoke is floating around the kitchen, but I know to get down low and crawl along the floor.

"Lauren?" I call. It's so hard to speak, let alone shout. "Lauren?" I call louder. I stop and listen. I hear something, I'm almost certain of it. A banging sound from upstairs. Someone's up there. Someone needs help.

I move to the kitchen door. From there, I can make out a long corridor, but the staircase is thick with smoke.

"Lauren?"

Once again, I hear a banging noise in response. I'm not imagining it. There's someone up there.

"I'm coming!" I call, but I have no idea how. I can't even keep my eyes open.

"Lauren? Can you get to a window?"

I listen, but the banging has stopped.

I climb the first few stairs, but the smoke makes me cough mercilessly. "Lauren?" I croak.

The smoke wraps its invisible hands around my neck,

Angel Dust

tighter and tighter. I can no longer tell where the smoke ends and I begin. It burns my eyes and fills my nostrils, covering me like a filthy cloth.

There must be another way. I climb back down and feel my way along. I'm not even sure if I'm going the right way anymore. My head feels so heavy, I can barely hold it up. I lie down on the floor. Just a little rest ...

❄

Sirens jerk me awake. My whole body feels like stone, but I force myself to keep going, crawling towards the noise. When I feel the cool tiles under my knees and I know I'm back in the kitchen, I pull myself to my feet and a gust of wind leads me back to the broken window, where I got in. I clamber out, tears streaming down my face as I see the fleet of bright red fire engines. I blunder out onto the front lawn and wave my arms like crazy. People come scurrying out of the surrounding houses.

Cowards! I want to shout. Where were you when the fire started? How could you let your neighbour's house burn down while you sat back and watched TV?

The fire engine doors open and the firefighters hop out, one by one.

"My daughter might be in there," I tell the startled crew. "She was kidnapped. I was given this address—"

"Try to stay calm," one of the firemen tells me, as if that's possible. "We're going to do our best to find her. You stay well back, OK?"

I stand on the pavement, shaking uncontrollably as I watch them spray powerful jets of water into the burning house. I bounce from one foot to the other, unable to keep still. I taught Lauren to get down low to the ground and not to touch the hot doorknobs. I taught her to plan an escape route from any building she enters. I hope she remembers everything she learned. I hope I did enough.

Another fire engine roars up and more firefighters leap out. They jump into action, setting up another hose. A group of firemen don breathing apparatus and break their way into the building, where the fire is still raging.

I stare at the blackened walls and think of my own childhood house. My life wasn't perfect, but I still love the place where I grew up. I've been back to visit it a couple of times. It feels weird to see another family living there and to see the moderations they've made. A childhood house is just a house, I know, but I would feel something if mine were destroyed. So how could Jody bear to set it alight? What terrible memories must lie within?

Not long after they go in, the firemen come out again. One carries someone over his shoulder.

"Found her in the bath," he says to his colleagues.

I step forward as they place her on a stretcher. Her face is obscured by an oxygen mask, but she's alive and clearly conscious. I'm at her side in an instant, oblivious to the firemen telling me to keep back. I look into the eyes of my daughter's kidnapper. She was never a large woman, but laid out in this pathetic state, she looks smaller than ever. Almost childlike.

"Where is she?" I demand. "What have you done with Lauren?"

A lazy smile spreads across Jody's face. I don't know if it's the effect of the smoke she's inhaled or if she's high. Her eyes are wilder than I remember – maybe that's the Angel Dust – and her face is paper-thin, almost translucent.

I move in closer. "Tell me!" I scream.

One of the firefighters takes my arm. "Easy," he warns.

"I'm not going to hurt her," I say.

I want to strangle her, but I can't because she alone knows the truth. And I still have to find Lauren.

"Please step back," a firefighter says to me. "Give her some air."

"I went back in … to find her," she gasps, then pulls the mask back on her face.

"She's faking," I say, with impatience. "She kidnapped my daughter."

I focus all my loathing and hatred into one menacing glare and I say, "Tell me where she is."

Another fireman runs from the burning building. He pulls off his mask and all I can think is that Lauren doesn't have a mask.

"No sign of your daughter," he says to me, "but we'll keep looking."

"Is she in there?" I scream at Jody. "Tell me!"

Jody shuts her eyes as if none of us is even here.

"Where are the police?" I sob. "She's dangerous. She needs to go to prison."

"The ambulance will be here soon," someone says, soothingly.

"She doesn't need an ambulance," I say. "She needs to be made to talk."

Why is there never a police officer around when you need one? What I wouldn't give to see DCI Penney. I feel like screaming, so I do. I scream and scream until my throat is hoarse. I don't care if I look like a lunatic. I fall to my knees and cradle myself in my own arms because my pain is so bad that no one else can comfort me. I feel the weight of a foil blanket being placed over my shoulders and I shrug it off. I don't want pity. I want action. I want them to put that bloody fire out, so they can find Lauren.

As I kneel there, fighting for breath, there's a commotion from inside the building and two more firefighters run out.

"Part of the roof collapsed," one of them gasps. "We only just made it out. We have to clear the area."

"No!" I cry. "Lauren might still be in there!"

"I'm sorry, love, but it's not safe for anyone to go back in for now. I can't ask my crew to risk their lives any more than they already have."

"Then I'll go," I say, desperately. "Lend me a suit or something."

"I'm afraid I can't do that," he says. "The building isn't safe."

I stagger backwards, towards the road. One of the firemen is herding people away. I glance down at Jody's stretcher. It's empty.

"Where is she?" I screech. "Where's Jody?"

I glance around, but I can't see her. I look at the small crowd, but she isn't standing among them. She's vanished and taken any chance of finding Lauren with her. Because if Lauren is not in the burning house, then only Jody knows where she is.

Think!

If I were Jody, where would I go? I didn't hear a car pull away. I look about. She could have ducked into one of the other houses, but the residents of this street don't look like the sort of people who would leave their doors unlocked.

Then where?

I scan the road again, my mind moving rapidly. There is one obvious place she would go. At the end of the cul-de-sac is a shortcut with a sign pointing towards the Thames Path. What better place to hide?

Nobody tries to stop me as I run towards the shortcut. It's not dark yet, but the streetlights have come on. The path is lined with buildings on one side and the river on the other. Modern, luxury apartments coexist with high-rise blocks of flats, built rapidly after the war and now crumbling into disrepair. There are a few people about – city professionals in their expensive suits and scruffy kids dragging their school bags – but no sign of Jody.

The treacherous Thames twinkles. Its deep waters are

simultaneously beautiful and deadly as it snakes through London. I walk through an urban beach that looks more grit than sand. A disco boat goes by, pulsing with music. There are people out on deck, sipping cocktails and chatting idly. It would make a good place to hide, I realise. Maybe Jody's on one of those boats now, or else waiting to catch one. I continue to roam, following signs to the pier. A sharp chill slices the air.

A pair of joggers brush past me, their breath visible as they puff along. There is a police dinghy out on the water and I wave wildly as it zooms past. It doesn't even slow down. People wave at boats all the time.

I continue to pick my way along the path, refusing to give in to the panic that threatens to overwhelm me. London has never felt as cold and uncaring as it does now. The kind of place where a little girl could disappear and no one would lift a finger to help.

I look out at the water, so dark and murky that you can only imagine what lies beneath. That's when I see what I hadn't known I was looking for. A head, bobbing in the water.

37

Her head is close to disappearing below the surface. If she goes under, I'll never find her. The water is almost black at that depth, and her clothes will soon drag her down.

I have to do something.

I grab a life ring from where it hangs on a board and hurl it into the water, but my aim is useless. It lands miles from the target, drifting quickly upstream.

"Help!" I yell. "Help!"

No one comes to the rescue. As I prepare to jump in, my mind takes me back to the moment I crashed through those train barriers. I think of how close I came to not making it. And how foolish I was to chase that van, which Lauren was never in.

Is there another way?

I remember the public safety advice they always give: Yell for help or use a pole to pull the victim to safety. Don't go in yourself, not under any circumstances.

Well, there's no convenient pole lying about. If I don't go in, she'll be swept away.

"Help!" I yell again, but no one comes to my aid. No one

Angel Dust

even sticks their head out of the window. The path is now devoid of all joggers, children and dog walkers. I yell again at the top of my lungs, my voice echoing over the rooftops. There is no response. The figure in the water sinks under and then back up again, desperately treading water. I can't wait. I peel off my shoes and coat and grab a second life ring. The last one.

I climb down onto the foreshore and take a tentative step into the swollen river. At first, I cling to the side, wary of the river's deadly current. Icy water numbs my toes, but I persist, never taking my eyes off the figure in the water. I hold the ring in front of me and kick as if I were in a swimming pool. The water is so cold that it makes my ears ache. I have swum in unheated pools before, but this is far worse.

A metal object brushes past me, just beneath the surface, and I try not to think about all the people who have fallen prey to this river before me. I keep my eyes trained on the prize as I plough through the freezing water. I can't do this for much longer, it's too cold. I need to go faster, faster, before it's too late for both of us.

There is a force that binds us together. We have a connection, Jody and I. How else would I have managed to find her? I swim to her, not because I want her to live, but because if she drowns, I may never find Lauren. Desperation fuels me, pushing my body to its limits.

I see a flash of recognition as I paddle nearer. I also see that she's clinging to a buoy. That's what's keeping her afloat. I kick my legs until I'm close enough to reach her. She is alert, despite the unnatural pallor of her skin and the blush of her lips as she coughs and splutters.

"Grab hold," I say, offering her the ring.

She looks at me with her sister's eyes. She looks so much like Alicia that it's hard for me to separate them in my mind. Jody is the one in the water, but it's Alicia who remains on my conscience, even now.

"Grab hold," I urge again. I hold the ring closer, afraid that any minute, I'll be swept away.

She reaches out a shaking limb, but she doesn't take it.

"You don't want to save me," she says, through her chattering teeth. "You only want to save Lauren."

"Can't I save you both?" I offer. Though she's right. Of course, she's right. I hate Jody with every part of my being. I'd host the Riverdance on her grave if only I could. But not until I knew that Lauren was safe.

She looks deep into my eyes. She has this freaky way of looking directly into my soul.

"What would you do to get your daughter back?" she asks.

"Just tell me what you want," I say, my body electric at her blatant admission of guilt.

Jody sneers, showing me her teeth. "You can have Lauren. I don't want her."

"What do you want, then?" I demand.

She grabs me by the hair and pulls me under. I struggle against her, but even in her frozen, panicked state, she is uncommonly strong. She is fighting for survival and so am I. I taste the putrid water as I plunge down into the murky depths. I push against her, but she has an iron grip. I fight back as hard as I can and for a moment, I surface and gasp for air, before she shoves me under again. This is the longest I've ever gone underwater. I don't know how much longer I can bear. I can't shriek for help, can't do anything to save myself. Only the thought of Lauren keeps me going. What if she survives, only to find me dead? I cannot allow that to happen.

This cannot be how I die.

My frozen fingers get a purchase on her clothing. I grasp her shirt and then her neck, and pull her under. Jody is like an animal. She struggles with a frenzy, continuing the fight underwater, both of us desperate for air. The dull thud that has rattled around in my head all week is gone, imploded by the pressure of the water.

Angel Dust

We have a death grip on each other, neither of us willing to let go. If I die, I'm taking her with me.

My life doesn't exactly flash before my eyes, but I do see a camera reel of images. Not momentous occasions but fragments of the ordinary, everyday stuff that makes up my life: me sitting at the side of the road after I broke down on the motorway; Deacon lugging bags of shopping in from the car and tripping over Fluffy; Lauren playing by herself in the garden. She was so often alone. Why didn't I notice that?

I keep hold of Jody, wishing it could all be over. If Lauren is dead, then I might as well be dead too. But if she's alive, then this is more than I can bear. How can life be so cruel that I could die, never knowing if she made it?

You were selfish to think you could have a child.

Those were the thoughts that haunted me as I held my screaming new-born in my arms and wondered how I was going to cope. I didn't know then that Lauren had colic. I just knew that she was rejecting me, and I thought it was no more than I deserved. I was alive while Alicia was dead. I had failed in my duty to protect her. I had the chance once and I failed to act, plunging her into deeper tragedy as I laughed about what she'd told me about her abusive father. I hadn't known the signs then. I didn't know how to spot a child in trouble, how to understand that the choices I made would affect both of us for the rest of our lives.

How could I have let Lauren come into the world, knowing that our mortal enemy was still out there, that Jody was quiet only in the way that embers are quiet in the fire, until someone stirs them up and they start to smoulder once more?

Jody has stopped struggling. She's been in the water longer than I have. The cold must have got to her. Her face is so blue, she could be dead, if it wasn't for the occasional flinch of her muscles.

Still clutching her arm, I smash through the surface and

gulp down air, gasping until my throat is like razorblades. It's not enough, but I feel myself going under again, and the second time, it's harder to find the way back up. My strength is fading and soon I will be as weak as Jody. If only letting go of Jody didn't mean letting go of Lauren. I could never do that. I would rather die.

I surface again and take another gulp of air, mixed with a mouthful of water. I spew it out like rotten steak, bile burning my throat. I take another gulp of air and change position, so I'm now holding Jody around the waist. She lets out a feeble kick and I bring her face to the surface, so she too can get some air. I'm not sure if she takes a breath or not. I barely feel her move, but I can't wait for too long because I need to breathe again myself. I try to find something to hold on to, but the buoy we were originally anchored to is long gone. We have been swept some way downstream, and I can make out a bridge ahead of us. The O2 is now visible on the bank to the right. Someone on the bridge is shouting something. I look up and see them waving their arms at me, trying to warn me of something. It's only then that I see the speedboat powering towards me.

Jody groans as I swim for the bridge. It's only a few meters in front of us, but in my exhausted state, it seems like miles. I flip over onto my back, one arm still clamped around Jody's torso, and I kick with everything I've got. The powerboat speeds ever closer, throwing up great quantities of foam.

This is it. They haven't seen us.

The people on the bridge shout louder and wave their arms as the water from the boat goes over my head. I think for a moment that I've been hit, but then I realise that I've been washed up against the bridge. I grab it with both hands, tears streaming from my eyes as I realise I'm safe.

Only then do I realise I've lost Jody. I look frantically around, but she isn't there. The motorboat stops, belatedly heeding the cries of the people on the bridge.

"Hang on, love! We're coming to get you."

Strong hands pluck me from the water. Somebody speaks to me in a calm, steady voice.

"Hey, take it easy! You're safe now. We'll get you out."

I spit out a mouthful of rancid river water. The vile taste lingers on my tongue like aged mouthwash. My limbs shake as my rescuer lifts me to safety. I lie on the bottom of the boat, flapping about like a fish, gasping for air. The next moment, I'm leaning over the side, hurling up water. I vomit violently until all that's left is the acid in my throat. Pins and needles run up and down my body, a painful reminder of the icy water. I collapse back into the boat, panting as I wait for my eyes to come back into focus.

When my vision clears, I see that Jody is also in the boat, wrapped in a thick, warm blanket. I've been given a blanket too, but I'm too numb to appreciate its warmth. Someone starts up the boat and we shoot off with great force, skimming over the water.

My rescuer asks me the usual questions: "What's your name? Do you know today's date?"

I answer as best I can, but there are more important things to relay.

"She kidnapped my daughter," I tell him, weakly. I try to point towards Jody, but my hands are too numb. I'm not sure my voice even works. My words don't have the desired effect.

"It's OK, love," he tells me.

I glance over at Jody. Of course, she doesn't look like a kidnapper. She looks like a victim – small and vulnerable under her blanket. How can I expect him to understand what she's done?

The boat zips along, carrying us miles from Cold Bath Lane and, presumably, Lauren, but I'm too weak to object. I watch Jody like a hawk, aware that any moment she might lurch back to life. Someone offers me a hot flask of tea and I take a grateful sip. I see Jody pull herself into a sitting position. I'm amazed she has the energy.

"Haven't you got anything stronger?" she asks, when she's offered tea. The crew laugh obligingly, but I don't think she's joking.

※

BRIGHT LIGHTS DAZZLE my eyes as we arrive at the dock. I look up to see an ambulance and a police car waiting.

"She should be in handcuffs," I say, pointing to Jody. My voice has returned now and I won't be silenced.

"She's not going to run off with hypothermia," our rescuer says.

"I wouldn't put it past her," I reply.

"Do you know what day it is today?" Jody asks, as the crew secure the boat.

"No, tell me," I say. Anything to make her talk.

"It's Alicia's birthday," she tells me. "She was my little sister, but she was more like a daughter to me. Did you know that?"

"No."

With effort, I shuffle myself closer. "I'm really sorry about Alicia," I say, "but Lauren had nothing to do with it. It was an accident. Surely you know that?"

Jody shakes her head. "No," she says. "There are no accidents."

I bite my lip. "Please," I say. "You've got to tell me where Lauren is. I'm begging you."

"What would you do to get your daughter back?" she asks

"Just tell me what you want."

She sneers, baring her uneven teeth. I never noticed how bad her teeth were before.

"You can have Lauren. I don't want her. I want your baby. The unborn one."

"What?"

I hadn't told anyone I was pregnant, not even Deacon. I'd barely even admitted it to myself.

How could she know? How could she possibly know? Because it wasn't supposed to have happened. Deacon had wanted a second child, but I hadn't. One was enough for me. More than enough. We'd just opened the shop, and OK, it wasn't the overnight success I'd dreamt of, but I still had plans. Big plans.

"You can have it," I tell her. The words froth like poison on my lips.

Her eyes glimmer like crazy diamonds. "You're absolutely certain?"

"Yes! Just tell me where she is."

Moments later, they load Jody into an ambulance and drive off to whichever hospital has agreed to take her. A local police officer arrives with my coat and shoes, which someone must have collected for me from the riverbank.

"Thanks," I say. "Now, please, can you tell me if there's any news of my daughter?"

She lays a gentle hand on my shoulder. "The house at Cold Bath Lane has completely collapsed, I'm afraid. We don't yet know if your daughter was inside, but if she was, there isn't much more that can be done."

38

I don't see Jody again once we reach the hospital. They deliberately keep us apart.

"Please!" I beg the police. "You have to make her tell you where Lauren is."

"We'll be taking a detailed statement from her, don't you worry," they tell me.

But I do worry. I don't know if they have enough skill to make her talk. I don't know if anybody does.

I dress in an old tracksuit one of the nurses kindly lends me when she sees that I'm serious about leaving. She understands that I can't travel home in one of those awful hospital gowns with the peekaboo backs. And there's no way I can drive, not in the state I'm in, so I ring for a taxi. I'll make arrangements to get Julio's car back tomorrow. I think briefly of ringing Siobhán and asking if I can stay the night at hers, but I decide against it. I want to sleep in my own bed.

All the way home, the taxi driver keeps squinting at me in the rear-view mirror, disturbed by my silence.

"Are you still there?" he asks at one point.

I close my eyes and pretend to be asleep, as the images of

the day run through my head. I got so close, finding Jody. When I saw that house on fire, I really thought it was all over. Instead, my torture continues.

❋

It's late when I arrive home. Deacon is outside, attacking the ivy on the front of the house. I open my mouth to greet him, but words fail me. I join him, tearing down the ivy in big, vengeful chunks. The pair of us go at it, ripping the life from the vines, shredding them until we have reclaimed a section of the wall.

Shattered, I sink down on the doorstep and stare at the great pile of leaves at my feet. Eventually, Deacon stops too. He rubs the sweat from his brow and looks at me.

"Let's go in."

The house is dead quiet. There's not even a sound from the pipes or the purr of the dishwasher.

"Is Erin–?"

"She's left," he says.

Good. But her perfume lingers.

I wait for him to disappear into his study, but he doesn't.

"You've had quite a day then," he says.

I nod.

I go upstairs and take a shower. I had one at the hospital, but it didn't seem enough. I scrub rigorously, desperate to wash the Thames from my pores. I change into some clean pyjamas and pull my dressing gown on over the top. I slip my tired feet into my slippers.

I find Deacon curled up on the sofa. Gone is my virile husband. He's breathless, like an old man. It's odd. You don't notice people aging over time because we all do it. He shouldn't look like this. He's barely forty.

"We should eat something," I say.

I go and have a look in the kitchen. The fridge contains little besides butter and milk, but the freezer bulges with casseroles and potato bakes that Kate and Rhett have dropped round. I take out the nearest one and stick it in the microwave, not caring what's in it. Focusing on food helps take my mind off the demons in my head.

When the microwave pings, I take the dish out and pile the bake onto two china plates. It's too much food, but I don't care. I grab a couple of forks from the drawer and carry it all into the lounge. Usually, Deacon insists we eat at the table, but today is an exception. This whole week has been an exception. The very worst week of our lives.

Deacon finds us a film to watch on Netflix and I pick up my plate and begin shovelling in food. I'm glad we don't have to talk. I can't bear to.

After we've eaten, we push the plates to one side and I lean my head on his shoulder. He wraps his arm around me and I don't push him away. This is the closest I've felt to him in a while, both of us too exhausted to put up barriers.

"There's something I need to tell you," I say, summoning up my courage. He looks at me, his face newly troubled as he anticipates what I'm about to say.

"Please … don't do this. Not now."

I take a deep breath. I've come to a realisation these past few days: real people are complex. It's not enough to love someone. You have to show it. I'm not going to start sharing everything that goes on in my head. I can't, but I do need to share more.

Before I can say another word, a Shy Boyz tune blasts out.

"Erin forgot her blazer," Deacon says. "I thought she might come back."

"Right." I stand up, annoyed at the interruption.

I yank the blazer off its hook and walk towards the door with it, keen to be rid of her. But when I open the door, Erin isn't there. And when I look down, I find the most pathetic little creature, with frizzy red hair and hazel eyes. She doesn't speak. She doesn't smile. I scoop her up in my arms and scream for Deacon.

39

"Lauren's home!" I scream. "She's home!"
Deacon is instantly on his feet. He darts over to us and hugs Lauren. He hugs me too.

Tears stream down my face, so many my vision becomes blurry, and I want to see her so much!

"You're squashing me," she complains.

"I can't help it," I cry. "I thought I was never going to see you again!"

I'm blubbing like a baby, completely unable to stop myself.

"What happened?" I ask. "How did you escape? Were you in the fire?"

"Mum!" she moans, pushing me away. "Way too many questions."

"Of course. I'm sorry."

I release my grip, but only long enough to get a good look at her. Her face is streaked with dirt and her hair is a big nasty tangle, but other than that she hasn't changed that much. She's definitely still my Lauren, attitude and all.

Deacon scoops her up and carries her into the lounge. I glance out at the road, but there's no one else there. I close the door and bolt it, locking out the outside world.

"How did you get home?" I ask, snuggling next to her on the sofa. "Why didn't you call us?"

"I did. So many times. You didn't answer." Her voice sounds accusatory.

"I don't have my mobile," I say. "But the police do. They should have answered."

Surely, they'd have answered?

I picture Penney, sitting bolt upright at his desk. He wouldn't have left anything to chance. If my phone rang, he'd have had someone answer it. Hell, he'd probably answer it himself. Maybe Lauren thought she was ringing me, but the phone can't have been connected.

"I'm just so glad you're home," I say, squeezing her hand.

We all sit close together on the sofa, and Deacon and I marvel at her.

"Is this is really happening?" I say to Deacon. "She's really back?"

"If it's a dream, then I'm having the same one," he smiles.

After a few minutes, Lauren starts to squirm and we reluctantly give her more room.

"What do you need?" I ask. "Do you want a drink? Something to eat?"

She looks at me with her new, unnerving gaze.

"Is Sophia dead?" she asks. "If she is, I would like to visit her in her grave. Can you take me there?"

My hand flies to my mouth. "Oh God, Angel, no! Sophia's fine. You can see her tomorrow if you want."

"I saw her lying in the road," she tells me. "She looked like she was dead."

"Oh no," I tell her. I feel awful that she's wrestled with this all week. "She hurt her collarbone, but she's going to be fine. She'll tell you herself tomorrow."

Lauren nods slowly, readjusting the counters in her head.

"Did she miss the concert?" she asks.

"What?"

"The Shy Boyz concert," she says. "It was Saturday night."

"Was it?" I ask. "Well then, I suppose she did."

"There will be other concerts," Deacon says.

"Not like this one," Lauren says.

"Course there will," he says. "Now, how about some hot chocolate with marshmallows?"

"Can I have some toast?" she asks.

"Of course. How do you want it?"

"Not too bready, not too toasty," she says, with the slightest smile.

Deacon goes into the kitchen while I stay with Lauren and try not to stare.

"You're alright?" I ask. I realise it sounds more like a statement than a question. I don't want her to lie to me and tell me she's alright if she's not. I don't know how to broach this. How do you speak to your child after they've been kidnapped?

"I missed my toys," she says.

"Oh, well I'm sure they missed you too," I say, trying not to feel hurt that it was her toys she missed and not us. Or maybe that's what she means. Who knows what's going on in her eight-year-old mind? She knows nothing of the hell we've been through, and we know very little of hers.

Deacon returns a few minutes later with a plate piled with toast and three mugs of hot chocolate. I glug mine down, desperate to feel its soothing warmth inside my stomach.

"We should call the police," he says. "They need to know she's safe."

"Do we have to?" I groan. But he's right. Even now, they could be working on her case.

"Give her a few more minutes," I say. "Let her finish her toast."

Lauren gobbles down her meal. She eats every last bite, even the crusts, and drinks all her hot chocolate. Then she sits back with a contented sigh. "That was the best," she says, eliciting a broad smile from her dad.

❄

Deacon rings Erin at home.

"Tell her she's too tired to be interviewed," I say. "She needs a good night's sleep."

He repeats this word for word down the phone, then falls quiet as he listens to Erin's reply. I can hear the sound of her voice, but I can't make out her actual words, much to my irritation.

"Well, what did she say?" I demand, as he puts the phone down.

"She said she'll pass the message onto Penney, but ultimately, it's his call."

"Great," I say. Just what we need.

I take Lauren up to her room.

"I don't want to sleep in here," she tells me. "I want to sleep in your room."

"Alright," I agree. Honestly, I'm not sure I'd be able to relax if she wasn't in the room with us. How can I know she's safe if I can't see her? How can we ever trust anyone again?

I sit with her until she falls asleep, her stuffed penguin tucked up tightly in the crook of her arm. She hasn't slept with a soft toy in ages, I realise, but it's not surprising she wants to now. I remember with guilt how many times I sent her back to her room after she asked to sleep in ours. I was always so worried about her regressing. It seemed so important to keep pushing her forward. Now I'd do anything I could to make her feel normal again.

Erin and Penney are on the doorstep when I come back downstairs.

"I've just put her to bed," I tell them, firmly. "She's very tired and needs to sleep."

"Has she said how she got home?" Erin asks.

I look at Deacon. "We haven't had the full story yet," he acknowledges. "We didn't like to press her for details."

"Has she been seen by a doctor?" Penney asks.

"I *am* a doctor," Deacon reminds them. "And I think what she needs most is rest."

"We'll need to question her in the morning," Penney says. "We need to make sure we understand everything that's happened if we're going to have a case against Jody McBride and Shane O'Leary."

"Of course," he says. "Now, if you don't mind, we're all very tired and I would like to go to bed."

I smile. It's good to have a flash of the old Deacon. Strong and assertive. Impossible to argue with. I know we're putting off the inevitable, but raking over it all is the last thing we need tonight. I appreciate that they've put a lot of time and effort into finding Lauren, and I don't want to sound ungrateful, but in the end, they weren't the ones who brought her home.

"You go on up," Deacon tells me once they're gone. "I need to ring Rhett and Kate to let them know she's safe."

I hadn't thought to tell anyone. My phone is still in Julio's car. "Can you text Mum and Julio?" I ask. "But make sure you turn your phone off after. We don't want Mum calling in the middle of the night, demanding to hear all the details."

He smiles weakly and I go up to join Lauren in bed.

Moments later, Deacon comes upstairs.

"Did you lock all the doors and windows?" I murmur.

"Of course," he says.

"And you set the alarm?"

"Yes. Is Lauren sleeping?"

"Like a baby."

He climbs into bed on the other side of her and we both watch her chest rise and fall, as we did when she was tiny. I remember tucking her into her cot each night, only to be

Angel Dust

awoken five minutes later by her raucous screaming, which no amount of feeding seemed to help. She was only ever happy when she was lying peacefully between us, like she is now. She looks the same as she always did, her mouth twisted into a slight smile. With her long lashes and pale skin, she looks more like an angel than ever. Perfect, I always used to think, though no child is really perfect. They all come with their own unique quirks and flaws.

Deacon falls asleep next, and eventually I follow. The three of us sleep through until gone seven in the morning, when Lauren climbs over me and patters into her room to find some of her things. I see her checking on all her treasures. She kisses the Shy Boyz poster on her wardrobe, then checks her notebook and pens are where she left them. She even lifts her Care Bear down from the shelf and gives him a big hug.

40

We are all still in our pyjamas when Erin and Penney arrive.

"I'll go and get Lauren," Deacon says.

Penney looks at me with that penetrating look of his, trying to read my mind.

"How much money did you raise while Lauren was missing?" he asks. "Out of interest."

"I'm not sure," I say. "Deacon dealt with it."

He narrows his eyes. "It's over a hundred grand. We checked."

Then why did you ask me?

"What are you going to do with all that money, Isabel?"

"We spent some of it," I tell him. "The campaign cost money. We put ads in the papers, abroad as well as here. We had to make sure Lauren stayed in the news."

"How much of that money is left?" he asks.

"I'm not sure. We'll have to go through it all."

"Still, there must be a fair amount left. What do you think you'll do with it?"

"I don't know. We'll probably donate it to a missing people charity."

"All of it?"

"Yeah, why not?"

He looks at me dubiously. He doesn't believe me. He still thinks I orchestrated my daughter's kidnapping for my own ends.

"Did you enjoy your time in the spotlight?" he asks.

I stare at him. "Are you serious?"

"There were some nice pictures in this morning's papers," he says. "Your family reunited, that sort of thing."

"Nothing to do with me."

Mairead or someone must have dug up those pictures on Facebook – probably the ones we had taken at Christmas. We weren't in any state to pose for new ones.

"I'll still be watching you, you know," he says, as I turn to leave. "There's something about all this that doesn't sit right. I don't know if it's just you or your whole family, but you give me a vibe, the wrong sort of vibe."

I hear Lauren coming down the stairs and I assume a more carefree expression.

"These police officers want to ask you a few questions," I tell her.

She pulls a face. "Do I have to?" she moans.

"You'll be alright," I assure her. "I'll be right here with you. Daddy, too."

We gather on the comfy sofas in the lounge. I want to hear Lauren's story as much as they do. I wish fervently that there was a way to get it without Lauren having to relive it all.

"How were you kidnapped?" Erin asks.

Lauren looks down at her feet. "Can't remember."

Penney leans forward. "It's important, Lauren. Try to remember."

Lauren looks at me uncertainly. I can tell she doesn't want to answer.

"It's OK," I say. "You're not in trouble. You mentioned a dog, didn't you?"

"In her own words, if you don't mind," Penney says, sharply.

Ungrateful twat. I was only trying to help.

Lauren clears her throat. "Can I have a glass of water?" she asks.

"I'll get it," Deacon says. "You begin."

She examines her fingernails, which seem to have grown miles in the short time she's been away. "There was a dog," she says. "He was a sweet little thing. But I lost him in the park. I never saw him again."

"The dog is fine," Erin tells her. "It never belonged to the man who took you. It's back with its real owners now."

Lauren's face fills with relief. "Good," she says, taking a sip of water. *Poor little thing. It isn't fair that she's had so much on her conscience.*

"So, you stayed at Jody McBride's house the whole time?" Penney says.

Lauren nods.

"How did you escape?"

"There was a fire," she says. "I think it might have been one of Jody's cigarettes. She was always smoking."

"How did you get out?" he presses.

"It wasn't easy," she says. "All the windows and doors were locked, except the one in the bathroom. I had to jump."

"Did you hurt yourself?" he asks.

"My ankle hurt, but I didn't care. I picked myself up and ran."

"How did you find your way home?" Penney asks.

"I followed the Thames Path till I came to Greenwich Station," she says. "I had a look inside the station, then I went on until I came to another one. I don't remember what it was called."

"Why?" Penney asks.

"Why what?"

"Why did you keep going? Why not stop at Greenwich?"

"There were police at the station," she says.

"Why didn't you go to them?" Erin asks. "The police are here to help you," she adds, a little self-righteously. I catch her disproving glance. She thinks it's my fault Lauren didn't trust them. Maybe it is.

"So, you caught the Tube?" Penney asks.

"Yes," says Lauren.

"Without a ticket?"

"No one asked me for a ticket."

He holds her gaze. "How did you know which train to catch?"

"I can read, you know."

"No one stopped you at the ticket barriers?"

Penney's scepticism is verging on rudeness.

"No one stopped me. And there weren't any gates at Queensbeach. I just walked through."

"That's very impressive," Erin says, "for a girl of your age to find her way home from London."

"I know," she says.

"Quite incredible," Penney says, giving me a look. He still thinks I was in on it somehow. He just can't prove it.

"So, you were in that house all week?"

I don't like the way Penney is speaking to Lauren, as if she's a criminal rather than a vulnerable little girl.

"Yes," she says.

"And how did you pass the time?"

Lauren wriggles as she is apt to do. "I don't know – I watched a lot of TV, did some sewing and drawing."

"What did you watch on TV?"

"Disney DVDs. Shy Boyz. Sometimes the news."

My heart lurches. "Did you see the press conference?" I ask.

But Penney speaks over me.

"Why didn't you leave before?" he asks. "What was stopping you?"

"The doors were locked," she says, "and I didn't have the keys."

He continues to look at her. He expects her to say something more. When she doesn't, he asks another question.

"What about the windows?" he asks. "There were windows on the lower floor that weren't locked."

"I didn't know that." She shrugs defensively. I feel defensive too.

"Are you questioning why she didn't escape earlier?" I ask.

"No, of course not," he backtracks. "My job is merely to ascertain the facts, whatever they might be. So, you didn't attempt to leave the house all week, until it caught fire?"

Lauren swallows. "That's right."

She glances at me. There's a strange expression in her eyes. It reminds me of the look on her face before she had her tonsils out, aged three. I remember how she cried out for help with her sombre green eyes and yet she said nothing.

Lauren

I have always known there was something my parents weren't telling me, and that something obviously involved fire. The way they talked about fire, you'd think one was about to start any moment, as if every time you turn your head, there could be a fire burning right behind you. My parents seemed surprised when it didn't happen, like when we went to the town bonfire and nothing went wrong, or that time when a small fire broke out in our neighbour's kitchen and the firemen put it out before anyone was hurt. The big fire was always going to come, but I never dreamt that I would be the one to start it.

There was something wrong with Jody, something I didn't understand. She wasn't the same after our strange night out. The kind, thoughtful Jody I had known left her body and I was left with this crazy person I didn't recognise.

"Fire releases you," she had told me. Fire was the key to everything. If I wanted to go home, there was only one way to make that happen.

I can do this, I said to myself. She showed me how.

I gave the lighter a flick and admired the amber glow. Then I walked over to the window and held the flame up to the curtains, but at the last minute, I pulled back.

Come on, you can do this.

I tried it a second time, but once again I pulled back before it was too late. After a lifetime of fire warnings, how could I break with my family's teachings? My brain was hungry for fire, but my body wouldn't let me do it. I tried a third time, but I caught the lining of the curtain by accident. I stared in wonder as it began to smoulder. Even then, I had to fight the urge to put it out.

I paced around the room, looking for something else to set light to, something made of wood. I noticed my pencils. My lovely pencils. And my notebook. All those hours of work. Could I really do it? But there would be many more notebooks, I told myself, once I escaped. It took me a while to get the fire going, but I felt such a rush when the pencils started to glow. It felt good, even though I'd set light to something I loved. The flames could have my drawings, just as long as I could go home. The fire would release me.

I hesitated in the doorway. Should I tell Jody yet? No, I needed to wait until the fire spread. Then she'd have no choice but to let me go.

All my life, my parents had warned me about the dangers of playing with fire. I had tons of books about fire safety on my shelves at home and a DVD of a firefighting elephant. And I'd been to more fire station open days than any of my friends. Yet, here I was, doing the last thing in the world anyone would expect of me. It was exciting, in a weird sort of way. Sophia once told me you get happiness dolphins in your tummy when you exercise. Well, I had those dolphins now.

I left the fire burning in the nursery and rushed into the bathroom. The bath was running, but Jody wasn't in there. She wasn't in her bedroom either. I ran downstairs and tried the front door and then the back. Neither one would open, and Jody was nowhere to be found.

The phone.

I raced back upstairs to the nursery, which was now filled with angry black smoke. I got down on my hands and knees, searching for the jeans I'd been wearing the night before. I found them scrunched up at the foot of the bed. I fumbled about in the pockets and pulled out Jody's phone with sweaty hands. It had 3% left on the battery. I dialled 999.

"Come on!" I muttered, as the deadly smoke snaked its way towards me.

I waited for someone to answer, but no one did. I looked at the phone again and saw that it had gone black.

What on earth am I going to do?

The smoke was so bad, I couldn't stand it a minute longer. I stepped out into the corridor and closed the nursery door, but the smoke followed me through the gap under the door. The corridor was filling with smoke, leaving me no choice but to shut myself in the bathroom.

The tub was full now and the water sloshed over the sides like a waterfall. I stepped over a puddle of muddy water and climbed up into the sink, the hard tap pressing into my back.

"I want to go home now!" I yelled.

I still hoped my parents would fly in on a magic carpet and whisk me off home. But they didn't.

A puff of grey smoke wafted under the door, curling around my feet. Smoke was the enemy, the wolf at the door. It demanded to be let in.

I'll huff and I'll puff…

I hopped down and rolled up the sodden bath mat, and placed it in front of the gap.

"Help! Help!" I yelled.

Angel Dust

Mum had often told me that I had a loud voice, but nobody came to the rescue.

"Help!" I screamed again, louder, longer, but my voice was lost in the wind.

"Jody? Where are you? We have to get out."

I heard coughing in the hallway, and then a rattling noise as she grappled with the doorknob.

"Quickly," I shouted, but she continued to cough and grapple with the door.

I grabbed a towel and used it to turn the knob. "Quick!" I said. "Get inside."

She stumbled in and I closed the door after her.

"Lauren?" she murmured.

She fell flat on the floor, and lay there, giggling.

"We need to get out of here," I said.

I bounded over to the window. It had frosted glass along the bottom half, so that people outside couldn't see when you were on the loo. I climbed up onto the cistern and took a closer look. The top half of the window opened when I pushed it. I opened it as wide as it would go and stuck my head out. I tasted the chill on my tongue and my nostrils tingled with cold. Down on the ground I saw the mushy aftermath of a recent snowfall and my heart lifted a little. I hadn't even known it had snowed. I imagined the feeling of crushed snow beneath my feet and it spurred me on. I pulled my shoulders out through the window, but what next? There was no soft landing there. Only concrete.

"What do you think?" I asked. "Should we jump?"

Inch by inch, I edged forward until I was balancing on my tummy. I didn't have a plan for what I was going to do next. All I knew was that I needed to get out.

"Help!" I yelled, as loudly as I could. "Help!" Then, remembering my parents' teachings, I yelled, "Fire!"

But no one came.

I looked down at the ground. It seemed impossibly far to

jump. I would break my legs. I might break my arms too, but what else could I do? Smoke filled the room. If I didn't move soon, it would lull me into a deadly sleep.

If I die, I can be a ghost like Sophia. We'll be ghosts together.

"We have to jump," I called to Jody. "It's the only way out."

I didn't expect her to answer.

"No," she said. "Not till your mother gets here."

"My mum doesn't know where I am," I said. I was certain of that now. There's no way she would just leave me here. I was stupid to think she would.

Suddenly, I felt Jody grab my ankles from behind.

"Let go!" I shrieked. "I'm going to jump."

"No!" she said. "Don't leave me!"

"You can jump too," I told her.

She was dripping with water from the bath. Cold droplets ran down my legs. I kicked hard, but she held on tight, her hands were like cuffs around my ankles.

"Get off!" I screamed, kicking as hard as I could, but she was stronger than me, ridiculously strong. She gripped my ankles so hard, I thought she might actually snap them with her hands.

I clung onto the window, desperate for someone to help, but the street below was deadly silent. It was as if someone had paid them all to go away. Eventually, I dropped down, exhausted into the bathroom. To my amazement, Jody took a cigarette from her pocket and lit it, as if there wasn't enough smoke in the room.

"Why won't you let me go?" I wailed.

Tears stung my throat, but I couldn't stop them coming. I wanted so much to go home to my family.

"Your mother has a choice to make," Jody said. "You can't go until she makes it."

"What choice?" I asked.

But she just shook her head and climbed into the bathtub, sending a tidal wave of water onto the floor.

"What are you doing?" I screamed. "We have to get out!"

Jody lay back in the bath and stared up at the ceiling, puffing on her cigarette, as if she had all the time in the world.

"What about your family?" I asked. "Don't you want to see them again?"

That's when it dawned on me. Maybe she didn't have anyone who would miss her. But I did.

My body was like a spring. I scrambled back up onto the toilet and up to the window. I hadn't known what to do before, but I had an idea now. I reached for a loose cable that hung down the side of the building. It was thin, but it felt quite tough, almost like rope. I didn't look back as I wriggled out the window, so I don't know if Jody ever got out of the bath.

I screwed up my eyes and rode the cable like a zip wire, fast, zooming down towards the fence. I let go at the last possible minute. It was still quite a drop and I hit the ground hard. Worse than the time Robyn pushed me off my swing. Pain shot through my body. Slowly, I sat up, then I stood gingerly on my ankle. It wasn't as bad as I had expected.

I staggered into the street, not knowing what to do next. There was nobody around, except the boy on his bicycle.

"Oy!" I called, as he rode past me. "Oy!"

Curiously, he stopped. "What do you want?"

"That house is on fire," I said, though it should have been obvious by now. "There's a lady trapped in the upstairs bathroom. She needs help."

The boy gawped at the building, and then back at me.

"I'll go and get my dad," he said.

I didn't wait for him to come back. I saw a sign for the Thames Path, and I followed it.

❋

TWENTY MINUTES LATER, I huddled inside Island Gardens Tube Station, staring up at the big screen. I needed to find a Tube train that went towards Waterloo. From there, I could catch a train to Queensbeach. I knew because I'd done it a few times with Mum. The trouble was, to get on a train, I'd need a ticket, and I didn't have any money.

I watched a couple of old ladies shuffle towards the barriers, dressed in warm woollen coats. They looked like the sort who'd have pockets lined with toffees, like the kind old lady I once met outside the butchers shop in Queensbeach. I remember her reaching into her pocket and bringing out a handful of soft, sticky toffees, which she pressed into my eager hands. I remembered my anger as Mum snatched them off me the minute she was gone. She threw them in the nearest bin, but I still enjoyed sucking the gooey bits off my fingers as she dragged me into Mothercare.

I took a step towards the old ladies. Maybe I should ask them for some money. Even if they could only spare a little, it would be a start. But then I saw the notice up on the wall in big, bold letters:

Police Message. Please do not give money to beggars.

Except someone has scrawled out some of the letters and spelled it 'buggers'.

While I was thinking about this, the old ladies rummaged in their pockets for passes and zapped their way through the barriers. I watched as they stepped onto the escalators and descended into the darkness below.

What now?

I glanced around the draughty station, conflicting messages running through my mind:

Don't talk to strangers.

But which ones were strangers? I was less certain than ever. Surely the ones in uniforms were OK. Or were they? My mind was still full of fire. I remembered how the smoke stung my eyes and made me cough. I'd had to get out, but I'd left

Jody behind. Would they blame me if I told them? Would they come and lock me up?

Just then, a group of young women walked in. There were only four or five of them, but they seemed to take up the whole station. They giggled and staggered about in their clicky-clacky shoes, handbags swinging from their elbows as if they didn't know the proper way to carry them.

"Will you help me?" I called after them, in a voice too quiet for anyone to hear.

One of them looked my way. Her eyes were two glassy marbles, the kind of eyes that could turn a kid to stone. I shrank back against the wall as she beckoned me over with her long scratchy fingers. They were bad women. I smelled the badness on them, worse than the way the beach smells after a storm.

"Come here," she called. Her voice echoed round the station. She walked towards me, arms outstretched, as if I were a stray kitten. I glanced about, but there were no windows, and the door was on the other side of the station. I pushed out my chin. Sensei Ling had never taught me how to fight people in heels, but fight I would.

A train rumbled in the tunnel below.

"Quick!" someone shrieked. "Hurry!"

The woman trapped me with her dead-fish eyes, refused to let me blink. I shut my eyes and wished her away. When I opened them, I saw her spin on her heels and dart off after her friends. I heard them trip-trapping noisily down the escalators, and onto the waiting train. Then all was silent again.

I scooted towards the door and sank down next to the ticket machines. It wasn't as warm as the other side of the station, but it felt safer. I looked at the posters on the walls. They still had Christmas ones up, and I really liked those. Colourful pictures of happy people opening presents and eating roast dinners. What I wouldn't have given for a roast dinner …

I'd been sitting there a while, wondering what to do, when a man came up to me, a short bloke with piercings all over his face.

"You on your own?" he asked.

I shrugged my shoulders.

"Where do you want to go?" he asked.

"Home."

"Do you know where home is?"

"Yeah, but I haven't got any money."

I tried that doll-face look Sophia does that makes grownups fawn all over her. Except I don't look as sweet as Sophia. There's something about my face that gives me away. I think it might be my freckles.

"You don't need money," he told me.

"What do you mean?"

"Do you like gymnastics?"

"Yeah."

"Did you ever use a pommel horse?"

I nodded, though I wasn't sure what he was going on about.

"Well then, it shouldn't be too hard for you to vault over the top of the barriers."

I stared at him. "I could do that?"

"I would if I were you."

I glanced around, to see if anyone was listening. "Won't it, you know, set off an alarm or something?"

"Nah! And even if it did, I don't think anyone would bother with a kid like you."

I nodded slowly. It was worth a try, wasn't it?

I walked up to the barrier and placed my hand on top. I pulled myself up and swung my legs over, expecting a shout of "Oy!" any minute.

I jumped down the other side. I jarred my sore ankle a little, but not too bad. I looked back at the man with the piercings. He grinned and gave me a thumbs-up.

Angel Dust

"Good girl!" he called. "Now run on home and don't stop till you get there."

Isabel: Two Weeks Later

"I had a call from Shy Boyz's manager," I tell Lauren at dinnertime. "She said she was sorry you and Sophia missed the show, and they'll send you tickets for their next tour when it's announced."

"Are you serious?" Lauren asks, her eyes lighting up.

"Yes, I am," I say, "but I don't know when that will be. It might not be till next year."

"I'll like them even more then," Lauren declares, with a passion. "I'll love them more and more every single day."

I smile and remember with fondness the inflexibility of youth. Believing that you already knew who you were and that nothing is ever going to change, that the things you like at eight will be the same things you will like at eighteen, that you would want to wear the same kind of clothes and keep the same friends. When, in fact, if you were transported into your life ten years later, there would be parts of yourself that you would barely recognise.

❊

PAM CONTINUES to clean for us. I can't believe I ever suspected her when she's always been so good to us. I can only put it down to my hysteria at the time. Lauren explained to me how she packed the jeans and jumper into her bag herself. Nothing to do with Pam. Her visit was pure kindness. Just typical Pam.

We edge slowly towards normality, but there are potholes along the way. Little reminders of the week we'd rather forget.

Erin's blazer still hangs on a hook by the door. She forgot to collect it the last time she was here. I ring her on her mobile, but she doesn't pick up. She no longer feels the need to answer our calls night and day, now that Lauren's safe. She's moved onto other things, other cases.

I know Deacon sees it there too and wonders why she never returns our calls. He offered to take her out for dinner to thank her for all she did for us, but he hasn't had a reply either.

"Are you really that bothered if she doesn't call us back?" I ask him.

"It seems odd, considering what we went through together," he replies.

"Maybe she's ill," I suggest, for the sake of his feelings.

"Oh please," he replies, not one to be fobbed off. Poor Deacon, I think he really thought of her as a friend.

"Or perhaps she's had to go undercover," I say, playfully. "Even now, she could be hanging around a street corner, pretending to be a prostitute."

Deacon gives me a look. "Now you're being mean."

Am I? Yes, I suppose I am.

"Mum, what's a prostitute?" Lauren asks, slipping into the empty seat beside me.

I steer Lauren away from the subject of prostitutes and try to interest her in her schoolwork instead. I haven't decided what I'm going to do about school yet. I was toying with the idea of home schooling, but given that she already has trouble making friends, it might not be such a good idea.

We work on the same maths problem for several minutes without much joy, then I close the textbook with a sigh. "Do you want to come shopping?" I ask. "We're out of everything."

"Can I have a treat?" she asks.

"If you're good," I tell her. I'm still fighting the urge to spoil her. It would be so easy to give her everything she wants, anything to make up for the days we spent apart, but I want our family to get back to normal. And giving Lauren whatever she wants would only create further problems.

The town car park is full, so I park at the library. It's a bit naughty, I know, but I have to park somewhere. We sit in the car, waiting for Lauren's Shy Boyz song to come to an end, when I see Erin coming out of the library. She's dressed down, in jeans and a jumper, more casual than I've ever seen her. She must be off-duty, I realise. A light blue Fiesta pulls up in front of her. I see the driver's head as he leans in for a kiss. It takes me a moment to register who it is. Penney. Erin is kissing Penney.

It all clicks into place: her strange behaviour towards me, that air of suspicion, the polite detachment. Erin is Penney's lover, which means she knows more about me than perhaps she should. She knows all about his suspicions, all about my past. Not just a passing description but all the gory details. All that time she was in my house, she was watching me, reporting back to him, waiting for me to slip up. No wonder she kept such long hours. I wonder how he feels now it's all over and it turns out I'm innocent again.

❄

LATER THAT DAY, we have another visit from the police. Paul Swanley this time.

"I was passing by," he says, looking a bit sheepish. "I thought I'd pop in and see how you were doing."

I look at his friendly blue eyes. I've trusted this man from the start, but after what I've discovered about Erin, I'm not so sure I should have. What if Penney's sent him over here, in one last ditch attempt to get the truth out of me? What if he isn't such a good guy after all?

"Would you like to come in for a cup of tea?" I ask, politely.

"That sounds lovely," he says. "And while we're about it, I can update you on the case."

He sits down on the sofa, while I make a pot of tea. I look

around for Lauren, but she takes one look at his uniform and disappears off to her room.

"What's happening with Jody?" I ask, spooning sugar into his tea.

"Jody's been released from hospital," he tells me, "and transferred to a maximum-security prison while she awaits trial."

"Good," I say, but I'm not taking any chances. I've already rung a private security firm and arranged for bodyguards to guard the house. It will cost an arm and a leg, but I don't care. I need to sleep at night. We all do.

"Why do you think she let Lauren go?" he asks, trying to sound casual.

"I have no idea," I say.

"Really? Because Jody said I should ask you. She made a point of it."

My mind flits back to the last conversation I had with Jody, in the lifeboat, while the crew were tying up the boat. I'd told Jody she could have my baby, but I hadn't meant it, of course I hadn't. I would have said anything to get Lauren back.

And then Lauren miraculously came back to me. That very night. I don't know if any of it was Jody's doing, but there was no way I was going to sacrifice my baby. With each passing day, I'd become more attached to the growing life inside me. I'd started to amend my plans, to fit them around the baby, the little bundle that would help us be happy again. I have given myself enough time to think about it, and I am certain now that this is what I want.

I wait impatiently for Swanley to leave, then I go and find Deacon in his study. He and Lauren are curled up in a corner, reading an old favourite, *Alice in Wonderland*. I thought she'd grown tired of Alice, but perhaps she finds it comforting to return to familiar ground. Or perhaps she can't bear to tell Deacon, just as she didn't tell me she'd grown out of her bears.

I let them finish the chapter and then Lauren skips off to wash her hands for dinner.

I sit down next to Deacon and take his hand, as I had tried to the night Lauren was returned to us.

He looks at me with sad eyes, as if thinking of all the pain we went through. We've both promised no more secrets. Well, I have one more to share.

"I'm pregnant," I announce.

"Are you serious?"

He reacts as I expected. Delirious. Ecstatic.

"I can't believe it! We're going to have another baby!" There are actual tears in his eyes, then he looks at me. "What's wrong?" he asks. "Are you OK?"

"I'm fine," I say, "really."

"What is it?" he prompts. "You *do* want to keep it?"

He can hardly bring himself to say it. There's no way I can tell him. No way I can admit what I've done. I force myself to smile.

"Of course I do," I assure him. "It's a bit of a shock, that's all."

He wraps his arms around me. "It's going to be fine," he tells me. "More than fine. It's going to be wonderful."

❄

LATER THAT WEEK, he sits by my side as an image of the baby appears on the monitor.

"It looks good," the sonographer says with a smile, after examining the baby's organs. "Looks a good size too."

Deacon grins from ear to ear. "Wait till we tell Lauren," he says. "I can't wait to see her face. I know we didn't plan this, but we didn't plan Lauren either, and she turned out pretty great."

I squeeze his hand as I relive that awful week when we thought we had lost her.

"And look, this doesn't mean you have to give up your shop. We can share the responsibilities. I'll take extended paternity leave. I wish I'd done that when Lauren was born. I want to be around more, for all of us."

"That would be wonderful," I agree.

If he thought I should give up the shop, this would be the perfect opportunity, but he hasn't said that. He's only thinking about what will make me happy and what will work for us as a family. I can't believe how lucky I am to have him. There's no need to tell him about the promise I made to get Lauren back. I would do it again if I had to.

I want your baby, the unborn one.

Over my dead body, Jody. May you rot in jail.

ALSO BY LORNA DOUNAEVA
MCBRIDE VENDETTA SERIES BOOK THREE

Cold Bath Lane

Who will pay the price for her silence?

Nine-year-old Jody is does well in school, despite living in a run-down part of East London.

Then one terrible night, her life changes forever, and Jody is forced to make an impossible choice between telling the truth and keeping her family together.

The police bring her in for questioning, and pressure her to tell them what really happened but is Jody ready to admit it, even to herself? Will the truth win out, or will Jody be sucked into a web of lies in order to protect her family?

This disturbing crime novel is utterly gripping and impossible to put down.

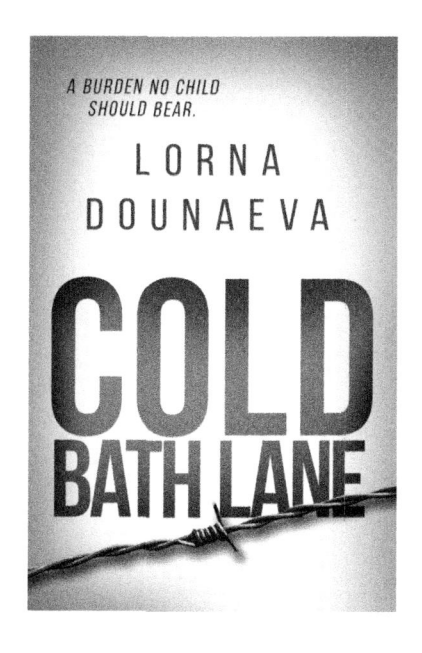

ALSO BY LORNA DOUNAEVA

THE PERFECT GIRL

She was beautiful, popular and successful, the one they all wanted to be. So who, or what, was she running from?

When reclusive writer, Jock falls for vivacious Tea Shop owner, Sapphire, he is amazed that she seems to feel the same way about him. He watches with pride as Sapphire is crowned May Queen at the town's May Day celebrations, but his joy turns to heartbreak when she runs off into the crowd, never to return.

As the days pass, he becomes increasingly desperate. Everyone he speaks to seems to love Sapphire. No one has a bad word to say about her. So why did she run away like that, and what is stopping her from coming back?

The Perfect Girl is a claustrophobic British thriller set on the English/Welsh border.

(The Perfect Girl was previously titled May Queen Killers)

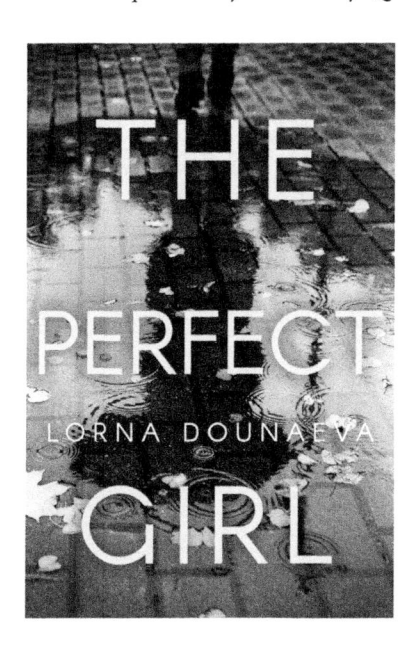

AFTERWORD

You can now join my readers' club to receive updates on new releases and giveaways at www.lornadounaeva.com

You can also contact me at info@LornaDounaeva.com

ABOUT THE AUTHOR

Lorna Dounaeva is a quirky British crime writer who once challenged a Flamenco troupe to a dance-off. She is a politics graduate, who worked for the British Home Office for a number of years, before turning to crime fiction. She loves books and films with strong female characters and her influences include *Single White Female* and *Sleeping with the Enemy*. She lives in Surrey, England with her husband and their three children, who keep her busy wiping food off the ceiling and removing mints from USB sockets.

facebook.com/LornaDounaevaAuthor

twitter.com/LornaDounaeva

instagram.com/lorna_dounaeva

Printed in Great Britain
by Amazon